Solar Storm
Survival EMP Book 1

Solar Storm

This is a work of fiction. All characters and events portrayed in this book are fictional, and any resemblance to real people or incidents is purely coincidental.

Copyright © 2017 Rob Lopez

Paperback Edition
First Edition April 2018

www.roblopez.co.uk

1

With the dusty, hard baked landscape and the two pickups in front of him, Sgt Rick Nolan could have been in Utah. He could picture clearly the scene from *Once Upon A Time In The West* where Henry Fonda walked slowly out of the heat haze, his grim smile and baby-blue eyes promising a slow death if he didn't get what he wanted. Wouldn't have involved the pickups, but it was a classic scene in Rick's favorite Western.

Except that movie had mostly been shot in Spain, and Rick had never been there. Kept telling himself he should go one day, but never got round to it. Most of the places he ended up in weren't where he really wanted to be. And where he wanted to be was home.

With thoughts like that, he knew he was getting old.

Tired.

"How are you?" he said, shifting the satellite phone to his other ear.

There was silence, and he imagined his wife in the kitchen of their home in North Carolina, near Fort Bragg, clearing the remains of breakfast from the solid oak table.

Then he remembered that she was due to fly to New York today for a seminar, and changed his mental image to that of her mother's house in Charlotte. Grandma would be looking after the children while Lauren was away.

"How's the kids?"

More silence. His eldest son, Josh, would either be on his Xbox, Nintendo Gameboy or his damn phone. Little Lizzy would be drawing. She was always drawing, and her scribblings – art, he reminded himself – were taped to the refrigerator, microwave, porch door and walls. She was either going to be a great artist or a terrible interior designer.

"Me and the guys are going out now. We'll talk when I get back."

With Lauren, the conversation would inevitably touch upon the subject of when he was getting out of the military. He was thirty five now. Lauren wasn't the kind to nag, but the conversation always went in that direction. Namely because he kind of steered it that way.

He'd been steering it that way for five years now with exactly the same results: nothing. He hadn't done anything about it. Hadn't felt inclined to do anything about it. Preferred not to think of it. He wanted to be home, and at the same time, kind of didn't.

It was a contradictory feeling he didn't fully understand.

"Take care of the kids. Love you. I'll see you again."

The satellite phone remained silent on account of the fact he had the battery in his pocket. He'd replace the battery when he got back to Camp Blazer near Kobani. He was too close to the front line here to risk being tracked or eavesdropped. Talking into a dead phone was part of his pre-mission ritual. Some of the Kurdish militiamen in the compound gave him strange looks, like why was the westerner having such a dry conversation on his phone, sitting in the shade of the olive grove and staring mournfully into the distance, while the other American soldiers sat around waiting for him to finish?

Rick's men understood, though.

They had rituals of their own. In years past, he'd imagined the conversation more vividly, listening to Lauren's voice as she laughed and blew him kisses. That only happened in these imaginary calls, but even that seemed distant now. The ritual had become more mechanical: a mumbled chant. The end part was real, though.

He would see them again. That was the point. The whole reason for the ritual. Some way of magically making sure he would return.

He could feel his family slipping away, however. Especially Josh. He was twelve now and entering that difficult stage of moodiness. Last time Rick saw him, he'd been a bundle of resentment.

Whether he resented his dad being away so much or for coming back home was hard to tell.

Rick stowed the phone in his gear and checked the breech of his M4 carbine. His men waited by the dusty, mud-smeared pickups. Five of them: dressed in cargo pants and tees, or Kurdish fatigues to maintain the pretense that there were no US 'boots on the ground' in Syria. The pickups were loaded with packs, spare wheels and armed with stubby grenade launchers. On the compound wall behind them, pockmarked with bullet holes, was the faded Arabic graffiti left by ISIS fighters before they'd been driven out of the area.

Definitely not Utah, then.

"Bird's in the air, Rick," called Leroy from the truck, patting his radio.

Leroy was a black Cuban from a family of exiles. He was armed to the teeth with at least two Glocks, a Bowie knife and a machete, besides his M4 and a ton of ammo. Being black, Leroy knew that if ISIS fighters got hold of him, they'd skin him alive. He wasn't going to go down without taking a lot of them with him.

The 'Bird' in question was the JSTARS surveillance plane that would be watching over them. They weren't taking the militiamen with them on this trip, so they needed to be able to call in air strikes instantly. The JSTARS carried radar capable of tracking every movement on the battlefield, cameras to obtain a visual image, and links to armed drones that would be circling below it. In contact with it, an AWACS airborne early warning plane flying along the Turkish border controlled and coordinated the movements of NATO fighter aircraft operating from bases in Iraq, Turkey and Qatar. One call was all it would take for Rick to unleash hell on any ISIS groups foolish enough to mess with his team. Climbing into the pickup cab, he opened a laptop on the dash. On the screen was the real-time satellite image of the target area. When the drones came online, he'd also have a thermal imaging overlay, day or night, that would detect anything hidden under camouflage netting. In addition to their own weapons and those of the Air Force, the six Special Forces operators could also call in cruise missiles from Navy ships stationed in the Gulf, not to mention air strikes from an aircraft carrier. Rick's tiny team had more firepower at their disposal than any equivalent squad in the history of warfare.

Somehow, he didn't think Leroy would need his machete, but if he wanted to look hardcore, that was his business.

Flynn, sporting shades and a beard, sat at the wheel. A veteran who'd joined Rick's team in Afghanistan, chasing the Taliban on horseback through the mountains, he was as calm under fire as he was now, just waiting for his cue. Staring out at the scrubby desert, Rick wondered if he too could see Henry Fonda.

Maybe not. He was more of a Chuck Norris guy.

"Let's go," said Rick.

Ready for anything, the two vehicles drove out of the compound and headed south.

Lauren toyed with her keys and phone, procrastinating. She really needed to head to the airport, but the smell of cookie dough dragged her back, triggering memories of her childhood.

It was early in the morning, but her mother was already baking the third batch.

"I think you've got enough cookies, Mom. I'm only going to be gone for the day. I'll be back late tonight."

Grandma Daisy Jones waved off her concerns. "I've got two hearty eaters in the house. I picked up some lovely steaks from the market yesterday. If the weather stays good, we'll have a barbecue. And I got some of that pasta that Josh likes."

"Josh isn't eating so much now."

"I know, but he should. He's getting thin. And I have some of that stringy cheese that Lizzy likes."

"It's junk, Mom."

"Yes, but she's got plenty of time to grow out of it. If she takes after you, she'll be an athlete when she hits high school."

"She's in first grade."

"I know that. You could do with a bit of meat on your bones, too, so I've packed you something for the flight."

She handed over a large, foil-wrapped package to Lauren. It was still warm: fresh baked cookies and toasted cheese sandwiches. Lauren could almost feel the weight of the calories on her hips already.

"That won't fit in my bag, Mom."

Lauren had her small military backpack. She hated to check in luggage, preferring to travel light. Even a wheeled carry-on was too much of an encumbrance for her.

"Of course it will. Now make sure you're not late for this meeting. It could be important."

"It's a seminar."

"That's a good thing. And it's even better that they're paying you to fly to New York to attend. They must think highly of you. I think you're going to be promoted soon."

"I have to go, Mom." She leaned down to kiss her mother's forehead, pushing aside the soft, white hair. She got the impression that she had to lean lower and lower with each year. Age was shrinking the old woman. She'd had Lauren when she was thirty seven, pretty late for her generation, and Lauren had always known her as frail, her back bent from a lifetime of tireless work. She'd always been energetic, and indeed something of an athlete in her own youth, but she moved slower now, her arthritic hip giving her problems that no amount of physiotherapy could cure.

Her cookies were still the best, though.

Lauren's father sat in the living room, watching sport on the TV. Since his operation the previous year, when he'd been fitted with a pacemaker, he'd assumed the 'license to loaf', exerting himself as little as possible, even though the doctor said that wasn't necessary. All he needed to do was stay away from magnetic fields, which weren't exactly all that prevalent in the neighborhood. Lauren suspected her mother actually liked it that way, because it meant her father didn't get in the way so much. The first few years of retirement were a little testy, to say the least. He'd spent the last years at the sawmill planning all the home improvements he wanted to do once he got the time. Mom hadn't taken kindly to finding the kitchen floor ripped up or tripping over the drill cord when new cabinets went up. She had a set routine and was relieved when the tools went back in the garage.

"See you later, Dad."

He waved the remote at her. "Take it easy, girl. Enjoy the flight."

"Try my best."

Josh and Lizzy were in the bedroom. Lizzy was unpacking the little suitcase she always brought, laying her pad and pencils neatly on the dresser. Josh, on the other hand, lay sprawled on the bed, shooting zombies on his Nintendo 3DS. He looked bored already.

"You guys be good for your grandma," said Lauren.

"We're always good," said Lizzy seriously. "What's the subject of the seminar today?"

"Domestic liquidity and aggregate demand."

Lizzy screwed up her freckled features. "Do you get cookies?"

"Always."

Lauren gave her a quick hug and kissed the top of Josh's unresponsive head. Lauren's old teddy bears looked down from their shelf, unmoved since she left to enlist. Dad wanted to turn the room into a games parlor, but Mom had fiercely resisted him, keeping the room exactly as she left it. Lauren thought she might at least have changed the bed into two singles, so that Josh and Lizzy didn't have to sleep together, but her mother was adamant it should stay, creaky springs and all. Lauren normally paid little attention to the room, but today she felt the pull of nostalgia as she looked at the framed pictures on the wall. One was of her with her friends at some outdoor concert where she smoked her first joint. The other was of her in uniform, graduating from Basic Combat Training at Fort Jackson, South Carolina. Her mother put that one there, maybe thinking that her daughter would continue to inhabit the room in spirit. Lauren felt a million miles away from the young woman in that picture. It had been a while since she left the military.

But there was something else. Something that was bugging her.

Dashing out to her car, she fumbled in her handbag for her keys, feeling the crumpled paper of another drawing that Lizzy had squeezed in there. Remembering that she already had the keys in her hand, she stopped, looking up the street. It was hot and someone was mowing their front lawn. Mr Henderson, taking time out from selling real estate, washed his car on the driveway, the sun casting a rainbow in the spray from his hose. Mrs King walked her two dogs, passing under the shade of the trees on the sidewalk. There were no kids about – they were at school – and half the people on this street were retired folks anyway, which was why Josh was less than enthusiastic about spending the day here, even though he was missing class.

Lauren felt pulled out of the scene, however, and her thoughts drifted to her husband in Syria.

Was she having a premonition of something? Was Rick okay?

She shook her head, casting away all doubts. She didn't need this right now. When she got in the car and started the engine, however, she took a last look down the street, like she was meant to be looking for something.

Whatever it was failed to emerge and she released the handbrake, pulling out. Probably just hormones, she thought.

She still found it hard to leave her kids.

Joe Butcher watched as the ejected plasma from the sun unfurled on his screen, reaching out into space like a fire serpent. He'd spent the whole morning at the Space Weather Prediction Center in Boulder, Colorado, observing the growing string of sun spots on the coronal hole. The tongues of fire initially bent back on themselves, held back by the turbulent magnetic fields and pulled by the sun's immense gravity. Then the image from the SDO satellite changed as the magnetic fields broke, and the mass of plasma erupted from the sun's surface, like a row of belching volcanoes. The computer modeling showed the fan of fire moving to intercept the orbital line of Earth, engulfing it like a tsunami hitting a dinghy.

"It's moving fast," said Joe. "It's going to hit Earth in thirteen hours."

X-rays flew on ahead of the surge, moving at the speed of light. Caroline watched the levels spike on her readouts. "It's big," she said. "Upgrading from an M to an X."

Brad, the team supervisor, sat behind them with his own bank of screens. "Okay, crunching the data," he said. His fingers clacked on the keyboard. "The Savani model predicts a range running from thirty two to forty seven degrees out of alignment. That makes it a G4. Going to be some beautiful auroras."

The closer a plasma ejection's magnetic fields aligned with that of Earth's magnetosphere, the less impact it would have when it hit. Aligning directly with the magnetosphere meant it would just slide over with minimal disruption. A G4 was a moderate geomagnetic storm in Earth's atmosphere.

"Are you kidding me?" said Joe. "Look at the readings from that thing.

No way is that going to produce a G4. It's at least a G7."

"Not according to the Savani model."

"The Savani model's still in beta."

"And it's been correct so far. Run the figures on an impact prediction."

Joe brought up the image of a world atlas and ran the simulator. Orbs of yellow appeared on the equator over Indonesia, turning green and spreading over the Pacific. More orbs appeared over the poles and the equatorial map began turning red. The expanding orbs met up like spilled paint on a smooth surface, and the atlas was engulfed in what looked like blood. "This could be bigger than the Carrington event. We could be talking G9+."

Brad looked up from his screen. "There's no such thing as G9+. What figures are you using there?"

"Worst case scenario of one hundred and eighty degrees out of alignment. That's more than just air traffic and comms. This could fry the grid."

Brad glared in annoyance. "Stop messing around. Use the Savani figures."

Joe did so, and the red turned green, with spots of orange briefly appearing at the poles, the Aleutians and over trans-pacific flight routes from California to Japan.

"That's better," said Brad. "Issue watch data to airlines and shipping, with a caution to the Department of Transportation, NASA and the grid."

Joe and Caroline glanced at each other. Last year, Brad had been chewed out by the Chair of the National Oceanic and Atmosphere Administration, who had herself been chewed out by a senate subcommittee for a red warning he'd given out that, according to the NSA, had triggered terrorist sleeper cells looking to take advantage of the anticipated disruption to communications and electricity. Two guys in Philadelphia had reacted to the gleefully alarmist reports on CNN by bringing forward a planned bomb attack on the transit system. The geomagnetic storm turned out to be minor and the two guys, who were being followed by the FBI, were arrested when they approached their lockup where some explosives were stored, and the CNN presenters got a good laugh at NOAA's expense, likening the doomsday scenario to the Y2K warnings. Since then, Brad had been on a tighter leash and forced to use the Savani model, even though it was still being tested. The problem for Brad, and everyone else at the Prediction Center, was that it was impossible to tell what the magnetic orientation of a CME would be until it hit the WIND satellite, about a million miles away from Earth. That only gave them sixty minutes before the CME wave hit the planet.

"What?" said Brad irritably.

Joe and Caroline looked mutely at him.

"We'll monitor it closely, okay?" he said. "Everyone's got their warnings. If they've got their procedures in place, they'll act accordingly. Now back to work."

Joe and Caroline returned to their screens.

"We've got another one," said Caroline.

On the screen, another bulge on the sun exploded, sending a plasma stream on the same trajectory as the last one.

"This one's moving faster," she said. "It's like it's trying to catch up."

Joe watched the magnetic readings on the sun. "I think a third one's forming. This could be a triple whammy."

They both turned to Brad, who threw his arms up in the air. "Okay, okay. Upgrade to a G5 and start crunching the data. And no messing with the figures. We report what we see, that's all."

"They call us the Prediction Center, you know?" said Joe wryly.

"Exactly. Not the Make It Up As You Go Along Center," retorted Brad.

Joe sucked in his lip. That had been the exact same remark made to Brad from the Chair when he'd been chewed out. The veins standing out on Brad's temple showed it still burned. He was doing what he needed to keep his job, but he wasn't happy.

2

Rick and his team spent the afternoon hidden in a wadi, twenty miles north-west of Raqqa, the self-proclaimed capital of ISIS. Underneath his camo net, he watched the drone feed on his laptop as it maintained high altitude surveillance on the Raqqa-Ain Issa road. A solitary T55 tank manned a checkpoint on the road, and Rick watched the crew take turns to man the turret, the other crew members sheltering under an awning. With the sun blazing down, it'd be as hot as hell inside that tank. Apart from the occasional pickup, nothing much else moved on the road, and the surrounding desert was featureless apart from an abandoned airfield pockmarked with craters and the wreck of an old Soviet MiG-21.

Rick's radio crackled. "Bird Two to Nomad, do you copy?"

"We copy, Bird Two. Go ahead," said Rick.

"Be advised. We have a warning of solar atmospheric disturbance: ETA, ten hours. Downlinks and communications will be affected. Support may not be available, and we'll lose the drones. What do you want to do?"

As mission commander, Rick had the latitude to decide what to do. It was his call to abort or not. "How long will the disruption last?" he asked.

"We've been warned it could be seventeen hours or more."

"How long are you going to be with us?"

"We've got tanker support. We'll be with you as long as you need us."

Rick mulled it over. It wasn't a critical mission. He'd planned to head out once it was fully dark and probe south, testing the reaction of Raqqa's defences. With the main offensive on Raqqa happening to the east, he wanted to find out what ISIS had left to guard their back door. A swift attack with the Kurdish militia might complete the circle around the city. It was speculative, though.

Next to him on the truck bed, Scott squeezed out cold ravioli and meat sauce into his mouth from the foil packet of an MRE. Scott was a hairy veteran of wars that went back to Somalia, and was older than Rick. The other guys in the team joked that Rick only brought him along because he made Rick look young. Age or not, Scott knew his stuff. "What do you think?" asked Rick.

Scott wiped his mouth and beard. "Up to you. Nothing saying we can't come back tomorrow, though."

That was pretty much what Rick was thinking. He hated to waste the moment they had here – at the least he wanted to take out that tank – but it wasn't worth the risk without dependable support. What bothered Rick the most was the effect a solar storm would have on the GPS satellites. At night, with their night vision goggles, his team had an advantage over most ISIS fighters – though the enemy had acquired and captured some NVGs of their own from the Syrian army. The first thing affected by any atmospheric disturbance would be the GPS signals, either cutting them or, worse still, introducing navigational errors. With pockets of ISIS all around them, Rick didn't want to stray into the wrong areas. Especially without drone support. The drones relied heavily on satellite uplinking.

"Roger that, Bird Two. We'll exfil at nightfall. Out." That gave them seven hours to get out of enemy territory – more than enough time.

"Good call," nodded Scott sagely.

"Didn't have to be so damned vague about it," said Rick.

"Don't need to be so damned prissy about it."

Rick smiled, cracking the layer of dust on his face. "Did you get all that, guys?" he radioed on his tac link.

The others were sprawled out on the lip of the wadi, scanning the desert with binoculars and sniper scopes. They each gave a silent thumbs up.

At least they'd get a beer when they got back.

"Wanna beer?"

Grandpa turned the steaks on the grill, giving Josh a sideways glance. Elena Seinfeld and her husband Max, neighbors from across the street, sat on the sun loungers, fanning themselves. The grass was yellow and parched. The fall heat was oppressive, and the Seinfelds wore their straw hats, the brims nodding in appreciation at Lizzy presenting her latest sketch to them. Grandma laid a cloth and coasters out on the table. The parasol was in the garage, and Josh knew he'd be asked to fetch it soon.

"Okay," replied Josh.

Grandpa quietly poured some of his beer into a plastic cup and handed it to Josh. "Don't tell your mom," he said.

Wasn't any chance of that, thought Josh. He didn't tell his mom anything anymore. And Dad might as well be on another planet for all the good he was. *Gee, Dad. Thanks for your service.* With Mom working longer hours for her new job, he was starting to feel like an orphan. He wasn't a cute, wide eyed kid anymore, worthy of everyone's attention. His teacher said his moodiness was a phase, and that it would pass. Just a part of adolescence.

It wasn't *his* phase, though. He didn't ask for it. It was like being given cabbage and beans on a plate instead of fried chicken. Hating the cabbage wasn't some phase. It was just that cabbage sucked. But somehow, having cabbage instead of chicken was his fault, not anyone else's. And if he claimed it wasn't fair, that was his fault too, like he should have known what he was signing up for. *Because life's like that, Josh.*

Well, screw life.

"Still seeing that girl? What was her name? Linda?" said Grandpa.

"Lydia," said Josh. "No, we were just friends."

"No making out, huh?"

"Don't be so gross. It wasn't like that."

"Sure."

"It wasn't."

"Ah, don't worry, sport. There's plenty more fish."

Grandpa was in his cargo shorts and his legs were stick-thin. The sight of loose skin over wasted muscles made Josh think that, over a certain age, people should be banned from wearing them. Nobody wanted to see that many liver spots in full view. Grandpa used to be a barrel of a man, and he was still pretty big, but he didn't walk much anymore. On the other hand, Josh himself didn't wear short pants anymore. His mom had bought him baggies for the summer, like he was some kind of surfer dude, but, in keeping with his mood, he preferred to wear black. And he hated being in the sun, preferring the shade. He just wanted to blend in and disappear.

"...and there's been another burglary on the end row," Elena was saying.

"No!" said Grandma in polite horror.

"Yes. They broke the lock on his garage and took his tools. Hundreds of dollars' worth, they say."

"Oh my, it's just getting worse. All these people coming to live in Charlotte now. It's getting out of control. We've got more crime than the rest of the country."

"No!"

"Yes. It was on the news. All those statistics."

"Awful. I think it was that Henderson boy, Rory. He took the tools."

"Really?"

"Oh sure. The police won't do anything, but he and his friends are always out in that Chevy of his, cruising or somewhat. They're into alcohol. And *drugs*," mouthed Elena ominously.

"Oh, but Rory was such a good boy when he was younger."

"They all start like that, Daisy. Then they play these crazy games on the internet and it drives them wild, I tell you. We've bought ourselves a gun, haven't we Max?"

"A thirty eight," intoned Max.

"How wonderful," said Grandma. "You should talk to Harry about that. You can compare models, and whatever else gun men do. He gets so bored these days. He needs something to get him out."

"I'm not a gun man," called Grandpa. "You make me sound like a terrorist."

Grandma dismissed him with a wave. "You know what I mean."

Lizzy approached Josh with her drawing pad. "And what do you want me to draw you, Josh?"

Josh sipped his acrid lager. "A hole."

"A hole," echoed Lizzy seriously, picturing it on the paper. "Why?"

"So I can jump in it."

"Josh," called his grandma. "Can you go to the garage and get the parasol? I'm cooking like a shrimp, here. And what is that you're drinking?"

Lauren waited uneasily in the New York boardroom of the Underwood Financial Services building. Plush carpeting, teak tables and tasteful art on the walls. Modern and minimal, with a view of steel and glass skyscrapers out the window. Lauren felt seriously out of place, wearing high heels with a black pencil skirt and blouse. Whoever said the outfit was coming back into fashion had never tried to wear the damned thing. The other women present wore looser and more comfortable looking pantsuits. And low heels.

Lauren helped herself to another canapé. Trays of them adorned the table, along with fluted glasses of white wine. Not a cookie in sight.

She thought about the food parcel still in her backpack. The airport security guy had given her a strange look when he spotted it on the scanner and she was forced to empty the contents of her bag and open the foil wrapping to show that it was food, not a bomb. She was tempted to throw it in the garbage after that, but she felt guilty. Her mother had taken the time to make that, and Lauren had been raised to never waste food. So the crushed parcel remained, the toasted cheese sandwiches coated now in cookie crumbs.

She was impatient for the seminar to start. At least she could focus her attention on something, then. This whole mixing and greeting thing wasn't her style, especially with these elite university types with their crisp accents and flawless hair. It wasn't until the catering girl came in with more trays that Lauren felt there was someone else in the room she could relate to.

A woman who looked like a model moved through the crowd, her legs striding elegantly as she wiggled her hips, a lipstick smile glued permanently to her face. She carried a sheaf of papers and homed in like a cruise missile on Lauren.

"Hi," she said. "You must be Ms Nolan from our North Carolina office."

Lauren wondered how she knew. Was it really that obvious?

"I'm fine with Mrs," she said, "and yes, I'm from the Charlotte office."

"You have such a cute accent," said the model with the corpse grin. "These are the modules we'll be covering today," she added, handing over a sheet, "all questions should be reserved until the end, and there will be a feedback session afterwards. Have a lovely afternoon."

"Thank you, I will."

One look at the complex sounding modules was all Lauren needed to confirm that she was in the wrong place. Hell, she was in the wrong job.

She only took the job because she was worried about how she'd raise the kids if something happened to Rick. She'd get a gratuity off the military if anything bad happened to him, tax free, but the fear haunted her for years, nevertheless. The fact that he told her repeatedly he was thinking of retiring only served to increase the fear, as if it was somehow tempting fate. His rate of operations had increased significantly in recent years, and the places he was visiting were getting more dangerous. Hearing about the deaths of the two operators in Benghazi in 2012 as they attempted to protect the ambassador from an attack on the Libyan consulate prompted her to think the unthinkable. A chance meeting with a friend last year got her an interview for the prestigious financial firm and a chance of starting a lucrative career. Her past record in Military Intelligence convinced them to take her on – she artfully neglected to mention she'd only been a linguist – and she'd been winging it ever since. Her stress levels had gone through the roof as a result, and just when she thought she was coping, she'd been invited to listen to a high level speaker flying over from some university in California. Apparently it would prepare her for some coming changes to her role. Maybe a promotion. It should have been good news, but in all honesty, it terrified her. Her original plan for stability and security was spiraling out of control.

What the hell was she thinking?

Breathe, she thought. *I can do this. Just means learning a whole lot more complicated financial shit.*

Yeah, right. She was struggling with her work as it was.

A balding man in a pin striped suit entered the room and approached a desk microphone at the end of the table. Switching it on, he tapped it once, then addressed the room:

"Ladies and Gentlemen. My apologies for the delay, but I regret to inform you that our keynote speaker has been forced to cancel his journey and cannot now attend. This seminar is postponed and we will send you the dates as soon as we have the details. Thank you all for taking the time to come today and we apologize for any inconvenience. That is all."

The hubbub that followed indicated that most people were okay with that, like it was just another journey to them. Lauren felt seriously pissed at first, but after a few minutes she felt the weight lift off her shoulders as she realized she could go back to her normal life now.

If nothing else, it would give her a chance to rethink what the hell she was doing.

People drifted out of the room and the catering girl returned to begin gathering up the trays, most still full of food. "What happens to all this stuff now?" Lauren asked her.

"It'll get thrown away. If you want, I can box some up for you as a carryout."

"Could you? That would be fantastic. My daughter would love this."

"Sure. Let me just get you a box."

For good measure, Lauren helped herself to a few unopened bottles of water from the table. She felt like a hick, but what the hell? Waste not want not.

The best part of the Underwood building was that it had its own employee gym. Lauren had read about it in the company brochure. Anticipating a wait before her 6pm return flight, she'd packed her sweatpants and hoodie. She was glad she did, because she had a lot more time to kill now, and wandering the noisy streets of New York didn't appeal to her. She wasn't interested in shopping at overpriced boutiques.

From the bank of treadmills at the window, Lauren had a great view over 42nd Street and the carousel and tables of Bryant Park. There was nobody else in the gym and she had the equipment all to herself. She couldn't find the remote to change the channel on the plasma screens on the wall, though, all of which were tuned to CNBC business news, with its rolling ticker tape of stock prices and shares across the world. The company clearly didn't want its employees to get too relaxed in their downtime. As she jogged for her ten minute cardio warm-up, she wished she'd brought her MP3 player.

But she never listened to music much, anyway, and she'd probably given it to Lizzy at some point and forgotten about it.

Tuning out the smug presenters on the TV, she ran through her workout routine, looking for that endorphin hit. The stress and worry fell off her as she locked herself into her sweat bubble and by the time she headed for the showers, she was buzzed and relaxed.

She totally missed the important message on the TV:

...what you heard there was Professor Kathy Taylor from the National Space Weather Prediction Center talking about the solar storm that's expected to hit the planet tonight. That's a geomagnetic storm that's going to fry the atmosphere and give us a beautiful light show if you live far enough north. Is this the extinction event all those preppers have been waiting for? Hell, no. You might drop a signal bar on your cell and get a bit of interference on your TV, but that's about it. If you're on a plane, you may be re-routed or delayed on account of the radar interference that might occur, but that's just a safety precaution. It's in the regs. What you really want to be looking at is the price of gold. This is spiking as people get nervous, and shares are taking a nosedive, but pay attention, because this is when you want to be buying. Scoop up those shares now and in the morning your investment will have doubled when the market rebounds. The fact is, Bruce, these doomsday scenarios never play out, so if you're smart, you could be laughing all the way to the bank...

Professor Kathy Taylor removed the microphone from her lapel and handed it to the technician. The camera crew were already dismantling their gear. The interview was over and they had other places to be.

Brad waited to one side, fidgeting. His shift was over but he was still hanging around.

"Any change in the figures, yet?" she asked him.

"No," he said glumly, "but I've still got a bad feeling about this."

"Stick to the facts, Brad. You know what happened last time."

"Yeah, but what if this time it's real? And we don't have all the facts yet."

"But we will. Look, we've put the warnings out, and it's on the network news. Everyone's as ready as they're going to be."

"But they're the same kind of warnings we always put out. People get complacent."

Kathy got impatient. "There's procedures and rules, and we're doing everything we're paid to do. I can't control how people respond. Go home, Brad. I'll see you in the morning."

3

Flight VT002 from London to New York was halfway across the Atlantic when it got its first warning.

"VT002, we're expecting a geomagnetic storm this evening that could interfere with the landing radar. Any chance you can expedite your arrival? Over."

Captain Harry Nills keyed the microphone. "Negative, JFK. We're experiencing strong headwinds and expect a delay to our landing time of an hour. Can you give us a weather sitrep?"

Flight Officer Lars sat up in the co-pilot seat. He'd been taking a nap. "Problems?"

"Geomagnetic storm," said Harry. "Check the systems. We might have to land on our own instruments."

As Lars scanned through his checks, JFK's flight controller came back to them. "Hi, VT002. You've got headwinds down to 23,000ft, but below that you've got a cyclone with crosswinds."

"What do you think?" said Harry to Lars.

"We could handle the buffeting if we drop lower, but I don't like the extra fuel use. We're light at the moment. Might be better to do a shallow dive to 32,000 and pick up a bit of speed. But if the beacons are working, I don't see a problem with the approach."

"No, me neither," said Harry. He keyed the microphone. "Thank you, JFK. We'll try and pick up a bit of speed. Keep us updated on the situation."

"Roger that, VT002. Assume procedural control on approach. The air will be clear of traffic, so steer a direct vector to runway 4R. We'll get you down as best we can."

"Doesn't sound very confident," said Lars.

"No, sounds like they're grounding all flights. Hit the seatbelt sign and make an announcement, informing connection passengers of a possible delay once we're on the ground."

"That'll make them happy," grunted Lars.

"Doesn't it always?"

Disconnecting the autopilot, Harry slowly pushed forward on the flight controls.

Lauren arrived at check-in at Newark Liberty airport to find a lot of people hanging around with their luggage, complaining in loud voices. Pushing through to the check-in desk, she got the bad news.

"Sorry ma'am. There are cancellations across the board. Your flight time's been moved to 5am tomorrow morning."

"Are you kidding me? Why?"

"Can't say. We're trying to get more information now. If you leave me your cell number, we'll be putting out texts for passenger updates. Again, my apologies."

Lauren blew hair from her face. Traffic had been bad from Manhattan and she'd had to run from the taxi, fearful she might be late. "What are the chances the plane could leave earlier?"

"I don't know. But they give us that time for a reason. You can wait at the check-in area, or try a hotel."

There weren't many seats in the check-in area, and some of the passengers were sitting on the floor amid their luggage. It wasn't an option that appealed to Lauren.

What the hell. She'd find a hotel and bill it to the company. It was the least they could do after wasting her day. Josh and Lizzy would miss another day of school, and Lauren would probably receive another letter about Josh missing valuable education time and the effect on his grades.

They weren't great all ready. She really needed to sit down with him and check his school work to find out what was going wrong. Maybe even hire a tutor for him.

Oh my God, listen to yourself. Are you some kind of rich socialite now who's too busy to spend time with her children?

With the longer hours she was working, the truth was that she couldn't. That hurt.

Wracked with guilt, she called her mother, toying with Lizzy's takeout box while she waited to connect.

"Scott, how come you never retired?"

Rick lay on the lip of the wadi, his low-light binoculars focused on the convoy of pickups that moved along the horizon, kicking dust up into dusk's fading light.

"Nothing to retire for," said Scott, focused on the same convoy. "I count two heavy machine guns and a twenty mil AA gun on the last vehicle."

Rick zoomed in on the last vehicle. He assumed the angular shape was a multiple rocket launcher, but he decided Scott was right. "Don't you ever get tired of this shit, though?"

"Sometimes. Tell me what's better than this and I'll take you up on the offer. Another vehicle coming up behind the convoy. That's six, now."

Rick turned to the new contact, seeing the black ISIS flag fluttering proudly on the vehicle. This was the second convoy they'd seen in half an hour. The empty desert was coming alive as the enemy sought the cover of darkness to move. There was more activity heading north than he expected, though. "Got anything waiting for you, back home?"

"My sister, an empty trailer and a drunken halfwit of a brother who keeps owing people money and wants me to bail him out."

Rick had two F18s on standby, plus a Predator drone armed with hellfires that would make short work of those vehicles. This was meant to be an intel gathering mission, however, and he didn't want to kick the hornet's nest.

Not yet.

"What happened to that business idea you were talking about?" he asked.

"That was Rudy's idea. Remember him?"

"Yeah, I remember Rudy. Said he was sick of sunshine. Moving to Canada, wasn't he?"

"Changed his mind. He wanted me to partner him in creating a contract firm to offer close protection to TV stars in Mexico City."

"Didn't appeal?"

"Nah. Goofy idea. And can you imagine me in Mexico? I'd stick out like a sore thumb."

Rick thought he stuck out wherever he went. Especially in Fort Bragg, which was where he lived. Even the local rednecks thought he looked strange, and that was saying some. Rangy and pop-eyed, he got into more bar fights than the rest of the unit put together. Rick knew the reason he didn't want to see his drunken brother again was because Scott'd likely be arrested after putting him in hospital. Or the morgue. Scott and his brother really didn't get along. And Scott liked to drink too. Rick suspected he didn't want to end up like his brother, which was why he stayed in. On operations, he never touched a drop.

"And what about you?" asked Scott.

"I don't know," sighed Rick. "I'm not sure what I'd do if I quit."

"Open a bar," said a voice behind him.

"Or a gym," said another.

Rick turned to look at Walt and Jamie, the two youngest guys in the team. Jamie certainly looked like he already owned a gym. Rick remembered a time when he too took abnormal pride in his physique, and, like Jamie and Walt, saw retirement as some far-off thing where he'd get a chance to spend all the money he'd accumulated. It was a comforting fantasy until it started to draw close.

"There you go," said Scott. "Open a gym with a bar. Throw in a shooting range and these guys'll be your first customers."

"Make it a brothel and I'll sign up now," added Leroy. "You do life membership, right?"

"Why do I get the idea you guys want to get rid of me?" said Rick.

"Might be something to do with the fact that you've been talking about retirement ever since your pa died," said Scott solemnly.

Rick fell silent for a moment. "He was a good father," he said.

And there lay the rub.

4

Brad didn't go home in the end. He just couldn't. The computer model on the screen showed the fiery serpent about to swallow the Earth in its gaping maw.

Of course, it was just a simulation, based on the known factors measured at the sun. What the ejected mass was doing in space was another matter, and they wouldn't know until it started to hit the satellites.

Emma Goodrich was the late shift supervisor, and she was impressed by Brad's nervousness.

"So you really think this is a Carrington?" she said.

"That name's being bandied about too much," said Brad, trying to resist chewing his nails. He needed to go outside for another cigarette. "We've got hardly any scientific data for Carrington. All we've got is news clippings of eye witness reports. We have no idea whether that was really a big deal for the sun, or just a taster."

The Carrington event was a geomagnetic storm that lit up the night sky in 1859. It induced massive currents in telegraph lines that melted platinum contacts and gave electric shocks to telegraph operators, setting fire to telegraph paper. In a world before ubiquitous electricity lines, that was all that made the news. There was no data regarding x-ray levels, polarity alignment or induced wattage.

"Carrington, super-Carrington, whatever," said Emma. "We've got shielded systems now. Forget the doomsday stuff. We've been testing the effects of nuclear EMPs, and scientists have shown that modern electronics in cars, for instance, just trip. After resetting, everything works fine. And the National Grid disconnects to control surges. It's a myth to say everything will grind to a halt."

Brad stared at her. "Nuclear tests induce EMPs lasting a couple of nanoseconds. That was impressive enough, although the majority of the data we have comes from the Soviet era. They didn't anticipate the kind of technology we'd have now, and we haven't done any serious tests since on account of the test ban treaty. But this isn't a nuclear bomb. When that CME engulfs Earth, it's going to take minutes, not nanoseconds, to pass through.

Look at the length of that thing."

"Yeah, and Earth's magnetosphere will shield us. That's what it does."

"It protects us from the proton storm, but when the CME hits it, it's going to turn into one big Van de Graaf generator."

"Okay, that's just too many certainties. In case you hadn't noticed, you've got no hard data either. The effects of this are above our pay grade, Brad. We let the computers make the predictions and we pass it up the line. Leave it to the scientists to analyze the results. You already got burned once for this. Each time this kind of thing happens, we learn from the results and adjust the statistical data. You know: science."

"Yeah, thanks for patronizing me," said Brad dryly.

"You're welcome," said Emma.

Brad rubbed his arms. "I'm going out for a cigarette."

Emma watched him go, feeling a little sorry for him. He hadn't been the same since the official reprimand – which was totally out of order. It smacked of political interference. Somebody up top clearly got worried about the effect on their funding, and Brad was the fall guy. Since then, however, he'd got strangely erratic. Emma got the sense he didn't trust the data anymore – nor what was done with it. It was like he was over-compensating by reaching his own wild conclusions.

She wondered if he'd built a bunker, yet.

What he needed was time-out. A sabbatical. When he came back and saw the world hadn't ended without him, he'd calm down.

"Data from the WIND satellite's coming through," called someone.

The satellite measured the solar wind, the stream of energized particles that flowed constantly from the sun. It also took more accurate magnetic readings. As the graphs surged upwards, somebody whistled. The computer took the new data and plotted the effects on the atlas. Emma stared in shock as the screen went a uniform red.

"What's the relative polarity?" she asked.

"Between a hundred and seventy two and a hundred and eighty eight."

Near opposite polarity to Earth's magnetic field.

"Give me a time for impact."

"Fifty three minutes."

"Put out the alert. Now!"

Brad came rushing back into the office, unlit cigarette still in mouth. Wide eyed, he watched the simulation on the big screen change as the computer adjusted. The fiery serpent bloated and grew.

"Mom said you had to sleep early tonight," said Lizzy.

"What for?" said Josh. "Don't need to get up tomorrow."

"Because Mom said."

The room was dark, lit only by the console of Josh's 3DS. He was sitting up in bed, with Lizzy curled up next to him.

"Don't forget to unplug it when you're done," said Lizzy.

"It needs to charge."

"Grandma doesn't like things plugged in at night."

"Grandma doesn't need to know."

There was a moment of silence. Josh had his headphones on.

"Does the light bother you?" he asked.

"No, I'm fine," said Lizzy sleepily.

"Better get back to sleep."

"Okay."

Josh battled zombies for a few minutes longer, then gritted his teeth when he died again. Seven attempts at the level, and he still hadn't gone any further. He wanted to pound his pillow and throw his 3DS at the wall.

If he was at home, in his own room, he would have.

Frustrated, he switched it off and lowered it gently to the floor so as not to wake his sister again. Easing himself under the sheet, he lay down and listened to her gentle breathing. Whatever anger he had subsided quickly and he touched her shoulder to wish her goodnight. Then he rolled over and dropped into a deep sleep.

5

"Mayday, mayday, we have multiple contacts. We need that air strike now!"

"Roger that, Nomad. We're working on it. Wait one."

"Jesus Christ," hissed Rick, releasing the radio button. Through his night vision goggles, the darkness around the vehicle seemed to be painted with green lasers. Loose equipment flew around inside the cab as Flynn drove fast over the hard dunes, jerking the wheel left and right to present a harder target. The suspension squeaked and pounded, and loose vegetation flew out of the night as Scott's vehicle swerved ahead of them, driving the same crazy evasive maneuvers. A slope loomed up ahead of them, and the packed earth disintegrated into plumes of dust as the machine gun and cannon rounds zipped past the pickups. From the back bed, the grenade launcher pounded triple salvos in return, though how Leroy was able to both aim and hang on was a mystery to Rick.

After leaving the wadi, they'd headed north and found more activity in the desert than Rick anticipated. The number of vehicles he saw didn't match the traffic data he'd got from the JSTAR. Near Ain Issa, artillery pieces and rocket launchers lit up the sky as they pounded Kurdish positions. Perhaps understanding the forthcoming interruption in air cover, ISIS forces were gathering for a surprise offensive, converging from different directions. Rick's team were spotted and, after a brief firefight, chased back south by increasing numbers of vehicles engaged in a well organized pursuit. Rick caught snatches of Arabic on the radio as he intercepted enemy messages. Whoever was coordinating the pursuit knew exactly who they were, and their value if caught. Without air support, there wasn't a lot to prevent the enemy achieving their objective.

Powering up the slope, Flynn launched the pickup over the ridge. A bullet shattered the windshield as they skidded down towards a rocky gully. Up ahead was a farm, surrounded by vehicles, and machine guns stationed there lashed the team with tracer fire, cutting off their escape. Flynn fought with the wheel as the pickup dropped into the gully. Sharp stones lacerated the tire, and the pickup pitched forward as it blew, pieces of rubber flying past Rick's window. Flynn stood on the brakes, and the pickup skidded to a halt, leaning at a dangerous angle. It looked like it was going to roll over. Rick kicked open the door and ran clear. The vehicle rocked, but stayed put. Leroy had already jumped down.

Tracer rounds kicked and whined. Scott, seeing them stop, reversed back up to them. Jamie, firing his grenade launcher from Scott's vehicle, bracketed the farm house with explosions, but the fire was unceasing, multiple tracer lines converging on Rick's position.

"Set up the M249 in those rocks there," called Rick to Leroy, pointing.

The M249 was the team's light machine gun and Leroy heaved it out of the truck, extending the bipod and racing to set it up. Flynn ran over to Scott's vehicle, but it was already taking hits. When the engine died, everyone bailed out.

The pursuing ISIS vehicles crested the ridge behind them, a line of headlights blazing. Leroy opened fire with the M249, halting them with a rapid buzzsaw of bullets that shattered windshields and sent ISIS fighters scurrying for cover. Rick crawled up the gully, adding fire from his M4 to the onslaught, but for every fighter he targeted, ten fired back, ricocheting bullets around the gully. Pinned down, Rick was helpless as a mounted 20mm cannon pounded his position and shredded his stricken pickup, igniting the fuel tank with a deep *whumph*.

Flying at 45,000 feet in Bird Two, Captain 'Skip' Saunders had a problem. The side-scan radar and powerful cameras on his modified Boeing 707 gave him the ability to spot and track ground targets for hundreds of miles, but he was suffering unprecedented interference from the ionosphere, and sending faulty data down to Nomad. The gathering proton storm in space leaked into the atmosphere, and the invisible proton particles were already whizzing straight through his aircraft. He knew that because he was seeing bright flashes as the particles plowed through his retinas. A glowing green aurora started to form in the dark sky, way further south than was predicted. Those same proton particles were cutting through the digital image sensors of the cameras, degrading the images. The computer compiling the data from all the sensors was thus producing contradictory pictures of the situation below, at one point contrasting sharply with the frantic radio messages from Nomad.

Unable to trust his equipment, Skip was also unable to vector a single aircraft to Nomad's aid. The F18s had been ordered to return to their carrier, and the Predator drone had developed a fault with its targeting sensors and forced to abort its patrol.

He was now being ordered to return to base himself.

"Negative, Control. We have a team trapped on the ground. Situation is critical. Repeat, situation is critical. Request urgent support by any means necessary."

"Control to Bird Two, geomagnetic storm is imminent, repeat imminent. You are to return to base immediately."

"No," said Skip. "I need air support in this area and I need it now, before it's too late."

Skip had already consulted his crew, and they were in agreement with him: they had to stay, even if it meant disobeying orders. If they left now, Nomad was toast.

There was a pause on the line. "Skip, goddammit! There's a major G-storm coming your way. If you don't land now, you'll endanger the whole aircraft."

That had to be Colonel Douglas. He must have snatched the microphone from the controller to break radio protocol.

"Colonel," said Skip, "we've weathered G-storms before. Our electronics are fully shielded." Not as shielded as he would have liked, but the aircraft was built for a nuclear conflict, and while nothing could stop proton strikes, the delicate avionics were still protected against the kind of EMP spikes expected back in the Cold War.

"You've never weathered this, Skip. We've been given red warnings. First time in my career I've received that. You're not going to make it back to Al Udeid. Put it down at the nearest airfield."

"With all due respect, sir, no. We're not leaving this team."

"Captain, that's an order."

"Colonel, I refuse. Give me something before we lose this team."

There was silence in the cockpit. Skip knew he'd just screwed his whole career, and his crew knew it too. Turning around in his seat, he looked at them all. They were kind of shocked that he'd actually said that to the colonel. Skip and Colonel Douglas went back a long way, and had close family connections, but this was crossing a line.

"There was some static on the last message," said Colonel Douglas. "I'm not sure I received it." There was a pause. "I'm authorizing a drone launch. It'll be with you in two hours."

Skip felt bad, knowing Douglas was stepping over a line himself in helping him. It wasn't enough, though.

"It'll be too late, sir. The team on the ground won't last two hours. On our screens we've got a fast mover in the area, tagged as one of ours. I just need one strike, sir. That's all I'm asking."

It was a tough call. The Air Force had perfected a complex system for combat missions, almost to the point of being bureaucratic, especially in a low pressure environment like the air war in Syria. Certainly, the army were inclined to think of the Air Force as inflexible and slow to respond, as well as a little soft and laid back. When it came to it, though, there wasn't a single pilot willing to leave troops on the ground in danger, and they were as ready as anybody else to lay their lives on the line for the guys they were supporting.

"I'll see what I can do," said Colonel Douglas heavily.

The crescendo of firing increased. In the light of the burning pickup, Rick could see Jamie pulling Walt to the cover of the gully. Walt had been hit, and that was bad news.

Scott was nowhere to be seen. Had he been hit as well?

They were all going to get hit if they didn't get out of there. Rick looked down the gully. There was a dry stream bed at the bottom of the slope. It didn't offer much cover. Rick ran through his options and decided he needed to get his team moving. But first he had to locate Scott.

"Jamie, get Walt to the bottom of the gully," he radioed. "Flynn, give him a hand."

He didn't need to say any more. When Jamie and Flynn got to the bottom, they'd cover the others as they followed. Leroy would keep firing until he got the word to move.

Steeling himself, Rick dashed out from the gully, sprinting to the other pickup. With the dust kicking up around him, he threw himself underneath the chassis.

"Scott. Where are you?"

"By the pickup," replied Scott.

"Where? I can't see you."

Scott leaned out from behind the front wheel. "Here."

"We have to move. Walt's been hit."

Scott shuffled forward. A fusillade of heavy bullets rocked the chassis above Rick's head, like it was being hit by hammers. Fuel started leaking down onto his helmet. Scott fired back at the machine gun while Rick rolled out into the open.

The 20mm cannon that ISIS used was mounted on the back of a truck and protected with a metal shield. The gunner spotted Rick's movement and swung the twin barrels towards him. Before Rick could take aim with his own rifle, the explosive shells rocked his position, showering him in dirt and shrapnel.

***

Lieutenant Merrill Kowalski was on his way back to base in his F16 when he got the call.

"Viper One, this is Control, we need you to divert one eight niner to fly ground support. Do you copy?"

Kowalski checked his instruments. He'd been in the air for two hours, stooging around, and he was low on fuel.

"Copy that, Control, but I'm near bingo on fuel, and I'm not configured for ground support."

He'd been on an airspace protection patrol over Northern Syria, armed with air-to-air missiles and tasked with deterring the Turkish air force from bombing Kurdish forces, which basically meant flying in circles at height while showing himself on Turkish radar and hoping the fellow NATO member wasn't prepared to trigger a diplomatic incident. It was a strange situation where the two allies were supposed to both be fighting ISIS, but they both backed opposing factions whilst doing so.

Then there was the matter of the Russians. Kowalski's wing man had already returned to base, but Kowalski had diverted towards a contact that turned out to be a Russian aircraft near the agreed demarcation line between their two air forces. Shadowing the aircraft and pinging it with his radar until it turned west, Kowalski banked east and throttled back his Pratt and Whitney engine, nursing the fuel for his return to Iraqi airspace.

"Viper One, we have a unit on the ground in urgent need of assistance, call sign Nomad. Situation is considered critical and there's nobody else to assist."

Kowalski sighed and scanned his instruments again, making calculations. It was pushing his luck, but he might be able to do something.

"Copy that, Control. Turning to one eight niner."

Kowalski throttled back the engine some more and pushed his sleek fighter into a gentle dive. Cocooned in his pressurized cockpit, with only the lights on his instruments visible, the pilot had no sensation of increased speed. Switching to the frequency assigned to him, Kowalski calmly thumbed the radio switch.

"This is Viper One to Nomad, do you copy?"

The engine hummed smoothly as Kowalski watched his altitude drop on his instruments. A shimmer of green appeared in the night sky above, which surprised him a little. He knew about the northern lights that would be triggered by the geomagnetic storm, but they hadn't been forecast to come this far south.

No matter. His fuel reading told him he'd soon be home, no matter what Control wanted. He wouldn't be able to linger long.

"Viper One to Nomad, do you copy?"

A scratchy, desperate voice came into his earphones. "This is Nomad. We need... we need a strike... sector Blue Seven Seven... coordinates five, one, zero.... zero, three."

Kowalski could hear the gunfire and impacts that interrupted the message. Nomad was clearly in trouble. Switching on a cockpit light, Kowalski checked the map strapped to his thigh.

"Copy that, Nomad. Inbound now from the north-west. Can you laser-designate your target?"

"Negative... I count six... seven soft vehicles on an east-west ridge... they're lit up, you can't miss them."

Kowalski begged to differ. From up here, it would be very easy to miss them, no matter how prominent they appeared from the ground. "Nomad, can you activate your beacon?"

There was no reply, but seconds later Kowalski got a reading on his panel and made a gentle turn. A tiny string of lights showed in the distance. Switching his HUD to his cannon sights, Kowalski lined up the target and swooped down towards it.

"Target in sight, Nomad. Can you confirm? Vehicles with lights. Tell me they're not yours."

"Negative... our vehicles are knocked out... on fire."

Kowalski saw the flames now, a little distance down from the ridge. "Copy that. You are danger close, Nomad."

"Don't give a damn... we're in cover... hit them now!"

Considering the volume of gunfire Kowalski could hear in the background of the message, Nomad was definitely in a tough situation. If not for that, Kowalski would have aborted the attack for fear of hitting his own side. Arming his Vulcan 20mm rotary cannon, he targeted the first vehicle in the line, aiming to sweep his shells across them. He calculated he had enough fuel for this pass, and maybe one more. After that, he had to go. The vehicle, a standard looking pickup, loomed in his sights. Kowalski pressed the trigger, unleashing a burst of heavy fire from the weapon housed in his wing root.

Lying pinned on the ground, Rick witnessed the tracers lancing down. It was like Zeus throwing a bagful of lightning bolts. The rapid lines of cannon fire stitched up the ISIS vehicles, tearing up metalwork, igniting fuel tanks and pounding the ground with exploding clouds of dust and shrapnel. Above it all, the night sky glowed red, as if the gods were ready to throw down more.

6

The sun's coronal mass ejection of plasma hit the Earth's magnetosphere and began flowing around it. Such was the force of the plasma's bow wave that it compressed the magnetosphere on the impact side and stretched the Earth's magnetotail on the trailing side. The massed electrons and protons reacted with the opposite alignment of Earth's magnetic field to induce terawatts of electricity in Earth's upper atmosphere that produced impressive, planet-wide auroras. Charging like a capacitor, the atmosphere discharged its power in the only direction it could – towards Earth.

When the first wave of plasma had passed, the stretched magnetotail snapped back within its original field lines, inducing a massive EMP spike that multiplied the charge already held in the broiling stratosphere.

Flight VT002 was nearly home. Turning over Long Island Sound to align with runway 4R, Captain Harry Nills watched in awe as the night sky erupted into lurid shades of purple and green. Updated by increasingly alarming messages from flight control, he'd been pushing the engines to their limit to make it down in time. His first thoughts over the Atlantic were for the safety of his passengers. At high altitudes, they were at risk from the cosmic particles that were set to increase during the geomagnetic storm. He was lower now, though, and felt confident that their exposure would be brief – well within FAA safety limits.

Approaching Long Island, the flight controller's voice broke up into harsh static.

"Can you repeat that last message, JFK?" said Nills calmly.

"Lowering flaps. AP off," said Flight Officer Lars.

"Applying speed brakes," intoned Nills.

The roar of friction as the aircraft decelerated mingled with the crescendo of interference in his headphones.

"JFK, are you receiving me?" he asked.

The sky turned a bright red, like an early sunrise, and the cockpit lit up, so he could clearly see his hand on the shaking throttles.

"Wow, look at that," said Lars. Every building in New York leaped out in sharp resolution under the blushing sky. The city lights gleamed like a thousand fires.

The instrument lights flickered and dimmed.

"Lowering undercarriage. Check the auxiliary power unit," said Nills, starting to sweat. The radar flashed up conflicting readings, and his headphones emitted only white noise.

"Two thousand feet," said Lars. "GS unit not responding. Rebooting."

A flash of lightning lit up the windshield. Nills wasn't expecting a thunder storm, and didn't appreciate being blinded. With nothing from flight control, and no signal from the beacon, he was making a visual approach.

"Undercarriage locked," said Lars, seemingly unconcerned. Nills took a deep breath, telling himself he had to be just as calm. Unusual weather event. That was all.

Tendrils of lightning suddenly appeared from the sky, arcing in multiple lines all across the horizon. The city lights went out, like someone had snuffed out a million candles. A series of terrifying bangs sounded in the cockpit – mighty hammer blows on the airframe from the lightning. Nills experienced complete whiteout. His headphones fell silent, and the instrument panel went dark.

Atmospheric power surges cradled Flight VT002 in a crackling death grip, the lightning sticks on the ailerons glowing bright red as raw electricity played between them. Exposed wires in the undercarriage bays burned off their insulating plastic and sparks flew from the turbo fans in the engine nacelles.

"The engines are dead," shrieked Lars, abruptly losing his cool.

Nills hit the restart buttons, but nothing responded. He pitched the stick forward in an automatic stall reaction, trying to put the aircraft into a gliding dive, but he got no response from that either.

"Goddammit," he yelled as centrifugal force pushed him up against his straps.

The one hundred and fifty ton aircraft dropped out of the sky, chased by its own tail of light. Whirling in a lazy pirouette, it smashed into the ground at the Harbor Links Golf Course at Port Washington, tearing up the tended greens and sandy bunkers and breaking apart. A single red-hot engine, still sparking, bounded onward into South Salem School, plowing through the empty buildings and coming to rest on a wooded path on the other side, setting light to dry brush.

The electromagnetic pulses glowing in the atmosphere induced blistering power surges in every wire and circuit board on the planet. Power lines glowed red as electricity jumped the insulators and earthed through the giant pylons. Barbed wire fences became active conduits, electrocuting nearby cattle. Bulbs blew and electronic chips burned out. Power station transformers exploded.

In Charlotte, a CityLynx light rail car picked up speed as power boosted through the overhead line, jumping the breakers and superheating the coils on its motors. Tyrel Watson, driving the car on its last night journey before returning to the depot, got an electric shock from the throttle lever as he tried to slow it down. The motors whined as the vintage-style streetcar hurtled down Elizabeth Avenue, the carriage rocking dangerously.

"Hey," shouted a bum from the back seat. "You trying to get me killed?"

The bum had been riding most of the night, preferring the shelter of the streetcar to a bench in the park. He ran forward now, showing none of the drunken awkwardness he'd displayed earlier.

"Can you hear me?" he demanded when he got to Tyrel.

Tyrel massaged his wrist. Ahead, a cab rolled out from the lot of Cuisine Malaya. The streetcar tore down the street like a fusion powered Delorean and ripped off the cab's front fender, shunting it aside.

"It won't slow down," said Tyrel.

"Jesus, ain't you got no brakes?"

Together the two of them pulled on the brake handle with all the strength they could muster. It made no difference. Trying the throttle lever again, they both jerked back from the shock.

Approaching the end of Elizabeth Avenue, the bum, sucking his burnt fingers, yanked open the doors and leaped out. Hurled from the speeding vehicle, he slid along the road, bumped up onto the sidewalk and hit a street light at sickening speed, breaking his back.

Tyrel watched in horror as the three-way intersection approached. The rails curved left, but he thought the streetcar wouldn't make it round.

He was right. The streetcar left the rails, slid along the ground and crashed through the pillared entrance of the Presbyterian Medical Center in a shower of glass.

One mile away, Josh, who'd slept through the lightning crashes, woke when his plugged-in 3DS blew up. Startled, he sat up, wondering what the hell was happening.

Kowalski was preparing for a second pass at the target when the lightning strikes enveloped his jet. The staccato pounding of his plane and the blinding flashes convinced him he was being hit by anti-aircraft fire.

Pushing the stick to one side, he began evasive maneuvers just as his instrument panel blew all its fuses. The engine died. His chaff and flare dispensers blasted off on their own, and his surging radar and avionics suite caught fire, filling the cockpit with smoke. Hitting the fire extinguisher button did nothing. With his eyes stinging and the bombardment of the airframe continuing, his electronically controlled flight stick flopped uselessly in his hand. With no control, the graceful jet fell from the sky like a brick.

Panicking, he yanked the ejection handle, igniting the rockets that blasted his seat and canopy into the air. As he flew upwards, crackling lines of static flowed like umbilical cords from the base of his seat to his aircraft.

Rick lay stunned by the geomagnetic storm's spectacular light display, his hair standing on end inside his helmet. The sky was so bright, he could clearly see the surviving ISIS fighters crawling about on the ridge, trying to get away from their burning vehicles. Away to the west, he saw the F16 knifing towards the ground, a bright parachute descending.

Taking advantage of the lull in the firing, Rick aimed his weapon at one of the enemy fighters.

Or he tried to. The red aiming dot on his reflector sight wasn't there. Switching it on and off failed to change anything.

Crawling towards the gully, he radioed Scott. "Moving out. Let's go."

He got no reply. His radio was so completely dead that he realized that wasn't working either.

What the fuck?

The ISIS fighters cheered as the F16 hit the ground and exploded. Leroy opened fire with his machine gun, cutting short their jubilation and forcing them to hit the dirt.

"Scott! Can you hear me?" yelled Rick.

Scott appeared beside him in the gully. He'd come via a different direction. "I think everybody can hear you," he said.

"Tell Leroy we're moving out. My radio's stopped working."

"Mine too," said Scott. "And my goddamn watch has stopped."

Rick checked and found his had also. "This is just weird." He shook his head. "Get to the bottom of the gully with the others. I'll tell Leroy. We need to reach that pilot before ISIS does."

Rick crawled up the gully until he reached Leroy, slapping him on the shoulder. "Time to go," he said.

Leroy quit firing. "Tried to call you but my radio's stopped working."

"Yeah, I know. Seems to be all the rage at the moment. Let's move while they're distracted."

Apart from the lightning cracks, the battlefield was silent. Even the fighters at the farm had ceased fire. One of them, manning a machine gun on a truck, pointed upwards. Other fighters came out of the building compound, gazing nonchalantly up at the sky.

Rick felt compelled to join in their focus. What he saw froze his insides.

A Boeing 707 spiraled down in a flat spin.

"Cover!" shouted Rick.

The JSTAR aircraft smashed down onto the hillside, bursting apart. Undercarriage wheels, engines and every other heavy component bounded away in all directions. Wing tanks ignited and flaps scythed like blades across the packed dirt. Seats and body parts tumbled in their wake. Face down in the gully, Rick and Leroy were buried in an avalanche of debris that swept away their damaged pickups.

7

Lauren woke with a start in her hotel bed. Thunder rocked and crashed outside, and her room lit up with flashes through the thin curtains.

Rolling over with a groan, she pulled the pillow over her head. It had been hard enough finding the hotel, and harder still paying almost two hundred dollars for a non-smoking room that stank of cigarettes and a carpet that smelled like it had been laid in the Civil War. Rooms were at a premium when so many people were forced to wait for the next day's flight.

Even shitty rooms.

With loud music from the room above and the noise from the elevator next to her room, she'd found it difficult to get to sleep. At least the music had stopped now, and the elevator was quiet. It must have been late.

Grabbing her phone from the night stand, she pulled it under the pillow to check the time.

She threw the pillow off when she couldn't get the phone to work.

Dammit. She needed to charge it. Getting out of bed, she padded over to her bag and found the charger. When she plugged it in, however, she still couldn't get the phone to work.

Outside, the mother of all storms continued. Lauren opened the curtains, marveling at the light display.

She didn't realize they had storms like this in New Jersey. It wasn't like anything she'd seen before. The cloud base glowed red, and she thought at first it was dawn. The baleful hue, and the flashes of light, brought to mind another image: Baghdad in 2003.

Operation Iraqi Freedom. She'd been attached to a recon unit as an interpreter back then, and with orders to halt outside the city, she'd watched as the air force bombed Baghdad. Streaks of anti-aircraft fire laced the heavens, and fires lent the city a hellish glow. For the first three months after she finished her tour, it was the one thing she had nightmarish flashbacks about.

She couldn't understand why, as she thought it looked beautiful at the time. She had much the same thought now, in spite of the interrupted sleep.

Somewhere in the hotel, someone was banging on a wall and yelling.

Lauren opened the window and immediately felt the static in the air. There was a strong smell of ozone. Looking down she saw the street lights were all off. She couldn't see a light anywhere in the city. She was thinking it was a pretty impressive power cut when she realized that the traffic wasn't moving either. On the road below, the vehicles had stopped and people were milling about.

"What the hell's happening, man?" she heard someone shout.

The banging in the hotel continued. It was coming from the wall by the elevator shaft.

Lauren tested the switches in her room, just to be sure. Nothing worked, so she got dressed in her gym gear, grabbed her key and left her room.

The door opposite was open, and Lauren saw the dim silhouette of a woman with a girl beside her.

"Are you out of power as well?" asked the woman.

"Yeah," said Lauren. "Looks like the power's down for several blocks."

"Do we have to evacuate, Mummy?" said the little girl.

"No, honey," said the woman. "We don't need power to sleep. They'll have it back in the morning."

"Excuse me, do you know what time it is?" asked Lauren.

The woman looked at her watch, then sighed. "It's stopped working. Honey, can you get my phone?"

The girl disappeared inside and returned with the phone.

"I can't believe it," said the woman. "This isn't working either. Do you have your phone, honey?"

The girl went back into the room, then called out. "I can't get it to switch on, Mummy."

"Well, isn't that the strangest thing?"

Lauren certainly thought it was. She walked over to the elevator and pressed her ear to the door.

A muffled voice was yelling for help.

Lauren made her way down to the lobby, where the polished floor was lit up by the lightning flashes outside the glass walls. At the marble-effect service counter, a black dude in shorts and a vest remonstrated with a young black concierge.

"I'm sorry, sir, but I can't do anything about the blackout. It's a storm. It's a natural event," said the concierge.

The dude was apoplectic. "My TV done blown up in my face! Boy, that ain't no natural event."

In the back room behind the counter, Lauren saw the smoking remains of a computer covered in white powder, with a fire extinguisher nearby.

"Excuse me," said Lauren. "I hate to interrupt, but there's someone trapped in the elevator."

"I'm sorry, miss, but the phones are all down. I can't call anyone."

The young man, no more than college age, looked worn out. His graveyard shift had turned into a nightmare, and he was alone.

The dude in the vest turned to Lauren, looking for support. "Can you believe this guy? I report an explosion in my room, and the first thing he tells me is I can't get no refund. Like it's my fault."

"Sir, that's not what I meant."

Lauren left them to their argument, wandering over to the revolving doors. On the street, delivery vans and cabs stood on the road. The drivers stood around, sharing cigarettes and exchanging opinions. Under the hotel entrance canopy, a homeless guy approached Lauren.

"You got any money?" he said.

Lauren waved him off, walking over to a man standing by his bakery delivery van, still trying to get his phone to come to life.

"What happened?" she asked.

"That's a really good question," he said. "Shame I ain't got no answers. One minute I'm driving along, the next, she cuts out on me. I can't even get the engine to turn over. It's like the battery's dead. Only it happened at the same time to every single vehicle here. What the hell causes that? The lightning's way up there, and I never even got struck."

Lauren had an idea what might have caused this, but she didn't really want to entertain it, as it made no sense. She remembered the army lectures about nuclear EMP attacks. That was the only thing that could explain the loss of personal electronic devices along with the grid and vehicles cutting out. There was nothing in the lectures about the weird light effects, though.

"Was there anything on the news last night about us being at war with someone?" she asked.

The delivery man snickered. "We's at war with just about everybody, but no, I didn't see nothing special on the news last night. Just some stuff about a solar eclipse, or something. Or a solar flare, I can't remember."

"A solar flare?"

"Yeah, they was grounding flights and talking 'bout interference on cell networks. But they never mentioned this. They were talking about some guy called Carrington."

"Carrington?"

"Yeah, some English dude. Maybe he owns shares in the networks."

"I don't think so," said Lauren, biting her lip.

Oh my God, she thought. A Carrington event? Seriously?

"I've got four hours to deliver all this bread," said the delivery man. "After that, customers are gonna be hungry. And pissed."

Back in the hotel, the residents were out of their rooms and hogging the corridors, complaining about the blackout. On her floor, Lauren found two men forcing open the elevator doors with a fire axe. The elevator shaft was pitch black.

"Anybody got a light?" said one of the men.

Somebody produced a box of matches, and one was lit and dropped into the shaft.

"I see the elevator," said the other man. "It's half on the door of the next floor down."

"Don't worry, buddy," shouted the first man down the shaft. "We'll soon get you out."

The two men moved purposefully to the stairwell.

Lauren entered her room. Her hands shook as she grabbed her bag. Please, please, please, she thought. Don't let this be what I think it is.

Tying her hair back, she took a deep breath. Disconnecting her phone, she packed it in her bag in a conscious attempt at denial. Picking up the canapé box, she pushed her way through the people in the corridor, dropped the key off at reception and strode through the revolving doors.

"Got any money?" said the homeless guy again.

Lauren ignored him, intent on getting to the airport.

The homeless guy didn't like that. "Fuck you, bitch! What do you want all your money for? The world's coming to an end. Are you saving for something?"

"Hey, motherfucker," the delivery man shouted at the homeless guy. "Watch your mouth!"

The atmosphere on the streets was mixed. For some people, it was a welcome change to the routine, like a major snowfall that stopped everything but which everyone knew was temporary. It was a chance to talk to strangers without having to introduce themselves first, because everybody was connected now by the freak occurrence.

Others wanted to bitch, because the change to the routine was a hindrance to them. But then, they were the kind of people who bitched about everything, and this was just one more opportunity.

And then there were others who were unsure about these events, like it might be a bad omen. They were the quiet ones, watching and wondering.

Lauren passed a group of such people gazing upwards at the Prudential office block. Lauren stopped and joined them for a moment, seeing the flames that licked the windows of the twenty fourth floor. Lauren could imagine the banks of computers and servers there, and realized there could be more fires in the other blocks that hadn't shown themselves yet. It was strange to see the flames and not hear sirens, and Lauren thought that probably everyone in the group understood they weren't going to hear them any time soon.

At the top of the building, their nation's flag flew, limp against the backdrop of the storm. Lauren didn't like the portent and hurried on down Broad Street.

At the next intersection, a Prius burned, flames licking out from the battery compartment. A truck driver took a fire extinguisher from his cab and went to help the Prius driver put it out while a gathering crowd watched. Today, at least, they weren't using their phones to film it for Facebook, and they looked kind of lost, like they should really be recording this somehow.

By the time she made it out of the downtown area, Lauren had counted three vehicles on fire, including a vintage station wagon that shouldn't have had any electronic engine management systems that were vulnerable to an EMP. The weirdness of the situation spurred her on faster.

The taxi that had brought her from the airport had entered the district from Highway 21. Normally, it would have been illegal for her to walk up the exit ramp, but right now all the traffic was stationary and people meandered the highway lanes, unwilling as yet to completely abandon their cars, but uncertain of what else to do. Because she seemed to be walking with a purpose, everyone she passed asked her what was happening.

She didn't want to be frank – nor admit her fears – so she feigned ignorance and kept up her pace.

After an hour of walking she arrived at the airport. Smoke rose from behind the terminal, and groups of people with suitcases gathered at the entrances, prevented from going further by security staff.

"All flights are canceled, people," shouted one of the security guards. "Go home until we sort this out. We'll message you."

"How?" shouted a passenger, holding up a dead phone.

"I have no idea," replied the security guard, "but nothing's happening here. All systems are down."

Irate passengers offered further opinions on the situation, none complementary, and Lauren grew more concerned when she looked around and noticed stewardesses and pilots in their prim uniforms in the crowd too. They weren't going anywhere, either.

Anxiously, she thought about her children, five hundred miles away.

8

"Harold!" was what Josh heard. An incredible scream that seemed to tear right through the house. It didn't sound like his grandma's voice, but it was.

He'd gotten used to a voice that was always so casual, and so certain in its authority, whether she was praising, berating or just offering her cast iron opinion on things. Everything was what it was to Grandma Daisy, and no amount of protesting was going to change that.

Josh had never heard his grandma call her husband Harold before. It was always a calmly dismissive 'Harry', or 'your grandpa'. Hearing his grandpa's real name screamed at the top of his grandma's lungs frightened him.

Josh froze, then remembered his mom wasn't at home to take care of things. Lizzy sat bolt upright next to him, looking like a startled rabbit. Josh realized he was the only other person in the house who could do anything.

Tumbling out of bed, he tripped over the charging lead of his smoking 3DS and staggered into the hallway. Flashes of light from outside lit the interior of the house like a horror movie. Still not fully awake, Josh careened down the hall, banging his shin on an ottoman. Cursing and hopping, he entered his grandparents' bedroom. Grandma Daisy was crouched on the bed in her nightdress, looking like she was making love to Grandpa Harry. Except she was screaming and shaking his shoulders, while Grandpa clutched his chest.

"Josh, call an ambulance!"

In the strobing light that illuminated the room, Grandpa's face was like twisted rock.

Josh ran out of the room and flicked on the hall switch.

Nothing happened.

Darting into the kitchen, he grabbed the phone and started to dial 911, thinking about what he should be saying. He'd never called emergency services before and found himself thinking about the number of cranky calls they received every year. Weirdly, he felt he had to get the words right.

He didn't notice there was no tone on the line.

Seconds passed as he recited what he should say before he realized the phone was dead. Letting the receiver fall from his shaking fingers, he ran into his room, looking for his cell phone. He cursed out loud when he saw that was dead too and ran back into his grandparents' room.

"The phones are out," he gibbered.

Grandpa was struggling to breathe and grimacing with pain.

"His pacemaker's stopped," said Grandma. "Please, Josh. Go to Elena. Ask to use her phone. We need an ambulance right this minute."

Still in his shorts, Josh unlocked the front door and sprinted out into the street, heading to the Seinfelds' house. Banging on their front door, he waited impatiently for Elena to get to the door. Instead, it was Max.

"Can I use your phone? Grandpa needs an ambulance real bad."

In his dressing gown, Max rubbed his face to wake himself up. In his hand he held his new .38 revolver. "Sure, kid. Through into the kitchen. Elena! There's problems with Harry."

Josh barged in and grabbed the wall phone.

"This one's dead, too!" he cried.

Elena appeared, her hair in rollers. "What's happening here?"

"Grandpa's sick. He needs the hospital and all the phones are down."

Elena paused for a moment to process that, then took charge. "Okay, calm down Josh. Max, get the car started. We'll take Harry down ourselves. I'm going over to give Daisy a hand. And put that silly gun away."

While Elena strode over the road, Max went to get his keys, muttering to himself. "Get a gun, she says. Only now it's a silly gun. Wasn't my idea, but now it's my dumb hobby. Why does she always turn things around so it's on me?"

Josh waited on the porch, restless.

"It's okay, kid, I'm coming, I'm coming." Max lumbered out. He was a big man and Josh had never seen him move fast. "We'll get your grandpa to the hospital. He'll be fine. He's a tough old bird."

He clicked the key fob to unlock the car, but there was no answering chirrup from the vehicle. Max clicked again and again, but no change. "Can you believe it?" he said. Waddling to the car, he manually opened the door, lowered himself heavily into the driver's seat and put the key in the ignition, turning it.

Nothing happened. "Goddamn it," he said. "Of all the times."

"Why won't it start?" said Josh, frantic.

Max shrugged. "I don't know. It was fine yesterday. Let me get the charger out of the garage."

Josh watched him lift himself out of the car and walk slowly to the garage. He couldn't believe things were taking so long. Grandma had given him the responsibility of getting help, and nothing was happening.

He drifted out onto the road, taking one dazed step, then another. Before he knew it he was running.

Lightning forked down and hit a street light with a terrible crack. The sky glowed like blood and Josh felt he was running witless through hell, but he couldn't stop himself. A sense of panic gripped him. People stood on their porches, looking at this half naked kid running barefoot along the road, but Josh paid them no heed. His feet were flying but he still wasn't going fast enough. All the while he thought this couldn't be happening. People didn't die in their homes so helplessly without someone doing something. There were nurses and doctors and paramedics who should be stopping this. He'd heard enough times about the things people paid their taxes for. Surely that was for something.

He was just a kid and he was running down the street because society wasn't honoring its obligation to take care of folks. What was the point of everything if it could just fall down so fast? Why the hell was he having to do this?

He ran down North Caswell Road, seeing transmission lines down and sparking. It didn't make sense to him. The street lights were all out and yet electricity flowed in sparks out of the cables. How was that possible?

He seriously considered that he was in a dream – the kind where he was being chased by bears or falling to no end. He'd wake in his bed soon and he'd make a point of not eating whatever it was that gave him nightmares. And he'd go to bed early. And not cuss so much. Whatever it took for him to wake up and find Grandpa was okay, wearing his ridiculous short pants and playing with the remote while he watched his stupid sports commentaries.

Josh hated sports, and hated running. He hated jocks and PT instructors. He hated having to do this, but he felt gripped. His fear powered him along like the biggest sugar rush of his life.

He reached the entrance of the ER at the rear of the Presbyterian Medical Center. Josh joined a line of people going in. Some were being helped to walk by their friends, several were badly burned. Inside there were candles burning. A triage nurse with a clipboard inspected everyone who came in. She took one look at Josh's cut and bloody feet and pointed to a corner. "You don't look so bad. Wait over there. Someone will bring bandages."

After all the fire of his run, Josh meekly did as he was told, overwhelmed by the vision of so many sick and wounded people. The room was packed and echoed with moans of pain. Josh was transfixed by the sight of one man whose face was so scorched, his pale white eyeballs seemed out of place, like they had more life than the charred skin stretched over his cheekbones.

Down the corridors, staff shouted instructions and orderlies walked around carrying fire extinguishers. Nurses with candles dripped wax on the floor, and moving gurneys trailed it in glistening lines that lit up whenever thunder flashes crashed outside.

Awkwardly aware of having given the wrong impression, Josh approached the triage nurse. "Excuse me, I'm not here for me."

The nurse, stressed out, tried to wave him away. "Just wait over there. Someone will see you."

Josh tried again. "It's my grandpa. He needs an ambulance."

"Got none of those," said the nurse, examining bruises on a man's face. "All ambulances are down. Can't do anything about it."

"He's having a heart attack."

"There's nothing I can do about that from here. I'd give you a defibrillator, but they ain't working either. If he wants help, you need to bring him in."

"I can't," pleaded Josh. "He needs an ambulance."

The nurse turned on him. "Listen, kid. I worked in the Sudan for a year, and the people out there didn't have ambulances. If they needed a hospital, their family brought them in."

Josh stared at her, as if he'd been slapped. The nurse half-turned away, looking guilty. "Hey, I'm sorry..." she began.

Josh didn't hear the rest. He pushed past the line and ran outside. In the parking lot, he burst into tears.

The journey home was the longest walk of his life. He'd been given his first adult test and he'd failed it. When he reached the house, he could hear the sobs and wails through the open door and knew his worse fears had been realized. Too embarrassed to enter, he sat on the stoop with his head in his hands, watching the blood dripping off his toes.

9

Rick felt blood dripping on his face. He knew it was blood because he could taste it. Lifting up the weight that pressed on him, he saw it was a headless corpse strapped to a flight seat. In the light of the flames, he saw the name tape on the shirt: Skip Saunders.

Throwing the corpse off, he rolled over and spat on the ground, trying to get rid of whatever might have entered his mouth. In spite of having seen enough dead bodies in his time he still had to fight the urge to gag.

Leroy emerged from under a scorched fuselage panel. "What the hell happened?" he said.

Rick didn't know. His first thought was that the plane had been shot down, but the JSTAR flew at too high an altitude for ISIS to reach. The lightning and the static in the air was the strangest phenomenon he'd ever experienced. Did this have anything to do with the solar storm he'd been warned about?

This was more than just a little interference.

"Are you okay?" said Leroy. "Have you been hit?"

Flinging the panel aside, Leroy clambered over the wreckage to get to him.

"It's okay," said Rick. "It's not my blood."

Leroy looked down at the headless corpse and the clumps of burning debris around them. "Jesus, this is like Armageddon. What the hell's going on?"

"It's not a drill. That's what's going on," said Rick. "We need to move. We'll figure this stuff out later."

Over by the farm, the fighters were in a jubilant mood. They considered this a great victory, and for the moment appeared to have forgotten the small team of special forces operators they were originally after. It wouldn't take them long to start combing the wreckage, though, looking for spoils.

Keeping low in the gully, Rick and Leroy made their way down to the dry stream bed at the bottom of the slope. From there, they were hidden from the farm.

Walt was sitting on the ground, naked from the waist up and a large dressing on his side, above the hip. Blood was smeared across his chest and stomach, and he looked pale. Rick glanced at Flynn.

"Did the best I could, man," said Flynn.

"Our radios are all out," said Jamie. "That's weird."

Rick tried out his night vision goggles, switching them on. They didn't work. As a final test, he got his satellite phone out and installed the battery. That didn't work either.

Even without its battery, something had fried its circuits.

"Check the second hand on your watches," Rick told the others.

"Mine's stopped," said Flynn.

"Mine too. What the fuck?"

"EMP," said Rick. "It's taken everything out. It's what's brought the planes down."

"EMP?" said Jamie. "That's a nuclear strike, right?"

"No, not a nuclear strike." Rick took his compass out, looking for a reading. The needle wavered, then flicked left and right randomly. "It's bigger than that."

Not wanting to explain further, Rick gave his orders. "We need to get to that pilot. I'll take point. Leroy, you've got the rear. Are you okay to move, Walt?"

Walt nodded.

"Good. Flynn, you keep an eye on him. Let's go."

The lurid sky meant they had no need for night vision goggles, even if they could get them working. Everything was scarlet. It reminded Rick of some scene on Mars. He was more into Westerns than Sci-Fi movies, but he could well imagine Matt Damon stepping out of his pod into the inhospitable, unforgiving landscape.

Or George Clooney in a spacesuit falling from the sky.

He had a feeling that was a different movie, but after seeing the JSTAR come down, it didn't feel like fiction no more. He wondered if the Skip Saunders he'd seen had known the risks of staying airborne. Surely the air force would have given them that information? Rick felt bad about not moving out earlier. And the haste that led him to blunder into that ISIS patrol was a noob's mistake.

Or just plain complacency.

If his heart wasn't in the job, he should have quit. Technically knowing his stuff wasn't enough. Not for this. Fact was, you had to love this job to stay alive. As soon as you strayed off the path, you were on your way to becoming a condolence telegram, and no amount of acting or kidding yourself would lengthen the odds.

He'd spent some time with the British SAS once at their base in Hereford, and was intrigued by the fact that they referred to themselves as Pilgrims. If they were alive, they felt that they'd 'beat the clock', meaning they hadn't had their names inscribed as casualties on the clock tower at the base. Because in the end, it was only a matter of time, and everyone knew it. It took a kind of religious vocation to continue in the face of that.

Not even stunning self-belief could survive such a continuous stream of hazardous operations. Ego was just a flaccid bag of hot air once the bullets started flying.

His failure to recognize he'd reached his limit was risking lives, his own included.

The stream bed dissipated into a series of runnels, then disappeared. Behind, he could see the farm and the roaming fighters clearly. It wouldn't be long before they wondered where the infidels had gone. The ridge ended in a steep scarp that overlooked a plunging valley of scrub and rocks before flattening out into a wide, arid plain. A red and white parachute lay draped over a worn pillar – some artifact that might once have marked the border of a province, or the beginning of a road.

Rick realized he still had his useless deflector sight on his rifle. Removing the quick release screws, he discarded the unit, going back to iron sights. The lightning flashes dissipated, limiting themselves to the cloud base. Distant peals of thunder rolled across the sky, and the shouts of jihadists carried across the desert.

Keeping low, Rick approached the parachute, finding the disconnected harness. The others dropped down behind him in a line while he searched for clues to the pilot's whereabouts.

Seeing no sign of him, Rick wondered where he might have gone. Undoubtedly, he was hiding, fearful of capture. Was he down in the valley or had he climbed the scarp?

"Rick!"

That was Leroy. Rick looked back and saw ISIS fighters following the stream bed. Rick made his choice.

He couldn't waste time searching. If there was going to be a firefight, he preferred the high ground.

The jihadists spotted them when they were still climbing. Bullets zipped and cracked as Rick clambered onto the ridge. From the top, he could see another line of pickups in the distance. The vehicles were stationary – stopped by the EMP – and figures sallied out from them, moving towards the gunfire. They were too far away, however, and Rick wasn't worried about them.

Not just yet.

Lying flat on the ground, he steadied himself and aimed his rifle at the ISIS fighters below. The stream bed offered them no cover, and Rick had a clear line of sight. There were only about seven of them, and Rick lined one up in his sights and squeezed the trigger.

The first shot kicked up dust to one side of the jihadist, causing him to flinch. Rick's second shot dropped him to the ground. The other jihadists stopped their confident spray of bullets and hit the dirt. Rick lined up another one as the rest of his team made the top of the ridge. One by one, they joined in, hitting the jihadists with precision shots. When Leroy set up his machine gun and opened fire, the small group of jihadists were pinned down, bleeding, dying or playing dead.

Rick used the respite to assess the situation. From the crash site, more figures were moving towards them, firing inaccurate shots at long range. Behind, over by the stationary convoy, more figures advanced in a ragged line.

The only way out for Rick and his team was across the plain. Rick didn't like that idea. Apart from having no cover, it meant heading west – or what he thought was west. That would take them deeper into territory governed by other factions.

In the kaleidoscope of militias that constituted Syria's civil war, it was hard to say who would be friendly and who wouldn't.

Rick peered over into the valley at the foot of the scarp. It didn't take long for him to see the F16 pilot, curled up behind a rock, his pistol out.

"Scotty. Get down to that pilot. Check him out. Let me know if he can walk."

Scott rolled over and slid down the slope while the rest of the team sniped at whatever moved in the stream bed. Rick wondered what he would do if the pilot was injured. He'd made it to his location from his parachute, but he might have crawled. If he'd broken his leg, or worse, Rick wasn't sure how they'd be able to get him across the plain. He was already worried about Walt. He seemed okay at the moment, but if he'd lost a lot of blood, the fast trek across the plain would be hard for him.

He definitely wasn't leaving Walt. As for the pilot... Rick didn't know what he'd do.

A heavy machine gun from the stationary vehicles at the farm opened fire, the tracer arcing high and falling onto the scarp, the heavy bullets punching chunks out of the hard soil. Rick ducked involuntarily. The weapon was off target, but the 12.7mm ammunition it used was powerful enough to take a man's head off with one hit. Sticking around much longer wasn't wise.

Scott reached the pilot and engaged in some hasty conversation. When he turned and gave the thumbs up, Rick was relieved.

"Okay, let's move out now. Go, go, go!"

10

Lauren wasn't happy with the airport security guard's cast-off reassurances. As someone pointed out, nobody was in a position to receive texts, and being told to go home was of no help to her. There wasn't much else the guy could say, obviously. He wasn't really in the loop.

Didn't mean she was going to pay him any heed, though.

Lauren walked along the express road until she reached an elevated section with a view over the runways. Stranded drivers stood along the rail, eyeing the spectacle. Lauren joined them.

An airliner stood burning at a terminal gate, dripping molten alloys. Ground control staff and mechanics crowded round a nearby aircraft, trying to push it away from the burning wreck. Towing vehicles stood near the baggage conveyors, totally useless. The crowd heaved, barely moving the heavy plane, then a fuel tank on the burning plane exploded, sending flaming aviation fuel in all directions. The crowd scattered, stumbling as they tried to get away, and lines of burning fuel caught on the wing of the plane they'd been trying to push.

Lauren had a feeling things weren't about to get back to normal for a while.

She knew enough about EMP effects to know that every circuit board, every avionics suite chip, was useless now. The only way to get the planes in the air again would be to replace every board, every radar, every radio on the planes.

Not to mention the electronics used by air traffic control.

New parts would have to be shipped in – but how would they get here? Hell, even the ordering system would be down. And if the machines that made the parts were controlled by computers, which they were, the problem was doubled.

Lauren wondered how far the damage spread. Was it just the east coast affected? Or more?

"Why are those guys not trying to put the fire out?" asked a spectator.

"Fire trucks won't move," said another. "Just like us."

A solemn silence descended on the group. The idea that everything could fail at once took some contemplating.

A turbaned cab driver with a fringed Sikh flag hanging from his rear-view slammed down the hood of his car after trying unsuccessfully to fix it. "I cannot believe it!" he said. "First Uber takes our fares, now this!"

The night's red glow segued into dawn's gray light, the overcast hiding the sky as if ashamed of what it had done. The lightning had ceased, but the smell of ozone persisted, and drivers got static shocks from their car doors. The air still felt electric.

Lauren walked among the vehicles on the freeway, watching the vain attempts to restart engines. Only an old dirt bike still ran, its engine putt-putting raggedly as it weaved through the traffic. Every now and again it cut out, and the rider would hammer the kick-start until it ran again. He would pass Lauren at a cautious pace, then Lauren would pass him as he sweated to restart it, over and over. Even simple electric coils had been damaged by the storm.

Back on Broad Street, acrid fumes were building as a smog settled on the city. There wasn't a breath of wind and the top ten floors of the Prudential building were ablaze. Like beacons in the fog, Lauren could see the upper floors of other blocks alight in the city. Firefighters trooped like a line of soldiers to the biggest fire, each carrying loops of hose. Without the engines, they had to carry their own equipment.

Connecting the hose to a fire hydrant, they tested the pressure. A jet of water shot up for about ten feet, then drooped as the pressure fell. With the municipal pumps out, the city's water supply was already dwindling.

A handful of cops tried to keep the crowd of gawkers at bay, urging people to keep moving back and closing off Broad Street.

Lauren detoured down Clinton Street, heading towards Penn Station. Showers of burnt paper floated down like snow. The glass fronted towers of the commercial district loomed ominously, each one potentially hiding another fire. Lauren hastened on to the train station, slowing when she saw the crowds gathered outside the closed doors.

One look at the electricity lines running above the tracks told her all she needed to know. She'd already seen the stranded freight trains from the elevated freeway and had kidded herself that a diesel train might still be running.

Until the tracks were cleared, however, nothing could move. It could take days. Maybe weeks.

Lauren still didn't want to believe what was happening.

It just wasn't possible.

Like a person in catatonic shock, she wandered aimlessly up the street, data switching back and forth in her mind. Reaching a small cafe on a corner, she opened the door and entered.

It was dim inside, and a buxom black woman behind the counter turned to her. "We're not open yet. Sorry."

Lauren staggered to a booth and sat herself down. "I just need to rest for a moment," she said.

"Honey, we got no power. I can't serve you nothing."

"It's okay," said Lauren quietly, putting her head in her hands.

"Might be to you. Ain't to me." The woman came out from behind the counter and locked the door. "People see you in here, they'll all be coming in. Then what am I going to do?"

"I'm sorry."

The woman gave her a pitying look. "What's your name, honey?"

"Lauren."

"Well, Lauren. My name's Patty, and today ain't a good day. No sir. Ain't had no deliveries and all I got is bread and water. Just another day in the corps."

Lauren looked up, noticing for the first time the pictures on the wall of a fit young woman in uniform, standing with a squad in front of a defaced statue of Saddam Hussein. "You were in the Marines?" she asked.

"Oh yeah," said Patty with undisguised pride as she sauntered back to the counter. "Did a tour in Baghdad, ran convoys to Fallujah and lived to tell the tale."

"Fallujah was a clusterfuck," said Lauren, falling easily back into military coarseness.

"Sure was. Were you there?"

Lauren shook her head. "Baghdad, Mosul and inbetween."

"What was your unit, honey?"

"101st."

"Screaming Eagles, huh? Well, in that case, I got soda and Danish, 'cept the Danish is from yesterday, so at your own risk."

"I'm fine," said Lauren, though in truth she felt the hunger pangs churn. She'd been running on empty all morning.

"Don't go getting all polite southern gal on me," said Patty, grabbing two colas from the fridge. "I can hear your stomach from here."

Bringing a plate of dull looking pastries to the table, Patty eased her ample frame onto a seat.

"Quite a mess out there," she said, looking out at the stranded vehicles. "How far from home are you?"

"Charlotte, North Carolina," said Lauren, cracking open a bottle.

Patty grimaced. "Honey, that is bad luck. Your family there?"

Lauren nodded heavily. "My children. With my grandparents. My husband is... overseas. On operations."

Patty looked at her with pity. "I guess you don't need me to tell you this is no temporary thing."

Lauren sighed. "I've been trying to tell myself this isn't so bad, but..."

Patty leaned back. "This is an EMP. You know how bad that is. I don't think most people out there know, but they will soon enough. Then they're going to be pretty pissed."

Lauren stared at her bottle. "I remember the looting in Baghdad after we liberated it. Some liberation that was. We had to stand there and watch as people tore their own city apart, looting the stores, the museum, even the hospital. I saw them take CT scanners out in carts."

Patty nodded at the memory. "Here, it'll be Nike Jordans and TV screens. Until people realize the power ain't coming back and they're getting hungry."

"What will you do?" asked Lauren.

"I got stock still sitting in my garage. I only came to check on the shop and see what I could salvage before I shuttered it up. I put five hard years into this." Patty looked wistfully around, then glanced at Lauren. "How you going to get home, girl?"

Lauren laughed bitterly. "Patty, that's exactly what I've been thinking about, and it scares me that I've got no answers."

A man in a suit, with a coat over one arm and a briefcase in the other, came to stand at the cafe window, looking in. Seeing the two women he tried the door, then tapped on the glass.

Patty didn't even turn his way. "We're closed!"

The man tried again, banging more forcefully, then gave up and walked away.

"Some people," said Patty.

She fell silent, and the two sat quietly, staring at the table.

"You know? Back in our great, great grandparents' day, if folk wanted to get about, they walked."

Lauren thought about the distance and shuddered. "They had trains then. And horses. And stagecoaches."

"For them's that could afford it, yeah. But the rest? They only had the feet that God gave them. If they wanted to get anywhere, they took the slow road." Patty thought for a moment. "Course, my great, great grandpappy was probably a slave, and he weren't allowed to go nowhere. But free folks had to get about. And we still got horses."

"Gone left mine in the saloon," drawled Lauren sardonically. "Sorry, don't mean to be churlish, but..." She put her head in her hands again. "It's going to take me weeks."

Patty gave her a hard look. "How old are your kids?"

"Josh is twelve, Lizzy's seven."

"Okay. Then you gotta get creative. No good sitting here, wishing things were different, or you'll end up like that guy in the suit, thinking he's still got to turn up for work. There's going to be a lot of people who try to keep to their routine. They don't know no better. Don't be that guy."

Lauren thought that was a bit harsh, seeing as they had no idea what the man was thinking or planning to do. But Patty was right. Every moment spent sitting in shock was a moment wasted. She opened her bag and pulled out her skirt and shoes. They were just taking up space now. "Do you want these?"

Patty laughed. "Have you seen my hips? I ain't going to get into those. Put them in the trash. Do you want these pastries? I can wrap 'em for you."

Lauren took stock of her inventory. "Thank you, I think I will. Do you have some bottles of water I can buy? I'll pay you for all this."

Patty waved her off. "Don't worry about that. You just make sure you take care of yourself." She put her hand on Lauren's. "And good luck."

11

Josh sat cross-legged in the shower, shivering. When he'd first turned it on, he got a blast of cold water, forgetting that, without power, it wouldn't be hot. The pressure had quickly dropped, however, and now it was just a dribble. Washing his feet, he picked out stones from his soles, watching the fresh blood swirl in the drain hole. The cuts weren't deep, and the bleeding soon slowed, but he remained where he was.

He didn't really want to get out to face the world.

Through the thin panel door, he could hear Grandma, Elena and Max discussing what to do about Grandpa's body.

Nobody seemed to believe him when he'd said there were no ambulances running. Grandma's grief gripped the house, and Josh felt sidelined. Max had gone out to the hospital himself, returning a long time later with the same news Josh had already told them. If they wanted to get Grandpa to the morgue, they'd have to move him there themselves. The Medical Examiner was currently unavailable, and until then, no death certificate would be issued. Legally, therefore, Grandpa was still alive, because they couldn't get anyone to admit he wasn't.

The conversation got heated at that point. Max suggested taking the body in a wheelbarrow. Grandma physically threatened Max. Elena calmed Grandma down and called Max an idiot.

Josh and Lizzy were left to their own devices, excluded from the adult talk.

Josh turned the water off and toweled himself dry, leaving red stains on the fabric. From the drug cabinet, he applied band-aids until they covered the soles of his feet, then gingerly pulled fresh socks over them. Getting dressed, he left the bathroom.

Lizzy sat alone on the bed, curled up against the wall, hugging one of Mom's teddy bears. Lizzy normally wasn't into teddies. Everybody remembered the time, two years ago, when one of Dad's army friends gave her one as a gift, and she'd archly replied that she was too old for cuddly toys. She was such a serious little girl that everyone figured she was either going to be a great artist or a fearsome lawyer.

Josh sat on the bed and she curled up against him. Outside the house, it was eerily silent. No lawn mowers, no traffic. The voices in the house were clearly audible as a result.

"He's going to decompose, dammit," said Max quietly, thinking he couldn't be heard.

"Max!"

"What? I'm just saying the truth."

Playing on his games, Josh was normally able to filter out the sounds of his surroundings. Now there was no escape.

"Why won't the ambulance come?" whimpered Lizzy.

"They're not working," said Josh.

"Why not?"

Josh wasn't sure why not. He'd never encountered anything like this. It was like a big hand had come down and just stopped everything, as if somehow none of it was real to begin with. Someone had flipped the switch and everything had ground to a halt. He watched a lot of sci-fi and dystopian fiction, but even in the *Walking Dead*, the vehicles still worked.

"Stuff will get fixed, I'm sure," said Josh.

"What about Mom?" said Lizzy.

"I don't know. Maybe the planes are still working?"

"What if they're not?"

Josh felt his heart beating rapidly. First his dad had been removed from his world, and now his mom. He felt utterly abandoned. It was fine being moody when he knew everything was okay, but his teenage urge to sulk evaporated in the face of this void he felt. What if neither Mom nor Dad ever came home again?

He took a deep breath. "Look, it's just a power cut, right? I'm sure they've got people fixing it. And they can repair cars in a garage, and... get more stuff from factories, I don't know."

Yeah, but garages and factories need power too, he thought.

The cuts on his feet started to itch, but he resisted the urge to scratch.

"Are you hungry?" he asked.

Lizzy nodded.

"You want cookies and milk?"

Lizzy nodded again.

"Okay, I'll get it for you."

The milk wouldn't be cold, and Josh decided it might be better to use a fresh carton.

And they weren't short of cookies.

***

Rick sipped some water from a hydration backpack tube. It was warm, and not exactly refreshing, but it was enough to keep his mouth from drying up. A strange haze in the sky diffused the sun, which made the heat a little more bearable, but there was no breeze. It was like the electromagnetic storm had put the weather in stasis.

Flynn, Scott and Jamie piled rocks for an all round defense while Leroy set up the M249. They'd only halted for a rest, but it was standard procedure never to be caught resting out of cover. If they couldn't find it, they made it. In the distance, telegraph poles shimmered above an empty road. Rick scanned the horizon with binoculars, confident the jihadists had given up their pursuit. Walt and Kowalski lay prostrate on the ground. The pilot, in his flight suit and soft boots, was not used to walking so far at such a pace. Rick expected that, and goaded the pilot to keep up. He didn't have time to be gentle with him, nor even introduce him properly to the team. Having escaped capture by ISIS, the pilot probably thought he'd been taken by a group that was just as bad, force-marching him to his doom. No matter. If they lived through this, there'd be plenty of time to explain.

Walt was the real concern, weakened by his wound, and it was because of him that Rick called for a rest stop. Kneeling down next to him, Rick proffered his water tube. "Take a couple of sips, bro."

Walt weakly lifted his head to suck on the tube. Rick peeled back the bloody bandage. The wound was clotting well, but Rick was concerned by how dirty it was. The bullet had passed straight through, and Walt must have been stretched over for the shot to have hit him beneath his body armor. He was unlucky. One inch to the left, and the bullet would have missed him completely. As it happened, Rick wasn't sure whether it had passed through any vital organs. The exit wound was pretty close to his kidney. Opening his own first aid kit, Rick pulled on some surgical gloves, then took an antiseptic wipe to the wound. Walt didn't flinch, which wasn't a good sign. Cleaning all round the wound, he swabbed up the blood on the stomach and chest and applied a fresh hemostatic gauze dressing.

"Scott, I need your plasma bag."

Scott brought it over, and Rick uncoiled its catheter tube and stuck the needle in Walt's forearm, taping it on. He then taped the bag to Walt's upper arm. "I'm going to need you to sit up, bro," he said to Walt.

Together with Scott, he helped Walt sit up against the piled rocks, and slipped a Dexedrine tablet between his pale lips.

Satisfied he'd done what he could, Rick took out his map. His compass seemed to be working properly now, but Rick guessed, from the route they'd taken, that he'd come further south than he wanted. He had no idea whose territory he was in right now.

"So what's the game plan?" asked Flynn.

Rick thought about his options. "From what we saw, I think they've taken Ain Issa. Looks like they're pushing north. Without air strikes, I don't think there's anything stopping them from carrying on. I think we're better off headed west." He consulted the map. "If we can get to the Tishrin Dam, we can swing north to Manbij. There's another team stationed there."

The Tishrin Dam was the only crossing of the Assad and Euphrates Lakes that cut across their path. Kurdish forces were supposed to be holding the dam. Rick hoped they were still there.

Scott looked thoughtful for a moment. "What if this isn't local?"

"What do you mean?" said Rick.

"The storm. What if the effects go further than we think?"

Rick removed his helmet to scratch his head. "I think you need to be a bit clearer in what you're talking about, Pappy."

Scott leaned forward. "You said last night this was bigger than a nuclear strike. I agree. So who else is affected besides us? The whole of Syria? Middle East? Europe? How far?"

Scott paused to let that sink in.

"What if it's everywhere?" he added. "There goes our air support, our resupply, our links to everyone." He looked at each man in turn. "How do we get home?"

Rick put his helmet back on. "We don't need talk like that right now."

"It's the truth, isn't it?"

"No. Here's the truth. Our comms are out, and we've got a wounded man who needs medical attention, pronto. That's our problem right now. I don't need to hear speculation about what might come after unless it affects our current tactical situation, do you hear me?"

Scott leaned back, studying Rick. "But you've been thinking about that, haven't you?"

Rick didn't want to discuss that either. He stood up. "Break time's over. I want to hit that dam before nightfall."

"You think Walt might need a little longer to catch his breath?"

Walt seemed to have perked up a little with the Dexedrine, but he still looked beat.

"We can't wait. If we need to, we'll carry him."

Walt put up a hand. "I don't need carrying yet. Could do with something to eat, though."

"We'll eat on the move," said Rick. "Let's get going."

Kowalski groaned as everyone stood up around him. "You want to carry someone? You can carry me."

Rick gave him a stony look. "Quit whining and get moving."

12

Outside Newark's downtown area, people opened their stores, placing *Cash Only* signs on their windows. Customers lined up, bags ready, awareness slowly dawning that the power could be out for a while.

It hadn't dawned on everybody, though. Lauren saw a line of hopefuls waiting outside a closed cell phone shop, somehow thinking that all they needed was a repair or a replacement. There was a line outside the bank, too, but that wasn't open either. Lauren wondered how long people would patiently wait before taking matters into their own hands. Especially if they were used to getting what they wanted.

Hastening down a side street, she saw her first body. The electricity lines were all down, the insulators a molten mass, and the body had been covered with a blanket. She guessed the person had been electrocuted when a cable came down on them. Or maybe they just got a shock from standing too close to the wires.

Lauren didn't stick around. She'd gotten directions to a bicycle store, and was relieved to see it was open.

The store owner wasn't overjoyed to see her, though.

"I won't be open long," he said. A lean, middle aged athletic type with a goatee, he was in the back room, adjusting the gears on a bike. Lauren noticed he'd put heavy security chains on the bikes in the front of the store, and a backpack by his feet was filled with smaller stock from his shelves. He looked to be in the process of locking up and bugging out.

"I need a bike," said Lauren.

"The card machine isn't working, and I don't do credit."

Lauren had the princely sum of fifty dollars in her purse. She'd hoped to elicit some sympathy for her plight – maybe add a few tears in order to get a major discount on the cheapest thing available – but she had a feeling it wouldn't work with this guy. She tried another angle.

"I see you're getting ready for the mob that's going to come breaking into your store. Smart move. Got anybody to move these bikes for you before it happens?"

The owner threw her an annoyed glance, then returned to his work.

"They'll be fine."

"You think? Won't take long for them to get through those chains if they've got a mind to. I don't think they're going to be worrying about the cops disturbing them, if you know what I mean."

"No," said the owner archly, "I do not know what you mean."

"Oh, I think you do. It'll be a pity to lose these beautiful bikes. Especially since claiming on the insurance is going to be impossible. It'd be a shame if you can't get anything for them."

The owner gave up working on his gears and turned with an exasperated look. "Excuse me. Is there any other reason you came into my store, other than to irritate me?"

"Yes," said Lauren, breaking out her most magnanimous smile. "I need a bike, and you need to be compensated. I only have fifty dollars in cash, but that's fifty dollars more than the looters will leave you."

The owner's mouth fell open. "But it's a Schwinn," he declared.

"I can see that."

"I can't sell one for fifty dollars. Even the pedals are worth more than that."

"But it's still better than nothing."

"No it isn't," said the owner adamantly.

"I think you'll find it is."

"No, really it isn't. Go away, and please don't insult me with further offers."

Undeterred, Lauren left and headed back down the street, determined to get herself a bike, whatever brand it was. She might not have been able to get herself a horse, but a bike was way more feasible.

She'd never ridden a horse anyway, and didn't want to test what the learning curve was.

She'd passed a hardware store earlier and now she entered. This time the store owner was a lot more friendly.

"Hi," he said, beaming. "How can I help?"

"I'd like a set of bolt cutters," said Lauren.

"Sure," he said, wandering over to a rack of tools. "We've got eight inch, fourteen inch and twenty four inch. Which one do you want?"

"Twenty four."

Still smiling, the store keeper brought over a long handled, heavy duty bolt cutter. "Good choice. We're running an offer on this one. That'll be thirty two dollars and sixty cents."

Lauren expected to be asked why she needed bolt cutters and had been preparing her story when she entered the store, but the store keeper was nonplussed and happily took her money. Maybe he was used to women coming in for heavy duty cutters. Was there a construction site of Amazons nearby?

"Looks like it's going to be another good day," said the store keeper. "Not too hot and not too cold. Just how I like it."

Lauren stared at him. "You know the power's out, right?"

"Oh sure, but that don't affect the weather. When I'm done here, I'll walk the dog and read a book in the park."

"You're not worried about your store?"

"No, business has been great. Sold out on all my sledge hammers this morning. Don't know why, but it's been a good day for sledge hammers."

Lauren looked into the smiling, innocent face and didn't know what to say. Was it better to be optimistic on a day like today? Or just plain ignorant?

"Enjoy your book," she said cautiously.

"Thank you. And if you need anything more, don't forget to come back."

Lauren had a feeling the people with the sledge hammers would certainly be back – probably at nightfall. Hiding the cumbersome cutters under her jacket, she hoped she was wrong.

The smog was thicker when she entered the downtown area: acrid, noxious and eye-watering. Pulling a collar over her mouth, Lauren hunched over, supporting the cutters under her jacket and feeling paranoid that onlookers would guess her intent. Onlookers were few and far between, however, having gone inside or cleared the area. The only ones she did see looked as furtive as her, hurrying from one place to the next, faces covered. Making her way to Penn Station, she went to where she had seen bicycles locked to a rail.

Presumably, they belonged to passengers who hadn't returned on the train today. Or at least, that's what she hoped.

Looking round to make sure she was unobserved, she shook out the cutters and used them on the cable lock of a nice looking commuter bike. The leverage provided by the long handles made short work of the lock. Dropping the cutters, she hopped on the bike and rode off, feeling as guilty as hell.

After thinking about all the looting that might take place in the city, the first example of looting she'd seen was her own.

She glanced back, expecting to see the irate owner chasing after her, but there was nothing. A little astonished at how easy it had been, she wondered how she would ever explain this to her children. After years of instilling in them the need to be honest and law abiding, she wasn't sure she could. Had she been religious, she might have begged forgiveness from God on account of her need. A Hail Mary and a few extra dollars in the collection plate, perhaps. Or a pledge to feed the starving.

Truth was, she hoped she'd also taught them to be smart enough to know when to bend or break the rules. That wasn't an easy one to teach, though, without being a complete and utter hypocrite.

Still, cycling out of the smog felt glorious, and weaving in and out of the stationary traffic brought a secret smile to her face. The freedom was exhilarating, and no van driver was going to cut her off or force her to the sidewalk today. Gleefully riding her stolen bike, she made it to the freeway ramp in minutes. Cycling up it, she passed over the stationary trains and past the smoking airport. The fact that the storm had halted the traffic in the night, instead of at the height of rush hour, meant the going was easy.

Approaching the toll booths of the New Jersey Turnpike, she got yelled at by some guy coming out of the control building. "Hey! You can't cycle on the tollway!"

She was through the booths before he could catch her, however. Ahead lay a smooth road south, and a place where some rules just didn't matter anymore.

13

Rick hadn't gotten as far as he'd hoped to by the evening. The land was becoming less arid, with fields, groves and villages appearing in the distance. Rick skirted them all, wary of being discovered. Ostensibly, this canton should have been under the control of the Kurdish dominated SDF. In reality, the situation was more fluid, and the loyalty of any village couldn't be taken for granted. Family ties ran deeper than any flag, and information flowed freely once money changed hands.

Walt was also slowing them down. As much as he pushed himself, they had to keep stopping for him to rest. He was getting weaker and Rick was getting worried.

On the horizon, he spotted an isolated farm: a walled compound with a couple of adobe buildings and small olive grove out the back.

"We'll check this place out for the night. Flynn, Scott, you cover the back. The rest of you, follow me."

Rick walked the dusty dirt track, his rifle ready. Flynn and Scott skirted round to the grove. The sun dropped low in the sky, burning the haze red.

Rick swung open the compound gate just as an old man opened the door to one of the huts. There was a well in the compound, straw for a horse, and a carriage made from a wooden platform, leaf springs and truck tires. The old man, his beard peppered with gray, froze as he watched Rick approach.

Rick saw the Henry Fonda scene from the opposite point of view.

He was Henry Fonda now: the menacing stranger with the armed gang visiting a lonely homestead in the desert, his baby blue eyes warning the old man that if he so much as moved, he was a dead man. A young boy would come running round the corner, skidding to a halt with shock. Maybe he would memorize the face of the stranger for the day when he would track him down to avenge the death of his family. The old man would hiss at him to get inside, knowing his own life could be measured in minutes, and a woman would appear, a hand rising to cover her horror-struck mouth.

Or none of those things would happen, because the man was used to gunmen visiting his home, whether they were ISIS, SDF or some other militia that called the shots, and he had nothing left for them to take.

"Salaam," said Rick casually, maintaining his guard. Behind him, Leroy entered the compound and did a sweep.

"Aleikum salaam," said the old man wearily.

"We are not here to steal anything," said Rick in Arabic, "but I need to check your house."

The old man grunted in response, like it was expected. Rick was glad he wasn't talkative. He'd learned his Arabic in Iraq, and from Lauren, but among the Kurds he hadn't used it much, so he was rusty.

Rick took his boots off, adding a modicum of respect to his coerced entry. Inside, the hut was sparsely furnished, with wood and wicker furniture, a mat on the dirt floor and blankets in the corner. No woman and no boy.

"We need to use your well," said Rick. "We have a sick man. We will be staying the night."

From his pocket he extracted a gold sovereign. He and his team carried them as survival payment if they ever got into trouble, accepted everywhere regardless of the currency. It was faintly disrespectful to offer the old man gold, since it was a Muslim custom to receive guests with freely given hospitality. On the other hand, the man was poor, and it was a stretch to describe the special forces operators as guests. He held it up and the man took it, again without a word. Rick stepped back outside.

"It's all clear," said Leroy.

"Get Scott and Flynn. We'll rotate two hour watches, patrolling the perimeter."

Walt leaned against the brick well while Jamie dabbed a wet cloth on his brow. Rick relaced his boots and walked over. A horse tied to a pole shifted, looking nervous at the influx of people, and chickens scattered into the shadows.

Jamie didn't look optimistic. "He's got a fever," he said.

Rick understood what that meant. Walt had an infection. He needed antibiotics and he needed surgery. Most of the team's medical equipment had gone up with the pickups. Rick looked at the rudimentary cart and made his mind up.

"We'll carry him tomorrow to the dam. They should have a medic there."

"Hey, don't talk like I ain't here," said Walt wearily.

Rick crouched by him. "Feeling left out?"

"Yeah, some."

"Don't be so boring, then. Come on, liven up. Tell a few jokes."

Walt cracked a smile. "Did you hear the one about the guy with septicemia?"

"No, can't say I've heard that one."

"Sure you have. You're looking at him right now."

"What's the punchline?"

"He died."

"See, this is why you get socially excluded, telling jokes that just ain't funny."

"It could happen though, couldn't it?"

"Flynn gave you an antibiotic shot at the scene. You'll be fine. You don't want to spend too much time thinking about these things. I need you functioning."

"I know. I'm just feeling morbid." Walt sat up a little more, drinking water from his tube. "I'll sleep it off. But if I don't," he added, "I want you to check on my kid."

Walt's girlfriend had given birth only two months before deployment. Rick was going to drop him from the team for this mission, but Walt had insisted on coming, saying it would give him more time afterwards when the baby was more likely to be crawling and talking. He'd teach him to call him Daddy.

"You know I will. Happy now?"

"Sure. I got to rehearse my own death scene."

Rick shook his head. "Not enough drama."

"Hey, you're the film buff. Give me lessons."

"Get some rest."

When darkness came, it was the blackest night Rick could ever remember. There was no light pollution, no stars, nothing. He'd gotten so used to using his night vision goggles that he forgot how dark it could get. He waited for his eyes to adjust, but it was like staring into a pit. Only the cold and the distant cry of a fox reminded him he was outside.

The old man came out with an oil lamp, bringing them falafel, olives and flat bread. It was generous, considering he was under no obligation. Rick wondered if he'd fed jihadist fighters like this, hoping to remain in their favor. It was probable. Basic survival. While Rick got to fly in and out on specific deployments, local people had to live with the civil war day in and day out. Got to the point where they really didn't care who won or lost, so long as it ended one day.

The old man left the lamp with them and Rick watched him go, limping from some unknown ailment. Out here, with his cart and his horse, the old man likely never noticed that the power had gone out. Even in cities like

Aleppo and Raqqa, people probably got used to water and electricity supplies ceasing suddenly. Those that couldn't afford trucks or gas used carts to bring their goods to market. Children played in ruins and refugees baked bread in brick ovens at the side of the road. A geomagnetic storm wasn't going to affect their lives much.

Back home in the States, though, most people had forgotten how to live like this. And with good reason: it sucked. No point in making things unnecessarily hard. But now? Rick shuddered to think of the effect – if Scott was right about it being global.

American cities were packed with more people today than could be fed with nineteenth century supply methods. Urban carrying capacity just dropped a hundred years in one night.

Maybe more than a hundred years.

Rick remembered the contingency planning for an EMP strike – there was none. Oh, there were congressional reports. And a few tests. But the whole thing was treated as such an unlikely occurrence that there was no urgency in coming up with solutions. It was treated as a theoretical problem, nothing more. If it wasn't worth votes, it wasn't worth devoting time and money to.

Not that Rick was any better prepared. He didn't have a cabin in the Appalachians, wasn't into fishing or hiking and had never tried to force his family to live closer to nature, even on vacations.

Resting between operations, it had never been his priority. If anything, it was when he was at his laziest. Back home, without a clear and defined objective, nothing warranted a sense of urgency.

Scott was afraid of becoming a drunk if he quit the service. Rick, on the other hand, was afraid of becoming a slob.

"Watcha thinking?" said Leroy, sitting next to him with falafel on flat bread.

"Nothing much," said Rick.

"Seen that face a billion times. I know you've got something on your mind."

"Not necessarily."

"Sure," asserted Leroy. "When you answer like that, I *know* you're running deep."

"Just stuff."

"I bet. You're thinking about your kids. And for the record, I am too."

Rick shifted uncomfortably. "I don't know if Lauren got back from New York before this all happened. I mean, if she's stranded there..."

"I know, I know, man. But if she's in New York, she's still closer than you are. That woman is so determined, she'll find a way to get back. Isn't anything going to stop her getting to her kids. And your kids are smart. Do you remember that time I gave a teddy bear to your daughter, and she gets up on her high horse and says she's too old for that shit? That was so funny. Your kids are tough and serious." Leroy offered him his last falafel. "They must get that from Lauren, because you're a mess, man."

Rick gave him a sideways glance. "Thanks."

"No problem," chuckled Leroy. "Seriously, though, they'll be okay. Hell, we don't even know if they've been affected by this. They're on the other side of the world."

Another voice joined the conversation. "For a storm that big, I guarantee you it's global. Earth's magnetosphere goes all the way round, kids."

It was Kowalski. Sitting in the corner of the compound, he was completely in the shadows. Rick and Leroy both turned to him.

The pilot continued, announcing airily: "Same light show we had here, they'll have had at home too. Planes falling from the sky, complete grid down. Couple of days, people are going to panic when they realize it's permanent. End of the week, they're going to be eating each other. Game over for the good old US of A."

"Don't need to sound so damned happy about it," said Rick acidly.

Kowalski's eyes flashed in the dark. "You told me to quit whining, so I'm trying to be upbeat. What else is there to say?"

"How about nothing?" said Leroy, disgusted.

"We don't need that kind of negative talk," added Rick.

"There's a lot of things we don't need," said Kowalski quietly, "false hope being one of them." He sighed deeply. "Got a girl waiting for me back in Florida. I don't know if I'll see her again, now."

"We've all got someone waiting for us," said Rick. "And we do not, I repeat, do *not* know what is happening outside of our area."

"It's basic science," said Kowalski casually, like he'd resigned himself. "I'm Kowalski, by the way."

"I know. It's written on your name tab. I'm Rick, and I don't see any reason to quit yet. Are you ready to pitch in or should I leave you here tomorrow?"

Kowalski gazed back at him. "You're a hard man. I helped you guys out."

"And we're grateful, but I'm giving you a choice. Are you in or out?"

"Seeing as you're so nice about it, I guess I'm in."

"Then you've got to keep up and shut up. And you might want to remove that name tab."

"Why? It's no secret who I am. Geneva Convention says I should give my name and rank only."

"This isn't Geneva."

14

Lauren made good progress until the cramp set in, then she was forced to dismount to massage her painful thighs. She'd only managed about twenty miles.

She wasn't as fit as she thought she was. Her legs burned and her ass felt like she'd been sitting on a porcupine. She hadn't ridden a bike for years, and in spite of the old adage, she found it wasn't so easy to get back in the saddle. Especially if it was a narrow one. A freeway that seemed so flat when driving had long gentle climbs that wore her out quickly. Traffic was sparse, but transmission towers draped their wires across the turnpike at frequent intervals, and burned out cables lay across the lanes that, when ridden over, made the bike saddle even more painful.

Earlier she'd passed drivers walking to the exit, and some had waved, amused at seeing someone cycle the tollway. Now, near dusk, the road was abandoned. Lauren hobbled onward, pushing the bike beside her. She needed a vehicle to stay the night in, but she didn't want to leave the bike outside.

Someone could take it as easily as she did – more easily, in fact – and bad as it was, cycling was still better than walking. She'd begun the journey optimistic, but was now appalled at the thought of how far she had to go. Keeping the bike safe, therefore, was imperative.

A mile ahead she could see an SUV, but it took her an age to get to it. When she finally got there, she was relieved to see it was empty. The owner, however, had locked all the doors manually before leaving it.

Lauren tested the tailgate. It opened fine, the owner having neglected to check it. Since the advent of powered door locks, it was easy to overlook. Crawling inside, Lauren lowered the back seats and pushed the bike in, pulling the tailgate shut. She settled into the front passenger seat which, after the saddle, felt like bliss. She even found a pack of candy in the glovebox.

Reclining the seat, she lay back, closing her eyes for a moment.

When she woke again, it was pitch black outside. She hadn't meant to fall asleep, and for a moment she forgot where she was. She sat up, startled, and cracked her elbow on the door. Her legs ached, but when she tried to stretch them, she hit the footwell.

Lauren lay back down, bringing her knees up to her chest to relieve the cramps. She was in a ridiculous situation, stuck in someone else's car, with someone else's bike, and no idea where she actually was.

Knowing her luck, she'd wake again in daylight with planes flying overhead, vehicles moving again on the freeway and a state trooper tapping on her window. She could then explain how she thought that, with the end of the world and all, she could just help herself to whatever she wanted and go where she liked, and no, officer, I don't have registration documents for this vehicle, I haven't been taking drugs and oh my God, I've missed my flight!

She clicked open the door and listened to the silence. It was almost reassuring to hear nothing at all. Stepping out onto the asphalt, she spun slowly on the spot, looking for any sign of life. Nothing moved around the indistinct boxy shapes of the other abandoned vehicles, and the horizon was devoid of any urban glow.

The distant crack of a gunshot made her flinch. She wasn't as alone as she thought. Straining her ears, she tried to pick out any follow up sounds, but nothing came.

Fencing lined the freeway, so she wasn't sure when she stopped whether she was still in the suburbs or in a rural area. She had a feeling there wasn't much rural in this part of New Jersey, but she really didn't know. She couldn't hear any voices or dogs barking. She couldn't even hear crickets. Uneasy, Lauren stayed out of the car, waiting for another clue, but the night didn't utter another word.

She wished she had her gun. Rick had bought her a beautiful Colt 1911 on their fifth anniversary – not exactly a typical gift, but she wasn't into flowers and stuff – and she'd been a regular on the range with it. But that was a while back, and since then it'd stayed in its locked box, hidden away from the children and promptly forgotten. She wouldn't have been able to take it on the plane anyway.

She got back into the car, clicking the door slightly closed. When it was this dark, staying quiet was the best thing she could do. Rolling slowly over on the seat so as not to squeak the suspension, she tried to get some more sleep.

Josh couldn't stand the silence. It only made the fact of a dead body in the house more ominous. The transition to the idea that it was just a corpse and not Grandpa had come quickly to Josh. Grandpa was gone. That thing in the house had no right to be there anymore.

It wasn't going anywhere soon, though. Elena and Max had remonstrated with Grandma in their own, contradictory ways, but Grandma didn't budge. That thing was her husband and she wasn't done mourning him yet. When the authorities gained control of the situation, he'd be dealt with in a decent manner. Max's suggestion that he be laid in the garage didn't fit that criteria, any more than the wheelbarrow did.

Grandma was sleeping in the spare room now, and that thing had the bedroom to itself.

Lizzy slept soundly, shielded from her imagination, but Josh remained staring into the darkness, getting angrier at the ineptitude of adults. It was obvious to him that things weren't about to get back to normal the next day, or the day after that. Nobody in the street had been able to get their car started, a couple of wooden houses in the next block had burned to the ground, and the chairman of the neighborhood association was openly carrying a shotgun, checking on each house. Josh had answered the door to him and, when asked, had told him everything was fine, even as Grandma argued with the Seinfelds in the background. The guy had shrugged and said, "I don't know when we're getting the power back, and I think the water supply's going too. Fill up any containers you might have, and if you've got food in the freezer, eat that first. But make sure you cook it right. If I hear anything, I'll try and let everyone know."

Josh filled a couple of jugs before the tap went from a dribble to a drip. Didn't even try to open the freezer since there was no power to cook with, and he had little idea how to cook anyway. If his mom didn't prepare it, he resorted to blitzing packaged slop in the microwave. It all tasted the same.

So the day was spent eating cookies and finishing off the milk.

Josh could bear it no longer. If no one was going to do anything about the decomposing corpse in the house, then he'd do it himself. There was no way he was going to sleep, otherwise. Getting himself dressed, he groped his way to the kitchen where Grandma kept her candles. Finding the matches next to them, he lit a candle, casting a flickering shadow of himself that caused him to turn, thinking there was something behind him.

A shiver ran up his spine at the thought of what he was planning to do, and his resolve melted a little. The idea of going back to bed and just lying there, knowing what was on the other side of the wall, stiffened him up again.

He had to do it.

Taking a deep breath, he counted to ten, then exhaled forcefully, inadvertently blowing the candle out. Feeling for the matches, he lit it again.

Letting himself quietly out the back door, he crossed the lawn to the garage. Inside, he found the shovel and took it out, lodging the candle on a post. The smell of burning lingered in the air, totally different from the odor of the barbecue Grandpa had tended yesterday.

Josh felt a moment of sadness, realizing he'd never see that again. But he reminded himself that the thing inside was no longer Grandpa.

Taking another breath, he steadied the shovel, then dug it into the turf.

The ground was dry and hard, and he didn't penetrate very far. Pulling on the handle, he ripped up a clump of grass.

It was no bigger than if he'd pulled it up by hand.

This was going to take longer than he imagined. He'd started, though. Before he could change his mind, he dug the shovel in again, more forcefully this time. Little by little, he etched out the shape of Grandpa's grave.

The labor took him a long time, and it was hot work. He kept returning to the kitchen to drink water from the jug until eventually he decided to bring it out with him. As the hour drew by, the hole deepened, the pile of discarded soil getting higher.

He kept thinking he was crazy, that he might be making a mistake. What if the authorities did sort things out? What would happen then?

Well, if they came for the body, they'd know where to find it. Driven by his increasing mania, he dug harder and deeper, ignoring the blisters growing on his hands. When at last he thought it deep enough, he leaned on the shovel, trembling from the exertion.

I've done enough, he thought. Surely I can't do this next part?

But he'd started it, and it would be dumb to walk away now, leaving an empty hole in the garden.

Besides, he wanted to sleep. He was exhausted, and no way was he going to do it with that thing in the house. It wasn't right.

Dropping the shovel, he entered the kitchen, went down the hall and stopped before his grandparents' door.

His heart thumped like a jackhammer.

How many times had he stood at this door in the past, knocking to wake them up for his breakfast, waiting for the voice telling him to wait a minute?

Breathing rapidly, he put his hand on the door handle and turned it.

The void opened before him, and a sickly sweet smell floated out.

Josh hadn't been sure what to expect, and realized he wasn't thinking straight.

Going back out into the garden, he retrieved the candle. Back in the kitchen, he grabbed a cloth and tied it over his mouth, then gingerly entered the bedroom.

Grandpa was in exactly the same position as Josh had seen him last, though the face was more relaxed now. Josh's heart was racing so much, he could barely breathe.

It's not Grandpa, he thought. It's not.

One foot in front of the other, he approached the bed, almost swooning. With quivering fingers, he grabbed one side of the bed sheet and threw it over the body.

That was almost too much for him, and he had to rest for a moment, but at least he couldn't see the body anymore. Walking over to the other side of the bed, he took that side of the sheet and threw it over to complete the loose shroud.

From the closet, he took a blanket and threw it on. He should have tucked it under, but he couldn't bring himself to risk touching the body. Gathering the fabric at one end, he pulled it towards the end of the bed.

The body was heavy, and again Josh realized what a stupid thing he was doing. He wouldn't be able to carry it to the garden.

He'd have to drag it. Wishing he could just stop now, he doubled over, tears in his eyes. None of this was meant to happen.

"Please, God," he said, "let this be over soon."

With a desperate, angry heave, he pulled the sheet, walking backwards towards the door. The body slid off the bed and landed with a sickening thud, one arm flopping out from under the blanket.

Josh dropped to his knees. "It's not fair," he said, sobbing. "It's just not fair."

There was a creak in the hall and Josh looked round to see Grandma in her nightgown, a heavy look on her face.

"I had to do it, Grandma," said Josh. "He's got to be buried right."

Grandma never looked as old as she did just then. She touched Josh's head. "I'm so sorry," she murmured. "And no, it isn't fair. Harry wouldn't have wanted you to have to do this. He loved you so much." Grandma wiped her cheeks. "And I've been feeling sorry for myself." She took a breath. "He was a man of dignity, and it was my duty to look after him, just as it was his to look after me. I wouldn't have forgiven him if he'd left it to my grandchildren to lay me properly to rest. And I know he wouldn't have."

"I'm sorry, Grandma."

"So am I, Josh. I can't do this alone though. I wish I could send you to your room, but I need your help, even if it isn't right."

"I've dug the hole."

"I know. I watched you. I am so ashamed, but you've been so strong. I should have acted sooner."

"The garage wouldn't have been right for him, Grandma. That's where you store junk."

Grandma broke into a strained smile. "No, you're right. Come on, let's do this together, before Lizzy wakes. I don't want her to see this, bless her."

Between the two of them they dragged the body through the kitchen, over the rough grass and into the hole. Josh filled it in as best he could, and Grandma took a handful of soil and scattered it over the rough mound. "Got no flowers for you, my love," she said quietly. "But I'll tend to you until they can move you to a better place. For now, you're home."

15

The old man took Rick and his team to the Tishrin Dam in his horse and cart. He didn't have much of a choice. Rick told him he could either accept cash for taking them, or Rick would take the horse and cart himself. They set off in the early hours, trundling over dusty tracks. By the time they reached the hill that overlooked the dam, the sun was high in the sky, the haze gone.

The old man refused to go any further, and dropped them there. Rick thought he looked wary of whoever might be holding the dam.

The dam stood at the end of a long causeway. At the beginning of the causeway was a checkpoint with two guards and a truck mounted anti-aircraft gun. The guards were armed with AK47s, but Rick saw no sign of black ISIS flags or armbands. Through his binoculars he could see scorch marks on the concrete above the hydroelectric generator vents. Cables dangled limply off the transmission towers at the nearby substation. The large transformers were blackened hulks, a debris field of twisted and melted metal spread beneath them. A few personnel were present on the dam, hanging around near a five story administration block on the other side. A parking lot of pickup trucks sat behind that, some with their hoods raised.

Rick handed his binoculars to Scott. "I'm going down alone. Stay here until I give you a signal. If anything bad happens, you're in charge. Try and make your way north to find another crossing point if I can't get back."

Scott peered through the binoculars. "Okay, it's your funeral," he said.

"Thanks, Scott."

"Can't cover you from here. You'll be out of range."

"I know, but it's got to be done."

"Rick, you've got kids. Stay here and I'll go down."

Rick slapped him on the shoulder. "I appreciate that, but I need you here. Besides, you'll probably scare the shit out of them, one look at you."

"Thanks."

"No problem."

"Good luck."

"You too."

Rick made his way down the scree slope to the modern road that ran towards the causeway. He'd considered leaving his M4 rifle behind, so as to present less of a threat, but decided against it. With his cargo pants, T-shirt and body armor, he looked every inch a Westerner. If ISIS had recaptured the dam, it meant they would shoot at him sooner, while he was still some distance away.

Which was preferable to being right up close. Even with the fearsome twin barrels of the anti-aircraft gun pointing in his direction, it at least gave him a chance.

It was a long walk. It wasn't exactly *High Noon*, but it was uncomfortable enough. The two guards at the checkpoint straightened up at the sight of the lone figure in the heat haze. Rick waved a couple of times in a feeble attempt to show he was friendly, but they didn't wave back. He kept his hands clear of his gun, letting it dangle on its sling, but it was cocked and ready, and it wouldn't take him long to snatch it up if he needed it. There was nobody in the cab of the truck, and the AA gun was unattended. Rick maintained a casual pace down the center line of the road.

When he got to within hailing distance, he shouted, "Salaam."

The guards gave a kind of half nod in reply. They looked mildly curious at his presence. They didn't, however, appear to be particularly welcoming of their supposed ally.

Rick guessed they were from the Arab contingent of the SDF. He hadn't worked with them much and had heard rumors that their alliance with the Kurds wasn't always congenial. They were here to fight against both ISIS and the Syrian government, but they could be touchy about the Kurds advancing so deeply into traditionally Arab territory. With the US heavily backing the Kurds, the Arabs were suspicious of American motives.

Propaganda efforts by the Turkish backed Free Syrian Army were often aimed at getting the SDF Arabs to change sides and fight against the Kurds instead. It made for a sectarian and ethnic soup that was difficult for outsiders like Rick and his men to navigate through.

Rick approached the barrier. "Peace be upon you and your family," he said: the usual Arab greeting.

"And on yours," said one of the guards, a young man.

"The storm two nights ago damaged our vehicles, and we have had to walk."

"There are more of you?"

"Yes, they are coming. One of our men requires medical assistance. Can you help him?"

The two guards exchanged glances. "You will have to talk to the commander," said the first one.

"Very well." Rick turned and waved to the others.

The guards watched the figures appear on the hillside.

"Why do they hide?" said the second one. "Do you not trust us?"

Rick turned to him. "Did not the Prophet say that you should trust in Allah but tether your camel first?"

It was meant as a joke to break the tension, but the guards didn't appear amused.

"ISIS has retaken Ain Issa," continued Rick. "I do not know where else they have advanced, so I had to be sure."

The guards shifted nervously. "Are they coming here?"

"I do not know. I will inform your commander. You may need more mujahideen here."

When the others arrived, Walt was pale and sweating. Thanking the guards, Rick led his team past the checkpoint and along the causeway. "You okay?" he said to Walt.

"Still alive," said Walt stoically.

"Okay, listen up, all of you. I don't know what the situation is here but I'm not getting good vibes. If they won't help us, we'll move on. Watch your backs."

The walk across the dam was sobering. Rick saw the extent of the fire that must have raged here. Melted globules of wire protruded from the disfigured connectors, and long cables dangled in the sparkling blue waters of the Euphrates. The hum and churn of turbines was absent, and Rick caught the sound of distant mortars. Militia men hung around the administration building, looking anxious. Another was working under the hood of a pickup. All the pickups were modern – courtesy of funds from the US and the EU – and their sensitive electronics rendered them useless.

The administration building was spartan inside, the furniture long gone. The partition glass in the lobby remained damaged from old bullet holes. The commander sat cross legged on the floor, looking over a tattered map, and fighters lounged around, waiting for orders.

The commander, a middle aged man with a trim beard, glanced at Rick's boots as they appeared by his map. "And who might you be?" he said in perfect English.

"We're advisers with the SDF," said Rick.

The commander, his face creased by too many days in the sun, looked up, noticing the Kurdish insignia on Flynn and Jamie's arm patches. "YPG, you mean," said the commander with a trace of disgust, referring to the

Kurdish militias.

"It doesn't matter," said Rick. "We're on the same side, and I have a man here who needs medical assistance."

The commander glanced at Walt, then back to the map. "I cannot help you. We have no supplies, and our radios do not work."

"Ours don't either. What's the situation here?"

"What do you think?" snapped the commander. "We have been abandoned."

"ISIS has retaken Ain Issa. They could be moving on the dam."

"Of course. We have ISIS advancing from the south, and the Free Syrian Army advancing from the north. Messengers I send out do not return, and your much vaunted air power is nowhere to be seen. What use are you to me?"

"What about Manbij?"

"Who cares about Manbij? Your friends are no longer there. They drive their convoys to show the flag, then they return to their bases in the east. They have not been seen for days. How convenient. Now the Iranians have detonated an EMP device, and nothing works, so there is little to stop the Kurds, Turks and Russians from dividing up my country between them. You were supposed to be protecting us, but instead you have made a deal with our enemies."

"It wasn't the Iranians."

"Do not give me your excuses. Look at this dam. It worked perfectly when it was held by ISIS. Now my people have no power. What are your promises worth, now?"

While they were talking, the militiamen took an interest in Kowalski, getting up close and prodding his flight suit. One of them pointed to his name badge and said, "Russki."

That really got their interest, and suddenly they were shoving Kowalski and hitting him.

"Hey!" yelled Flynn, savagely pushing a militiaman back.

Militiamen reached for their rifles, then froze as the Special Forces operatives aimed their weapons at them, safety catches clicking ominously.

Rick found himself aiming his rifle at the commander's head. It was an instinctive action, and the commander slowly raised his eyes.

"You have a Russian pilot with you," he said acidly.

The Russian air force wasn't popular here, having hit the SDF units a couple of times when they clashed with Assad's forces.

"He's not Russian. He's an American pilot," said Rick. "Tell your men to stand down."

The commander was unfazed. "I have more men outside. You are outnumbered. Give us the Russian, and I will let you go free."

Rick imagined exactly what they would do if they handed the pilot over, and pressed the barrel of his rifle forcefully against the commander's head. "Order your men to stand down, or you'll be the first to die, and we'll cut through any man who stands in our way. Do you understand?"

The commander weighed the odds, and read the intent in Rick's eyes. Finally he barked a command in Arabic, ordering his men to lay down their arms. Rick eased back the rifle from the commander's skull, but kept his safety off. He contemplated disarming them and tying them up, but that would involve shouting and alerting the others outside. Rick chose instead to have his team casually withdraw. "You have a good day," he said to the commander.

The commander gave him a weary look. "Go home, American."

They edged out the door.

It was a tense few minutes as they made their way across the parking lot. Rick nodded and salaamed the militiamen outside as casually as he could, while maintaining three-sixty awareness. The militiamen were mildly confused, curious at this group of Americans moving in tactical formation. Then a man came out of the building, shaking his rifle at them and shouting.

"Stay easy," murmured Rick to his men, waving back with a fake smile.

The militiamen grew agitated as pertinent information passed quickly through the group, injured pride hardening their faces. More started to shout.

"Easy now," said Rick. They were nearly at the concrete barriers on the other side of the parking lot.

The man who'd come out of the building leveled his AK47. A staccato punching ripped the air as Leroy opened fire with his M249, a line of exploding concrete chips and ricocheting bullets appearing in front of the militiamen, who immediately ducked and scattered.

The commander came running to the door, seeing his men taking cover, and barked angry orders at them.

Rick thought he might be ordering them to attack, but when they remained in position, watching the Americans with sullen looks, he realized the commander was restraining them, worried about the consequences of a shootout.

Rick tipped him a salute, and the man glowered back. By now, the team had reached the concrete blocks and the raised parapet of the exit road that led past the substation and towards a junction. To the southwest were a line of hills, beyond which were ISIS. To the northwest, along a wide road, lay

Manbij.

"Nice going," said Rick to Leroy, still walking backwards and keeping an eye on the militia.

"Yeah, it worked," said Leroy. "Used up the rest of the ammo in the box, though."

Leroy tossed the machine gun over the parapet, where it slid down the bank towards the water, and unslung his M4.

"Kowalski," said Rick.

"What?"

"Tear off that name tape before I shove it up your ass."

16

Lauren doubled up her jacket and tied it to the saddle to make the ride more bearable. Her legs still ached when she woke, but the feeling passed. Under the hot sun, however, she felt thirsty, and began to worry about her water supplies. Food was running low too. It was hungry work, cycling. When she saw the sign for the Molly Pitcher rest stop, she thought it worth checking out.

The baking hot concrete of the parking lot shimmered the air. A handful of abandoned cars were parked, but the majority of the vehicles in the lot were long haul trucks. Their drivers had obviously been sleeping in the cabs when the storm hit. Lauren dismounted and walked her bike towards the service building. A trio of truckers sat in chairs outside the entrance, soaking up the rays and shooting the breeze. One of them had a baseball bat propped by his chair.

"Howdy," said Lauren as she got close.

"Hi there, young lady," said the one with the baseball bat. He was completely bald, with a short white beard and a patterned tattoo covering most of his scalp. His eyes creased as he scrutinized her, but Lauren didn't get a sense of menace from either him nor the others.

"Not so young, but thanks. This place open?" The door was wide open, but she thought it courteous to ask.

"I believe it is. Better talk to Ralph here, though."

Lauren had assumed Ralph was a trucker, but he wore the green shirt and pants uniform of the service station company. He must have been the night manager when the power went down. His pants were creased, like he'd been sleeping in them, and the shirt underarms were stained by two large sweat patches. "Go right on through," he said, "but pay me out here. The cash register's out. And don't touch the Starbucks machine. That's a franchise and I promised to leave it as it is. Useless without power anyway, but you've no idea how many people keep trying."

Lauren looked around the empty lot and wondered who those other people were. Had there been a constant stream of highway refugees?

Lauren took her bike inside. It was dim, and hot as hell without the air conditioning. She made her way to the bathroom. It was bliss to use a toilet after squatting at the roadside, and she made a point of taking some of the toilet paper for later. She flushed the toilet by habit, forgetting that the water system wouldn't be operating anymore. She was thus surprised when water cascaded into the bowl. Taking the empty bottles from her bag, she filled them at a basin, then splashed water onto her face to remove the caked-on dust. It was warm but heavenly, and she drank her fill from the faucet.

The shelves in the store were almost empty, most of the good stuff already having been taken. Lauren grabbed a few bags of potato chips and some candy and granola bars. It was the kind of junk that put weight on her hips, but today wasn't a day to worry about that.

Outside, as she paid Ralph, she realized that maybe he wasn't the manager. He could have been the janitor taking advantage of a free payday. The three together looked as if they'd taken ownership of the place and, apart from the baseball bat, had the appearance of three old boys manning a garage sale.

There were chairs available, so Lauren sat down to eat. "I'm surprised you've still got water running," she said.

"It's the water tower," said Ralph, jerking his head back towards the structure at the back of the service area. "It'll be good for a while."

"How long do you plan on staying?"

Ralph shrugged. "Till there's no reason to stay. Right now, there's no reason to go nowhere."

"Home?"

"It's just an apartment. I'll make that long walk when I have to."

"And where's home to you, young lady?" asked the guy with the bat.

"North Carolina," said Lauren, picking oats from between her teeth. "And the name's Lauren."

"North Carolina? I'd give you a ride in my truck, if it was working. I brought a load up from Georgia. I'm Sam, by the way. And this is Earl. Poor guy came all the way from Louisiana."

Earl looked like a sad puppy.

"His daughter's about to get married," explained Sam, "and he's worried he'll miss the wedding."

"It ain't right," murmured Earl.

Lauren doubted the wedding would take place now, but she didn't want to fan the flames of that particular discontentment. "What about the other drivers?" she asked.

"Ahh, the local boys made their way home on foot. One dude from Michigan hung around for a while, waiting for help. Lost patience in the end and set out this morning. Good job, too. Guy did nothing but bitch. We got a nice little community here. Gotta make the best of it, right?"

"You're going to hole up here?"

"Sure. Why not? No point running around all scared. There's warehouses around here. One of them will have food. Need a Buddhist frame of mind, that's all. Keep the energies flowing in the right direction, and things will work out. There's people out there fixing stuff. Might take a while, but it'll all come good."

"Go with the flow," muttered Lauren.

"Exactly. That's what I've been saying the whole time."

Lauren wasn't sure whether to admire such faith, or pity it.

On the far side of the rest stop was a police station house, its red and white radio mast sticking up beyond the gas station. A lonely state trooper ambled casually across the parking lot. He looked the same age as the truckers and wasn't in any hurry.

"How are you doing, Pete?" called Sam to the trooper.

Pete looked beat. He dropped his heavy frame into a chair and mopped his brow with a handkerchief. "So so," said the trooper. "Made it as far as Concordia today. Most folks are calm, though they got a million questions I can't answer. Even saw some guys on the golf course. Some people don't care what happens so long as they get to play their holes. Still short of about fifteen troopers who failed to report for shift yesterday, but they live a hell of a long way out. If no one else turns up, I'm going to have to start deputizing. Get some of the fine folks from these gated communities to start wearing out some shoe leather. That's going to be fun."

Sam leaned across to Lauren. "We've already been deputized," he assured her. "Keeping the peace in our little neck of the woods."

"Just so long as you don't go swinging that bat where you shouldn't," said Pete. "So who's the newcomer?"

"This here's Lauren – or so she tells us – and she cycled here off the freeway."

Lauren wondered if Pete was going to give her a ticket for that, but instead he just nodded. "Good call. I could do with a bike right now. Live local?"

"No, just passing through," said Lauren.

Pete seemed amused by that. "Stranger rolling into town. Maybe I should check you against my wanted posters."

Lauren shifted uncomfortably, thinking about her stolen bike.

"Just kidding," said Pete. "Where you headed to, anyway?"

"North Carolina."

Pete whistled. "Well good luck. You carrying?"

"No."

"You wouldn't have a permit, anyway," reasoned the trooper, "but you want to be careful out there, a woman traveling alone. Can't call 911 now."

Lauren didn't see the point in restating the obvious, and just said, "Thanks."

Pete looked around, like he was missing something. "Are you guys going to make a coffee for me?"

"Oh now, come on," said Ralph, "I promised Sally I wouldn't touch her stuff."

"It's just a few capsules," said Pete. "I could do with a Starbucks now. Put it on the station tab. Hell, we've given her enough good service. And where's Martha?"

"She's getting some wood," said Sam. "Soon as she gets here, we'll brew some water."

A huge woman with the meatiest arms Lauren had ever seen waddled out from behind the building, carrying an armful of firewood. "Howdy, Sheriff," said Martha with a toothy grin.

"Have these deadbeats been leaving you to do all the work?" said Pete.

"Sure have," said Martha.

"She volunteered," protested Sam.

Pete narrowed his eyes at him. "You, sir, are no gentleman."

"Not ever," called Martha cheerfully.

Lauren got up from her chair, suspecting it was Martha's. "I'll be on my way," she said.

"You sure?" said Pete. "If we get a good coffee going, you could be in luck."

"Thanks, but I've got a long way to go."

"Okay. Happy trails, pardner."

Lauren left them chuckling over the asinine joke. She wondered whether they'd be laughing in a couple of days time when the food and water ran out. Sam's optimism about people 'fixing stuff' was touching, but misplaced.

She felt sorry for Earl, though. Somewhere out there, his daughter was wondering when he'd return to walk her down the aisle. Such thoughts led her to dwell on her own children. Spurred on by that, she pushed the pace as she hit the freeway.

Josh ached all over. His feet stung, his hands were blistered and his arms and shoulders hurt, but he felt good, which was strange.

Tending the barbecue, he looked towards Grandpa's grave. Dawn's light showed that it hadn't been covered properly, so he'd added more soil this morning, making it look neat and even. Grandma had asked a neighbor if she could cut some flowers to put on the grave, and the blooms rippled in the fresh breeze.

Stoking the coals, Josh felt, for the first time in his life, like a man.

I buried Grandpa, he thought.

The implications of that blew his mind. The memory of the night before felt surreal, and after years of lethargy, it was manic. It was like he'd gone crazy. He should have felt remorse. Or haunted. Instead he felt decisive. Something needed doing and he'd done it.

He wasn't useless anymore.

Grandma staggered out with a bucket of murky water.

"What's that?" he asked.

"Brine," she said. "My, I haven't done this since I was a little girl. My own grandmother showed me how to do this, but I never dreamed I'd have to do it myself."

"We're just barbecuing, Grandma."

"No, this is different. Pay attention. Back before they had refrigerators, they had to salt and smoke meat to preserve it. Push the white coals to one side, and add more in a line around the edges. Leave the middle clear. Did you soak the wood chips like I asked you?"

"Sure."

"Good boy. Sprinkle them on the coals."

Josh did so, and Grandma dug her hand in the bucket and pulled out a disgusting looking piece of meat. She'd rescued everything from the freezer, but Josh thought it smelled too bad to bother with. Grandma begged to differ. She slapped all the meat onto the rack. The wood chips were already smoking, and the drips from the meat sizzled on the bottom of the barbecue.

"Close the lid now and open the vent just a touch."

Josh did as he was told. "And now?"

"We leave it for the rest of the day. We'll have jerky and smoked ham for the rest of the week."

"And after that?"

Grandma put her hands on her hips and took a deep breath. "One step at a time, please, Josh. My word. Your grandpa wanted us to buy a small homestead when we retired. I told him not to be so ridiculous. When you're old, fetching food from the store is enough work. I couldn't imagine spending my time with chickens and the like. And your grandpa certainly wasn't about to chop wood for the stove. I wasn't taken with the romantic image, but now..." She glanced at the grave, and the suburban image around her. "Well, it's too late now. I need to go lie down for a spell. See if you can cheer your sister up. She's still not herself."

Lizzy was in the bedroom, hugging her knees to her chin and staring at the wall. Josh sat on the bed, but she didn't move closer to him.

"Hey," he said gently.

Lizzy didn't respond.

"You okay?"

Silence.

"You haven't been drawing today."

"Can't draw," murmured Lizzy.

"Sure you can. Why don't you draw the teddy bear there? Put him in the woods. Or something."

"Don't want to."

"I'll draw him, then."

Josh picked up her pencil and pad and began sketching eyes and a nose, adding fur.

"Can you draw me a hole?" said Lizzy.

"To jump into? That's easy."

"No, I want a portal. To take me somewhere."

Josh raised an eyebrow. "That's deep. Got someplace in mind?"

"I want to go where Mom and Dad are."

Josh didn't know exactly where his dad was – it was always some secret destination – but he guessed it was somewhere in the middle east. "I don't think you want to go where Dad is."

Lizzy turned to him, her eyes red from crying. "But he can come through the portal and be here now. And Mom too."

Josh rubbed a salty tear from her cheek. "I'm sure they've got their own kind of magic way of getting here."

Lizzy deadpanned him. "They don't."

"Sure they do. Dad's, like, a special operator. He's trained to do all sorts of weird stuff."

"But he's not magic."

"No, but he's got skills. They teach you how to use your initiative. And Mom was in the army too."

"What's initiative?"

"It's where you think of things."

"Like how to build a plane?"

"Not that kind of stuff, no. Least, I don't think so. I mean, it'd be pretty

85

cool, but, uh, no."

"So what's going to happen to us?"

"Nothing," shrugged Josh. "Yesterday was scary, but that's done now. Grandma's better now, and she knows what to do. And the neighbors are all helping, you know? Everyone helps each other. We just have to wait. This is why you've got to keep drawing. Got no TV now."

Lizzy picked up the pad. "Your bear looks funny."

"I can't draw."

"He looks like a cat."

Josh scrutinized his efforts. "Does a little. You'll have to show me how to do it right."

Lizzy toyed with the pencil. "Do you think Mom will be here soon?"

"Yeah, sure. You know Mom. She's so fit, she'll be running home. Why don't you draw a picture of that?"

"Running?"

"Of course. With a bear. On the highway."

"Like Thelma and Louise?" said Lizzy, referring to the movie.

"Uh, yeah. Only, without the ending where they drive off the cliff. Or the car." Josh scratched his head. "Just add the bear."

Lauren covered a lot of miles before she hit trouble. Pedaling hard through the gap between two trucks, she was surprised when a figure stepped out in front of her. Jamming her brakes on, she squealed to a halt just before him.

A barrel chested dude put his hand on her handlebars. She tried to pull back but she could feel his strength locking the bike in place.

"This doesn't have to be painful," said the man in a deep baritone. "I just need your bike."

Lauren stared into his eyes and saw no compromise there. Cautiously, she dismounted, taking a couple of steps back. She glanced behind her, but there was nobody else. If he came closer, she could run.

The man, seeing her fear, gave her a cold smile. "I'm sorry," he said. "It's just the way it is." Mounting the bike, he pedaled calmly away.

Lauren's horror turned slowly to anger. The one thing that would get her to her children was being taken from her.

Girl, do something. He's right there. Are you just going to let him get away?

Waiting until he'd picked up a little more speed, she broke into a sprint. He didn't look back, so he didn't see her gaining on him. Pumping hard to catch him, she grabbed hold of his hair and pulled him sideways. Off balance, he veered to one side, struggling to keep upright, then toppled off the bike.

That wasn't enough. Using his falling momentum, she slammed his head hard down against the concrete, leaped over his body and grabbed the bike, still running. With her heart in her mouth, she jumped onto the saddle and pedaled hard.

The man rolled over on the concrete, and, with a look of fury, rolled back up and chased after her. Lauren's thighs protested against this sudden effort, but she didn't let up. With the sweat popping on her face, she switched up the gears. He got to within a foot of her when she started to pull away, then he stumbled and stopped, dizzy from his concussion.

"You bitch," he screamed.

Damn right, thought Lauren, still pushing hard. She didn't relent until she'd covered another mile. When she stopped, she was trembling from the effort. The half-digested granola bar came back up her throat, and she puked her guts up on the road. Wiping her mouth, she leaned on the bike, trying to stop the shakes.

She walked for a while after that, taking deep breaths and glancing behind her. When she found a car with an unlocked trunk, she raided it for a heavy lug wrench, and told herself she was not going to be caught unprepared again.

Giving every vehicle a wide berth from that point on, she witnessed a gang of youths looting a truck on the opposite highway. The driver, who'd been sleeping in his cab, staggered away, his face dripping blood. The youths passed out boxes of electrical goods to waiting hands. Lauren didn't waste time rubbernecking.

17

"I thought vehicles that didn't have fuel injection or onboard computers weren't affected by EMP?" said Rick.

"That's the theory," agreed Flynn, lifting up the hood.

It was a battered old Ford pickup on a dirt road that Rick had spotted from the main highway. Rick could see where sparks from the battery had burnt a pinhole in the hood. Flynn leaned over to examine the engine bay.

"Course, that might not apply to the big old storm we witnessed. Check out the starter motor," said Flynn.

Rick peered in. The starter was a blackened hulk. "What the hell happened to that?"

"My guess is that the storm induced a powerful current in the wires. The longer the wire, the more powerful the current. The winding on that motor constitutes one hell of a long aerial."

Scott rapped his knuckles on the steel panel of the pickup. "I heard that vehicles are supposed to act like natural Faraday cages to protect what's inside."

"So are plane fuselages," said Flynn. "Didn't help the air force, did it?"

Rick glanced at Kowalski, but the pilot was still bummed by what happened at the dam, and didn't feel inclined to give his opinion.

"Besides, this isn't a complete cage," said Flynn, pointing to the open ground beneath the engine.

Rick checked round the vehicle. The keys were still in the ignition, and empty propane cylinders lay in the truck bed. The driver had abandoned the vehicle in a hurry, probably thinking the whole thing was going to blow.

Rick scratched the stubble on his face and looked to where Walt sat in the dust, head bowed with exhaustion. "Pity," said Rick. "Could have done with something that still worked."

Flynn looked thoughtfully at the engine. "The plug leads look okay, and the ignition coil is buried beneath the air filter. Doesn't look burnt on the outside. If we push-start it, we might be able to get it to go."

"Yeah," said Leroy, "or we can end up pushing some heavy ass piece of shit for no reason."

Rick looked at the bumpy dirt track. "It's worth a shot, but we'll have to push it to the road."

"Oh, now you're just making me feel even better," said Leroy.

Rick slapped him on the shoulder. "You know I have your best interests at heart."

"Yeah, sure."

"Walt! Jump in the cab. You're steering."

Walt dragged himself to the vehicle and took the wheel. Rick examined his face, putting a hand on his brow. "How you feeling?" he asked.

"Cold," said Walt.

Rick could feel the fever on his skin. "How's your vision?"

"Okay, I think," said Walt, squinting.

"Hang in there. We'll get help soon."

They pushed the pickup over the bumps to the road. Once on the smooth surface, Walt switched on the ignition and engaged second gear.

"Everybody ready?" said Rick.

Everyone nodded, and they started rolling the vehicle forward, picking up the speed until they were running with it. Walt released the clutch and the pickup juddered, digging its nose in, and the engine fired.

Flynn listened to the ragged engine note. "Doesn't sound like it's firing on all its cylinders."

"Don't care," said Rick. "Take over the wheel. Walt, move up. Everyone else in the back."

The pickup rocked like a nervous horse as it set off up the road.

An hour later, Rick banged his fist on the roof of the cab to halt the pickup. Ahead sprawled the dusty white buildings of Manbij. Rick trained his binoculars on the checkpoint on the road.

The sandbagged emplacement appeared to be unmanned.

"Jamie," said Rick, nodding towards the checkpoint.

The two jumped down and began walking, one each side of the road. Rick eased off his safety catch, scanning as he walked. Behind the emplacement was an adobe hut, and parked by that were two pickups. Sparse olive groves flanked both sides of the road. Rick halted and crouched, turning to see that Leroy and Scott had already dismounted, rifles aimed. Waving at them, Rick directed them into the groves.

The last time he'd encountered this checkpoint, a Kurdish flag had been flying. That was soon replaced by the more diplomatically correct flag of the Manbij Military Council, a cobbled together entity of rival militias. No flag flew now, however, and that made Rick cautious. Nodding again to

Jamie, he resumed his advance.

The emplacement was empty, with boxes of machine gun bullets, but no machine gun. The door to the hut lay open, but that too was devoid of any life. A pornographic magazine was tossed on a bunk and a bowl of fresh olives lay uneaten on the desk.

Rick checked the vehicles, but they were dead, streaks of soot marking the edges of the hoods. Military grade radios were rendered useless.

"Looks like they bugged out," said Rick.

"In a hurry, too," said Jamie.

Checking for booby traps, Rick entered the hut, sniffing at the olives.

"Hey, look at this," said Jamie. "They got halal MREs."

Cases of US army meals-ready-to-eat were stacked in a corner, all marked as halal. Jamie opened a case, extracting the foil packages. "Lamb and Barley Stew, Black Bean and Chicken, bagel chips and fruit loops. That's real thoughtful."

Rick searched the hut for a first aid kit, but came up empty handed. Stepping outside, he waved at Flynn to bring the pickup in. Leroy and Scott emerged from the grove.

"So what we got?" said Scott.

"A lot of nothing," said Rick. "They've abandoned their post and I don't know why."

"Spooked by the storm, do you think?"

"No, they left this morning. We'll take a break to eat, then move on. There should be a Ranger unit by the Al Sab barracks. They'll have a medic."

Jamie came out with a pack of sunflower seeds, cracking shells in his teeth and spitting them out.

"Got anything else besides bird food?" asked Leroy.

"Inside, man," said Jamie. "Enough MREs to constipate you for a week. No pork, though. All halal."

Flynn halted the truck outside the hut. Rick leaned into the cab. "Keep it running," he said. "Grab what you can to eat." He opened the door and peeled back Walt's bandage to examine the wound. It looked bad and smelled bad.

"It's just a matter of time," said Walt languidly.

"Don't give me that shit," said Rick. "You drinking plenty?"

"I don't remember," said Walt, looking genuinely disorientated.

Rick examined his eyes and snapped his fingers in front of them to get them to focus. "Fight it, Walt. Don't quit on me." Unhooking Walt's water tube, Rick shoved it between Walt's lips. "Drink. We've got more water inside. Stay hydrated."

Jamie and Leroy brought out the cases of MREs and laid them in the truck bed, while Scott brought out a plastic water cooler container. While everyone squeezed the contents of the foil packages straight into their mouths, Kowalski handled his gingerly.

"Isn't there any way to heat these?" he asked.

"No time," said Rick, wiping his mouth.

"But it looks like dog food."

Scott laughed. "Air force don't like army chow."

Kowalski narrowed his eyes at him. "Just not used to this."

"You hungry, ain't ya?"

"Yeah, I'm hungry, smartass."

"Stop bitching and start eating, then."

"Stop arguing," said Rick. "Top up your water containers and fill your pouches with as much food as you can cram in."

Kowalski wrinkled his face, then pulled out cold chunks of meat with his fingers. Delicately, he tasted it. It wasn't to his liking, but he started eating anyway.

The city of Manbij had been fought over by almost every faction in the Syrian civil war, and it showed. Buildings carried the effects of bombing campaigns and entire blocks had been bulldozed to rubble. Some semblance of normal life should have returned by now, however, and Rick was disturbed at how deserted the streets were. Abandoned vehicles sat at junctions, and people peered cautiously from the windows of their apartments, as if they expected something.

Rick called a halt outside a shuttered pharmacy.

"Tell me you've got a bad feeling about this," said Scott.

"I'm not saying it," said Rick. "I'm not Harrison Ford."

But he felt it, nonetheless.

Dismounting, he signaled his men into combat ready positions and strode over to the pharmacy. He gave the shutters a hopeful shake, but nobody responded from within. Taking a wrecking bar from the pickup's toolbox, he inserted one end into the padlock at the bottom of the shutter, then stamped on the bar to break the lock. Raising the shutter noisily, he looked inside.

It was an open booth, with creams, sunglasses and shampoo. Rifling through the packs on a medicine shelf, he read the inscriptions in Arabic and English, finding only mild painkillers and flu remedies. Smashing a wooden cabinet at the back, he searched in vain for antibiotics.

"We've got company," said Flynn.

Rick came back out and saw a large body of gunmen filtering into the street from the junction at the end. They were casual about it, but one of them carried an RPG.

"Any idea who they might be?" said Rick.

"Your guess is as good as mine."

Rick walked forward. If they were local fighters, it would be better to forestall a misunderstanding early.

He never got the chance to introduce himself. The gunmen raised their rifles, and the one with the RPG dropped to one knee and aimed his rocket launcher.

"Cover," shouted Rick.

The RPG fired with a backwash of dust, and the rocket streaked down the middle of the street and slammed into the pickup. The explosion blew the vehicle apart in a hail of flame and debris.

Crouched in a doorway, Rick shrank down as shrapnel pattered against the walls.

18

Walt had been in the pickup. With his ears ringing from the concussive blast, Rick turned in horror, seeing the smoking wreck. Time slowed down for a moment, and he remembered Walt's last words about it only being a matter of time.

And the fact that he had a baby waiting for him back home.

Rick felt the shame of having made a bad call. He should have ordered Walt out of the truck when they halted. He shouldn't have been so complacent. The warning signs were there, but he'd ignored them.

Then he saw a figure crawling in the dust away from the vehicle. It was Walt, and his leg was on fire.

Time snapped back into place, and Rick turned towards the threat. The RPG gunner was loading another rocket into his tube.

Rick locked him in his sights and fired three rapid shots, all impacting on the man's chest. The gunner sat back on his ass, looking shocked, then slumped down dead.

Another gunman ran out to retrieve the RPG. Rick dropped him with a single shot. By now, the rest of his team had the street covered with precision shots and the remaining gunmen had taken cover. Rick turned again, saw Jamie dragging Walt to a doorway, and assessed the situation.

There was no way back. The street was too straight and with too little cover. Ahead, however, was an alleyway.

"Scott! Leroy! Secure that alley. And give me smoke."

The volume of fire increased as the gunmen recovered from their setback and began spraying the street with bullets. As Scott and Leroy prepared to move, Rick and Flynn switched to automatic fire and began putting down bursts at every enemy head that appeared, forcing them to flinch back. Scott and Leroy sprinted forward, bullets ricocheting around them, and dived into the alley.

"Reloading," called Rick as he pulled another magazine from his pouches.

Flynn kept him covered until he was ready. As Rick leveled his rifle to resume firing, a smoke grenade sailed out of the alley, bouncing into the middle of the street, spewing out fumes. When the street was obscured, Rick slapped Flynn on the shoulder. "Get to the alley. Secure the other end."

Watching Flynn go, Rick steeled himself, then ran across the street to Jamie's position. Although the gunmen couldn't see him anymore, they continued to fire blindly through the smokescreen, and Rick ran through a hail of zipping bullets, sliding to a halt against the wall. Jamie poured water over the burns on Walt's leg, having already cut away the pants leg. Kowalski cowered behind him, bewildered by the noise and bleeding from shrapnel impacts on the side of his face.

Rick, with no time for finesse, lifted Walt's head up roughly. "Are you okay?" he said.

Walt blinked. "I think that woke me up," he said.

"Can you make it to the alley?"

"Yeah, I can walk."

"I need you to run, soldier."

Walt locked eyes with him. "Well, sure, why not?"

Rick nodded, satisfied that Walt was still with him. All he needed were his legs and a sense of humor.

"Kowalski, help him up."

The pilot looked at him as if he were mad.

"Kowalski! Move it."

Kowalski moved it.

Running bent double, the group dashed across the street, bullets still skipping across the hot asphalt. Running through the swirling tendrils of smoke, they made it to the alley where Scott and Leroy traded fire with gunmen advancing from cover to cover, attempting to overrun their position.

"This ain't a good place to stay," said Scott, pulling his head back as rounds chipped at the corner bricks.

"Who are we fighting against?" asked Rick. "Is this the SDF or the FSA?"

"I don't know, but they ain't friendly."

"I don't care what letters of the alphabet they are," said Leroy, "this is Dodge, and we gotta get out."

Rick took one look out to assess the situation and nearly got his head shot off. Pulling back hastily, he concurred with Leroy. "Gentlemen, it's time to go." The street was crawling with gunmen.

Flynn was already posted at the other end of the alley, and by the time the team got there, he too was flinching from the heavy return fire. "They're trying to flank us," he said.

Across the street was a row of flat roofed houses. "Jamie," said Rick. "Get into one of them houses. We'll cover you."

Sprinting out to an abandoned car, Rick took up position behind it, firing to suppress the gunmen. Jamie ran past him, across the street, and barreled into a wooden door, smashing it open. Disappearing inside for a moment, he re-emerged, firing towards the gunmen.

"Go, go, go!" said Rick to the rest of the team.

With Kowalski supporting Walt, Leroy and Scott moved with them, jogging sideways and firing bursts until they reached the house. When they were safely inside, Rick called to Flynn, who remained at the alley. "Move," he said.

Flynn fired off his last shots, then turned to run. Too late, Rick saw an RPG rocket streaking towards him. Shouting a warning, he ducked down. The rocket slammed into the wall by the alley and detonated, sending out a blast wave that rocked the car Rick was sheltering behind, showering him in debris. When he looked up he saw Flynn lying sprawled in the dust, his arm blown off and his helmet rolling on the ground. Rick ran to him immediately and was hit by a bullet that flipped him round and knocked him off his feet.

Gasping for breath, Rick lay on the ground. He'd been shot in the back, and the pain was spreading. Bullets zipped by him as the gunmen tried to finish him off, and Rick started to crawl, disoriented. He found himself face to face with Flynn. The dead eyes staring back at him eliminated any doubt about the condition of his friend.

Leroy and Scott appeared on either side of him and after checking Flynn, they grabbed Rick's arms and began dragging him at a run, still under fire. Rick recovered his balance halfway across and ran with them until he was through the doorway and inside the house.

Breathing heavily, Rick leaned against the wall. "I've been hit," he said. "Check the damage."

He dreaded what they'd find, thinking he'd end up like Walt. Or worse. But after checking his back, Leroy announced, "There's nothing there." Producing a squashed bullet head, he added, "Found this in your body armor, though. Went right through the Kevlar and was sticking out the other side. You've got a bruise, but nothing else."

Rick laughed grimly, then stopped when he remembered Flynn.

It didn't seem right, leaving him there, but the rest of the team was still in danger. They weren't in any position to retrieve the body.

In the dim recess of the house, Rick saw a woman and two little girls huddled in the corner, apprehensive at the sight of foreign soldiers in their home. He also saw a back door.

"We need to keep moving. Scott, take point."

Rick didn't bother explaining anything to the woman. As soon as Scott pronounced the rear exit as clear, the team fled out into the street and took off down another alleyway.

The image of the mother with her children remained with Rick, however, and he began to think of Lauren.

19

Riding the turnpike down through New Jersey, Lauren felt she was on a giant zipper, and she was the slider that pulled it open, revealing elements that had previously been hidden under civilization's skin. As the miles rolled on, she encountered the occasional looter. Someone was also trying to siphon fuel, for reasons that were not immediately apparent to her. A guy waving a club yelled at a distant group dancing on the roof of a bus, and a bunch of kids from a nearby suburb dashed between the vehicles on their skateboards, perhaps fulfilling some long held fantasy.

Apart from chance encounters, however, the tollway was deserted, with a couple of burned out wrecks in between the stalled early morning traffic flows. Birds perched on roofs fluttered off as she rode by, sweating in the heat that rose from the asphalt and emanated from the sheet metal car bodies. The backpack chafed her shoulders, and her butt still hurt, but her legs felt stronger, and she watched her shadow gradually flip from one side to the other as the sun moved overhead, passing signs that indicated exits to Trenton in the morning, then Philadelphia in the afternoon. She was eating up the miles, but unfortunately she was eating through her food supplies too. It wasn't long before she was consuming the last cookie-flavored toasted cheese sandwich, and she still felt hungry.

The majority of the vehicles on the tollway were trucks, making night time deliveries to the stores for the morning. Lauren realized that, with the store shelves being rapidly emptied in the cities, most of the food available was actually here on the highway. She couldn't have picked a better route home. It would take a while for most people to realize that, but until then, she had a free hand.

With her mind set on getting home, she hadn't wanted to delay her journey by scavenging, which was time consuming. On the other hand, once she calculated that her journey could take over a week – and maybe more – she castigated herself for not thinking long term. If things were going to be as bad as she thought, she needed more than just food. She needed a complete range of survival supplies, which included the ability to light a fire. She didn't even have a box of matches on her.

She'd learned a few survival techniques in basic training in the army, but because she hadn't gone on to the advanced infantry course, she hadn't picked up much more. And basic training was such a blur, she'd forgotten it all anyway.

It was going to be a pain in the ass to learn all that shit again.

Coasting to a halt, she picked her first vehicle to loot: a white van that appeared to have been targeted already. The rear doors were half open, and cardboard lay on the road, but as it was clearly unlocked, she thought it worth a look.

The lug wrench she'd picked up stuck out of the top of her backpack, strategically placed so she could reach back and bring it out in one swing. Doing so, she approached the van, listening out for any lingering occupants. Gingerly, she swung the doors open. When she saw what was inside, she uttered a mirthless laugh.

The van was full of bicycles, folded up and packaged in plastic and cardboard. After arguing the toss with Mr Schwinn, she now had more bikes than she could shake a stick at. Hell, this might even be a shipment for his shop.

For a brief moment, Lauren considered replacing her own bike with one of the newer ones on display. It was evident from the discarded packaging that the van driver, finding himself stranded, had assembled one of the bikes and ridden off on it.

Slightly deflated, Lauren decided to stick with the bike she already had. It had proven itself so far, and she was growing attached to it. She was on the verge of walking away when she realized that she needed spare parts more than she needed a bike. Delving back inside, she found a box filled with tire repair kits and tools. She also found something she hadn't considered: panniers and racks.

She spent the next few minutes fitting a rack to the back of her bike and filling the panniers with everything she thought she needed for a long-distance trip. She even found a pair of padded lady's cycling pants – not the most flattering of things, but her ass was crying out for a solution to its woes.

Suitably attired and feeling smug, she pedaled away, glorying in the improved comfort.

As deserted as the tollway looked, she was surprised to see some truckers had remained in their cabs. She thought perhaps they were owner operators reluctant to abandon their vehicles. Maybe they didn't want to leave what they saw as their homes. Or maybe they harbored some faith that the company would come to rescue them – or feared they'd be fired and made liable for the lost goods. She considered asking them politely if she could look in their trailers, but there was no way that was going to come out sounding right.

She cycled for a couple of miles before she found an abandoned rig that looked like it might contain what she wanted. Unhooking the back doors, she found pallets stacked high with supermarket products and wound with plastic wrap. Without a forklift truck, however, she had trouble getting to the pallets deeper inside and conducting a proper search. Crawling over piled pet food, toiletries and cleaning products, she struggled to reach down for canned food and soda. What she really wanted to find was bottled water and energy bars. After sweating for half an hour, she gave up and settled for canned fruit, dog treats and soda pop.

She was anxious about being caught by other looters, preferring to stay on the move, so she filled her panniers and set off, feeling the extra weight as she pedaled up a long incline. After a mile she reached the summit and freewheeled down the other side. She was enjoying the breeze in her hair when she pulled her brakes on and halted, startled by an odd sight.

A large RV sat in the middle lane, bikes strapped to the rear fender. The side awning had been pulled out and under its shade, a couple sat at a picnic table while their two children played ball nearby. A dog leashed to the camper noticed Lauren and barked. The couple turned to look, unperturbed by the appearance of a stranger.

Lauren coasted down towards them and stopped at a respectful distance. "Howdy," she said.

"Hi," said the man, looking her over. "Can we help you?"

The dog continued to bark, and Lauren felt she was intruding. The couple were tanned and about her age, and they looked completely relaxed about where they were, like it was Lauren who was weird for cycling on the freeway. The children continued to play.

"Kind of," she replied. "I'm looking for water. Do you have any you can trade for a couple of bottles of soda? For the kids?"

The man glanced at his children. "I don't like them drinking that junk. Just makes them thirsty."

"I've got canned peaches and dog treats, if any of that interests you."

The man looked to his wife, who gave a languid nod. "Okay," said the man. "I can fill a bottle for a couple of cans."

Lauren guessed the RV probably had a storage tank for potable water. Delving into her panniers for a bottle and two cans, she took out an additional can for herself. "Do you have a can opener?" she said.

The man, looking bemused, said, "I think we can find one of those round here somewhere. Why don't you take a seat?"

Lauren glanced at the barking dog, an angry looking German Shepherd. "I don't think he wants me to."

The woman dismissed her fears with a wave. "Don't worry about him. If we're okay with you, he'll be okay too."

The man stood up, and Lauren noticed for the first time the revolver in his waist band. The sanguine coldness of the two worried her for a moment, and she realized this wasn't a good time to be trusting people, especially if the vibes weren't right.

"Actually, forget it," she said. "I don't want to bother you, and I have to be going."

"Bother us?" laughed the man, spreading his arms and looking around. "There's nothing here, and nothing to do."

"But we can play," said one of the children, a tousle haired boy who ran to the dog and gave him a hug. "Shush, boy."

The dog ceased barking and licked the child's face.

The image in Lauren's mind of the creepy family that might be ready to abduct or murder lonely hitchhikers melted away, and she realized she was still paranoid after the guy tried to steal her bike that morning.

The man entered the RV and emerged with a folding P-38 can opener, which he tossed on the table. "Here, you can keep that one. We've got others. No point having a bag of cans and no can opener, is there?"

Lauren took a seat while the man went to fill her bottle. With her stomach rumbling, she opened her peaches and began eating them with her fingers, dribbling juice on her chin. "I'm sorry," she said, "but I'm just so hungry."

The woman handed Lauren a tissue and shouted back into the RV, "Larry! Bring out a fork."

Duly equipped, Lauren attacked the rest of the can, then drank the sweet syrup left in the bottom. The whole family watched her, even the dog, and Lauren knew she was being rude, but she couldn't help herself. As soon as she tasted the first peach, she just had to consume the rest without pause.

Larry placed the cans she'd given him back on the table. "Looks like you need these more than we do," he said.

"If you'd come by earlier, I'd have cooked you something," said the woman. "We've still got propane in the tanks. I'm Mary, by the way."

"Lauren," said Lauren, opening another can. "I've got some dog treats in the pannier if you want to get some."

"Nah," said Mary, "He's eaten, and he'll only get fat. How far have you come?"

"New York. Heading to North Carolina."

"That's a ways," said Larry, settling back into his chair. "But we've got you beat. We were heading to Georgia."

"How are you going to get home?"

"This is home. We park up the RV for a couple of months at a time, then move on. I run an online website design company, and Mary runs a YouTube channel. We home-school the boys, and do pretty much what we want. Or we did. I made the mistake of bugging out from the last campsite on the night of the storm. If we'd have stayed where we were, we'd have a better view, a lake and some woods. At least we stocked up on food before we left, and there's a creek over yonder behind the trees. And we can siphon gas for the generator. We'll be okay for a while."

"We never wanted to stay in one place," explained Mary. "Before the boys came, Larry and I traveled about, offering work on farms."

"Might be time to do that again," said Larry. "Must be a farm hereabouts where we can trade labor for eggs."

It sounded a little too idyllic to Lauren, but for all she knew, they might have been right. "There's a truck about a mile that way, full of food and stuff. If you use your bikes, you might be able to get some before looters clean it out."

"Might be an idea. Hey guys, wanna go for a ride?" said Larry to the boys.

The two boys, neither older than ten, looked excited. Lauren thought that, to them, this must be one big adventure. Maybe it was better to look at it like that.

"I'd better get moving," said Lauren. "Thanks for the water."

"No problem. Good luck out there."

Lauren cycled away, feeling thoughtful. She wasn't sure whether Mary and Larry were deluded, or just very, very smart. They had a plan, if it could be called that. Or maybe it was an old fashioned sense of being able to weather everything as a family. At least they were together, and had lived closely for a long time. It shone a spotlight on Lauren's own family.

Rick's long absences had come to feel routine, and her own absences a hectic necessity. Which seemed fine when transportation and communication systems were working. Not so, now.

Or maybe it wasn't, even then. And deep down she'd always known it. She had no desire to pack her family into an RV, but right now, if she and Rick were at home with the kids, and the storm had gone down, it wouldn't have been as big an issue. Together, they too would have weathered the consequences. With everyone that she loved close to her, nothing else mattered. The career and the financial security was just chaff in the breeze. Regime change in some far off land was simply a waste of time. The storm made all that stuff completely irrelevant.

She rode until nightfall, and made her bed in the trees at the side of the highway, preferring to be hidden rather than in a vehicle. She was still wary of scavengers. In the gloom she felt profoundly depressed. Aching and exhausted, she wasn't sure what was right any more. The gloom deepened as she tried to get comfortable, feeling cold now. Too tired to think, she drifted off, shivering.

When she woke to dawn's light filtering through the trees, she hardly felt she'd slept at all. Tree roots on the uneven ground made her body hurt even more than the day before, and the thought of cycling another mile made her groan. The bright sunlight, however, banished the dark mood of the night before, and once she got moving, her optimism returned.

Within an hour she was cycling over a suspension bridge across the Delaware River. In the sparkling waters below, a police launch puttered along, towing a string of rowing boats, each laden with boxes. Other small boats with simple engines cruised the same route, all carrying supplies to the city of Wilmington, its charred towers still smoking.

People were getting organized, and Lauren wondered if the worst was over.

20

Rick was surrounded by food. Dangling from the branches above were succulent peaches. The orchard was full of them. Reaching up to pluck one, however, was a hazardous activity. Machine gun bullets zipped through the trees, angrier than the wasps that hovered and fed over the fallen fruit. From the edge of the orchard, stretching towards an ancient ruin of pillars and collapsed walls, lay a field of cotton, the soft white bundles looking like freshly fallen snow.

They'd escaped Manbij and shaken off their pursuers in the night, but they were in a dense agricultural area, surrounded by villages and farms, and it wasn't long before they were spotted again. In the distance, Rick saw an old Volkswagen camper pull up and drop off a group of militants in an attempt to cut off their retreat before driving off to pick up some more. As the militants entered the cotton field, the machine gun ceased firing so as not to hit their own men. Rick adjusted his sights and fired a series of shots towards the militants, forcing them to hit the dirt and disappear among the cotton balls. Shortly after, the machine gun began firing again, probing the trees.

Walt lay holding his rifle, his face an unhealthy pallor. "Are you ready?" Rick asked him.

"I'm not going to make it," murmured Walt. "You go. I'll cover you from here as best I can."

"Bullshit. We're getting you out of here." Turning to the others, he said, "We're going to crawl to those ruins."

"Good place for a last stand," observed Scott.

"There'll be no last stand," said Rick curtly. "We keep moving and that's that."

With no further way north, and with ISIS coming up from the south, Rick was determined to push south-west towards Aleppo. Al Bab was closer, but held by the same militants trying to kill them now. He wasn't sure he could expect better treatment by the Syrian government forces in Aleppo, but he knew the Russians were there too, and being interned by them was better than being captured by militias who were only loyal to the nearest warlord. At least Walt would get medical treatment, and if that was the only thing he could salvage from this mission, then all well and good.

Rick took point, crawling out of the orchard and between the cotton plants. It was punishing work, crawling for hundreds of yards on the hard packed earth, and he knew it was harder still for Walt, but he had no solutions for that. He still hadn't located the machine gun that was keeping them pinned, but if they weren't out of here by the time the camper returned, they were all screwed.

Hustling forward, he froze when he heard the sound of metal dragging over a stone. Ahead, the cotton plants waved as they were pushed aside. Rick sighted his rifle, and a youth with a black bandana appeared, hauling an AK47 on its sling. Rick fired two shots, exploding the youth's face in a red cloud. The machine gun bullets immediately began probing his position, raining snowy cotton over him. Rick doubled his efforts, trying to get out of the beaten zone.

The ominous whistle of a mortar bomb forced his face into the dirt. The explosion nearby showered clods of earth in a wide radius. Rick turned to see if his team was okay. They were strung out in a line behind him, and with a wave of his hand he ordered them to scatter. Shuffling forward a few more feet, he froze again as the next bomb was lobbed over, the earth shaking beneath him.

If there was anything that infantrymen hated most, it was mortars. The horrible whistle and the random location of the impact made it difficult to anticipate, and there was no way to stop it. Rick lifted his head to see if he could locate it. It sounded close. A puff of dust from the ruins indicated it was firing from behind the broken walls, out of sight. At the same time he spotted the machine gun that was giving him so much trouble. It too was in the ruins, nestled in the gap between the blocks of a fallen pillar. The gunner spotted him and swiveled the weapon on its bipod, stitching up his position with ricocheting near misses. Rick tensed up, flinching with each crack that zipped by his ears. As soon as it paused, he slithered forward like a lizard, past the dead body of the militant. He could hear shouts in Arabic as the machine gunner called corrections to the mortar operator. He made a few more yards before the whistle came again. The round landed behind him, tearing apart the body of the militant and flinging limbs into the air.

Rick crawled faster as the bombs rained down on the field, panting like a dog as he exerted himself. Reaching the edge of the crops, he saw the ruins twenty yards away. The machine gunner, eyes wide, spotted him and swiveled his weapon towards him. Rick had his rifle ready, and he hosed down the gunner's position with a long burst, hitting him in the head and chest and jerking him backwards out of sight. Jumping up and sprinting across the gap, Rick found the militant rolling on the ground. He emptied his magazine into him, just to make sure.

Behind the ruined wall and down some steps was a small amphitheater. Two militants manned a 60mm mortar. On seeing Rick, they reached for their AKs. Rick picked up the machine gun and, at close range, fired the weapon from the hip, unleashing a hail of bullets. When the box magazine clunked empty, the militants lay contorted and still.

Scott emerged from the field as Rick reloaded his rifle. In the distance, trailing a plume of dust, the camper was returning with a fresh group of fighters. Without thinking further, Rick jumped down to the mortar and turned it around, pulling the pin from a mortar bomb and dropping it down the tube. There was a hollow *whump*, and the bomb launched, landing fifty yards in front of the vehicle. The camper halted, and the militants inside jumped out. Rick spun the dials on the mortar bipod to adjust the range and dropped another bomb down the tube. Before the militants could get clear, the bomb sailed down and impacted on the camper, blowing it out and scattering their bodies.

There was a moment of utter silence, and Rick palmed his face with a groan. Scott reached his side. "You know?" he said, "we could have used that vehicle."

Rick sagged back onto his haunches. "I know," he said. "I was trying for a near miss."

"Maybe you should have tried to hit it. You'd have missed, then."

Rick glanced sideways at him. "You're real helpful."

"I aim to please. Unlike you."

The remaining militants emerged from the field, running away, and Scott turned, firing snap shots at the fleeing figures. None of them dropped. "Now that's how to miss," said Scott ruefully.

Walt emerged from the crops, looking like he'd just swum the Atlantic. Kowalski was behind him, looking in even worse shape. There was no sign of Leroy or Jamie.

Rick ran back into the field, keeping low, heading for the plumes of dust that hovered over the blasted cotton. Scott's rifle cracked, firing towards the orchard over Rick's head. Rick dropped lower, calling out in a hissed voice for Leroy and Jamie.

He found them by a crater, their bodies covered in earth and cotton blossoms. Sliding onto his knees by Leroy, Rick turned him over. His clothes had been shredded by the blast, and blood leaked out of the corner of his mouth.

"Leroy!"

Leroy's eyes were open, but he had difficulty focusing on Rick. His fingers flexed, as if he was trying to lift his arm, but it wouldn't move. "Hey there," he murmured.

Rick tore off Leroy's body armor, frantically looking for wounds. "Rest easy, we'll get you out of here."

Leroy tried to chuckle, but his mouth was filling with blood. Spitting it out in a spray, he said, "Get home to your children."

Rick lifted Leroy's head to prevent him choking, but by the time he did that, Leroy's eyes had rolled back. Rick pumped his chest to get his heart going again, but only succeeded in spraying more blood out from the shock-damaged lungs.

Jamie was easier to assess. His head had separated from his neck and lay a few feet away.

Rick quit pumping, defeated. Angry and frustrated, he closed Leroy's eyes and held his hand over his friend's face, trying to hold his own tears back.

Josh walked half a mile to the creek that ran through the suburb, carrying a five gallon plastic container. Water had ceased dripping from the faucets now, and Grandma was worried about their supplies running low.

"Get it from the creek," she'd said, "but don't drink it. We need to boil it first."

Well, duh, thought Josh, feeling cocky again. Even he knew that. Squatting on the stones by the creek, he dipped his container in until it was full, lifting it up to see the particles swirling in the brown water. Even after boiling, he wasn't sure he wanted to drink it. Grandma said she was going to revive a copper distiller left in the garage, stored there after Grandpa gave up his fantasy of making his own moonshine. Josh wasn't sure how that would work, seeing as he assumed it was only for making alcohol.

Capping the container, he lifted it up, a little shocked by how much it now weighed. Well, there was no rush to get home. He'd never been that strong, and if he needed to rest on the way back, he could do so.

The creek ran through a wooded area that Josh remembered from when he was younger. Grandpa used to bring him down to fish – or at least pretend to fish, because they never caught anything and Josh had never seen anything in the water. It was fun, though, and he could make-believe they were out in a real rural area, with bears and shit. It was harder to maintain the pretense these days, as developments had grown on the banks of the creek. New low-rise apartment blocks and parking lots lay nearby.

As Josh hauled his container home, a kid with a baseball bat came over from the blocks.

"Give me that water," shouted the kid.

Josh glanced at him. The kid looked about ten years old, all puffed up and scared as he waved his bat.

"Get your own," said Josh dismissively.

"I'm warning you," said the kid, his voice rising in tone.

"Yeah, right," said Josh. He wasn't about to take some punk-ass kid all that seriously, especially one whose voice hadn't broken yet.

It was a mistake. Walking away, Josh didn't see the kid coming up behind him. The *thwack* of the bat across the side of his head took him by surprise. Stunned by the impact, he found himself on his knees, his head ringing. A series of blows rained down on his back, but none measured up to the first one that had him struggling to keep his balance, his vision blurred.

By the time he recovered, the kid was dragging the container back across the parking lot. A group of youths stood waiting near a block entrance, arms folded. Other, older faces peered out of windows. Nobody lifted a finger to do a thing about what they'd just witnessed.

Josh staggered away, still in shock. When he got home, there was pandemonium when Grandma saw the blood on the side of his head. Lizzy started to cry while Grandma sorted through drawers for some bandages, urging Josh to sit down in the kitchen.

Josh felt no pain, only dizziness. What he was really conscious of was a deep shame. He felt vulnerable and worthless, unable to stop even a ten year old kid from beating him up and stealing his stuff. He couldn't believe it had happened.

The front door opened and Elena and Max entered the house, carrying a plastic bag of goods.

"We went to the store, Daisy," called Elena. "They only let us have two items per person, but I got you some flour."

She came into the kitchen and saw Grandma cleaning Josh's wound.

"Oh my word! What happened?"

While Grandma explained, Max mooched around the kitchen, agitated. "They had cops outside the stores," he said. "They frisked me and found the gun. Confiscated it. Told me I was lucky they didn't arrest me for carrying a concealed weapon. Can you believe it?"

Elena helped Grandma with the bandage. "Josh, are you okay? Can you see my fingers clearly?"

Josh stared straight ahead, feeling removed from the scene.

"Is anybody listening to me?" said Max. "They took our gun. What are we supposed to do now?"

21

Lauren eyed the tunnel with foreboding. She'd followed the I-95 to Baltimore, but the tollway dipped beneath the harbor and she wasn't sure she wanted to follow it anymore. It was pitch black and clogged with vehicles, and before she stopped, she thought she heard the echo of voices inside.

All was silent now, but she had the sense someone was waiting in there.

On either side of the tollway were rail yards, coal heaps and port warehouses. In the distance, a pall of smoke hung over the city. The wisdom of arriving at a big city in the middle of the crisis began to gnaw at her conscience.

The big problem was that she had no maps, so couldn't plan her route well. The couple at the RV probably did have maps, and she realized too late that she should have asked if she could take a look at them. Until she reached North Carolina, she had no idea where she was off the interstate. Detours were an invitation to get lost.

She wasn't going through the tunnel, though. That much was clear. She didn't want to go through the city, either, but the approaching rumble of a vehicle with a throaty exhaust prompted her to make a decision. As she wheeled her bike towards the concrete barrier dividing the highway from the rail yard, a '69 Dodge Charger with tinted windows arrived at the toll booths and stopped, engine idling.

Lauren lifted the bike over the barrier and hastened across the tracks, glancing nervously back. The Dodge sat there, possibly contemplating the blocked passage to the tunnel, then it turned around and burbled back up the tollway.

Lauren had no particular reason to be cautious about it, but she was nevertheless glad to see it go. It conjured up images of *Mad Max*, and on the bicycle, she felt vulnerable. Other vehicles would undoubtedly have survived the EMP, and she wondered for how long it would be safe to travel on the major highways.

Not much longer, probably. She wanted to cover a lot more miles before she was forced off them.

The streets near the port showed all the signs of gentrification, with factories and brick warehouses converted to apartments. Old row houses had been cleaned up, and community corner stores converted into homes. She passed hipster cafes and art galleries, but most were closed. The smell of burning hovered in from downtown, plus the persistent crack of gunfire. Students and white collar workers sat out on the stoops, just as the poorer dock workers had done in the past, but there were no children running around. The faces appeared gloomy or apprehensive. Expensive cars sat uselessly on the roadsides, and transmission poles bore the evidence of fires where the transformers had blown. Lauren wasn't sure how desperate people were yet, but she avoided places where she saw small groups congregated, turning down side streets until she was completely lost. The nature of the streets changed the further she progressed, old buildings replaced by apartment projects and new builds that nevertheless looked shabbier and dirtier. Grass grew more profusely on the sidewalks, with houses abandoned and boarded up. She'd reached the poorer areas of Baltimore, and still she couldn't see any traffic signs to the I-95.

Turning onto a main street, she heard the distinctive exhaust of the Dodge, cruising slowly. She pulled over quickly, dismounting, and rolled the bike into an alley, hiding herself behind a pile of trash. The vehicle drove by, maintaining its leisurely pace. Lauren peered out to watch its progress, trying to shake off the feeling that she was being stalked.

She wasn't prepared for what happened next.

Two black youths in hoodies jumped out at a corner, in front of the car. One, wielding a pistol, pumped five shots into the windshield. The vehicle slowed and the other youth ran round to the driver's side, yanking open the door and pulling out the limp body of the driver. The youths jumped into the car, and the exhaust roared as they drove the Dodge away at speed, leaving the body of some ordinary looking middle aged white guy in a plaid shirt – not Mad Max, nor any other kind of road warrior.

"You is in the wrong place," said a voice.

Lauren turned suddenly, seeing an elderly black guy behind the chain link fence of his yard. He scrutinized her with a mix of curiosity and fatalistic bemusement.

"Is there a right place?" she said.

"For white folk like you, anyplace outside the neighborhood is a right place. At least you got a choice."

Lauren wasn't sure what to make of that. "I'm trying to reach the I-95. Which direction is it from here?"

"You wanna go back that way, and quick."

"I've just come from that direction. The tunnel's blocked. I need to head south."

"Then you wanna go downtown, but I wouldn't. They be rioting there. Crazy people. And the cops are even crazier. Shoot you as soon as see you."

"Have you witnessed that?" asked Lauren.

But the old man ignored her question. "They're afraid," he intoned. "These are the End Times. Prepare yourself and make your peace with God."

Without another word, he turned around and shuffled back into his house. Lauren stared for a moment, conscious of her rapidly beating heart. The street was clear again, but she hesitated to venture out. Slowly, she reached to her pack, pulling out the lug wrench, its weight a comfort in her hand. Checking out every shadow, every doorway, she stepped out and made her way along the shady side of the street. Cycling on the road made her too conspicuous, so she pushed the bike. Her mouth was dry, but she didn't want to pause, and certainly didn't want to advertise that she had water, or anything else people might want.

Passing the body of the driver, she saw two police officers at an intersection. They hadn't come to investigate the crime, though. White cops, they moved warily, turning circles as they walked. One wielded a shotgun, the other pushed a shopping cart with bottled water and cereal boxes. An overweight black woman harangued them as they walked away.

"Wotcha going do?" she yelled. "We need help here! We *need* assistance."

The cops paid her no heed, intent on getting out with their rattling cargo.

"This is genocide," screamed the woman. "You hear me? You leaving us *to die*."

Lauren considered approaching the cops but realized they were bigger targets than she was. Hated in the neighborhood and unable to call for backup, they picked up the pace as a shot echoed in a nearby street. A dog barked, and the woman kept on shouting. Lauren detoured down a side street, determined to get as far away from any disturbances as possible.

Two blocks on, she witnessed two black guys dragging a young black woman down the street by her hair. The woman screamed and kicked, but the two guys, looking around warily with guns in their waistbands, were unwilling to let their prize escape their grasp. Faces in windows turned away, drawing blinds. Folks sat on stoops got up hastily and entered their houses, bolting the doors. A small child ran up the street, crying hysterically, trying to catch up with the men. The guys dragged the woman into a corner house with boarded windows and slammed the door in the child's face.

"Mommy!" screamed the child, battering frantically at the door.

Lauren stood transfixed. The twisting of her gut, and the adrenaline coursing through her veins, urged her to run. She couldn't take her eyes off the child, though.

She remembered Josh at the same age, crying on his first day at school. That had broken her heart, back then, and she hated the memory.

But this was worse. Legs trembling, she gripped the handlebars tight until her knuckles paled.

She couldn't walk away. Anger boiled inside her.

Dropping the bike, she strode to the house. The front door looked solid, so she went round the back, climbing the fence from the alley. Garbage and weeds filled the yard, but the rear door had been kicked in at some point. Lauren entered, clutching the lug wrench in both fists. Broken bottles, pieces of foil and discarded needles littered the kitchen floor. Screaming came from the front room.

"Hold her down," yelled a voice. Then: "You like this, bitch? I'm going to fuck you good, then you're gonna tell us where you stashed the shit."

Lauren hesitated for a moment, her heart pounding, then barged into the front room. One of the men was holding the woman down, punching her in the face. The second guy stood watching, wrapping a belt around his fist. Lauren came up behind him and swung the wrench with all her might. The heavy tool smashed into the man's skull with a loud crack, and he dropped to the ground.

The other guy, seeing his comrade fall, reacted instantly, leaping up. Lauren swung the wrench, but the man caught it in his hand and tried to wrestle the weapon off her. Taller than Lauren, he forced her back and down. Lauren kicked at him and grabbed his other arm to stop him punching her, attempting to push back, but his strength was too great. She kneed him in the groin, eliciting a grunt, but the man freed his right arm and punched her in the face. Stumbling backwards over the body of the other guy, Lauren tumbled to the floor, losing her grip on the wrench. Dazed from the punch, she squirmed, kicking out, but it was like landing blows on a tree trunk. Her attacker paused to knead his groin, evidently feeling the pain, then switched the wrench to his right hand and loomed over her, arm raised to strike.

Curling up in a futile attempt to weather the blow, Lauren's hand fetched up against a pistol on the floor. It had fallen from the prostrate guy's waist band. The weapon was a Beretta M9, the same weapon Lauren had been issued with in Iraq. Closing her hand over the familiar grip, her thumb moved automatically to the safety, clicking it off. As the wrench swung down towards her, she brought the pistol up and fired three times, the report echoing loudly in the room. Three spurts of blood leaped out from the man's chest, and the wrench clattered down onto the bare floorboards. Before Lauren could roll clear, the man's body tumbled down on top of her, crushing the breath from her lungs.

Heaving the body off, she lay gasping, her ears ringing, the realization of what she had just done dawning on her. Her cheek stung, a deep pain surfacing slowly along her jaw, and the dead man's warm blood soaked through the front of her hoodie.

The woman she'd rescued coughed and moaned, and Lauren crawled over to her. The woman bled from her nose and cuts to her chin, and appeared dazed. Opening her eyes wide, she looked at Lauren and said, "Who are you?"

"Doesn't matter," said Lauren. "Are you okay?"

The woman worked her jaw. "I guess."

Another groan signaled the waking of the man Lauren had hit with the wrench. As he rose to his knees, Lauren aimed the pistol at him. Clutching his head, he seemed surprised when he pulled his hand away and found blood on it. Taking in the scene in the room, his eyes fell on the barrel of the pistol pointing at his head. Falling backwards in shock, he scrambled up, stumbled over his feet, then staggered over to the front door. Yanking it open, he stepped out, falling off the stoop. The child, waiting outside, rushed in and threw his arms around his mother. The mother clutched him tight, whispering reassurance. The guy outside picked himself up and lurched out of sight. The mother took one look at Lauren and said, "You should have shot him."

Lauren was still struggling to comprehend the situation she was in. "He was no longer a threat," she said. "Rules of engagement."

"That shit don't count round here," said the woman. "He's going to get his brother and the rest of the gang, and they ain't going to be so merciful."

22

"Name's April," said the woman. "And thanks."

Lauren searched the body of the man she'd shot, finding a Ruger 9mm, but no extra magazines. She also found his ID and a wad of money. She didn't want to know the identity of the person she'd just shot, and she was about to shove it back into his pocket when April spoke up.

"If you don't want that money, I'll have it."

Lauren appraised her. She placed April in her mid-twenties, and her kid about five, a little younger than Lizzy. An attractive woman, in spite of her bruises, and seemingly unfazed by her experience, like it was just another day in the hood.

And maybe it was. She had a determined look in her eyes, though.

"Mind if we split it?" said Lauren. "I might still need some."

She wasn't sure how much longer cash would be worth anything, but she considered it worth having something, even if she was only going to be lighting fires with it.

With that thought, she continued searching through the man's clothes until she found a lighter.

The woman seemed amused. "Seeing as you're going to be so polite about it, sure."

Lauren peeled off some notes and handed over the rest. "You'd better get home quick," she said.

Holding her new guns ready in the pouch of her hoodie, Lauren peered out of the front door. The guy who'd fled the house was gone.

Unfortunately, so was her bike.

"Crap," said Lauren. Her heart sank.

"You're not from round here, are you?" said April.

"You think?"

April looked to the bag on Lauren's back. "Where were you headed?"

"Home," said Lauren.

"Is it close?"

"No."

"You'd better come with me, then."

April took the child's hand and led the way out of the door. Lauren, for want of any better ideas, followed her. Staying off the street as much as possible, they moved through cluttered back alleys until they reached the rear entrance to April's ground floor apartment. The door was already slightly open, the wood splintered around the handle. April looked cautiously through the back window before pushing at the door, listening carefully. Inside, the closets had been emptied, clothes and boxes scattered all over the floor. Floor boards had been levered up and a couch had been slashed.

"You'd better watch from the front door," said April. "We don't have much time."

Lauren opened the door a crack and stood guard, her stomach tight. The flash of anger that led her to go on the rampage earlier had subsided, and now she dwelt on the consequences. The loss of the bike gnawed at her as she thought about the distance she still had to cover. Being the target of a gang only compounded her pessimism. Could she have shot the guy before he got away? Executed him? Should she have even got involved in the first place? And what if she saw the gang members walking up the street now? Was she prepared for a shoot-out?

With a screwdriver, April levered up the lid of a dented, rusting washing machine and pulled out a small backpack.

"Is that what those guys were looking for?" asked Lauren.

"No, this is my bug-out bag," said April. "What those guys were looking for doesn't exist here."

"But I guess you couldn't persuade them of that?"

"No."

Gathering scattered tins, bottles and noodle packets, April threw them into a wheeled carry-on case and thrust it towards Lauren. "Here, you take this."

Lauren took it. "Why would you have a bug-out bag?"

"If you lived here, you'd understand."

Lauren chose not to pursue the matter further. April unfolded a three wheeled jogging stroller, snapping it into place. "In you get, baby."

The boy had clearly outgrown the stroller, but he got in nevertheless. April threw a blanket in with him and grabbed a couple of thermal jackets and some other clothes, thrusting them into the stroller basket.

The street remained clear, but they left via the back door and into the alley. The cracks of gunfire seemed closer now.

"Which direction were you headed?" asked April.

"South. The I-95."

"I can get you there."

Lauren eyed the stacked stroller. "And then?"

"Don't care. I'm leaving the city and never coming back."

"Don't you have relatives or friends you can go to?"

"I had a friend. His name was Choo, but he's dead now."

"How did he die?"

"You shot him."

Lauren wasn't sure she wanted to know more. At the end of the alley, they peered out, checking the street was safe, then dashed across to the next alley. Not far away, they could hear shouts and the blast of gunfire.

"You've arrived in the middle of a war," said April in a matter-of-fact voice.

"Are people fighting over food and water already?" said Lauren.

April laughed. "Food and water? Hell, no. These people are fighting over drugs. Ain't no more shipments coming to town. The Lafayette Crew and the Johnsons are fighting to raid each other's stashes, just so's they can sell drugs to the freaks and crackheads who ain't gonna get their welfare checks at the turn of the month anyway. It's a crazy war for crazy people. Once the dumbasses realize this ain't no temporary situation, the desperate loons on the street are going to be stealing people's food to barter for cocaine. Then they'll die. It's going to be fifty shades of ugly, and I don't want to see it."

Lauren thought it looked pretty ugly already. As they neared the downtown, they saw the riots. People smashed windows and shutters and broke into stores and restaurants. Boxes and bags were carried out. Sports equipment, clothing and TVs were clutched in people's arms. Shopping carts carried away a lot more. Youths with masks over their faces looted cars and hurled Molotov cocktails at the Children's Museum for no reason that Lauren could see. Waves of choking smoke filled the streets. A police cruiser was crushed as a gang jumped up and down on it. Police presence was minimal, and as they passed the harbor, Lauren saw a thin line of them, watching impotently as looters emptied a pharmacy. Youths ripped up stones from the sidewalk and hurled them at the cops, forcing them back. The police appeared poorly equipped, with only a few riot shields between them, and they were more interested in self-preservation than taking offensive action. Heavily outnumbered, they yielded ground until they became distant and irrelevant. The youths celebrated with whoops and shouts, and Baltimore burned.

April led the way down the Inner Harbor walk. The old harbor was a tourist attraction, with the *USS Constellation*, a civil war sailing ship, moored on its own. Burning embers floated on the breeze, and Lauren thought it was only a matter of time before they caught on the ship's rigging or wooden structure. The only tourists around now were the scavengers and opportunists who ran in and out of the harbor malls. It was an intimidating atmosphere to be pushing through and at one point, a guy with a knife ran up to them and yelled, "Give me that bag!"

Lauren pulled both guns out of her pouch and aimed them at him. "I don't think so," she said.

The would-be mugger didn't waste time expressing his dismay. He took off, looking for easier targets.

"Should have shot him, too," said April phlegmatically.

"Just get us out of here, okay?" said Lauren, pocketing the guns and keeping a nervous all-round watch.

"You look pretty badass, with all that blood on you," said April. "Like *Kill Bill*."

"I hated that movie. How much further?"

"Entrance to the freeway is two blocks that way."

A guy with a leather jacket and a cash register tray decided he didn't have enough. Coming out of a kitsch store and museum, he spied Lauren's bags and waved a revolver. Lauren, on edge, pulled out the Beretta and, in a two handed stance, fired two shots to center mass. The man, discharging the revolver into the air, fell backwards, the cash tray tumbling and spilling coins. Nearby scavengers dashed for cover, and April sped up. Lauren backed after her, keeping her gun on the guy. He twitched, leaking blood on the paving, but didn't get up.

"Got myself a kick-ass soccer mom," said April gleefully.

Lauren's head reeled. She hadn't planned to shoot, but it was instinctive. Running with April across a highway, she pocketed the gun again, feeling the hot barrel against her stomach. Down a side street she glimpsed the police discharging their firearms while retreating, possibly reacting to the shots she had fired, though they were shooting at the rioters.

"Can you not be so damned cheerful about this?" she said to April as they ran.

"Sorry," puffed April. "I get sarcastic when I'm nervous."

Her kid in the stroller leaned forward, a stony expression on his face. He looked like a figurehead on the prow of a ship, and Lauren could only wonder what was running through his mind. From the moment they'd left the house, he hadn't shown a trace of emotion.

23

Josh held Lizzy's hand at the back of the crowd as more people emerged from their houses for the impromptu street meeting. The atmosphere was tense.

"When is the power coming back on?" yelled someone.

The chairman of the neighborhood association stood in the middle of the road next to a cop, who had his bicycle with him. "Please, everyone," said the chairman, "save your questions till the end. Officer Copeland has taken the time to visit as many neighborhoods as possible, and he has to visit more, so let's keep this brief."

"What about the water?" called someone else.

The police officer, looking a little weary, held his hand up. "Settle down, everybody. I'll answer your questions as best I can, but we've all got to stay calm. We're doing our best to make sure people get what they need, but understand that we're kind of stretched right now. If you're willing to help, we'd appreciate your assistance."

"Are you working on the power yet?"

The officer tried to see who'd asked the question, but there were too many faces. "We've got engineers working around the clock at the McGuire plant, and they're doing the best they can, but there's been a lot of damage."

"Isn't that a nuclear power plant?"

"Yes sir, it is, but don't go worrying about that now."

"Are you kidding me?" said another voice. "If the pumps are out, the core's going to melt down. It's going to blow."

A wave of consternation rippled through the crowd.

"Please," said the officer, "we've got our best people working on it. Last I heard, they were using generators to pump water from the lake to cool the reactors. These people are dedicated and professional. They know what they're doing."

"So did the people at Fukushima."

"I don't know nothing about that. I've just come to tell you that you haven't been forgotten. We're coordinating relief operations with the Red Cross and the military at Fort Bragg, and we're going to try and get supplies into the city. As soon as we've got distribution centers set up, I'll be round to let you know. In the meantime, be patient and help each other out."

"Are we under martial law?" said another voice.

"No, sir, we are not. This is a State of Emergency and all normal laws apply. Please don't consider taking the law into your own hands. I know some of you are armed, but permits for concealed handguns are still required for compliance with the law. Please do not be tempted to break this law."

"Yes, but can we rely on you to protect us? You're the first police officer I've seen in three days. When are we going to see more?"

"We're doing the best we can, ma'am. Some of us have families too."

It was Grandma who'd asked the last question, and like everyone else, she didn't appear convinced by the answer. The chairman, meanwhile, shook the police officer's hand, bidding him goodbye, and the officer mounted his bike and cycled away.

Someone near Josh turned and said, "We won't see him again for another three days now."

"Three days?" replied another. "More like never. He'll cycle right out of town and he won't come back."

"I'm sure that won't be the case," said Grandma, not liking the speaker's tone. "He's an officer of the law and he has a duty."

"Duty my ass. A few more days without pay or water, and he'll use that badge and gun to look after his kin, and nobody else."

"Listen up, everybody," called the chairman. "I understand there are concerns, and believe me, I share them, but we can get through this. You heard Officer Copeland's news, so be assured that the authorities are doing everything they can to return things to normal. In the meantime, let's look out for each other, especially the elderly folk. If you think anyone needs help, don't hesitate to offer. We've got a few hours of daylight left, so I propose we hold a swap meet, right here in the street, and we can barter excess goods and services. If you've got useful skills, bring them to the table. And one last thing: if anyone takes water from the creek, make sure you boil it first. We don't want anyone getting ill. And if you're using candles tonight, please take precautions. I cannot stress this enough. The last thing we need is a house fire, right now. That's everything. We'll set up some tables and see what people can bring. Let's have some community spirit."

As the crowd dispersed, the speaker that Grandma didn't like muttered, "Damn plant is going to blow and this city's going to glow like Chernobyl, but hell yeah, let's have some community spirit and worry about candles."

Josh felt a tug at his elbow and turned to see the Henderson boy, Rory. A freckle faced teen, Josh had watched him from a distance, growing over the years. From an ordinary looking youth, he'd acquired muscles and the confidence that seemed to go with it, cruising with his bros at the weekend and hanging out with girls – the complete opposite of Josh. Close up, though, his demeanor was tender and respectful, and nothing like the hooligan image Elena had painted.

"How are you doing?" said Rory, concerned. "I heard about what happened at the creek. That was a bad deal."

Josh stared mutely at him.

"Sorry to hear about your grandpa," continued Rory. "That must have been tough."

Josh didn't know what to say. Behind Rory stood some of the older kids in the street, gazing at him in fraternal unison.

"Look, I just want to say that, if you're going to go down to the creek again, you should get one of us to go with you. We can't let the creeps from that neighborhood get one over on us, you know? We've got to stick together."

Josh recognized the faces from his many visits to his grandma, but he didn't really know any of them. In truth, he'd felt intimidated by them. He didn't make friends easily.

Rory scratched the imaginary stubble on his smooth cheeks. "Me and the boys are going over to the Jackson highway tonight, see if we can check out some of the trucks left there. Supplies for the community, you understand. We could use an extra pair of hands, if you're willing. If there are enough of us, it should be okay. Wanna come?"

"Yeah," said one of the boys. "You coming?"

Josh gazed blankly at them, his insides icing up.

He was saved by his grandma. "Come along, Josh," she said, casting a harsh glance at Rory.

Josh allowed himself to be meekly led away. Any other time, he would have felt ashamed. For now, he simply felt numb.

Elena and Max joined them in the house.

"Well, that was a load of nothing," said Max bitterly.

"What do you expect?" said Elena. "They're doing everything they can."

"What's that exactly? Look how many transmission lines are down. You see anybody coming to fix them? No. And how could they anyway? The trucks won't move. And all that crap about concealed licenses don't take away from the fact they took my gun. What am I going to do? Holler 911 and wait for some cop on a bike to get out to us?"

Elena rolled her eyes. "Always complaining."

"And why shouldn't I? They got nothing for us. I tell you, nothing."

Grandma looked over at Josh and Lizzy. "You children had better go to your room," she said tenderly. "Play a board game, perhaps."

Without a murmur of protest, the children about-faced and sloped into the room, lying down on the bed. Whatever talk Grandma was protecting them from, however, could still be heard through the door.

"You heard him talk about the nuclear plant," said Max. "If that blows, we're all going to be growing two heads."

"If it allowed you to think better," said Elena, "that would be an improvement."

Josh stared at the ceiling.

"I'm glad you didn't go with those boys," said Lizzy. "I don't want you to join a gang."

Josh turned thoughts over in his mind. The image of the crazy kid with the baseball bat, of Grandpa stretched out stiff and cold, and that nurse's disdain, all churned together in a kaleidoscope of images that already seemed distant. The few friends he had back home felt a million miles away. And Mom and Dad... were just gone. It was like he and Lizzy were orphans, shipped out to some strange place. People talked past them or behind them, not knowing what to do with them. Yesterday he felt like a man. This morning he felt like a child. Now he didn't know what he was. He was just drifting.

Taking his sister's hand, he squeezed it tight.

24

"He hasn't spoken much since his father left," said April.

Lauren sat on the ground, her back against a tree. Through the sparse woods, she could just see the raised highway of the I-95, and glimpsed the silhouettes moving along it against a darkening sky. Ever since leaving Baltimore, they'd encountered other refugees fleeing the troubled city, and many of the vehicles on the tollway had already been broken into, the contents of glove boxes and trunks strewn over the concrete. Cargo tarps on truck trailers flapped in the breeze after desperate hands had ripped them away to facilitate the looting of boxes. A single body lay by an open door, a jacket covering its chest and face and no clue as to how the person had died. Lauren, for one, didn't want to investigate. She realized now that she should have, in order to assess the risk of staying on the highway. The road led directly to Washington DC, and Lauren expected that soon they would meet refugees coming the other way. They were trapped between two cities, with suburbs close by in every direction. She had to make a decision about when to strike out west to detour around the urban areas, but she had no idea which roads would be best. She badly needed a map. She also needed to find a way to move faster. She estimated they'd made maybe fifteen miles on foot. If she planned to make her way home via minor roads, or in the hills out west, progress would be even slower.

"How long ago did he leave?" said Lauren.

They were eating Powerbars and drinking Gatorade from April's bug-out bag. April wanted a fire to cook some hot food, but Lauren vetoed the idea, worried that a fire would attract unwanted attention.

"It's been two years," said April. "We had a nice place in Highlandtown, but after he left, I couldn't afford the rent, so I had to move somewhere real cheap. Only reason it was cheap was because no one else wanted to live there. My boy's seen too many bad things since then, and he just don't want to speak now. The social worker said he needed speech therapy. I told her to get the hell out. The only therapy he needed was a safe place to grow."

"Why were those men beating you? What did they want?"

April's hand drifted to the bruises on her face. "I made a dumb mistake.

Me and Choo had a thing together. It only lasted a couple of weeks. He seemed a nice guy at first, even though I knew he was in a gang. I thought he was different – you know, the way you always do when you want to believe a guy ain't like the others. Didn't take long to see I was wrong, and we had no chemistry anyway. After we broke, we stayed on good terms. It was amicable. Then I found he'd hidden a stash of drugs in my apartment. They do that sometimes – it's like insurance. As soon as I discovered it, I threw it in the trash. Didn't want any of that shit round my boy. Eventually I forgot about it. Then the power goes out, the street price goes up and Choo's thinking to get himself an advantage. He wasn't so happy when I told him it was gone. I should have bugged out earlier, but I was too late."

Daniel, the little boy, slept peacefully in the stroller, his little hand resting on a half eaten Powerbar.

"What made you intervene?" asked April. "That was a big risk, and you don't know me."

Lauren nodded towards the stroller. "Your boy. I have two children and I couldn't bear the thought of what would happen if they were forced to witness the same. I guess I just saw red."

April stroked her child's head, causing him to stir. "When I saw you coming in with that tire iron, I thought I was hallucinating. Couldn't believe it. Nobody else would have gotten involved like that. They're too afraid of those gangs."

"If I'd have lived there, maybe I would have too," said Lauren thoughtfully. "I didn't have so much to lose."

"You lost your bike."

"There is that. Mind you, if I'd have carried on my way, I'd be eating dog treats now, so maybe that's not a bad thing."

"I owe you."

Lauren shifted uncomfortably. "Don't think that. How's your blisters?"

April wiggled her bare feet. "Stinging like hell."

"What are you going to do?"

April studied Lauren. "You're worried that I'll slow you down, aren't you?"

Lauren averted her gaze. "I didn't say that."

"You don't have to say it. It's written all over your face. In your position, I'd be thinking the same. Hell, I'd have left already."

Lauren looked at her. "No, you wouldn't."

April gave a resigned little shrug. "Easier to say than do, I guess. But we got us a real problem here. How far are you from home?"

"I don't know. Three hundred miles? Maybe more."

"Exactly. And I ain't got no place I've got to be in a hurry. In fact, I got no place to go at all. Makes no difference to me whether I go fast or slow. But like I said, I owe you, so here's the deal. I'll keep up with you and help you out. It's safer for two than one, right? As soon as you find some transport, you take it and you go."

"And what about you?"

"I was thinking of getting away from the east coast and heading into the mountains."

"You ever been up there?"

"No, but I've been watching prepper videos and they say that, when the shit hits the fan, you want to get out of urban areas. So that's what I'll do. Build myself a little cabin, do some fishing and live wild. I've been learning survival skills."

Lauren tried not to laugh.

"What?" said April.

"Nothing."

"You don't think I can do it, do you? Black girl from the ghetto up in redneck country, fighting off the bears and hicks?"

This time, Lauren did laugh. The mental image she conjured up kept her chuckling until she couldn't stop. April looked aggrieved at first, then started to crack. In seconds they were both laughing.

"I'm sorry," said Lauren, wiping her eyes. "I didn't mean to be rude, but I couldn't help myself."

"You're just so cruel," said April, still giggling.

Lauren took a breath. "I think it's the tension. I needed to get it out." The shadows deepened around them as darkness crept across the sky. "I killed someone today," said Lauren suddenly.

April sighed and gazed at her. "And it feels bad?"

"I don't know. I'm kind of thinking I should be feeling something, but... I don't know."

April shook her head. "Girl, he was trying to kill you. And if you hadn't shot him, we'd both be dead."

"I suppose."

"Suppose nothing. It's true."

"I know. It's just I don't feel as bad as I think I should be. I'm kind of conflicted."

"Better that than a victim."

Lauren remained unsure. "Taking a life should be the hardest thing in the world. That's what I've been taught. Even in the army they push you to prepare for it. Never thought it would actually be easy. Doesn't seem right."

April leaned forward. "You've got too much time to think. That's the real problem. I say we forget about it and get some sleep. Got a lot of miles to put behind us tomorrow."

Having sat still for so long, Lauren felt the night's chill. She shivered. From the highway a voice called out. Seconds passed but there was no answering call. Lauren dropped her voice to a whisper. "We need to take turns keeping watch tonight."

Taking the pistols out of her pouch, she weighed them in her hands, deciding to keep the Beretta.

"Are you familiar with firearms?" she asked.

"No," murmured April. "I ain't really a ghetto girl."

"That's okay. I'd be no good in the mountains, either. This is a Ruger SR9. It's got a gazillion safety features so it should be okay for a novice."

April reached out her hand to take it, hesitated, then pulled her hand back. "I don't know if it's a good idea. Maybe it's better if you keep it."

"No. We need two pairs of eyes and two guns ready. Like you said, it's safer for two than one. We look out for each other. Perhaps now's not a good time, but in the morning I'll teach you how to handle this."

"Now you've got me conflicted."

Lauren chuckled softly. "Okay, so we get to share the pain. If this is as bad as it gets, we'll be fine."

25

Walt murmured in his sleep. Rick checked his temperature and felt the heat rising off Walt's brow before he even put his hand on it.

After holing up till nightfall, they'd hoofed it through the darkness to avoid detection. Walt was in a state of near delirium, and Rick and Scott had taken turns holding him up as he walked. It wouldn't be long before he was unable to walk at all. Kowalski lagged behind, increasingly tired, and Rick worried constantly about losing somebody in the dark. They maintained total silence and a deep gloom descended on the little group, unable to share their thoughts. As the stars wheeled slowly overhead, Rick felt his own reserves of energy drain away, and when Walt's legs buckled completely, Rick called it a night, despondent. He took the first watch and sat cradling his rifle, his head nodding as the others breathed heavily in their sleep. Whenever Walt's murmurings grew too loud, he'd nudge him, dragging him back from his deep slumber, hearing his breathing quicken. Feeling the sweat on Walt's brow, he dripped some water into his open mouth to keep him hydrated. They were running low on the precious fluid. He had a squeeze-bag water filter with him, but streams were few and far between on the flatlands, and the creeks that ran through the cultivated areas were a magnet to the local population who had their own water needs.

Rick ran logistical issues and strategies through his mind. He'd learned to do this even when tired, his brain ticking options off like a machine, but he was running into dead ends now. The noose was tightening around his squad, his solutions becoming less adequate. He'd been trained for all eventualities, but he'd become so used to having technology and the backup of the biggest military in the world that the narrowing of his options was becoming deeply frustrating. He'd lost three men and he was convinced he was going to lose another very soon, and there wasn't a damn thing he could do about it. Unable to express his anger externally, he internalized it as dark resentment, and he wondered then if this was how Josh felt.

The sudden leap from his current predicament to his son's state of mind startled him, like a piece of domesticity had just intruded on a tactical situation. His bleak rage deflated like a balloon, and icy depression seeped into him. The stark fact that he was never going to see his son again descended like a blanket on his shoulders, and suddenly all his worrying and planning seemed pointless.

He wasn't going to be able to tell him what he meant to him, nor explain why they'd drifted apart. He'd never be able to say out loud that he didn't understand the reasons himself, but that he wasn't happy with the kind of father he'd become.

He hadn't lived up to the kind of man his own father was.

And it wasn't just the absence. He'd lost the link. Not just to Josh but to Lizzy and Lauren too. The distance never mattered before, because he'd been able to connect with them and slot right into family life, but the past few years were different. He didn't know whether it was the tempo of operations, his increased responsibilities or the fact he'd become jaded. His instinct knew something was wrong. He just couldn't put his finger on it.

Or maybe he was too afraid to admit it.

If so, he was a fool, because he'd lost his chance to tell them how much he loved them. Or perhaps how much he should have loved them, if he'd been smart. The obligatory letter in his pack back at base was never going to be delivered now, even in the event of his demise. They were all stuck in this goddamn country, and the chances were he'd be buried in it.

Or just left to rot. Like Flynn, Jamie and Leroy.

The dying embers of his anger flared up again and he plunged his thoughts into them, determined to forge new ideas to get them out of this.

Scott stirred and woke. "Dude," he said, "you should have woken me. It's nearly dawn."

Rick looked up and saw the sky lightening from the east. He was in such a state of tension, he hadn't noticed the passage of time. "I couldn't sleep," he said quietly, scratching his beard growth.

"Get yourself some," said Scott, sitting up.

"No. We need to move soon."

"We need to do something about Walt."

Rick glared at him. "What's that supposed to mean?"

Scott cocked his head. "I was thinking we need to get him some transport. Why? What did you think I meant?"

Rick retracted his claws. "Nothing."

"You thought I was going to suggest leaving him, didn't you?"

"Didn't say that."

"I bet you were thinking it, though, getting all tetchy with me."

Rick rubbed his face. "I was just pissed, that's all."

Scott looked out at the emerging horizon. "Yeah, we've got ourselves a situation here."

"Tell me about it. I've been trying to work out how we get out of this."

"Me too. Been feeling like a pin ball, bouncing from one mess to another."

A clang of metal rang out in the distance. Rick slipped off his safety catch, craning his neck to see what might have caused it, but a dirt berm blocked his view.

"Maybe we should try entering a town," mused Scott. "Steal a cart. Or maybe find a doctor. There's got to be someone."

"That's a shitty idea."

"Every idea's a shitty idea. Our options range from small piles of crap to great steaming mounds of poop. Hold your nose and take your pick."

The clang came again.

"Wake the others," said Rick.

Crawling to the berm, he peered over. A dust-blown runway stretched off into the distance, with two hardened concrete hangers off to one side. There were no aircraft stationed at the runway, and there was no control tower. Rick judged it to be a disused satellite field, but about twenty gunmen clustered around the entrance to one of the hangers, hammering at a lock on the sliding doors. Taking out his binoculars, he focused on the group.

Scott crawled up alongside him. "Holy crap," he said. "Is this what we were sleeping next to?"

"Yeah, it's a good job it wasn't a working base."

The gunmen broke the lock and slid back the doors. Inside, the nose and propeller of a light aircraft protruded from the gloom. As the gunmen entered, Rick noticed the cans of gas some of them had brought.

"They're going to try to get it flying," he said.

"Smart move," said Scott, observing through his own binoculars. "With everything else grounded, they'll have instant air superiority and no worries about ground to air missiles. Do you think we can hijack it?"

"With all those guys there? What do you think?"

"It's a shitty idea."

"Exactly."

The gunmen wheeled the aircraft out and started topping up its wing tanks with fuel.

"It's not as shitty an idea as walking, though," said Scott.

Rick worked through scenarios in his mind for taking the aircraft, each more unlikely than the next.

"It is," he concluded.

Scott disagreed. "Mount a distraction and we could draw some of them away."

A militant entered the cockpit, waving the others away from the prop. After a few moments, he stuck his head back out, gesturing. A gunman stepped up and took hold of the prop, pulling it round. After several attempts at trying to get it to start, another man joined him. Together they yanked the prop over and over, but nothing happened. After five minutes the militant in the cockpit called a halt and climbed out. The engine cowl was lifted up and curious faces peered inside, poking occasionally. A brief argument broke out, the engine cover was dropped back down, and a few more minutes spent trying to prop-start the aircraft. After sweating and arguing a little more, the gunmen gave up.

Disappointed, Rick lowered his binoculars. "You know, for a second there, I was warming to your distraction idea."

Scott sighed. "It just ain't fair, tempting us like that. There's got to be something here that works."

"They're not doing it right," said Kowalski dryly.

Rick and Scott both looked at him. He'd snuck up on them uninvited.

"Say again?"

"They're not doing it right. You can't just turn the ignition on and roll the engine to start. It's a Cessna 172, not a Pontiac."

"You know that plane?" said Rick.

"Yeah. Most common plane in the world. My cousin's got one. Taught me to fly in it."

"So what are they doing wrong?"

"They're not priming it right."

"Think you can do it better?"

Kowalski thought for a while. "I could try, but I can't guarantee nothing."

Scott rolled his eyes. "Way to go, Mr Confident. We're better off walking."

Rick turned on Kowalski. "We need to get out of here pretty damn quick. Can you fly that plane or not?"

26

Kowalski stared back for a moment. "All I can do is try."

Scott face-palmed. "All the pilots in his squadron, and we had to get the one with no balls."

"That's nothing to do with it," replied Kowalski testily. "Your ego might make you feel tough, but in the air force we learned that engines don't run on testosterone. Different approach, soldier boy."

"Okay, cut it out," said Rick, checking the plane out with the binoculars again. Part of the group had broken off and were walking up the runway, heading towards what appeared to be a town on the other side of the airfield. A few others drifted away to enjoy a cigarette away from the gas cans. "We'll stick it out until these others leave, then make our move."

"What makes you think they'll leave?" said Kowalski.

Rick nodded towards the mosque tower in the town. "Morning prayer."

Scott leaned in front of Kowalski and tapped his own skull. "See? Clever."

"Yeah," said Kowalski. "Him, not you."

Rick crawled over to Walt. The wounded soldier looked at his lowest ebb, but surprisingly he still held his rifle and was trying to keep watch over the fields that stretched out behind them.

"Hang in there," said Rick. "We're planning on flying you out of here."

Walt turned his head slowly to face him, his eyes barely open. "Yeah?" he croaked. "They're sending a bird out to us?"

Rick realized he'd forgotten about the solar storm, and so delirious he was maybe thinking that a helicopter was being sent out to evacuate him.

"Something like that," said Rick quietly.

"Cool," breathed Walt.

"Just one last effort, okay?"

"Sure."

Rick sat with Walt for a while until Scott hissed for him to come over.

"They're moving," said Scott as Rick reached the berm. The gunmen had pushed the aircraft back inside the hanger and were closing the sliding doors. Standing around, they talked for a while, then made their leisurely way down the runway, laughing at some joke. Rick watched impatiently until they climbed over the berm at the other end and crossed some waste ground into the town.

"Let's go."

Carrying Walt between them, Rick and Scott crossed the runway at a jog. The lock on the doors was broken, and Rick forced them slowly open until there was just enough room to squeeze in. The light of the rising sun revealed a rusted and aged aircraft.

"Jesus, that's a pile of shit," said Scott.

"Yeah, but it's better than a mound," said Rick. "Your words, not mine."

Kowalski inspected the craft, tugging at the ailerons and flipping the rudder back and forth. Rick looked inside the cockpit. The 70's style seats were ripped and the blocky flight controls chipped and scratched. The radios were missing, the wires hanging out, but it appeared to have a full panel of analogue instruments, though Rick had no idea what any of them were for.

"I think she'll fly," said Kowalski.

"Are you kidding me?" said Scott. "Thing's probably been sitting here for years. No wonder they couldn't start it."

"Not so," said Kowalski, lifting the engine covers. "There's not much dust on it." He checked the oil. "This has been topped up recently. This thing's been flying during the civil war."

"How come it hasn't been shot down?" asked Rick.

"It's small. Low radar profile. And we had orders not to shoot at them, as they were classed as civilian aircraft. Militias used them to ferry supplies sometimes, and sometimes militia leaders going to meetings. If we didn't have intelligence of who was inside, we didn't touch them. Some of these guys were on our side."

"Supposedly," said Scott.

"Yeah, well. This was probably captured when ISIS were pushed out of the area."

Some of the gas cans still had fuel inside, and there were coils of tubing nearby.

"Have they been siphoning the fuel from somewhere?" asked Rick.

"Yeah. This model runs on auto gas. There's plenty sitting round in tanks now."

"What's the range?"

"Fully topped up? About eight hundred miles. It'll get us to Incirlik easily."

Incirlik was an airbase in Turkey being used by the US air force to fly missions against ISIS. Paradoxically, it was also being used by the Turkish air force to bomb the Kurds, whom the US supported. After the recent coup attempt in Turkey, it had become something of a diplomatic headache, with US movements restricted after being held under suspicion and the base locked down under tight Turkish control.

"Forget that," said Rick, finding some flight charts in the pocket of a door. He opened them out. "The Russian base at Latakia is closer. Do your thing and see if you can get us airborne."

Walt was eased into one of the rear cockpit seats, Rick and Scott pushed the hanger doors open and the plane was rolled out. Rick loaded the full gas cans inside. Kowalski leaned into the cockpit and said, "Master switch is off. Turn the prop slowly three times."

Rick took hold of the two bladed propeller and began to turn it. "You sure this thing's not going to start with me holding the prop?" he asked.

"No, it's safe. Just turn it real slow."

A dog wandered across the runway. A mangy mongrel, it looked suspiciously at the humans.

"I've done it," called Rick. "What now?"

"Hold on," said Kowalski, rooting around in the hanger. "I'm looking for some chocks."

The dog began to bark.

"Rick," called Scott.

Rick turned and saw a boy standing on the berm. "Kowalski, you'd better hurry up."

The boy ran off towards the town. The dog continued to bark, keeping its distance, and Scott took up position by a dilapidated wooden hut. Rick ran to join him.

"What have we got?" he said.

"Nothing yet," said Scott, aiming his rifle. "Wait..."

Movement appeared by the buildings on the edge of town that soon translated into bobbing heads.

"Kowalski! We've got company!"

Rick moved to the other side of the wooden hut and sighted his M4. A man appeared at the berm. As soon as Rick saw he was armed, he squeezed off a shot. At long range, his bullet kicked up some dust on the berm, causing the man to flinch. More gunmen appeared, running on the other side of the berm, down the length of the runway. Scott fired some shots and the men disappeared as they crouched down.

Kowalski, meanwhile, was chocking the wheels of the Cessna. Grabbing the prop, he yanked it down, stepping back as he did so. Nothing happened.

Stepping forward, he repeated the maneuver. The Cessna didn't start.

Tactically, Rick was in a bad position. The wooden hut was too flimsy to use as cover, and if the gunmen kept using the berm for cover, they would pop up on the opposite side of the runway and turn the hut, and the plane, into a colander. Taking a chance, he dashed across the runway and threw himself against the berm. Leaning over, he saw the gunmen running towards him, bent double and hugging the berm. He took aim at the lead one and squeezed the trigger twice for a double tap. The lead gunman stumbled and slipped. Laying flat on the ground he lifted his AK and returned fire. The other gunmen, unperturbed, scattered. Some threw themselves down to lay down fire, others dashed over the berm and onto the runway. These gunmen, Rick noted, were professional, spreading out and aiming carefully with single shots as they advanced in relays. A couple of pale faces in the group indicated they were Al Qaeda mercenaries. Scott pinned a couple down on the runway, but the rest seemed determined not to lose their plane. It was likely they were also quickly aware that they faced only two shooters. Rick was forced to hug the dirt as he faced incoming fire from both sides of the berm. His initial tactical advantage had been turned against him and he had no cover now.

Kowalski yanked at the prop again and the engine chuffed once, then twice, before falling silent. As the fire turned to the plane, he ran to the side and leaned into the cockpit. Rick thought he was taking cover, but the plane was just flimsy metal. He thought of the cans he'd just thrown into the back – not to mention the wing tanks full of fuel. The gunmen thought that maybe turning the plane into a fireball was better than losing it to the infidels and concentrated their fire on the target.

Rick couldn't see how they could miss. And Walt was in the plane.

Rick ran forward, firing on the run, trying to close the range and get the gunmen's attention. It didn't take long. Throwing himself down onto the concrete and scuffing his elbows, he endured withering return fire that zipped past his ears. From the other side of the runway, Scott mimicked him, taking the fight to the militants until he too was forced down. A crazy mid range gunfight ensued, and during that time the Cessna's engine chuffed again, caught and then roared as the engine started.

Rick chanced a glance and saw Kowalski dragging the chocks away and leaping into the cockpit, altering the engine note to a steady rumble. That should have been the signal to pull back, but Rick couldn't move. In spite of firing repeated short bursts at different targets, he couldn't suppress them and prevent them from firing back. Through the heat haze and the weeds rising off the concrete, he caught the muzzle flashes as they kept him pinned down, and occasionally one gunman would get up and run a couple of yards before throwing themselves down again. By such methods, they got closer and closer.

The Cessna engine roared again, and the plane waggled its wings as it moved forward onto the runway, then the engine pitch rose as the plane turned its tail to the gunfight and began taxiing to the far end of the runway. Rick couldn't work out what Kowalski was doing. He was tempted to get up and run after the plane, but he knew he'd be cut down in seconds.

Kowalski spun the plane round at the end of the runway, then opened up the throttle. The aged plane suddenly looked the picture of grace as it accelerated towards everyone. Before it even got close, the wheels lifted off the ground and Kowalski lifted the nose and banked the wings, veering off over the hangers and away.

Rick was stupefied. He looked across at Scott, who appeared just as surprised as him. Even the militants ceased fire for a moment. The plane climbed up into the sky with an ebbing drone.

Rick knew he was screwed. Taking one look at the militants, he leaped up and ran away, weaving to present a hard target, but a burst of gunfire clipped his calf and brought him down again, sprawling in the dust. Rolling over into a shallow drainage ditch at the edge of the concrete, he brought his rifle up. He was still in shock that Kowalski had left them.

On the other side of the runway, Scott attempted to shuffle back towards the hut, but a renewed concentration of fire chipped up the concrete around him. Rick adjusted his sights, targeted a militant head, and pounded rounds in his direction until he went down. Rick couldn't tell if he was hit or just ducking, and at that moment didn't care. His only chance was to suppress a couple more and take a chance on running again. As he swapped in a new mag he knew that if he didn't, he was finished. Dreaming up every single insult he could think of for the air force, he switched to another target.

The militants inched forward, first one man, then another. Another popped up behind the berm, trying to see where Rick was, and Rick twisted and stitched up his face with close range rounds that threw him backwards. In the distance the Cessna wheeled gracefully in the sky, then arced down towards the ground until Rick couldn't see it anymore. He didn't see an impact, but it looked like the plane had crashed.

Maybe the engine had cut out.

Rick didn't dwell on the karma. With his eye glued to his sights, he sought out targets, the recoil hammering the butt into his shoulder as he burnt through his ammo. He didn't notice at first the bird-like silhouette that floated over the town.

It was the Cessna and it appeared to be gliding down for a landing, as Rick couldn't hear the engine. The plane hovered through the heat haze, getting closer, the engine roared suddenly and the militants turned, alerted to its presence.

The plane came in low, but it was accelerating, not slowing down, and the wheels were almost touching the deck. It didn't even look like it was flying anymore, but it came on faster and faster, heading directly for the militants. The gunmen lay poised, thinking the plane would fly low over them, but as it skimmed the concrete, they realized even lying down wasn't enough. Panic stricken, they leaped up and ran out of the way. The plane roared by like it was on rails, then soared back up into the sky. Rick didn't wait to work out what was going on. As soon as the gunmen had ceased firing, he sprinted away, ignoring his burning calf. Parallel to him on the other side of the runway, Scott ran too.

The plane climbed until it was hanging from its prop, did a hammerhead stall, and fell back down, twisting round until it was pointed to the earth. Flaps down and flaring, it touched delicately down on the runway, rolling towards them. Rick pounded his feet on the concrete, running faster than he'd ever run in his life. Bullets began zipping by, but he ignored them, his eyes fixed on the approaching plane.

Kowalski didn't slow down. Rick, sprinting hard, grabbed the strut under the wing and swung himself in to grab at the door handle. As soon as he got it open, he pitched himself in, his boots dragging along the runway. In the back seat, Walt was barely conscious, and Kowalski stuck to his controls, so Rick had to drag himself in. When he saw Kowalski steer towards Scott, Rick opened the door on the other side of the cockpit and leaned out, arm outstretched. Scott, his face flush with the exertion, grabbed his hand and got dragged along as the plane picked up speed again. With his legs hooked around a seat base, Rick grabbed the front of Scott's body armor and heaved him in.

In the confines of the cockpit, the engine screamed as Kowalski mercilessly opened the throttle. The wheels hopped up off the runway and Kowalski kicked the rudder pedal to send the plane in a fast drift over the ground, heading for the militants again. The gunmen fired a few more shots, then ran for the berm, throwing themselves over as the plane roared over, inches above their heads. Shuffling the plane's tail left and right to present a harder target, Kowalski climbed until he was over the town and away.

"You goddamn asshole!" shouted Rick above the cabin noise as he strapped himself into the front passenger seat. "What the hell were you doing?"

"Keeping the plane safe," shouted back Kowalski, not taking his eyes off the sky ahead. "It's what you wanted, wasn't it?"

Rick leaned down to pull up his pants leg, checking his wound. The bullet had bored its way through the edge of his calf and out again, leaving a neat trough. There was little blood as the hot round had cauterized the wound, but Rick's hands were shaking. Leaning back in the seat, he took deep breaths, his heart beating fast from the adrenaline still coursing through his veins. The thrumming of the engine echoed in his ears, and he had to make an effort to stop the bile rising from his stomach. Clutching his water tube, he sucked on it greedily to remove the acid taste from his mouth. A chill ran through him at how close he had come to not making it, and he trembled, his muscles spasming. Laying his palms on his thighs, he continued his breathing exercises until his heart slowed down and a wave of exhaustion dulled his senses. Lulled by the vibrations he sank into a fitful sleep.

He woke when Scott shook his shoulder. The Syrian coastline lay ahead, the blue waters of the Mediterranean shimmering in the sun. Turning, he saw Walt sagging in his seat, head back, mouth open. Scott, gray faced and weary, drew a finger across his own neck. Rick sighed deeply.

"I can see the Russian airbase," called Kowalski. "A few more minutes now."

"Forget it," said Rick. "Keep going."

"What?"

"I said forget it! Walt's dead. Just get us out of this goddamn place."

Crossing the coastline, they passed over waves that broke on the beaches. Offshore, two Russian missile cruisers sat anchored in the bay. Their elaborate superstructures, festooned with aerials, were blackened by fires that had turned two sleek and majestic warships into lifeless hulks, listing and low in the water.

"Where to now?" asked Kowalski.

Rick imagined the US fleet in the Gulf had met the same fate. All that military might, all the bases and their capabilities, had gone up in smoke. Trillions of dollars spent on the greatest command and control systems in history were now worth nothing. From the highest ranking admiral to the lowest grunt, everyone was stranded. They were all on their own now.

"Take us home," he said.

27

Josh couldn't pinpoint where the smell of burning was coming from, but it was pervasive. There was no smoke anywhere, but the still, hot air was heavy and suffocating. The wind had dropped to nothing. The heat at night made sleeping difficult. It was impossible not to do so without having the windows open, but Grandma worried about security. Strangers drifted by on the street during the day, some dragging suitcases. There was talk of setting up barricades and checkpoints at both ends of the street, but there were few volunteers willing to sit for hours in the heat of the sun, away from their houses, and none willing to sit through the nights, which were pitch black. Grandma loaded up Grandpa's revolver and insisted they slept in the same room together. Josh lay awake for hours, listening to her snoring. Daily life had become surreal. The streets were so quiet that Josh could hear conversations in nearby houses, and occasionally arguments as short fused tempers flared. Kids used to play on the street while adults, who had nothing better to do, got to know their neighbors better than they ever wanted to. Polite talk got more serious as disagreements were aired, and the kids soon got bored and disappeared inside. The shortage of food meant less and less visible activity as people saved their energy and worried about supplies. As soon as night fell, however, everything stopped and it was like the world had ceased. No more lights in windows or late night TV shows. No sound from the nearby rail line or highway. If he wasn't listening to his grandma's snoring, Josh listened to those of his neighbors, carried freely out of their open windows. Or from their porches, for those who dared to sleep outside, unable to bear the oven-like interiors. Josh remembered when he and Lizzy used to camp out in the garden, but the darkness felt too sinister for that now, and his sister refused to go into the garden anymore, on account of knowing that Grandpa was buried there. Josh didn't want to admit it, but he was starting to feel the same way.

That was the beginning of the first argument in the house, when Grandma suggested the digging of a latrine pit in the garden. Unable to flush, the toilet had become unusable, but Lizzy was adamant that there was no way she was going to go anywhere else. Grandma tried to reason with her, then got snappy, and Lizzy put on a foot stamping performance that almost earned her a slap. Josh saved her ass from getting a paddling by offering to go to the creek with the bucket and bring back water to pour into the toilet. Grandma assented, though the tension between her and her granddaughter remained. It was not something Josh had ever witnessed before. Coming to Grandma's for a night or two had always been a blissful experience, and Lizzy, being the cute young one, had been treated with something approaching reverence. And then they went home.

There was no going home now, and the strain was showing on Grandma's face. She'd aged visibly and looked tired all the time.

Josh was glad to get out of the house. Carrying his bucket in the shade of the oak trees that lined the street, he hefted the nine iron he'd liberated from the garage. He didn't remember Grandpa ever playing golf, but he was grateful for his hoarding habits. If the punk kid by the creek tried to steal his water today, he'd wrap the nine iron round his neck. That was the fantasy he'd played over in his mind when he'd been unable to sleep. In fact, it was one of the thoughts that prevented him being able to sleep. The injustice and the shame burned, inflamed by the lonely darkness. He wanted payback – to not be so weak.

In broad daylight, much of that anger dissipated. He was just a kid with a golf club, not some avenging warrior. He felt conspicuous as he passed folks sitting out on their porches. Disinterested eyes tracked him as he walked by.

Among the single story houses in the neighborhood were larger, more lavish homes. Every time Josh came to visit his grandma, another small house was being demolished, the builders utilizing the lot to throw up a medium size mansion as wealthy new owners took advantage of the fact that house prices here lagged behind the more affluent districts like Dilworth. The chairman of the neighborhood association stood outside one with two other guys, pointing and talking, like he was trying to sell it to them. Josh lowered the golf club down by his leg, trying to make it less obvious. He fully expected a reprimand, even though the group all toted shotguns. It wasn't like he could pretend he was going to play a round.

Trying to look casual, he sauntered by.

"We've got to get the bodies out," said the chairman.

"Joe, I'm not sure that's a good idea."

"You got a better one? Those people deserve a burial."

Josh stopped, arrested by the subject matter, and the chairman looked at him, clearing his throat. "There's nothing for you here, kid. Just run along."

Josh looked towards the house. "I'm not a kid," he said quietly.

"Doesn't matter. This shouldn't concern you."

"No point sugar coating it, Joe," said one of the other men. "This concerns everyone. Two elderly folks just died of heat stroke in their own home. People need to be warned."

The chairman sucked his teeth. "I don't want a panic. We've got a lot of old folks here."

"All the more reason to let them know."

"These new builds are like hot boxes," said the third man. "They're not designed to manage without air conditioning."

"Yeah, but the bodies," said the chairman.

"They're cooking now."

"And it'll only get worse the longer we put it off."

"Fine. You go right on inside and pull the bodies out. I'll bury them."

The chairman frowned, hesitated, then hitched up his jeans and strode towards the house. Opening the front door, he leaned in cautiously, then wheeled back out, retching.

"I told you they were cooking," said one of the other men smugly.

Josh drifted off lest they ask him to go in next. Hauling one body to a grave had been more than enough for him.

Directing his thoughts to the creek, he hefted the nine iron again, preparing himself for a confrontation. He imagined the kid with the baseball bat waiting there for him. It was a ridiculous notion, considering the kid had his own container now, but then he remembered the gang looking on.

Maybe they'd claimed ownership of the creek.

That also seemed absurd. There was water there for everyone and it hardly seemed likely that taking another bucketful would make a difference, but Josh slowed his pace, his mind filled with images of a picket line held against him. His resolve wavered and he paused. He thought about going back and asking the chairman for an escort. He considered the possibility of digging a well in his garden instead. Eventually he turned down another street, looking for another place to access the creek.

Near the highway that bordered the northern part of the neighborhood was an old supermarket building that was up for lease. Behind it ran the creek, but Josh hesitated again when he saw people clustered around the building. Moving away into the shelter of the trees at the back of the lot, he found a quiet spot by the creek. Looking behind to make sure no one was sneaking up on him, he dipped his bucket.

"People use that creek as a toilet," said a voice.

Josh jumped up, waving his club. In front of him, on the other side of the creek, a teenage girl stood calmly in the shade of a tree, looking at him.

Seeing Josh's reaction, she giggled. "Didn't mean to scare you," she said.

Josh stared, wondering why he hadn't noticed her. Her dark clothes and dark hair blended into the shadows, and she was pretty enough to make Josh avert his gaze for a moment. "Doesn't matter," he stuttered.

"What? That I scared you, or that people shit in the creek?"

"Both," muttered Josh.

"You'd better check your bucket, just in case."

Josh glanced into the bucket. The water looked just as murky as it always did. "It's fine," he said.

"You from this neighborhood?"

Josh looked up. The girl didn't look much older than him, but she had a nose ring and a confident gaze.

"Kind of."

The girl looked wistfully through the trees at some of the houses. "Looks a nice neighborhood. I'm Skye, by the way."

"Josh," grunted Josh, feeling awkward.

"Hi, Josh."

Josh mustered a smile, feeling her eyes on him again. "Hi." She was unbearably cute and he felt like a dork as he struggled to get his words out. "You're not from round here, then?"

Skye shook her head, and Josh was mesmerized by the swish of her hair. "I'm from Cincinnati," she said. "Mom wanted to come look at some property down here and we got stuck on the highway. Came here with everybody else and someone opened up the building for us. Kind of like a refugee center now."

"Huh," said Josh dumbly.

"Some church folks brought us some food. It was nice. I like this neighborhood."

Josh coughed. Part of him wanted to get back with his bucket, but the other half didn't want to go yet. "Not my neighborhood, really. Staying with my grandma."

"Cute," said Skye, "so we're both outsiders. We have a connection."

Josh blushed. "Yeah. Kind of."

Skye laughed, and to Josh it sounded as fresh as a mountain stream.

"We should hang out," said Skye.

"Yeah," said Josh, and Skye laughed again.

As much as he wanted to stay, Josh couldn't think of anything else to say. His brain seemed to have frozen. Skye, appraising him with keen eyes, said, "I guess you need to be getting back."

"Yeah," muttered Josh. "My sister, and stuff." He gestured with his bucket.

"Okay. Maybe we can talk again."

"Sure. Uhm. When I get more water."

"Cool. It's good to talk. Gets boring here." Skye shuffled her feet, suddenly looking shy. "I'd give you my number, but, you know..."

They both laughed, and to Josh it felt as intoxicating as a physical embrace.

"I'll be back," he said, feeling more confident.

"I'd like that," said Skye.

There was a moment of awkward silence. "Gotta go," said Josh with his best attempt at a casual shrug.

"Okay."

"I'll see you."

"Sure."

Josh turned away, giving her a little wave. She waved back, eyes shining in the gloom of the shade.

He practically skipped all the way home, his heart buoyant. A drone in the air made him look up and he saw an ultralight soaring over the streets, its wings a vibrant red. He waved at it and the helmeted pilot waved back. Josh wanted to jump up and fly with him.

Mr Henderson sat out on his porch, head in his hands.

"Good morning, Mr Henderson," called Josh.

He got no reply, but he was too happy to care. Back in the house, he tossed the golf club into the umbrella stand.

"I'm home, Grandma."

Grandma was mixing flour and water into a sloppy dough. She cocked an eyebrow at him. "Someone's happy," she said.

"I got the water."

"I'm afraid all we can manage is some tortillas today and a tin of hot dogs."

"That's okay."

"You hate tortillas," said Lizzy, coming out of her room.

"Doesn't matter."

"Grandma was worried about you."

"Why?"

"I'm not sure you should go out on your own, Josh," called his grandma.

"Why not?"

"It's not safe anymore. The Henderson boy's been stabbed."

Josh's smile faded.

"We think he's going to die," said Lizzy. "He got in a fight on the highway."

Josh's insides froze. "I didn't go near the highway," he lied.

"It's better that we should stay together," said Grandma, kneading the dough.

Josh thought of Skye. "Grandma, I can take care of myself. And we need the water."

Grandma turned on him, her face stern. "You'll stay in the house, and that's the end of it."

28

Lauren had shown April how to handle the Ruger, and had made her practice dry-firing it. Glancing at her now, she wasn't sure it was enough.

They were back on the tollway, making their slow way south with the other refugees. Along the highway, individuals and small groups were strung out, some pulling mobile luggage, others pushing shopping carts. They were not alone, however. Sitting on side embankments or posted on overhead bridges were others, watching and waiting. Like vultures.

Lauren recognized them as predators looking for easy pickings, waiting to swoop. Most were young men. Suitcases broken open with their contents spread on the highway showed where they'd struck. A woman in a gray pant suit sat disheveled and sobbing at the side of the road. One of her high heeled shoes lay broken by a torn bag. "They took my laptop," she cried. "Why would they do that?"

Lauren maintained her pace as she strode past. "Walk with us," she told her.

"They took everything I had," the woman continued. "Where are the police? Why aren't they stopping this?"

"Shut up and walk with us," called Lauren back to her.

April leaned in to her. "What are you doing?" she asked. "We don't need another mouth to feed."

Lauren indicated the predators waiting on a nearby bridge. "Safety in numbers," she said.

"She ain't no good to us," said April. "Look at her. She about ready to quit."

The woman didn't get up and Lauren wasn't ready to slow down and coax her into moving. "Okay, forget it. Let's try and catch up with that group up ahead. And look alert. Make the bastards think we're not worth the trouble."

"Get my gun out and they'll know we ain't worth it."

"No, keep it hidden for now."

"I get it," said April, nodding. "The gray man look."

Lauren turned to her. "What the hell are you talking about?"

143

"Prepper logic. You don't want to draw attention to yourself, so you be like a gray man. You blend in. Except we're gray women. We don't look like we've got much, but we're not going to trigger someone's defenses by looking like a threat."

"We've got bags. That's enough to make some people want to take a look. And in case you hadn't noticed, that woman was in gray."

"The color don't matter, it's the type of clothes. With a suit and shoes like that, she's just screaming to be robbed."

"You know, you could be accused of blaming the victim, there."

"That PC shit don't matter no more. We're in a real world situation now."

Lauren couldn't argue with that, so they walked in silence for a while, looking around to let the watchers know they couldn't be snuck up on. Fatigue made Lauren's eyelids heavy, however, and it was getting harder to stay truly alert. The previous night had been uncomfortable and cold, and in between watches, Lauren found it hard to sleep. She wished she could have crawled into Daniel's stroller. He certainly looked comfortable in it, and when he wasn't sleeping, which he did a lot of, he was simply staring. Lauren was so used to children complaining, fidgeting or running around that she found it a little creepy. Cute as he was, there was something not quite right with Daniel.

"How long have you been prepping?" she asked April.

"Only a few months."

"Why?"

"I told you. Living where I lived, it seemed a pretty good idea."

"It's just strange. I mean, did you have any idea this was coming?"

"Are you kidding me? If I'd have known that, I'd be in the mountains by now. Why you asking?"

"No reason, really. I was just wondering if there were any signs I'd missed. Some kind of premonition, maybe."

"Something that would have made you stay at home?"

"Maybe. I haven't been paying attention to many things. Even when my flight was canceled, I never thought to check whether there was anything I needed to know."

"It was on the evening news."

"See? I could have checked that."

"There wasn't a lot of information. Just telling people to look out for some great northern lights."

"It's not just that," sighed Lauren. "I just feel like I've had my head up my ass for months now. Well, years actually."

"You're thinking about your kids, aren't you?"

"Yeah, it's kind of an obsession."

"Tell me about it. Before I had Daniel, I never gave a crap about anything. Afterwards, it's all I can think of. Guys get it easy."

Lauren thought about Rick, and the resentment that had been slowly building inside her. It was what propelled her into a career she didn't want. "Maybe," she said.

If she'd been open about it instead of bottling it up, she wondered if it would have made any difference. She didn't know. As a loyal army wife, that was a conversation she'd never wanted to have. Divorce rates had rocketed since 2001 in Rick's unit alone, and Lauren didn't want to add to that statistic, but with Rick being away so often, the burden and guilt of raising the kids alone had put a strain on the marriage that remained unspoken. She felt angry at the increasing distance between them, angry that he was resisting retirement, and angry that she hadn't made her case more forcefully for him to quit.

She also felt guilty at the times she wished he could sustain an injury that would bring him home – a dreadful secret she hated to admit even to herself.

It was such a mess, and now she was here, he was there, and everyone was nowhere. One premonition, one spoken word, and everything might be different now.

Or it might not, and she was wasting her time with stupid fantasies. She knew the risks when she married Rick – knew that he'd be deployed overseas countless times as the War On Terror intensified. All the military wives knew it, and she couldn't kid herself that she didn't. As a reservist, she knew she could have been called up for deployment herself, but still she chose to raise a family. April was right – this was no time to play the victim.

All roads lead to Rome, it was said. In this case, they led to Washington DC. Lauren was alerted to the fact when she heard the distant drone of engines, and saw light aircraft in a holding pattern. The I95 had reached the Beltway, and the highway was being used as a landing strip. One by one, the light aircraft landed. A few boxes of supplies were unloaded and the planes took off again, heading back over the capital and towards the navy yards by the Potomac River. Soldiers posted along the tollway waved the refugees on, directing them to the exit ramps.

Lauren, suspicious about where they were being directed to, climbed the wooded embankment at the side of the tollway. From there she looked out upon a patchwork of fields hemmed in by the suburbs and gasped.

It was like an aerial view of a rock festival, only without the bands. Refugees teemed in the fields, with more lined up to join them. A few tents had been set up, but most people were out in the open. FEMA flags flapped in the breeze. Soldiers strung fences up and dug latrines. Officials in high visibility vests carried boxes down from the planes, escorted by armed police.

"Holy crap," said April after struggling to get the stroller up the bank.

"Yeah," agreed Lauren. After all the chaos on the road, it was pleasing to at last see some sign of organization. "I think you'll be okay here."

"Say what?"

"You wanted a safe place. And let's be honest, you were never going to make it to the mountains."

April looked at her in disbelief. "You're saying you want to split, now?"

"That's not what I'm saying."

"Then what are you saying?"

Lauren turned to her, surprised by the sudden hostility. "You said you had nowhere to go. They're distributing food down there, and... well, they'll be setting up shelters soon, I'm sure."

April took a good look out at the fields. "It's a concentration camp," she said.

Lauren, taken aback, replied, "I know there's a lot of conspiracy theories about FEMA, but you don't seriously believe them, do you?"

It was April's turn to be surprised. "No. Take a good look. You see how many people there are down there? Look at the lines. They're backing up right through the suburbs, and you know there's plenty more behind us still coming from Baltimore. You think a few little planes can keep all them people fed? How many of them are ill? What about medical supplies? Water treatment? Cholera, dysentery and all the other stuff they can get? That there is a humanitarian disaster waiting to happen."

"I know it looks bad, but..."

"Bad? It's a total mess. What the hell makes you think I'm going to take my boy down there? It's no better than what I just left."

"It's your boy I'm thinking of. The journey south's going to be hard. I can't give a guarantee that we'll be better off than those people down there."

"I don't need no guarantee," said April haughtily. "Let me ask you one question. Would you take your two children down into that camp, knowing it could be the last place you end up?"

Lauren hesitated. "I don't know."

"Take a good hard look, Lauren. They're searching people at the gate, making them hand over their weapons. They're looking through their bags and taking their food. Oh sure, they're going to tell you it's for fair distribution, and that you're going to be looked after. That's what they told them folks at the Superdome during Hurricane Katrina, and look what happened. Rapes and murders, that's what happened. You going to feel safe as a lone woman sleeping there at night with no lights? You think your kids are going to feel safe?"

"Okay," exclaimed Lauren. "I get the point, and I don't have any answers, all right? I'm tired, and I was just thinking it could be a good place for you. It was just the first thing that entered my head."

April gave her a hard look. "You were thinking you'd be better off without me, that I wouldn't be a burden for you."

"That's not what I was thinking!"

"Sure you were."

Lauren clamped her jaw. She was confused by her thoughts, dismayed by the picture April was painting and angry at being accused. The dramatic change in the tone of their relationship was a shock to her, and she hadn't seen it coming.

Like so many things.

"You go where you want now," said April. "Me and my boy are heading west. Good luck."

"Wait," said Lauren.

"Ain't waiting for nothing. I see how things are, now."

"Goddammit, you're reading me wrong."

"I don't think so."

"April, listen to me! I made a mistake, okay? Cut me a break here. Are you going to go off on your own because of some stupid argument?"

April paused, studying Lauren as if wondering whether to give her the benefit of the doubt.

"You're tired," continued Lauren, "and we're both stressed. If we're going to survive, then we're going to have to be able to disagree on stuff without hitting the nuclear option every time."

April softened. "There's people down there looking at us," she said with a sideways glance.

Lauren didn't bother checking if it was true. "Good. Gives them something to occupy their time."

"So what do we do now?"

"I don't know, let's just get the hell out of here."

29

They buried Corporal Walter E. Stimson at sea. There were no flags available to honor a fallen comrade, nor a casket and bugler. Only the respect and care of fellow comrades-in-arms. Scott tucked Walt's stiffening arms into the armored vest. Rick tied Walt's boot laces together. As Kowalski held the plane low over the sea, its shimmering shadow surfing across the waves, Rick and Scott opened the cabin door and held it against the slipstream as they slid Walt's body out. As soon as the weight was gone, Kowalski pulled the plane into a gentle climb while the door was secured.

Rick sat back in his seat, staring down at the collection of dog tags in his hand – Walt's, Flynn's, Leroy's and Jamie's. Four soldiers lying scattered across foreign climes, never to return home. Rick held the tags tight in his fist, determined to get these at least back to US soil.

Kowalski leveled out at five thousand feet in a cloudless sky, the compass swiveling as he altered course. The land mass of Cyprus lay under the left wing, but he continued onward. The air speed indicator, altimeter and attitude indicators worked fine, the needles quivering in the engine's vibration, but the gas and oil gauges were dead. It was imperative they get over land again. Kowalski flew for an hour before the Turkish mountains appeared on the horizon. By then, Rick was asleep, the vibrations combined with his own weariness putting him out like a light.

He woke as Kowalski drifted the Cessna down over a highway that ran through some hills. The highway looked modern and pristine, with only two vehicles sitting on it. Side-slipping to avoid transmission wires on one side of the road, Kowalski appeared determined to land on the cars. Throttling back, he skimmed over their roofs and landed perfectly on the smooth concrete, braking to a swift halt. Switching the engine off, he turned to Rick. "This is where we refuel," he said.

Rick turned to see Scott was also asleep.

"How long have we been flying?" asked Rick.

"About seven hours," said Kowalski, massaging his eyes. "We've passed over most of west Turkey and crossed the Dardanelles. We're near the Greek border now, I think. Might even have passed it, I don't know."

"You want to make sure one of us is awake next time," said Rick. "Last thing we need is for you to fall asleep too. This vibration is brain numbing."

Climbing out of the plane, Rick looked around. Apart from the ticking of the hot engine, everything was silent. Scrub trees covered the hillside, giving way to dusty fields as the road descended into a wide valley. On the far side of the valley, on the hill slopes, white houses were dotted. Rick leaned into the plane and slapped Scott's leg. "Wake up. We've got gas to siphon."

One of the cars was damaged by fire, and they didn't get much out of its tank. The other was a beautiful looking Mercedes with automatic transmission and a full tank. Walking back and forth between the car and the plane, they filled up the plane's wing tanks in relays. Didn't take long before there was no more to pour in, and they still weren't full.

"That was what I was afraid of," said Kowalski. "Without a fuel gauge, I can only estimate the range from full tanks. We're going to have to stay low over the roads and keep looking for opportunities to fill the cans."

"Where are we going, exactly?" said Scott. "We can fly across Europe, but this thing won't make it across the Atlantic. Shouldn't we be looking for a boat? Or a bigger plane?"

"Won't get us across the Atlantic," said Kowalski, "but it will get us across the Arctic."

"What?" said Rick.

"It's the northern ferry route for light aircraft. Up through northern Europe, across to Iceland, Greenland, then over to Canada."

"You sure? Sounds... complicated."

"My cousin did it. Bought a plane in Stuttgart, Germany, and flew it back to the States. Lots of pilots do it."

"But you haven't?"

"Always a first time for everything."

"I'm liking the idea of a boat better," said Scott.

"Can you sail?" asked Kowalski.

"I don't fucking care. This piece of crap ain't going to make it to Greenland."

Rick looked the plane over. "He does have a point. It's looking kind of beat up."

"The engine works and it's got wings," said Kowalski. "That's all I need. Do you want to go home or not?"

Rick and Scott exchanged a glance.

"I want to go home," explained Scott, "and I don't want to die in some shit-ass plane."

Rick had his doubts, but this was neither the time nor the place. "Get us as far as you can," he said to Kowalski.

Scott rolled his eyes. "We're going to end up on an ice floe. If we do, I swear I'm going to feed you to the polar bears myself."

Kowalski looked at them both in their T-shirts. "Yeah, we're going to have to get you guys some warmer clothing."

Josh went shopping with Grandma and Lizzy. It wasn't a normal shopping excursion. Crossing the bridge over the highway, they entered the commercial district around Central Avenue and found migrating refugees and scavengers instead of shoppers. Driven by a desperation to keep things normal, Grandma led the children by the hand to her favorite store, the Home Market.

It had been gutted. A sign pasted to the wall apologized to its customers, saying there was no stock left. That hadn't stopped people smashing the entrance in and ransacking the empty shelves. The dollar store next door suffered the same fate. Pulling the children along, Grandma limped awkwardly but resolutely down the avenue, past boarded up restaurants and shattered glass.

Josh resented being made to hold Grandma's hand. She hadn't permitted him to bring his nine iron for fear of being stopped by the police, but there wasn't a cop in sight. He could have carried a rocket launcher and no one would have given a damn. Refugees, pulling or pushing anything with wheels, headed east, away from the blackened towers of the uptown financial center standing like bleak monoliths against a persistently blue sky. Beyond the towers, a distant plume of white smoke rose high, spreading and dispersing to form the only cloud in the heavens.

"Lady, what are you doing?" said a baggage laden passerby as Grandma pushed against the tide on the sidewalk. "The nuclear power station's blown. You're going the wrong way."

Grandma ignored him, heading down a side street to another pillaged store. In the parking lot, two men and a woman fought over a plastic bottle of soda until it dropped to the floor and cracked open, the contents hissing out onto the concrete. The woman immediately dropped down to lick at the puddle, joined by one of the men. The other man snatched up the remnants of the bottle and ran.

Switching direction, Grandma tried the 7-Eleven, but to no avail. Every store was empty.

Opposite the 7-Eleven was the Army Reserve center, with a small parking lot of Humvees. Upgraded to turbo electronic ignition, they were as useless as every other modern vehicle. Whatever staff manned the center had gone – if they'd even been able to turn up for work. Every semblance of authority had vanished, and the displaced citizens of Charlotte streamed by, keen to distance themselves from the small but ominous radioactive cloud behind them.

Visibly agitated and struggling with her arthritis, Grandma returned home to witness the signs of folk on her street packing their belongings and preparing for an exodus. Elena Seinfeld was waiting for her.

"Where have you been? You missed a street meeting. People are getting out. The chairman says the army have opened a camp on the east side of the Rocky River and we should all try to get there. They've organized food distribution and medical facilities."

Grandma entered the kitchen and sat down heavily at the bare dining table.

"Did you hear me, Daisy? We have to go. Come with us."

Grandma rubbed her head and stared at the strands of white hair she'd pulled out.

Elena leaned over the table. "Please, Daisy. They say things are going to get worse. You can't keep the children here."

"I'm waiting for my daughter," said Grandma in a hollow voice.

"Leave a note for her. Tell her where we're going. Please."

"This is my home. Harold's here."

Elena took a deep breath and put her hand on Grandma's arm. "I understand how you feel, but Harold's gone and he wouldn't want you to just give up like this. It's not safe here. Not anymore."

"Get your hands off me," snapped Grandma.

"Daisy..."

"This is my home! If you want to quit and run, go. And take your worthless husband with you."

Elena straightened up, mortified. Struggling to breathe for a moment, she opened her mouth, closed it again, and then, with a final indignant flourish, turned on her heel and left.

Grandma shut her eyes, her face graying over. Putting her head in her hands, she started to sob.

Josh and Lizzy watched the tragic transformation of the doting, angelic figure in their lives. Maker of cookies. Dispenser of gifts. Fussing carer. Now all too human and helpless. Lizzy crept forward to touch her fingers, stroking the back of her hand, and Grandma pulled her into an embrace.

Josh felt awkward. "I'll go and fetch water," he said.

He got no reply. Hesitating for a moment, he turned, grabbed the nine iron and bucket, and ran out of the front door.

The trees on the sidewalks flashed by, his passage a grim vortex of images as serious, defeated faces looked at him. His heart heavy with guilt, his mind thought of only one thing: seeing Skye again. Fearful that she was leaving too, he pushed himself, recalling his nightmare run to the hospital. Pieces of his world were breaking away and he was frightened he was going to be left with nothing. Racing to the creek, he skidded to a halt among the trees, looking around. A solitary, dark figure sat crouched on the other side of the creek, and a pale face looked up, shining a shaft of light into his darkness.

"Hi," he said breathlessly.

Skye blinked, as if rising from a deep sleep. Focusing her eyes, she gave Josh a quizzical look. "Hi," she said.

Josh's heart sank, thinking she didn't recognize him. Euphoria and longing ground inside him like a millstone. "I, uh, came for more water," he said. "Remember me?"

Skye gazed at him for a while, her face impassive. "Sure."

Chest heaving, Josh gazed back. "I thought you might be gone," he murmured. "With the others."

Skye sniffed and wiped her nose. "No. My mom's sick."

Josh sucked his lips in. "I'm sorry," he said.

"That's okay," said Skye absently. She cocked her head, as if seeing Josh properly for the first time. "Did you run all the way to see me?"

Josh struggled with his reaction, moving from a frown to a half smile. "No. Yeah. Kind of. To see how you were. Obviously."

Skye smiled wanly in return, and Josh felt his heart soar.

"Because," he added, "you know, I'm not leaving either. Because... just not."

"You're sweet," said Skye.

Josh blushed. "You too. I mean, as a person. And it's good. I... I like that."

Skye's smile faded, but her eyes continued to shine. "I like it too," she said quietly.

"So. Are you okay?"

Skye's gaze drifted towards the makeshift refugee building. "There's a few jerks around."

Josh's face fell, and he looked towards the building too. "Really?"

"It's not a big deal," said Skye. "Just worried about my mom." Picking up a stick, she poked the ground with it. "They say the radiation's coming."

"Uh, yeah."

"That worry you?"

Josh hadn't really thought about it. "I don't know."

Skye snapped the stick. "Not like we can do anything about it, right? It just happens."

"I guess."

"Can't change anything, really."

"Guess not."

"I'm sorry. I'm not really good company today."

"No, it's okay," said Josh hastily. He wanted to wade across the creek and touch her. Take her in his arms. He pictured himself doing so, but he remained rooted to the spot.

"You'd better go," she said. "Your sister and all."

"Hmm," muttered Josh, his mouth suddenly dry.

"Don't forget your water," she said.

And she turned away.

Josh walked disconsolately back through the streets, torn up inside. He didn't know why she wanted him to go. Didn't understand what was wrong.

He wanted to run back and tell her he'd fallen in love with her. That he couldn't think of anything else.

Instead, he trudged back to the house, feeling emptier than ever, the pieces still falling.

30

Lauren stopped to consult her map, a road atlas she'd liberated from an abandoned garage. The garage shop had been cleared out of anything edible, but key chains and maps were still in plentiful supply. They'd spent the rest of the day bypassing the DC metropolitan area and darkness was falling, but Lauren wanted to get across the Potomac before they stopped for the night. The nearest crossing was the Chain Bridge, and coming down off the wooded heights, through affluent, winding suburbs, everything seemed quiet. The houses were dark and it was hard to tell which were occupied and which were not. Lauren was tempted to explore a couple, but the last thing she needed was to encounter a scared homeowner with a firearm and a nervous trigger finger. Between her and April, they still had ample food supplies anyway, especially since they were rationing it. It meant they were always hungry, and that made the miles more tiring. It also made tempers a little tetchy, so they'd entered an unspoken agreement to simply avoid talking unless it was absolutely necessary. This was one of those moments.

"Bottom of the hill we turn right. We'll soon be at the bridge," murmured Lauren.

April just nodded.

Lauren led the way, sticking close to the trees at the side of the road. In the gloom she could see the river, the large island that ran the length of it, and the black ribbon of the Chesapeake and Ohio canal that ran parallel to it. The hum of crickets filled the air.

Several vehicles lay abandoned on the approach to the bridge, their doors and gas fill caps open. Weary and looking forward to finishing for the night, Lauren didn't catch the significance of that. There was a strange smell in the air that also failed to ring any alarm bells.

A low whistle snapped her out of her complacency, and she stopped immediately, scanning the wooded embankment on the other side of the road. That's where she thought the sound came from, but she couldn't see anything in the twilight under the trees. A hundred yards away lay the parapet of the bridge. A shadow unfolded itself, becoming the silhouette of a man.

A man who'd been waiting.

"It's okay. It's safe," he called.

The hairs on Lauren's skin prickled. She realized what the smell was.

It was the sweet odor of rotting bodies.

"Turn around," she whispered harshly to April.

"Why?"

"It's a trap."

"It's okay ladies," called the man. "We'll look after you."

"Run," hissed Lauren.

As soon as they bolted down the road, the undergrowth on the embankment exploded as someone, the whistler, dashed through the trees to keep pace with them. Lauren pulled the Beretta out, catching the fleeting glimpses of a running shadow. Halting and dropping her suitcase, she brought up the pistol in both hands and fired three shots in quick succession, tracking the shadow, the blasts echoing loudly in the night. There was a thump as something fell. Grabbing the suitcase handle, she raced after April, her heart pumping hard.

They ran for what seemed like miles. When they came to a halt, exhausted, they looked behind. The crickets chirped and nothing else moved on the road.

"What the hell happened?" gasped April.

"I don't know," said Lauren. "I thought..."

But she was no longer sure what she thought. There had been no pursuit, and the only person shooting had been her. She started to wonder whether she'd been imagining things. The weariness, the hunger and the darkness had triggered her paranoia. The strange smell was still in the air, and she realized it was probably rotting wood in the canal. Or the dry weather lowering the water level and exposing something.

But the man and his strange comments. That was odd. She was certain she hadn't hallucinated him, but then she wondered if she had.

And the movement in the trees could have been an animal.

She realized she needed to rest. Wandering the twilight half asleep wasn't a good idea.

"What do we do now?" said April, spooked.

Lauren didn't want to approach the bridge again. "I don't know. Let's keep going until I think of something."

The next bridge was in the metropolitan area, and Lauren didn't want to venture there. She didn't want to be trapped on this side of the river, either. She wondered whether she was desperate enough to swim. It might at least wake her up. Dwelling on the fate of April and Daniel quashed that idea.

Unexpectedly, they came upon another bridge – a small one next to a gravel parking lot that crossed the canal. Lauren strained her eyes to read the sign in the parking lot: Fletcher's Cove National History Park. More importantly, she saw the words, 'Boat House'. Leading the way across the bridge and into the trees, she found wooden picnic benches, a locked building and a wooden dock that led out to the cove and the Potomac. The river didn't look that wide at this point, but the opposite bank reared up in a steep, wooded slope, at the top of which was a road. Taking out her lug wrench, she attacked the padlock on the boat house, straining until she popped the screws out of the wood. Within the dark interior were row boats and canoes.

"Fold down the stroller," she said to April.

Grabbing at the gunwale of a row boat, she attempted to drag it out. "Jesus, this is heavy," she gasped, only managing to bring it forward a few inches. April ran back to give her a hand. Between them they managed to lift it and shuffle it in stages towards the dock.

Daniel wandered around the folded stroller as the crickets chirruped and the women grunted and strained. "Mommy?" he said, sounding frightened.

"Not now, baby," panted April.

"Mommy," repeated the child plaintively.

Lauren decided she preferred it when the child was silent. Sweating profusely, she staggered into the water by the dock and dropped the boat. Catching her breath, she listened intently for any sign that someone had heard them.

"Load up the boat," she whispered, hurrying back to the boat house. She paused, staring into the trees, again listening hard. Her paranoia was tripping and she expected someone, or something, to step out. Seconds passed, but nothing happened. Trying to get a grip of herself, she grabbed a pair of oars and dashed back.

She wasn't that familiar with boats, and it turned out April wasn't either. Rocking unsteadily on the water, she lifted the oars onto the row locks. In the confined space, April held onto Daniel, with the stroller, bags and cans piled in the prow. Lauren pushed away from the dock, her heart skipping a beat as the boat lurched dangerously over to one side. Steadying herself with the oars, she dipped the blades into the water and pulled, drawing away from the shore.

As soon as they left the cove, a light current caught them, turning the prow, but Lauren glanced back at the opposite shore, confident they could reach it in a couple of minutes. The knuckling of the row locks was alarmingly loud, and the oars slapped on the water as she struggled with the angle of the blades. Adjusting her grip, she dipped the blades more gently and dragged the oars slower.

The crack of a gunshot was followed by an angry zip, and something plopped in the water near the boat, sending up a splash.

Lauren was stunned for a moment. She didn't see where the shot came from, and couldn't see anyone near the dock they'd just left. In the distance she could see the straight, hard line of Chain Bridge in the growing darkness, but it was almost a mile away, and she didn't think anyone would be able to see them from there.

There was another crack, and something zipped by, close to her head. Yanking at the oars, she heaved with all her strength. The third shot thwacked into the side of the boat, splintering the wood and causing April to yelp.

Lauren rowed like a crazy woman, the oars flailing the water. The narrow river now seemed as wide as a lake, and her back muscles protested as she worked to propel the craft, dreading the fourth shot.

Whoever was shooting had used the first two shots to gauge the range, bracketing the target. The third one was spot on. The fourth would be the killer.

It never came. The boat crunched up against a gravel shore and Lauren leaped out, grabbing April's hand.

"Come on," she urged.

Together they ran to the shelter of a rocky outcrop among the trees.

"Stay here," whispered Lauren hoarsely. "And stay down." Grabbing her pistol, she scrambled up the slope.

The shooter wasn't on the bridge. Nor on the north shore by the dock. The angle of impact on the boat confirmed that. The shooter was on the south bank – the same place they were – and shooting from a high position.

Slipping and sliding in the darkness, Lauren punished her legs and lungs in her anxiety to get to the top. Dizzy from her exertions, she reached a low brick wall.

It was the parapet of the George Washington Memorial Parkway, a scenic road with rest stops for the majestic view over the river. Lauren suspected the shooter was at one of the rest stops, and that the reason the fourth shot never came was because he had a limited view up the river. Lauren expected him to be coming down the road now, trying to estimate where they'd landed. Wiping away the sweat that dripped into her eyes, Lauren steadied the pistol on the parapet, waiting to take him out. All thoughts about whether she'd been hallucinating were banished. Someone had indeed been waiting at the bridge for them, and someone was now willing to shoot them. If it wasn't the same someone, it meant there were more of them out there.

It didn't really matter who or why.

Lauren waited, her breathing steadying, her eyes adjusting to the gloom. In the distance, an engine revved and died, and she thought she caught the sound of a vehicle driving away, but nothing else happened. She lingered there until the heavy hum of crickets mocked her for wasting her time.

Giving up, she engaged the pistol's safety and made her slow way back down the slope.

"Jeez, what took you so long?" asked April when she got to the bottom.

"Had a theory that didn't play out," said Lauren, sitting on a rock and kneading the small of her back.

"Did you see who it was?"

"No."

"This is just crazy shit."

Lauren didn't disagree. While she'd been gone, April had set up the stroller, and Daniel was asleep in it, gently sighing. "Is there anything that kid doesn't sleep through?" she said. "Man, I'm so tired I could drop down right here."

April looked around at the rocks and water lapping nearby. "Somewhere a little more comfortable might be good."

"I was joking. We need to get out of here. They might return to search this location."

"What the hell did they want with us?"

Lauren moved her hands to massage her neck. "Well they sure as hell weren't interested in drugs. Might have been looking to rob us."

"I think they wanted to do a lot more than that."

"Maybe. But in the end they just wanted to waste bullets for... nothing. I don't know what they wanted and I don't really care. We need to get ourselves – and that stroller – up this slope."

"I got the bags ready. They gotten wet, though. That last bullet went right through the bottom and started flooding the boat. Any more time on the water and we'd have sunk."

Lauren looked up. "I forgot to ask. Were you hurt? I heard you call out."

"Nah, I was fine. I thought you were hit until I saw you haul your ass up the hill."

"Ah. Well, gotta do it again now, but I think there's a park on the other side of the highway."

"You sure you don't want to wait out the night down here? We'll be able to hear anything that comes."

Lauren stood up and stretched her back. "No. One more effort, then we'll rest. We can do this."

31

Rick crouched next to the chocked front wheel of the Cessna, listening to the crickets in the darkness. He'd enjoyed the warmth emanating from the engine earlier in the night, but now he was cold. They were somewhere in the Balkans. Kowalski thought they might be in Slovenia, but he'd been dog tired when they landed on the road in the hills, and the landing had been bumpier than his normal efforts. He was sleeping in the trees at the side of the road, and his snoring was loud. Rick let him sleep, splitting the watches between himself and Scott.

Security was a worry. Landing near abandoned cars, siphoning fuel and taking off again wasn't a problem. Staying on the ground overnight, however, was. The sound of a plane coming in to land had the potential to draw attention from miles around. People were hungry and desperate, and the arrival of an aircraft, after days of seeing nothing else in the skies, promised salvation. It didn't matter that a light plane couldn't carry much. Didn't matter if Rick and Scott insisted that they weren't in a position to help anyone. And it didn't help that they couldn't speak the local language. The Cessna represented the return of civilization, and the chance of escape. They'd chosen an isolated spot in the hills, looking only for an abandoned vehicle, but an hour after they landed, people turned up, either from houses hidden in the vast forests, or simply because they were refugees already on the road. When a small group of men turned up with an old woman in tow, Rick and Scott had been forced to turn them away, attempting to communicate with them at first, and finally aiming their weapons at them until they got the message. It was harsh, and Rick felt sorry for them, but they only had enough food for themselves, and not much of that. They certainly weren't in a position to ferry someone to a hospital, which is what he thought the men wanted him to do, pointing frequently at the old woman. They left, grumbling among themselves and casting hateful glances back at the foreigners with their plane. Rick worried they might come back in greater numbers. Smashing the windshield of the nearby car, Rick scattered the glass along the road, twenty yards in front of, and behind, the plane. In the darkness, if someone tried to sneak up on them, through the woods or along the road, he'd hear them crunch either the undergrowth or the glass. So far, the night had been quiet.

For the first time, Rick gave some thought to his own house. He'd been concentrating so hard on staying alive that he hadn't seriously contemplated actually walking into his own home. It was a distant fantasy. Now that he had the means to actually get there, he began to wonder.

If things were as bad as he thought they might be, his house probably stood empty. Looters might even have cleared it out. His extensive DVD collection would be scattered across the floor. Sofas would be slashed in the hunt for hidden valuables, closets searched. Lauren's jewelry would be gone. The watch his father had left him that he'd worn at the wedding would be taken. The kid's toys... well, nobody would bother with those. Lauren had kept Josh's collection of toy soldiers in a box in the garage, but that was more for her nostalgia than his. The boy had lost interest in military stuff. Rick hadn't kept any military mementos himself. He hadn't retained his Ranger cap badge or anything like that. Had never tried to bring back knives, spent bullets or disassembled AK47s from Iraq, like some of the guys did. He wasn't interested. Going out on deployment was just another day in the office, and hoarding those things was the equivalent of holding onto paper clips and staples. Rick saw that kind of stuff every day and didn't really need it hanging around at home. Out in the field, it was junk. Didn't make sense to try and bring it home.

The house held no attraction for him, really. He led a nomadic existence, and material things ceased to have much value. He'd bought the house the year before they got married, more because it was the done thing than because he wanted it. He let Lauren do most of the choosing. As long as she was there, he didn't really care. They had sex in every single room after moving in, like dogs marking their territory. The place ceased to have any significance for him after that. They could have moved out a year later and it wouldn't have bothered him. One house was the same as the next.

Waking up with Lauren next to him in bed, with the sound of the kids running around outside, that was something else. That was worth saving.

Or so he'd thought.

The truth was, things had changed. Last few years, he'd wake up and Lauren would have set out early for her new job, and Josh wouldn't be running around anymore. He'd be on his console, and Lizzy would be doing her own thing. The house would be silent and he would look up at the blue ceiling and wonder when it stopped being white. He'd open the closet to access his meager collection of shirts and trip over boxes of files.

He'd see the extensive array of makeup and beauty products in the bathroom and wonder if Lauren was seeing someone else.

The house managed pretty well without him, and as time went on, so did his family. Walking back into Fort Bragg, he'd hit the gym, check the rotas and wonder when his team was going to go back out again. He didn't want to find out if Lauren was being unfaithful. Didn't want to investigate why his son barely spoke to him. Afraid to open Pandora's box, he'd kept the lid shut, knowing he wouldn't know how to handle it.

Got a dozen useless citations for courage in combat, but was too afraid to peer through the looking glass at home, in case he saw what he'd become. Like an aging vampire, he couldn't see his reflection in his family any more. Invisible to them, he'd all but vanished.

Rick shifted his position by the wheel, scanning the surroundings with his peripheral vision, checking that all shadows and silhouettes remained in their place. Kowalski's snoring dropped to a heavy sigh, and he twitched in the undergrowth. Rick wondered what he was dreaming about. Did he think of home? Did he think of anything? He'd mentioned having a girlfriend back in Florida. How much did she mean to him?

If actions spoke louder than words, Rick couldn't claim that his own family meant much to him. They were in danger now, but he hadn't prepared them. The children could be alone right now, but he had no idea of their capabilities, of whether they were strong enough to bear the brunt of what may come. He was in the wrong place at the wrong time, and relying on Lauren. Leroy had been right, she was a determined woman, but if she was unable to make it back from New York, Rick knew it was partly his fault. He knew he'd driven her to take the job and all it entailed. Knew that, without him, she needed a successful career to provide security for the children. He hadn't liked her choice but had been unable to criticize it.

He wasn't in any position to say anything. Not without being a douchebag.

As the sky brightened in the east, Rick jumped up from his position and strode over to kick Kowalski awake.

Kowalski stirred, rolled over, then reacted angrily when the kicking continued. "What the hell man? It's still dark."

"It's nearly dawn," said Rick. "You can take off soon."

"What's the rush?" said Kowalski, yawning. "I flew for sixteen hours yesterday. Do you know how tiring that is? It's not safe to do that much flying. I need to be able to concentrate. I'm not a machine."

Rick kicked him again. "Quit your bitching. We move in ten."

"Ten minutes? Are you kidding me?"

"No. Now move your ass."

Getting home now was more imperative than ever, and he didn't want to waste a minute.

Lauren was trapped in suburban hell. The map said Fairfax County, but it felt like a continuous extension of Washington DC. Whichever way they turned, they encountered leafy avenues and abandoned cars. One car had been rolled across the head of a street, with 'Stay Out' crudely painted across it. Lauren and April detoured, seeing faces in windows giving them uncompromising looks. Reaching a bridge that crossed the I66, they saw the lanes crowded with refugees, all headed towards Arlington and DC.

On the bridge, a barricade had been set up, manned by armed men: ordinary folks with shotguns and hunting rifles. One of them shouted out, "Turn around. Go back the way you came."

Lauren and April turned around, looking for another way to cross the highway. Finding a road that went underneath it, they passed families sheltering under its concrete roof, cooking on propane stoves. Lauren glanced at them, seeing the blank stares of the children, the unrolled sleeping bags. A bulked out Latino guy in a vest said, "Keep moving," thinking Lauren was looking at the cook pot. Lauren said nothing and kept walking.

Two guys attempted to free a bicycle from a coin operated bike station, trying to force the lock. The other bikes had already been released. Lauren and April crossed the street to avoid them. Ahead, a line of refugees trudged towards the exit ramp of the I66, looking to join the exodus. Again, without needing to consult each other, Lauren and April turned aside down another street to stay clear of them.

Permanently weary, Lauren thought they were never going to get out of the urban areas. Cracks of gunfire echoed in the distance. Following the signs to downtown Falls Church, she stopped dead when she saw a body hanging by its neck from a street light. April turned the stroller around so that Daniel could not see it.

"Sweet Jesus, what is happening around here?" she uttered.

Lauren didn't know, but she took it as a warning. They detoured again.

Walking down a once pretty street with gabled houses and picket fences, she saw what appeared to be a barrier of garbage up ahead, cutting across the road. The houses grew increasingly blackened the further they progressed until they came across the charred stumps of homes that had burned to the ground. There was nobody around, and the garbage seemed surprisingly colorful. It wasn't until she drew closer that she saw it wasn't just a pile of trash.

Curved white panels lay around, like giant pieces of egg shell. A serving trolley lay upside down. Bags and suitcases torn open. Airline seats were scattered across gardens and lawns. The tail fin of an airliner leaned over against a smashed tree. Deep furrows had been dragged across the ground. According to Lauren's map, they were a few miles from Dulles airport. This was one plane that hadn't made it.

The seats were still occupied, clouds of flies hovering around them. Crows picked at the remains. April turned the stroller around again.

Josh walked slowly down the street, dragging his nine iron disconsolately along the sidewalk. The houses were eerily silent. Drapes were drawn, like the occupants were just away for a vacation, but Josh wondered how many of these houses were actually tombs. A couple had notices pinned to the door. He suspected they'd been put there by the chairman, warning people of what might lie inside. The chairman was gone now, and his status had likely gone with him. He would be just another refugee on the road, though Josh could imagine him still trying to keep people together as a group, fussing over them, urging everyone to help each other. Josh hadn't wanted to go and was glad Grandma had stood her ground, but he started to wonder now whether that had been wise. Bereft of support, it suddenly felt lonely in the house, even though Josh had never given a second thought to anyone outside it before. They weren't eating much anymore, and his stomach was growling. The futile shopping trip yesterday laid bare the reality that there would be no more food coming from anywhere.

He still didn't want to leave, and it wasn't because he was thinking of his mom coming back. He was thinking more of Skye, though *thinking* wouldn't be the right word to describe the powerful sensations that drew him back to the creek. He was aware that morning that he should have felt more frightened, more worried, about the current situation. He could see it in Lizzy's eyes, and in the lines of Grandma's face, but instead he felt what could only be described as an all consuming addiction. Skye was all he could think about. The thought of her made him feel all mushy inside. Any idea that she might have lost interest in him was like being stabbed in the stomach with a hot fork. Feeling such sharp edges from his emotions disturbed him.

It also invigorated him. Walking quickly, then running, he arrived at the creek in a torment of anticipation. Failing to see her, he walked along the bank, peering anxiously through the foliage. When at last he saw her, his heart took a leap.

Skye leaned at the back of a tree, hugging herself tight. At the sound of his voice, she turned. The plaintive look she gave him twisted his tormented emotions further.

"Skye, what happened?"

Her face was heavily bruised. She bore livid scratches on her neck, and her clothes were torn. She hid herself behind the tree.

Josh entered the creek and was stopped dead by her cry: "Don't come any closer!"

"Skye..."

"Leave me alone! Just get your water and go."

"But..."

"Please! Just go."

Confused, Josh took another step forward.

"I don't want to see you anymore, okay?" she shouted. "Get out of here."

Breaking cover, she dashed away through the trees. Pinned by her words, his feet in the water, Josh watched her go. He wanted to chase her, but her rejection burned like a slap. He couldn't work out what just happened. Tears pricked his eyes. He wanted to call out to her, but the words died on his lips.

Unable to bear it any longer, he turned away, forgetting to get his water. Stumbling, he looked at his empty bucket, returned to the creek and then stared at the trees for a good while, waiting for her to materialize, to apologize, to be happy to see him again.

None of these things happened and he returned home, his bucket heavy with water and his heart heavier still. In a state of shock, he dropped the bucket by the bathroom, dragged his feet to the bedroom and fell onto the bed.

Grandma emerged from the garden with a plate of barbecued tortillas. "Dinner's ready," she said curtly.

Lizzy came into the bedroom. "Josh?" she said.

Josh didn't move. Face down, his tears seeped into the quilt.

Lizzy came closer. "Josh," she whispered. "I'm worried. I haven't seen Grandma eat. She's making us food but she's not eating."

Josh didn't move.

"Josh, please. This is serious. If she doesn't eat, she's going to die."

32

The little Cessna flew over the Austrian Alps. Barely able to get over the snow dusted peaks, Kowalski was forced to detour round the bigger mountains, flying through lush alpine valleys and over picturesque lakes. The sky was no longer clear and blue, and as the cloud base lowered, the plane was forced lower still, unable to take the risk of flying in the clouds lest they smack into the side of one of those beautiful slopes. Hugging the ground and leapfrogging transmission towers, Rick gazed out upon idyllic scenes of pastoral life. With cattle, mountain streams, and forests, he figured that people here might do okay. What it would be like trying to make it through a winter, Rick didn't know. The ski resorts this year were likely to be pretty empty.

As they left Austria and crossed into Germany, the population density increased dramatically. The autobahns were choked with refugees, and sprawling camps littered the banks of the Danube, small boats ferrying supplies for hungry mouths. Rain streaked the Cessna's windshield and Rick thought 'of the UN refugee camps he'd seen in Africa; in Sudan, Liberia, Sierra Leone, and imagined the same scenes with the addition of mud and a colder climate. He wondered how long it would take for warlords to rise, staking a claim to resources and carving out a territory. Chances were, even those idyllic pastures in the alps would become part of someone's fiefdom. It was tempting to think of Europeans as being soft and peaceful, but Africans preferred to live in peace, too. Everybody did, no matter where they lived. It only took a hardcore of ambitious groups who reveled in violence to dominate them all. Rick had seen them rise in every power vacuum, in every social breakdown. Failed States grew violent groups the way dung heaps grew mushrooms. There might not be as many guns out here to arm those groups, but Rick had witnessed first hand the atrocities that could be committed by a small band with machetes. Bullet, blade or club, the result was the same. No ideology required: simply hunger, self-interest and will. The rest could be made up on the fly, and often was.

Only one thing was certain: a lot of people weren't going to make it. Old tractors could be hand cranked to keep plowing the fields, but when the fuel ran out, as it eventually would, the complex agricultural system that kept the cities fed would break down. Harvesting would need to be done by hand and horse, and Rick doubted there was enough expertise, nor horses, to make that work any time soon. In the Hundred Years War, famine, disease and roaming armed bands killed off two thirds of Germany's population. In France, half. And that was before the industrial age, when peasants were hardier and more manually skilled than modern populations. It didn't bode well, and Rick felt overwhelmed by the implications.

He just hoped he was being too pessimistic.

"Do you want to fly?" said Kowalski.

Rick snapped out of his thoughts. "What?"

"Do you want to learn to fly?"

"I don't think that's a good idea."

"I disagree. I'm getting tired. If you want us to fly non-stop, you've got to pitch in."

Rick looked down at the ground, suddenly thinking of the mysterious forces that were keeping the plane aloft. Mysterious to him, anyway. In a big plane, and even a helicopter, it was tempting to think of reliable, brute-force technology being the only reason he could fly. In a tiny plane with a buzzsaw engine, that idea wasn't so credible. Not from the cockpit.

"I don't want to screw things up," he said.

"You think I do? All I want is for you to learn to hold the controls and let her fly."

"I bet it's not that easy."

"No, but it ain't that difficult, either. Now landing, that's difficult. Taking off is a challenge too, but I won't ask you to do that. Just hold her straight and level. She's trimmed and stable. Put your hands on the controls."

Gingerly, Rick wrapped his hands around the vibrating flight controls. Kowalski took his hands off his.

"Hey!" said Rick, "what the hell are you doing?"

Paralyzed with fear, Rick clung to the controls, not daring to move a thing.

"See?" said Kowalski with a smirk. "It flies itself."

"Yeah, okay. Great demonstration. Now get the hell back on the controls!"

"You're doing okay. Let's get a little more adventurous."

That wasn't what Rick wanted to hear.

"Without pulling or pushing on the yoke, turn the wheel slightly to the left," said Kowalski.

"No."

"Come on, you can do it."

"This isn't necessary."

"If you want to help out, it is. Turn the yoke."

Taking a deep breath, Rick turned the yoke a tiny fraction.

"You can turn it a little more than that," assured Kowalski.

Rick turned it a little more and felt the plane tilt slightly.

"Now that might not seem a big deal to you," said Kowalski, "but if you look at your heading on this dial here, you'll see we're turning left. The artificial horizon also shows your angle of tilt, if you like. Now turn it back the other way until the horizon on this ball-reading is perfectly level."

Relieved that he hadn't sent the plane into a spin, Rick turned the yoke the other way, eyes fixed to the artificial horizon.

"Okay, that was simple enough. You've turned the plane a few degrees to port, and you've leveled out. Now I want you to turn the other way, taking us back to our original heading. Keep your eye on the compass reading."

For the next hour, Kowalski put Rick through his paces, telling him what to do and instructing him in the hazards to watch out for, like hills and low cloud. After practicing the gentlest of maneuvers and handing the controls back over, Rick sagged back in his seat, sweating, mentally exhausted, but, though he was loathe to admit it, invigorated by the experience. He turned to see what Scott thought of it, and discovered that his comrade had slept through the whole experience.

Which was probably just as well, as Scott wasn't the keenest of flyers.

Dropping back into a light sleep himself, he woke when Kowalski put the plane into a steep bank.

They were over a coastline, with a gray sea under gray skies stretching away to the horizon. Running along the coastline was a levee. Picturesque windmills dotted the landscape, and canals crisscrossed the green fields.

They were in Holland, and Rick wondered how long he'd been asleep. He had to find a way to keep from snoozing.

Kowalski was angling to put the plane down on a perfectly straight stretch of road. It could have been a runway were it not for the fact that a canal ran right next to it. Along the bank of the canal were a line of wind turbines, and they looked uncomfortably close to the road as Kowalski brought the plane in to land. Rick watched them flash by, glad that he wasn't at the controls.

As the plane braked to a halt behind an abandoned Volvo, he looked out at the incredibly flat landscape. The objects he'd mistaken for wind turbines were actually wind operated pumps that kept the land from being flooded, extracting the water from the fields and depositing it in the canal. With all the major pumping stations out of action, this ancient form of technology was the only thing preventing the sea from reclaiming most of Holland.

In the distance, an actual wind farm with turbine generators turned out to be less useful, the solar storm having fried the generators and set them alight. They looked like a field of burnt matches.

Rick and Scott set to work siphoning the gas out of the Volvo, filling one can and running to pass it up to Kowalski on the wing as the tube drained into the next can. Dripping the last of the gas into it, Rick took the barely filled can over. "We're going to need more than this," said Kowalski. "Especially if we're going to go across the sea. That's the last place I want to run out of fuel. I was hoping our course would take us closer to northern France so we wouldn't have to cross so much water, but I miscalculated our heading. I'm too used to GPS."

"That don't make me feel good if we're flying to Greenland," said Scott. "You know I'm serious about feeding you to the polar bears."

"It's not ideal," admitted Kowalski. "I need better charts. The maps in the plane don't extend this far."

"That's information we could have done with earlier. What were you planning to do? Ask the penguins for directions?"

"There's no penguins in the Arctic," said Kowalski phlegmatically.

"So what *are* you going to do?" asked Rick.

"I've got some ideas. Have a little faith. Go get me some more gas."

There was another car about half a mile down the road. Scott and Rick took the gas cans for a stroll.

"Can we trust that guy?" said Scott as they walked.

"He's got us this far, hasn't he?"

"He missed his landing target by two countries. Seriously, do you think his idea is any good?"

"You're right. I vote we should go with your idea."

Scott looked at him. "What idea was that?"

"Exactly," said Rick. "You don't have any. Quit bitching and get with the program."

"I joined up to bitch. It's not just a right, it's a pleasure."

"Gets a little wearing after a while."

"So see a therapist. You in love with Kowalski now? That's nice. Let me know when the wedding is."

Rick gave him a side glance. "You're an asshole."

"Best way to be, now, the way things are. Don't trust anyone who isn't.

Anyone perfect is hiding something."

They reached the car, which turned out to be another Volvo. "Just for that, I'll let you suck the gas out of the tube."

Scott took out his knife and snapped open the fill cap. "See? Even you can be an asshole. I had to do the last one."

Rick took hold of his rifle and looked around. "Means you're getting good at it. Why waste a valuable skill like that?"

In the far distance were two large, industrial sized barns. From that direction Rick spied figures approaching on bicycles.

Scott spat out a mouthful of gas and dipped the tube in the can.

"Heads up," said Rick. "Cyclists approaching."

Scott straightened up and aimed his rifle, looking down his 4x ACOG sight. "They're all guys, and they look pissed."

Rick had already deduced that from the furious way they were cycling. Moving away from the flammable can, he positioned himself near the front of the car. Scott moved a few paces out, forming a blocking line with Rick. The cyclists closed the gap quickly, braking hard a few yards away when they saw the rifles. There were four guys, varying in ages. Two wore bib-and-braces overalls, the others dirty jeans and wool shirts. One of them dropped his bike on the ground and took two steps forward, gesticulating and yelling. Rick didn't understand a word he said, but he gathered the guy wasn't too happy about the gas being siphoned. He didn't bother replying, checking instead for possible weapons in the group.

The yelling guy tried to make a move towards the gas can, and Scott aimed his rifle, clicking off the safety. "You back the fuck up," he said in a tone that needed no translation.

So this is how it begins, thought Rick. Two groups squabbling over a rare resource that they both needed. Maybe this was the guy's car. Maybe the farm claimed ownership of it since they considered it to be in their territory. Or simply because they thought they needed it more. The weapons, in this case, decided the issue. One side had them, the other did not. These guys couldn't call the police, and once they'd flown off, Rick wasn't worried about receiving an extradition notice. No such thing as property law now. Ownership belonged to whoever could take it and keep it, whether by force or by guile. In spite of centuries of law and order, most people quickly understood that, whether they agreed with it or not. That's when they realized that rights were a fiction, a comforting myth that meant nothing without force to back it up. The next logical step was the forming of protective groups or gangs. Everything flowed from there: from the coalescing of tribes to the creation of nations. Niceness only came from full stomachs, and morality was just the frosting on a very dirty cake – the generous indulgence of the victors.

When it came down to it, civilization was but a thin veneer.

The guys backed up as Scott requested, and the gas continued to trickle into the can. Studying the looks on Rick's and Scott's faces, they turned away and returned to the farm.

Rick didn't have to think about whether he would have shot them if they attempted to fight. He knew he would have. And they knew it too. Just for a can of gas.

Scott was right. This was the Time Of Assholes.

33

"What do you mean, you're not gonna let us through?" shouted Lauren, exasperated. "We're just following the road. Who do you think you are?"

The gruff woman behind the barricade thrust her shotgun towards Lauren's face. "I am telling you one last time. You are not coming in."

"You don't own the goddamn road!"

Lauren was dead on her feet. Having finally cleared the metropolitan areas and the suburbs, she and April found themselves tramping through the lush wooded hill country north of the Bull Run river. Million dollar properties with winding drives and several acres nestled in the forest, some dating back to the civil war. The area looked too genteel to be comfortable with refugees. Lauren had already found one road barred against her, some small town deciding that they didn't need any more strangers coming through. Now, having detoured several miles, she found another obstacle. The Union army had been stopped twice at Bull Run, and it seemed Lauren wasn't going to have any better luck.

The woman at the barricade wore a shooting vest and was flanked by two guys who let her do all the talking. One of them carried a Bushmaster M4 carbine, and even in civilian semi-automatic configuration, it was enough for Lauren and April to feel they were considerably outgunned. They kept their own pistols hidden.

April stepped forward before Lauren blew up completely. "This woman is trying to get home to her kids," she said. "We're not asking for help. We just want to pass through and then we'll be on our way."

"I've heard that story before," said the woman haughtily. "Go back to where you came from. You'll find nothing here."

Lauren looked ready to hit her when one of the men, an older, bearded guy, put his hand on the woman's shoulder and said something quietly to her. The woman, as highly strung as Lauren looked to be, backed away reluctantly, glaring at Lauren and April.

The bearded guy, smiling wanly, took her place. "Sorry ladies, but this is officially a no-go area, by order of the town council. If you back up a few miles and take the next right, you should be able to find a road that'll take you where you want to go, wherever that is."

"We've been that way already," said Lauren, fuming. "We got the same treatment."

"Then you'll have to go the other way and head through the city of Manassas."

Lauren didn't want to go through another urban area. "We're just trying to pass through. If you're that uptight about it, you can escort us. You can't seriously think we're a threat to you."

The guy put on the airs of a man who was just obeying orders. "Sorry, but you've got to understand. We've had a little trouble, and some robberies. Folk who simply passed through could have acted as scouts for some of the badder elements. We're just trying to take care of our own. In our shoes, you'd do the same."

April touched Lauren's arm. "Okay, we'll go. Thanks for your time."

"There's Federal camps being set up. Maybe you're better off going there."

"Again, thanks," said April, trying to pull Lauren away.

"You ladies should be careful on your own. There's some real bad dudes out there. We've had reports of a couple of them in an old pickup going around robbing people. Even tried to kidnap a girl from our neighborhood, which is why Mary here is so protective. So take care, out there."

"Asshole," muttered Lauren as she walked away.

"Keep smiling, girl," said April between her gritted teeth. "Soon as we're out of sight, we'll try and cut through the woods."

Grandma Daisy sat on the edge of the bed, staring at the wind-up carriage clock. Ticking loudly, it was the only thing working in the house. Inherited from her own mother, it was something Harold disliked, on account of the ticking. When he was angry he threatened to remove it, but he never touched it. Daisy compromised by fashioning a cover cut from an old blanket to muffle the noise at night.

When Lauren was very young and had trouble sleeping, Daisy put the clock in her room to soothe the nightmares away.

It was a shame it wasn't doing much to fend off this particular nightmare. Daisy winced as the stomach pain came again. She wanted to lie down but that made the pain worse. She'd suffered from gastric ulcers in the past, but they'd eased in recent years, so she didn't have any medication stocked. The tablets she took for her cholesterol and her heart had nearly run out, and her thyroid problems left her weak and tired. She still had half a bottle of pills for her hypothyroidism, but her hormone levels must have dropped further due to the stress. It had happened before, necessitating a visit to the doctor to alter the dose, but that was no longer possible. The arthritis in her hip meant she couldn't walk far without pain, and the joint contributed to her tiredness by not letting her sleep.

None of that, however, was worse than the grief over Harold's sudden passing, or the anxiety she felt for her daughter. For those things, there was no medicine at all.

The clock ticked steadily, willing her to take a nap and let the heavy eyelids close. It would have been bliss if she could, but her stomach ulcer had other ideas. She really needed to go and rest in an upright position. Picking up the burdensome revolver, she heaved herself up and dragged her feet to the chair in the living room.

From there, she had a view of the street, but it only served as a sorry reminder of the mess she was in. On the opposite side, Elena's house stood empty. Daisy bitterly regretted her final words to her. If she had any sense, she would have gone with her. At the very least she could have promised to join her afterwards. There was no need to lose her temper like that.

But she hadn't wanted to go. She still didn't. The chairman had come to persuade her to leave, but she'd remained adamant. Her daughter was coming home, and she would be here for her. She couldn't bear the thought of her little girl arriving to an empty house, wondering where her mother and her children were.

The poor girl didn't yet know that her father was gone.

Daisy rocked away the ache. It didn't matter that her daughter was a grown woman. She would always be Daisy's little girl. When she'd joined the army and gone away to war, Daisy had worried herself sick, pestering her with messages and frustrated with the communications difficulties. The nightly news was filled with images of soldiers on the move and journalists reporting from rooftops as Baghdad shook under bombardment. Daisy watched avidly, looking to catch a glimpse of Lauren. She lost weight thinking about what might have happened to her. Every day for a year, she heard reports of the brutal insurgency and the roadside bombs. She stopped caring about the rights and wrongs of the war. She just wanted her daughter to come home. When Lauren finished her tour, Daisy wept with relief for three days. A weight had been removed from her shoulders, and her little girl appeared taller and hardened by the experience. She'd been a little worried when Lauren introduced Rick to her a few months later, wondering at the wisdom of having another soldier for a partner. Daisy hoped it wouldn't influence her to return to Iraq for a second tour, as many soldiers were doing. The announcement of a pregnancy, and of her engagement, banished her fears. Lauren was going to leave the army and raise a family, and that was music to Daisy's ears. Becoming a grandmother was bliss, especially knowing her daughter was staying in the area. Rick's continual deployments were a concern, but Daisy got over that. If anything happened, she would always be around to help her daughter take care of things.

There were no images on TV now, no journalists to explain what was happening in the world. The fate of US personnel overseas was a mystery. The whereabouts of her daughter, equally so. She'd initially assumed it was just a matter of travel, that transport systems would be fixed or improvised. The awful silence in the house and on the street told a darker story. Everybody had left and Daisy felt abandoned. The hope that her daughter would make it home grew fainter with each tick of the clock.

She didn't feel strong enough to be the sole carer of two grandchildren. It wasn't fair that they should endure this, but she really didn't know how to ease the situation for them. The food was running out, and each day left her weaker and more frail. Her determination to keep them safe for Lauren's return clashed with the realization that her own time was running out. And if she couldn't make it, what would happen to them?

Daisy dried her eyes.

"Are you crying, Grandma?" said Lizzy.

She'd approached so quietly, Daisy hadn't noticed her. "No, honey. Just something in my eye."

Lizzy unwrapped a napkin, revealing the remains of a tortilla. She held it out. "You have to eat, Grandma. Here, I saved this for you."

Daisy's eyes welled up again. "Sweety, you shouldn't have."

"Please eat, Grandma."

Daisy didn't have the heart to tell her that eating only aggravated her ulcer and made the acid pain worse. "Don't you want to share it with your brother?"

Lizzy appeared ashamed. "He's not here."

Daisy caught her breath. "What do you mean?"

"He's gone out. I'm sorry, but he told me not to tell you. He's gone to see a girl."

Daisy hadn't heard him go out. The children were as quiet as mice these days, and Josh had been acting strangely. She berated herself for not paying enough attention. Heaving herself out of the chair, she gripped the sideboard to steady herself. "Pass me the gun, Lizzy. Quickly now. And fetch me a walking stick."

Josh hid in the trees by the creek, staring at the makeshift refugee building. He'd hung around, waiting for Skye to turn up, but it was getting late now, and she hadn't shown. He hadn't been sure what he'd say to her if she did. He only knew he needed to see her.

The highway by the building was quiet, and he hadn't seen anyone around. He wondered if maybe she'd left, and the building was empty. He didn't really want to discover that, because that meant he'd lose her forever, so he hesitated to check it out. In the end, however, if he wanted to know either way, he'd have to risk disappointment.

And rejection.

He'd spent the afternoon interpreting and reinterpreting what she'd said. Unwilling to come to the obvious conclusion, he'd agonized over the possible meanings until he could stand it no longer.

He needed to tell her how he felt.

Gripping his golf club, he padded to the side door of the building.

It was open, so he walked right in, and the smell hit him immediately. It was just like the smell he'd encountered upon entering Grandpa's room. The skylights gave the interior a diffuse, dim glow, and when his eyes adjusted, he saw the bodies.

They lay in different positions, their postures indicating complete indifference to where they died. Some were half covered in blankets, others were not. Josh covered his nose with his sleeve, unable to comprehend the horror. Stupefied by the sight, his heart pounding with a rising panic, he finally remembered what he'd come in for.

He might not want to know, but he had to be certain.

Disturbing clouds of flies, he wandered the vast floor, craning his neck to try and identify the bodies without getting too close. The old supermarket retained some of the old signs, hanging from the ceiling with wires, and it was obscene to witness corpses lying under Fresh Meat notices, or reclining on Special Offer posters. Gagging on the stench, Josh kept moving until he spied the body of a girl.

He knew immediately from the clothing it was her. Shuffling forward, he leaned over, hoping she was just curled up in sleep, and she looked indeed as if she'd just laid down to rest. The shard of glass and the pools of blood from her slashed wrists told a different story. She lay with an arm across the chest of a bloating corpse, and Josh guessed that was her mother. But only from the hair, which looked the same as Skye's. The face was an unrecognizable mess.

Josh reached out with shaking fingers, daring himself to touch Skye's skin. He couldn't believe she was dead. If she still had a pulse, he could maybe save her.

A corpse nearby moved, and a head lifted up. It was another woman, and her face was pale and ghastly, but her eyes retained life, and she locked Josh in her awful gaze. "Go," she said, coughing. "Before he comes."

Josh saw her ripped clothing, just like Skye's. Saw some of the same bruises on her face. And realized why Skye had rejected him and forced him away.

She was trying to protect him.

It took slow seconds for this to dawn on Josh, and he turned too late to see a man bearing down on him.

The man must have been hiding, or sleeping, in a back office. Unshaven, haggard and wild eyed, he held a chef's knife in his hand.

Josh ran towards the door, but the man anticipated him and moved with surprising speed to block him. Josh backed away, not sure what to do next, and the man leered and pointed the knife at him. "You look well fed," he said. "You got food somewhere?"

Josh darted to one side, making another attempt for the door, but the man matched his movements, preventing his escape.

"You think a few scraps from the church was going to be enough?" continued the man. "You thought it'd be okay to let us starve while you rich, pious bastards hoarded food? Tell me where it is, boy, and I'll let you live."

Josh backed away, stumbling on a corpse. Skye's corpse.

"You liked her?" sneered the man. "She was sweet, I can tell you. More than you could have handled. Lead me to the stash, and I'll make sure you get a chance to be with a girl for real. It'll be our secret. What do you say?"

Furious at the man's words, Josh bellowed at him and charged, swinging the club at the side of the man's knee. The man jerked, his leg giving way, and swung his knife at Josh as he passed. Josh ducked under the blade and swung the club again, slamming it into the man's back. Seething, he wanted to smash the man's head, but the flailing arms blocked his target. Charging again, he brought the club down with all his might.

The man, one knee down, gripped the club and held it. Josh tried to wrestle it free, but his puny arms were no match for the man's strength. One wrench, and the club was torn from his grip. He dodged to one side, narrowly avoiding the blade, then took his chance to run.

The man, running at a limp, chased after him, but Josh outpaced him, his legs pounding like pistons.

"Come here you little swine," screamed the man.

Josh ran like the wind.

***

Grandma, with Lizzy in tow, had made it as far as the Henderson's house. She'd heard the scream, a distant echo, and feared the worst. Minutes later she saw Josh sprinting up the street towards her like a boy possessed. Throwing himself into her arms, he sobbed. "She's dead Grandma. She's dead."

Grandma consoled him, not having the faintest idea who he was talking about. Down the street, there was no further movement. Releasing Josh, she pulled the revolver out, conscious of her poor eyesight as she scanned the deepening shadows.

"Back to the house, now," she said. "I don't think it's safe out here anymore."

Lauren lay flat on the ground among the ferns, peering out from the trees. They'd lost a lot of time trying to cut through the woods. It was no place for a stroller, and frequent detours were necessary to avoid the fenced private estates. Guard dogs barked at the noise they made, and at one point someone fired a warning shot. It was nowhere near Lauren and April's location, but clearly, people were nervous. Reaching a road finally, they headed south on what appeared to be a clear route to the bridge across Bull Run. The sound of a truck engine as dusk approached sent them back into the trees.

The pickup that appeared shone no lights, and was traveling slow and quiet. There were two people in the cab, and a third standing on the bed with a hunting rifle slung across his back. He was barely a silhouette, but Lauren thought he bore a striking resemblance to the figure who'd called out to her, back at the Chain Bridge. It was impossible to be sure, but it was obvious they weren't refugees. Lauren initially thought they might be running a patrol for a settlement, but their stealthy progress, with the engine revs kept low, indicated they were more likely on the hunt for something. Or someone.

Lauren watched them disappear around the corner, heading south. The engine idle ceased abruptly, and Lauren's heart sank. It could be that the trees masked the sound, but she was certain the engine had been switched off, and she knew why.

The bridge was being held against them as the marauders set up an ambush at another choke point.

Lauren let out an exasperated sigh. There was no other crossing for miles in either direction, and she felt weary and frustrated. Soon, it seemed, it would be impossible to travel anywhere without meeting an obstruction. Or trouble.

34

Under the Cessna's port wing lay the green patchwork fields and moorland of Scotland. Under the right wing, off a craggy coastline, the North Sea and white capped waves. An offshore wind blew hard, and Kowalski had to keep his foot on the rudder to crab the plane sideways and keep it over the coastal cliffs.

They'd followed the coastline of Britain since crossing the Channel, and it meant they no longer had to follow the compass. When visibility was poor, Kowalski dropped his altitude. He didn't want to risk flying in cloud in case they drifted out over the sea, and until they reached northern England, there were no hills to worry about. Seaside towns huddled miserably in the rain, holiday trailer parks looking forlorn and unwelcoming, and the piers and amusement parks lay deserted. Once they hit Scotland, the wind blew the cloud cover away and the Cessna rose over the majestic peak of Edinburgh Castle, the mighty fortress standing guard over a gloomy and still metropolis, the evening shadows creeping into the streets. From there onward Scotland grew more mountainous and less populated until, in the final stages of the journey to Wick, they saw only tiny towns and villages.

Wick itself was a small fishing port that barely warranted a second glance. Etched out on the landscape next to it, however, were the runways of a small airport. Kowalski touched down and taxied to the end of the runway.

"I don't see why we need this," said Rick. "We can land somewhere more remote and attract less attention."

Kowalski turned the engine off. "We need this," he said. "Wick is one of the essential stops on the northern ferry route. They've got a lot of experience handling light aircraft to and from the States. I need the exact bearings and distances to Iceland and Greenland. Without them, I'm not sure I care to venture over the North Atlantic. Iceland's a small target and we can't afford to miss it."

They stepped out of the plane onto a landscape that seemed almost as flat as Holland, apart from the dark hills on the horizon. A cold wind blew across the gray runway. Nearby stood a cluster of World War Two era buildings, silent sentinels with broken windows and grass growing on their flat roofs. In the distance were two large, discolored hangers, piles of scrap metal leaning up against their walls like drifted rusty snow. A squat air control tower sat atop a more modern industrial building. Out over the sea cliffs, gulls screamed their indifference to mankind's current predicament.

"You stay with the plane," said Rick to Scott. "Anybody gets too close, discourage them."

Scott shivered in the breeze. "Unless they've got whiskey. For that, I can get very friendly right now."

"Stay antisocial until we've checked the place out."

Rick and Kowalski walked across the concrete pan. Rick felt like he was in a black and white movie, and fully expected someone in an antique car to drive up and tell them to scramble to meet the hun at fifteen thousand feet. Or offer them tea. The stroll through an alternate timeline ended when they reached a smart terminal building with colorful advertisements on the windows for the Pulteney Distillery, which appeared to be in the town. Rick was glad he'd left Scott with the plane.

"Can I help you fellas?" called a voice.

A bearded gentleman with a coat and wellington boots walked out from behind the terminal.

"Actually, you can," said Kowalski. "We need directions to Iceland."

The man's bushy eyebrows rose a fraction. "Are you asking about the supermarket, or the island?"

"The island."

"You're focking mad," said the man, glancing at Rick's rifle. "Where have you boys come from?"

"Syria," said Rick.

The eyebrows rose a little higher. "You're yanks, I see."

"Yes sir."

"And you want to be getting to Iceland now," said the man, like it was a concept that, although absurd, might have its merits.

"Exactly."

The man frowned, dispensing with any idea of optimism. "Totally mad. No radios, no GPS, no beacons. And the weather's turning bad. That your plane? You won't have a lot of reserve fuel if you drift off course and have to conduct a grid search."

"You know your stuff," said Kowalski. "I assume you work here."

"I maintain the grounds, that's all. I don't need to be a genius to see you're taking an unnecessary risk."

"We're trying to get home," said Rick.

The man focused on him for a moment, then grunted. "Understandable, I suppose. Anyway, I failed to introduce myself. I'm Stuart."

"I'm Rick. This here's Kowalski, and the loon by the plane is Scott."

Stuart looked across to the Cessna. "We'd better get that into a hanger. I assume you're not planning to fly tonight, and the whole town heard you coming in, so there'll be some interest. I imagine every man and his dog will be here soon."

Rick expected a mob. Instead they received a growing group of curious well-wishers. The first visitor to the airport office was a smiling chairman from the town committee.

"An invasion, is it?" he said upon seeing the guns, shaking Rick and Scott by the hand.

He didn't have a dog, but he had brought his young daughter with him. She hovered shyly behind his legs, peering out at the strangers.

"Must seem that way," said Rick as he wondered what the girl was thinking. No doubt, rumors would soon be flying among the other children.

"Don't worry," said the chairman, amiably. "Stuart can lock them in the office for you. We have some vacant rooms at the hotel waiting. We'll walk you down."

"You sure?" said Rick. "We don't want to be a burden to you. I'm sure you've got your own problems to deal with."

The chairman waved away his concerns. "I run the hotel, and we haven't had visitors for a while. I'm curious to hear news from the outside world, and I daresay others are too. Stuart says you flew in from Syria."

"Yeah, more or less."

"We have a chap in the town whose grandson is in Syria. Special forces, I believe. Rather like yourself. He may be keen to talk to you. He has been a tad concerned."

"Not sure I've got much in the way of good news for him," said Rick. "I started out with a squad of six. Now it's Scott and me, with Kowalski in tow."

"Ah," said the chairman. "Perhaps not a good idea to say too much, then. Still, on behalf of the town, I'd like to welcome you to our community and hope we can make your stay comfortable."

"Do you have a bar in this hotel?" said Scott.

The chairman laughed. "We do, but everything is strictly rationed. I hope you understand, service is not up to our usual standards, but we'll see what we can rustle up."

Rick removed the magazine from his rifle and cleared the breech. For good measure, he stripped down the rifle and removed the bolt carrier, putting it in his pocket. He decided to keep hold of his pistol, tucking it away in his body armor. He'd seen *The Wicker Man*, and preferred to stay cautious.

Kowalski stayed behind with Stuart, both poring over a chart spread out on the table. It turned out that Stuart had a pilot's license too, so they had a lot in common, and much to discuss. Rick and Scott followed the chairman and his daughter into the town.

It was like returning from a moon landing. News had traveled fast and people came out of their houses to shake their hands. Children accumulated, giggling and gossiping at the sight of the two grizzled looking veterans. The chairman seemed to grow a couple of inches taller as he proudly paraded his new guests before the town.

With so many happy people about, Rick had to wonder how they were coping without power and supplies, and the chairman explained that, with farms surrounding the town, and a fishing community in it, they were not actually short of food. Being so isolated, they weren't inundated with refugees from the cities either. In coordination with the police, they'd implemented a strict rationing scheme, using the voting register to make sure everyone got a fair share. Access to clean drinking water, on the other hand, was more of a problem, as were medical supplies. The chairman seemed confident that power and transport links would one day be restored, but in the meantime, the town had adapted to the situation.

"Not everybody is happy, of course," said the chairman, "and we do have an antisocial element in the town. Fortunately, we have a large police station that serves the county situated right here in the town, with many officers living nearby. Without their cars, they have to return to beat policing, which is something we've been asking for, for years. We've also raised a temporary volunteer constabulary to assist with patrolling the streets and maintaining the nightly curfew, so I think it's fair to say that people feel safer than they ever have."

Rick wondered whether the Brits were too polite to say the words 'Martial Law', or whether they were simply more sanguine about it. The people who came out to greet them certainly looked happy enough, and it occurred to Rick that they perhaps saw the arrival of the Cessna as the first sign of normality returning, or a sign at least that the outside world hadn't forgotten them. Maybe they hoped the next plane to arrive would be bigger and laden with supplies.

The bar and lounge in the hotel was the kind of place Rick had only ever seen in pictures, with oak beams, wide armed chairs and a log fire. The Scots didn't consider it cold enough to need a fire yet, so Rick and Scott were donated wool sweaters. A small glass of warm ale was followed by a plate of freshly caught crabs. By the light of candles, the two operators were interrogated by what seemed half the town that was crammed into the bar, and Rick felt increasingly drowsy as the long day caught up with him. When he was finally allowed to retire for the night, he pressed down on the soft mattress in his room with something akin to awe. He didn't think he'd have any problem sleeping.

He was wrong. Relaxing for the first time in a week, he woke as the nightmares jerked him around, the images of battle, Leroy's dead face and the sight of a dark mist swallowing up his laughing children plaguing his thoughts. Snapping upright on the bed, he leaned forward, gasping for breath. A cold touch of dread gripped him. In the claustrophobic silence of the room, all he could think of was that, no matter what he did, he was too late. His family was in danger and he'd failed them. Wrapping himself in the blankets, he stared out of the window, willing the night to end.

At dawn the Cessna was rolled out of the hanger and Stuart helped them refuel. "I've topped up the oil," he told Kowalski. "You want to be careful. That engine's not so tight."

As the engine was started, a small crowd gathered to watch them go. Everybody in the town seemed to have a stake in the plane's success, and a small girl with a handful of daisies ran forward to present them to Rick.

"Damn, I'm going to miss this place," said Scott.

Rick said nothing. The night's darkness was still with him. It was an emotional sendoff, and some of the faces in the crowd seemed to understand the risk they were taking. He felt like Lindburgh on the eve of his transatlantic flight, and realized that, right now, they probably shared the same level of technology when it came to navigation aids. Basically, there were none.

"You've got no de-icing on this plane," shouted Stuart above the roar of the engine as he leaned into the cockpit. "Stay low. You'll use more fuel, but at higher altitudes you risk getting blown off course and your wings icing up. You cannot, I repeat, cannot miss the island. Everything's laid out on the chart. If you don't hit land at the speed and times I've given you, then for God's sake, don't keep going. Start a search. You will not make it to Greenland in one hop."

He handed Kowalski a thermos flask. "It's only hot water, I'm afraid, but you might need it where you're going." He also handed over a tiny plastic bottle of amber liquid. "This is the good stuff: whiskey. That's my ration, so go easy with it. And good luck."

Taxiing out to the runway, Kowalski lined up the aircraft. Opening the throttle, he trundled down the runway, and Rick looked back.

The crowd was already dispersing, and Stuart was a solitary figure. He wasn't waving. Hunched against the wind, he looked resigned and mournful.

35

Kowalski didn't ask Rick to take a turn at the controls this time. Flying low over the waves, eyes darting from the compass to the view ahead, he was silent and grim. The gray cloud base was low, and drizzle reduced visibility.

The atmosphere in the cockpit was tense, and the air reeked of gas fumes from the full canisters in the back. Rick stared at the sea, knowing that if they had to ditch, their life expectancy could be measured in minutes, and the further north they went, the shorter that time would be.

That would probably be a blessing of sorts, because they had no ability to send an SOS, and nobody would be able to respond to it anyway. A quick, numbing death would be the best they could expect.

After three hours, they spotted land off the starboard wing, and Rick thought they'd made their destination, but Kowalski flew on. Checking the charts, he saw they'd passed the Faroe Isles. This far north, and usually dependent on mainland supplies, he wondered how the occupants were faring.

He decided it wasn't wise to dwell on that.

With nothing else to do, Rick contemplated sleep. The sight of the vast ocean chilled him, however. In spite of not being able to make a difference, he felt it was imperative to stay awake.

"Grandma, it's him!" hissed Josh.

Daisy moved as fast as her hip would let her. "Josh, get away from the window."

The drapes were drawn and the house was under lockdown.

Or as close to lockdown as she could get it. A sideboard had been pushed up against the front door, the kitchen table against the back. They weren't able, in Daisy's judgment, to access the outside grill. If they weren't spotted, then the smoke from the coals would give them away. They therefore hadn't eaten anything, apart from a spoonful of sugar and the last, stale cookies in the barrel.

They'd heard, rather than seen, the scavengers in the night, breaking windows to get into some of the houses. Daisy and the children had spent a sleepless night, waiting for the inevitable. For some reason, it didn't come, and dawn brought an empty street again, but Daisy remained wary about venturing out. The tall trees on the sidewalk shaded the house, making it bearable in the heat, but they were low on water, and the thirst was constant.

Peering out while trying not to disturb the drapes, Daisy saw the man Josh had described, and the sight of him swaying down the street with the knife in his hand made her feel faint. With both thumbs she cocked the revolver and waited.

The man had a wild look about him. At any other time, Daisy would have had him down as a drug addict, desperate for a fix. She supposed the hunger gave him that appearance now, but on the other hand, he could be an addict. Or an alcoholic. It was impossible to tell.

Daisy wasn't sure if he'd been the one breaking the windows in the night, but he looked quite bewildered, as if he was lost. The appearance of a cat, however, galvanized him into action, and he gave chase, swinging the knife like a sword. The cat got away easily, and the man stopped dead, dejected. Suddenly, he looked toward the house and Daisy froze, certain she'd been spotted, but the man's eyes wandered onto other houses, perhaps trying to assess the chances of finding food. Or drugs, if that were possible on this street.

Seeing nothing that held his interest, he shambled off until he was out of sight.

Daisy glanced at Josh and Lizzy, who stared back at her. They looked terrified. Josh especially was traumatized after finding that dead girl. Struggling to de-cock the revolver, Daisy sat down heavily on her chair, conscious of her rapidly beating heart.

Josh returned to his vigil by the window, unable to take his eyes off the street.

Lauren stared at the bridge for an hour, lying among the trees in a bend on the road. Nothing moved across it or near it, but she couldn't shake off the feeling that the guys in the pickup were still there, perhaps hidden in the woods on the other side, like she was. She saw a lot of wildlife: a long legged heron wading near the banks of the Bull Run, jabbing its beak to spear a wriggling, silvery fish; a Kingfisher darting back and forth along the shore; and even an owl leaving its roost at dawn, its great wings flapping slowly to propel it over the trees. None of them seemed perturbed by the presence of humans nearby, suggesting that maybe it was as quiet as it looked.

But neither April nor herself had heard the sound of the pickup starting up and driving away.

The mud she'd rubbed on her face started to itch, but she resisted the urge to scratch. If there really was somebody else watching, the flash of movement would give her away. It didn't take much to draw the eye.

Inching slowly away, she slid backwards through the undergrowth until the bridge disappeared from view.

"Anything?" whispered April when Lauren got back to her.

Lauren shook her head. "I don't like it, though."

"You've got a bad feeling about this."

Lauren glanced at her. "I'm not Harrison Ford."

"What's that supposed to mean?"

"Nothing. I just think it's too risky."

April pondered the situation. "Do you think we're being too paranoid about this?"

"We got shot at, remember?"

"Oh yeah. Okay, screw the bridge. If we go back the other way, we've got to go through Manassas. Is that better?"

"No."

Lauren spent some time thinking. It was frustrating that a simple matter of walking on roads had become so complicated. According to her map, nearly all the roads ran east to west. And numerous rivers ran west to east, from the Appalachians to the sea. Cutting through all that meant a lot of meandering. And a lot of bridges. It was like she was in a war zone now, and everything was a tactical decision.

"Can your boy swim?" she asked.

April gave her a pained look. "With floaties."

On her own, Lauren could have swum the river easily. She didn't want to admit it, but April and her kid were becoming a hindrance. "I saw a sign for a hiking trail through the woods. We'll follow the river and see if we can find a fording point downstream."

April cheerfully agreed, and Lauren wondered how long it would be before she had to tell her they needed to go their separate ways. Maybe she shouldn't have tried so hard to reassure her, back at the FEMA camp.

Too late, now.

They took to the Occoquan Trail and found it wide enough and flat enough for the stroller. They made good time, but the river got wider past the bridge, and Lauren couldn't see any easy way across.

On the opposite bank, palatial properties nestled in the trees, each with their own private dock. Lauren stopped when she saw a canoe tied up.

"We can use that," she whispered to April.

April squinted her eyes to peer through the foliage. "You mean to ferry us across?"

Lauren opened her atlas. "No. I mean to go downriver. Getting tired of these dead end roads." Lauren traced her finger along the Bull Run, then up a tributary that looked like it would take them to the southern edge of Manassas. "This is perfect," she said.

Stripping out of her clothes, she tiptoed through the ferns, looked out to see that nobody was around, then waded into the river.

It was refreshingly cold. After living and sweating in the same clothes for so many days, it was bliss to immerse herself in water. She was tempted to wash herself more thoroughly, but instead she struck out smoothly for the opposite bank. It didn't take her long to reach the dock.

A path led up to a house, but she could only just see it through the trees. There was no activity, and she couldn't tell whether it was abandoned or not. She decided it was better to be quick rather than to explore, especially if the owners had dogs.

The canoe was fiberglass, with two oars locked in the bottom. The fallen leaves indicated it hadn't been used for a while. Untying it, she towed it back across the river.

Little Daniel stared at her naked body as she hauled herself out of the river. April handed her a blanket to dry herself with. "We should be able to get our stuff in there," said Lauren, "but I'm afraid we've got to leave the stroller."

She was hoping that April would protest at that point, giving her a reason to suggest separating, but April appeared to be in agreement.

"It means Daniel will have to walk after we leave the river," added Lauren, testing for a reaction.

"No problem," said April. "My boy can walk anywhere." She turned to Daniel. "You're okay with that, aren't you baby? You want to go on a boat ride?"

Daniel gave a rare smile, and Lauren's heart sank a little. She wavered on whether to explain things a little more forcefully, then gave up. Pulling on her dirty clothes, she hid her disappointment.

After they'd cleared Manassas, she'd broach the subject again, giving April the option to go west to the mountains. Or rather, she wouldn't give her the option.

She'd just insist. Her own children were waiting, and she couldn't afford to be slowed down any further.

Getting into the canoe, with Daniel sitting on the bags between them, they pushed out. In less than half a mile, they found the tributary that snaked south and turned into it, paddling against the current.

The cruise liner drifted forlornly, bucked by the waves, the viewing decks empty. As they flew over it, Rick could see the lifeboats were missing. There was no sign of them on the vast ocean and he wondered if they'd made it to land. The polar explorer, Shackleton, rowed with his crew from the Antarctic to the Falkland Islands, but they were tough motherfuckers. That kind of tenacity was rare now.

Or maybe it was just something people would learn with enough determination. Rick wasn't sure. Special Forces training was grueling, and the pass rate was incredibly low. Rick had a lot of admiration for folks in the past who lived with such hardships every day. He imagined the villagers in the Afghan mountains would take this new world in their stride. The Innuit of northern Canada too. The pioneers who trekked across the midwest of America were certainly made of sterner stuff than their descendants. On the other hand, they died in large numbers from diseases people had forgotten about.

Rick guessed they were about to be remembered again. The romantic life of the cowboy was going to be laid bare for the fiction that it was.

The blower from the cockpit heater wasn't working, and the warmth that seeped weakly from the vents wasn't enough to overcome the cold. Rick was glad of the sweater, but he was still acclimatized to the tropics. Shivering, he tried to get comfortable. The chill of the seat's vinyl cover seeped into his legs.

Kowalski remained fixed in his posture, his concentration never wavering. If he felt the cold, or the hunger, he didn't say, and Rick felt a new admiration for him. Soft as he'd appeared when they first picked him up, he was a different person behind the controls. His navigation, in spite of Scott's fears, was spot-on too. After another hour, the land mass of Iceland appeared, a white capped mass rising from a slate sea. As they crossed the coast, a snow-tipped mountain loomed ahead. Banking the aircraft, Kowalski turned to follow a long and empty coast road. As soon as he spotted a lone vehicle, he touched down on the asphalt and rolled gently to a halt. Switching the engine off, he sagged back in the seat, mashing his eyeballs with the heel of his hand.

"Well done," said Rick.

"Could have been better," said the pilot. "Was aiming for the airport at Egilsstadir. We're miles west of that."

Scott stretched in the back seat. "I don't care. You did good."

Kowalski turned. "That's fair praise coming from you."

"Yeah, well. Make the most of it, Air Force. I don't give them things away easy."

They shared an MRE from Rick's pack, then opened the flask of hot water and passed round the cup. When Rick stepped out of the plane, the cold wind cut right through his sweater.

Working quickly, they topped up the tanks from the gas cans, then made their way to the car, siphon tube in hand. As soon as Scott broke open the fill cap, however, he wrinkled his nose.

"It's diesel," he said.

"Have we got enough already to make it to Greenland?" Rick asked Kowalski.

"Yeah, but I would have preferred a reserve."

Rick looked along the road that curved gently away into the distance, in the shadow of craggy, gray peaks. Immediately he thought of Ben Stiller, longboarding through the picturesque Icelandic landscape in *The Secret Life Of Walter Mitty*. It was one of the few movies he and Lauren enjoyed together. What was the tag line? Stop dreaming and start living, or something like that. It was one of those life-affirming movies, with great photography. Rick didn't even like Ben Stiller, but he enjoyed the movie a lot.

The scenery didn't look quite so panoramic from where he stood, but it was still pretty amazing, especially when he realized that what he'd taken to be a mountain in the distance was actually a volcano, and he was standing near a lava flow to the sea, the ground a plain of crushed charcoal.

Given the turn of events his life was taking, he wondered if, in a reversal of the tag line, he'd actually stopped living and started dreaming. It was certainly a surreal and unexpected destiny.

"We'll follow this road and see if we can find some gas on the way," he said. "Do you think we can fly near that volcano before we go?"

Kowalski looked at him. "Sure, but why?"

Rick couldn't help but grin like a kid. "Just want to recreate a moment from a movie."

Leafy trees dangled their branches in the water, sandbanks created channels in the river and insects buzzed over the mud of dry lagoons. To Lauren's mind, it created a scene reminiscent of *Deliverance*, a cult movie Rick had once urged her to watch. She'd hated it, and she certainly didn't need the reminder. With every meandering river bend, she expected to see armed figures waiting on a shore, accompanied by the sound of banjos.

If she felt vulnerable cycling, she felt a lot more vulnerable in a boat with the shore so close. Paddling upstream also proved tiring, and there were moments when she thought it would be faster to walk. Running aground numerous times, she was tempted to quit and just beach the boat once and for all. Cursing under her breath, she bent her back to paddle harder.

They'd passed under one bridge already and another loomed ahead. According to her map, they had one more bridge to go before they reached another tributary that might take them south. On the map, however, it was just a thin blue line, so she had no idea whether it was navigable. Nor even worth trying.

"We'll take a break after this next bridge," she said.

She lacked the upper body strength for this kind of endeavor, but maybe it was just a matter of practice. She was determined to keep going for as long as it was possible.

They crossed the shadow of the bridge, and Lauren steered closer to the shore where she'd seen swirls of debris on the surface. She figured the current was maybe stronger in the center of the river, and that it would be smarter to hug the shore.

"Lauren," hissed April urgently.

Lauren glanced back and saw a pickup glide across the bridge. It appeared to slow down for a moment, but then continued on its way.

"Is that the one you saw last night?" said April.

Lauren wasn't sure. Most pickups looked the same to her, and what were the chances that this was the same one?

Given that most were no longer running, she guessed that the odds were pretty high.

"Forget the break," she said.

She hadn't seen anyone standing on the pickup bed, but it was possible he was setting up his rifle and scope right now.

The impetus that thought gave her saw the boat's speed pick up until she'd rounded a bend. She paused to glance once through the foliage, but the bridge remained deserted. That in itself meant nothing, she decided. Eager to get completely away from the area, she plowed on.

An hour later they reached the third and last bridge, and by then Lauren wasn't sure she could row much further. April, sat behind her, had either stopped rowing or was putting less effort into it, because Lauren felt she was dragging the entire weight of the canoe. With the tunnel vision induced by her efforts, she didn't see that she couldn't have gone further, even if she wanted to.

A low concrete dam had been built across the river. Passing under the bridge, Lauren didn't notice until the boat ran aground on a sandbank that had built up in front of the dam. Stupefied, she looked up at the structure, her last reserves of energy giving out at the sight.

"I think you've come far enough, ladies," said a voice.

Lauren turned sharply, seeing the man from the pickup just a few yards away, his rifle pointing at her chest.

"Don't make a move," said the man quietly.

Lauren was indeed going to make a move, her hand reaching for her pistol as she twisted in her seat, but then she saw two other guys further back on the shore, one with a shotgun, the other with a large caliber revolver. She had to have paddled right past them to reach the dam.

The man doing all the speaking tutted and shook his head. "I wouldn't do that if I were you. Hands behind your head. Do it now, because if you reach for that piece I know you've got there, I'll put this thirty-aught-six bullet right through your chest and, unlike you, it won't be pretty."

Lauren looked at the size of the bore on the rifle, and the finger poised on the trigger, and knew she didn't stand a chance. April was hugging Daniel tight to her belly, eyes wide with fright. Reluctantly, she raised her hands, her cheeks burning with humiliation. Her muscles hurt and her legs felt weak. The main speaker watched her intently, seemingly fascinated, and Lauren averted her gaze, not wanting to give him any more information about how she felt.

The one with the revolver had a large band aid across one cheek. Sticking the weapon in his waist band, he pulled out a sheaf of zip ties and waded into the river, coming behind Lauren and pulling her arms down behind her back, binding them. Sticking his hand into the pouch of her hoodie, he triumphantly pulled out the Beretta.

"So it was you who grazed my cheek," he leered, prodding her face with her own pistol. "Maybe I ought to do the same to you."

Lauren didn't respond, and the man left her to do the same to April.

"She's clean," Lauren heard him say. As a bag was thrust over her head, blocking everything out, she realized something was odd.

Daniel, the little boy who'd screamed the sky down when his mother was dragged away in Baltimore, failed to utter a sound.

36

The moment the engine died was the moment Rick thought he'd killed them all.

He was at the controls of the plane, cruising at three hundred feet under Kowalski's watchful eye. He hadn't wanted to fly the plane, but Kowalski insisted he give it a try, saying they had enough altitude to recover from any mistakes. Looking at the vast ocean beneath them, Rick doubted it. The waves were peaked white, and a squall was blowing them sideways. Under Kowalski's instructions, Rick nudged the left rudder pedal to keep them on course, keeping his eyes pinned on the instrument panel. Try as he might, he couldn't help glancing down at the dark water.

That was when the engine suddenly cut out. For a brief moment, the prop continued to turn, then the engine picked up, faltered and roared again. Kowalski's hands were immediately hard on the controls, and Rick thought he'd made some sort of mistake that had nearly doomed them.

Kowalski altered the fuel mixture, opening the throttle a little, watching the instruments with concern.

"What did I do?" asked Rick, moving all his limbs away from the controls.

"Nothing," said Kowalski, looking increasingly worried.

"What happened, then?"

"Don't know," responded Kowalski curtly. "Fuel impurity, maybe."

Rick wasn't reassured. They'd managed to refill the gas cans before leaving Iceland, but the business of siphoning gas was not a sterile procedure. If water droplets had got into the fuel...

Kowalski was on the same wavelength, and immediately started to climb towards the cloud base above them. Rick realized he was trying to gain height in case they were forced to glide. Rick wasn't sure how that was meant to work out, but as far as he could see, there was nowhere to glide to. According to Kowalski's calculations, they were still two hours out from Greenland.

Rick was no expert, but he was pretty sure the Cessna would not be able to glide for two hours.

Kowalski ascended into the clouds, and the cockpit grew dark as they were surrounded by a gray wall. Scott leaned forward between the front seats but said nothing. Nobody spoke as Kowalski stared at the instruments, watching the altimeter needle wind slowly round. The engine faltered again, and again he reached for the mixture control, but the engine resumed its drone.

The climb through the cloud took a long time, and when they broke through the top into a pure blue sky, it was like surfacing from a dive into the ocean.

Rick felt a deep chill as he realized they nearly *had* taken a dive into the ocean.

Kowalski continued climbing until he reached the aircraft's maximum altitude of ten thousand feet. The engine was running well, but below them the cloud was like a frozen plain that stretched to the horizon.

"Shit," exclaimed Kowalski.

"What?" said Rick, thinking something else had happened.

"We've got to descend through cloud for the landing."

Rick wasn't sure what that meant. As far as he was concerned, a controlled descent was better than plunging down after losing all power.

They flew for another hour, Kowalski's face growing more concerned, when suddenly he exclaimed, "Shit, shit, shit."

The air speed indicator needle was dropping rapidly. Kowalski had taught Rick about not letting the air speed drop below the stalling point, and he looked on in horror as the needle passed the stalling point.

The aircraft was still flying, however.

"The pitot tube's frozen," said Kowalski.

Rick had no idea what that meant. "Is that bad?"

"Means I have no idea what our air speed is. Can't trust the altimeter either."

Seeing as the plane was still aloft, Rick wasn't sure how big a deal that was.

"Our navigation's dependent on knowing what our air speed is," explained the pilot. "I need to know how far along our bearing we've gone before I descend through the cloud and I calculate that by knowing our airspeed."

Rick opened the chart, and Scott leaned over his shoulder to look at the penciled line. "Have they got mountains in Greenland?" he asked soberly.

"They don't have much else," said Kowalski.

The sun coming through the canopy should have been a relief after the drab chill below the clouds, but it did little to alter the icy atmosphere as

Kowalski weighed up his options. Without radar or radio control, and with half the instruments inoperative or unreliable, descending into zero visibility was a potential death sentence. Maintaining his course in the hope of finding a break in the cloud, Kowalski was eventually forced to give up.

"Guys, we've got a decision to make," he said grimly. "I don't know where we are. Somewhere under that cloud is land. Or maybe not. We can carry on looking for a break until our fuel runs out, or we can descend and hope for the best."

"What's your professional opinion?" asked Rick.

"Honestly? If I was in my F16, I'd turn around, bail out and wait for a pick up. With the way things are, that's not an option for us. I haven't been trained for the level of technology we've got here, so my professional judgment isn't worth a lot. Take your pick."

"I say we go down and get it over with," said Scott.

Rick didn't like the finality of that option. It meant crossing a point of no return. On the other hand, there seemed to be no benefit in putting it off. The cloud cover looked solid for as far as he could see. "Agreed. Let's do it."

Kowalski looked at them both. "Okay. Whatever happens, I just want to say it's been fun traveling with you guys."

"Wish I could say the same," said Scott.

With a wan smile, Kowalski pushed forward the controls, putting the Cessna into a shallow dive. Rick took his last look at the azure sky, thinking it looked more beautiful than ever. Streams of cloud drifted across his sight, and the blueness was snuffed out as the plane plunged into a gray hell.

Rivulets of water streamed over the windshield and a chill seeped into the cockpit. Ice crystals formed on the corners of the canopy, and the engine coughed and stuttered, the RPM needle flickering back and forth. Kowalski gripped the controls like a man possessed. In spite of the cold, Rick noticed he was sweating.

Turbulence rocked the plane, and he felt his stomach shift as the Cessna rose and fell. The repeated tribulations of the engine set his teeth on edge and he had to make a conscious effort to relax his muscles. It was like being in a dream and falling. If there was nothing he could do – and he was completely helpless – he might as well be calm. Try as he might, however, it was an ambition he was unable to fulfill.

The cloud swirled beyond the prop, and a snow covered mountain slope appeared ahead of them. Kowalski yanked back the yoke and slammed the throttle home. Rick was pinned to the seat by the g-force as the plane screamed into a climb, the jagged rocks coming at them like a meteor shower. Kowalski side slipped and banked hard, the empty gas cans in the back slamming into each other, and a peak shot by. The wings looked as if they were about to drag through the rocky slope, and Kowalski pulled extra gs until the entire airframe creaked. Tendrils of cloud flashed across their vision, and another slope of black rocks with snow patches loomed before them. Kowalski threw the plane into an opposite bank, and the Cessna skirted over a ridge so close, it looked as if it were going to tear its undercarriage off. The ground fell away and Kowalski pushed the nose down, peeling away from the cloud base. All around them, valleys of moon rock nestled between peaks that ascended into the cloud. Kowalski twisted the little plane down through the valleys and emerged over water. Chunks of ice floated on the sea, and a mist hung like a veil over islands and fjords.

"Holy crap," breathed Scott.

Unsticking his head from the side of the canopy, Rick had much the same thought.

They weren't out of the woods yet, though. As the engine faltered, they looked around for a flat place to land and saw none. Everything was either jagged or frozen. Kowalski gained height to pass between the peaks of another island.

"Everybody look out for a runway," he shouted.

Rick glanced out of the cockpit. There didn't seem to be anything flat enough for a picnic blanket, never mind a runway. "How far away are we?" he asked.

"I have no idea. Look for houses. Look for a road. Anything."

The engine blipped and surged, and Kowalski looked desperate. Channels of ice strewn water flashed beneath them, and he banked the plane, following the jagged coastline, but everything looked the same. Scott tapped Rick's shoulder and handed him his binoculars, and together they scanned the terrain while Kowalski nursed the aircraft onwards.

"There! I saw a house," called Scott.

Rick swung round, trying to catch a glimpse of what he'd seen, but all he could see were more islands, peaks and icebergs.

"Turn left," called Scott. "I tell you, I saw something."

Kowalski banked the plane and gained height until he was just under the cloud base. Crossing over a large island, they flew over a lake and towards more mountains.

"There's a road," said Rick. "A track."

It was a regular line in an angular landscape and Kowalski banked the plane again. Whatever Rick had seen disappeared into its surroundings, and he scanned again.

"Structures at three o'clock," said Scott, and Rick turned, seeing them too: Tiny, red colored houses on the edge of a bay. Kowalski dipped a wing for a better view, and they all saw the long, unnaturally straight line across the landscape: a runway in a rocky plain.

"Well I'll be dipped in shit," said Kowalski.

"Get us down, and I'll happily do it," said Scott.

Kowalski throttled back, and the engine immediately cut out. "Shit. Buckle up, this is going to be rough."

He put the nose down, turning gently as the air whistled past the now quiet cockpit. Unable to line up with the runway, he aimed towards it, looking to land at an angle. Rick didn't think they'd have enough room to land that way and braced himself.

The Cessna rocked in a crosswind, and Kowalski fought to keep its nose pointed correctly. A couple of airport buildings grew into view, white buildings springing out from the rocky turf. At the current heading, the plane looked like it was going to charge across the width of the runway and straight into them. Unable to bank hard lest they lose too much altitude, Kowalski was handling the plane like a basket of eggs.

As gentle as the glide seemed, the ground rushed past at incredible speed as the plane got lower, and for a moment it looked as if they weren't going to make the runway. Holding the plane aloft as long as he could, Kowalski crossed the marker lights and put it down on the gravel runway, the vibration shaking the canopy. With a foot pressed hard on the left rudder, and the flaps down, he applied the brakes, trying to kill the momentum, but the plane rolled right across the center line, towards the other side of the runway. Without engine power, Kowalski could do nothing else. The Cessna bumped off the edge of the runway, across the rough ground and onto the hard apron in front of the airport building. Pressing savagely on the brakes, Kowalski growled curses under his breath until the plane slowed to a halt, feet away from the terminal building.

37

"I don't know whether to kill you right now, or offer to have your babies," said Scott. "Hell, make it twins. The stretch marks will be worth it."

They sat in the Cessna, too stunned to move.

"I'll take it under consideration," said Kowalski wearily.

The hot engine ticked and the wind whistled through the door gaps.

"I really don't want to do that again," said Rick.

They waited quietly, expecting activity from the airport building, or curiosity from the village, but nobody came. A bright yellow forklift sat on the apron with a luggage cart attached. A fuel tanker was parked by the terminal building. Both were littered with bird droppings. The control tower atop the terminal building appeared to be unmanned.

"I don't think we're going to have trouble with customs today," observed Scott.

Getting out of the plane, the trio wandered around the terminal. Every door was locked. Through the windows they could only see chairs and a customs counter. The garage at the end of the building housed a pristine fire tender. Down a long path, they could see the village of scattered and brightly colored wooden houses by the shore of a bay. A couple of boat trailers sat by the wooden docks, but there were no boats. As they walked down to the village, not even a barking dog greeted them. Two seal carcasses hung from a pole, fed on by seabirds. Every house turned out to be empty, though in good order.

"They evacuated everyone," said Rick, looking around.

"Not surprising," said Kowalski. "Winter's coming. They probably thought it was a good idea to get out while they could. Pretty isolated here. Most of the settlements are on the west coast. Nobody lives in the interior, which is just one big glacier."

Rick peered into a house, seeing a seal skin coat hanging up.

Innuit. If they didn't think they could survive here, nobody could. Rick kicked in the door.

"That was someone's pride and joy, once," said Scott dryly.

"I don't think they're coming back," said Rick. He tried on the coat. It was a little tight under the arms, but it was a hell of a lot warmer than the sweater. He turned to Kowalski. "What about the plane? Can you fix it so it doesn't try to kill us again?"

"I don't know. If we can find some tools, maybe I can do something."

"Make sure you do, because we're stuck here with no other transport. I mean, even Shackleton had a boat."

Scott started a fire and roasted the seal meat while Kowalski worked on the engine. He'd drained a quart of fuel from each of the wing tanks to eliminate the chance of water droplets in the gas and was now dismantling the air filter.

"Pass me that wrench there," he said.

Rick passed it up. They'd found tools and a box of spares in the airport workshop. Being the most common plane in the world helped a lot at a time like this.

"See if you can find me some anti-icing fluid," said Kowalski.

"What does it look like?"

Kowalski peered out from underneath the engine, an incredulous look on his face. "It'll be labeled?"

"Right."

Rick mosied around the workshop until he found a plastic container with green fluid in it.

"Get a cloth and rub it liberally along the wing edges," called Kowalski.

The smell of cooked meat drifted across. The light was fading and Rick was anxious about getting the engine going again before it got too dark. He didn't want to wake up with the thought of still being stuck here.

"And don't forget the pitot tube," said Kowalski.

"Which part's that?"

"It's a tube. Right there. Underside of the wing."

Feeling like a dummy, Rick set to work.

"Hey guys, this meat's nearly ready," called Scott. "And it's delicious."

"How about not eating it before we get there?" said Rick.

"Couldn't help myself. Had to test it."

Rick's stomach growled as he swabbed the wing. "What's it taste like?"

"Like the greasiest burger you've ever had."

Rick wished he hadn't asked. Images of giant burgers floated through his mind.

"I got it," called Kowalski.

Rick turned. "What?"

Kowalski held up a rusted metal frame with a grille. "Air filter's split, and the drain hole in the air box is blocked. Rusty as hell."

"That's what caused the engine to fail?"

"I hope so, because I don't know enough about this engine to strip it down further. I can change the filter, dry out the plugs and drain the carb. Then we'll see."

It seemed, to Rick, to be an incredibly minor thing, considering the potential effect in the air. He remembered Scott's comments about the state of the airplane back in Syria. "Is this still airworthy enough to get us to the States?"

Kowalski pouted. "To be honest, I'm surprised it's gotten us this far. Didn't want to put you guys off or anything, but I thought we'd get stranded a lot sooner."

Rick didn't need that kind of honesty right now.

"What did he say?" called Scott.

"He said it'll get us there easy," explained Rick.

Kowalski grinned. "Oh, sure," he said loudly.

"You lying fuck," said Scott. "You get that thing started or I'm going to eat your share of the meat."

Kowalski feigned shock. "First you offer to have my babies, now you want to eat my meat. If I didn't know better, Scott, I'd say you had a thing for me."

Rick laughed hard. Twenty minutes later, Kowalski primed the engine and swung the prop. It caught first time and there were grins all round as the motor chugged steadily.

As the night set in, they sat round the fire and ate until they were full. Rick proffered the small bottle of whiskey. "Gentlemen, I think we've earned this."

Overhead, the last of the cloud passed and the stars glittered in the frigid air. "Here's to the last leg."

38

Daisy woke to the sound of distant thunder. The slow rumble sounded like the night sky was crumpling. She hoped it heralded rain. There wasn't a drop of liquid left in the house, and it was still too dangerous to go down to the creek. Her mouth was parched and she worried about the children's needs. Another day was probably all they could stand. After that, she would have to risk a walk down to the creek. She refused the idea of sending Josh – he'd suffered enough – but her hip twinged already at the thought of the journey.

No matter. If they did not get water soon, they would die. It was a dreadful choice, but soon it would be no choice at all.

The thunder rumbled again. It was late in the season for such things, but she hoped it was an overdue summer storm. It might not mean rain, however. She remembered the lightning on that dreadful night of the solar flare, and wondered if this was the same. Perhaps it had altered the climate, making dry thunderstorms more likely now.

Lying next to her in the bed, Lizzy breathed steadily, sleeping soundly. Josh, however, on the other side of the crowded bed, had stopped his heavy sighs, and Daisy guessed he'd woken up and was listening, just like her. He'd grown tense and jumpy, and she worried about him. She was no longer able to comfort him like a little boy, and he'd long refused hugs, but the haunted look in his eyes made her want to gather him to her.

Drifting off to sleep, she snapped awake again at the sound of another crash.

It was not the thunder this time, however. It was too close.

Another thump echoed through the house, waking Lizzy and making her sit bolt upright. Daisy put a hand to her shoulder, hoping she'd stay silent.

Someone was trying to break down the front door. Slowly, Daisy stretched out a trembling hand to the revolver on the dresser. The sideboard against the door was heavy: at least for her and the children. To a strong person, it might not prove to be much of an obstacle at all. Daisy listened to her palpitating heart, wondering if this was the moment she would have to confront an intruder.

The shattering of the bedroom window startled her, and Lizzy screamed. Barely able to breath, Daisy pulled back the heavy hammer. Another piece of the window broke, a heavy object thudding against the drapes, and Daisy pointed the gun and fired.

The boom was tremendously loud in the room, and another piece of glass shattered as the bullet flew out. Deafened, and blinded by the flash, Daisy gasped for breath and fumbled with the hammer, expecting the intruder to climb in.

Nothing else happened, and as her hearing cleared, the house resumed its silent slumber. Through the broken window, the sound of crickets returned.

Had she hit the intruder? Was he dead?

Daisy dared not investigate, and in fact was too afraid to move, lest she make a sound with the bed springs. The clock on the other side of the house ticked steadily, and the distant thunder rolled again. Seconds turned to minutes, and the minutes drew forth into an hour, but neither Daisy nor the children would sleep more that night. Instead, Daisy, clutching the revolver, prayed for the dawn.

39

Lauren too wanted the dawn to arrive, if only to alleviate the spooky atmosphere of the inside of the old saw mill being lit with candles. The broken roof high overhead had enough steel sheets on it to block most of the stars, and the rusted saw blades sticking up from the piles of fallen beams, and the chains that hung from the iron gantries, gave the place the flavor of a horror movie.

"It looks pretty, doesn't it?" said the guy with the hunting rifle. "It gives it a certain ambiance. This place doesn't look much during the day, but the mixture of decay and candlelight highlights the romance."

Lauren knew the guy's name was Neil. The chubby guy with the shotgun was Tyrone, and the salivating brute with the band aid was Bud. She knew because Neil had taken the time to introduce them all. Neil had taken a liking to her and was trying to be nice.

It hadn't prevented Lauren from having her hands and feet tied and dumped on the rough mill floor. Bud had taken an interest in her, caressing her cheek with a Bowie knife and trying to thrust his hand down her pants. She'd struggled hard against him, kicking out, and when he tried to lie on top of her, she'd bitten him. That was why she was now gagged with a dirty cloth. In his outrage Bud had slapped her about until Neil pulled him off and sent him away.

Lauren wasn't fooled by the apparent kindness. It was a good cop, bad cop routine, and the look in Neil's eyes told her what he really wanted.

He didn't just want to rape her. He wanted a certain compliance. Maybe he wanted to kid himself that she'd prefer to give herself to him in return for some leniency and protection.

Lying on her side, her legs ready to kick out again, she glared balefully at him.

April lay a few feet away, her boy sitting close beside her, unbound but clutching his stomach, like he had a bad belly ache. Tense and watchful, he stayed quiet. April, on the other hand, wouldn't stop talking. Fidgeting constantly, she'd offered herself to the men if only they'd cut her loose and suggested all kinds of favors she could do if she had her hands free. Lauren listened with faint disgust. Back at the river, she'd put on a performance to prevent them taking Daniel from her, screaming hysterically. Now she was the smooth tongued diva, surrendering herself to the compromises a woman had to make to please a man. Or so she said. Lauren, seeing a different side to April, wondered if this was how she'd behaved with that gang member back in Baltimore. If so, it hadn't helped, and when these guys finished their eating, it was going to get ugly.

They ignored April for the time being, however, preferring to concentrate on Lauren. Neil regarded her as the greatest prize, and the others deferred to his judgment, letting him make the first move before choosing. Considering how they looked across to her from the fire, it was clear they'd already made their choice. April might be the dessert, but Lauren was both starter and main course, a veritable buffet for their pent up carnal desires. What would happen after that was not clear, but Lauren wasn't optimistic. The men seemed to be using the mill as a base, but once they'd harvested everything within range, they'd probably move on, and they likely wouldn't want burdensome captives who'd need feeding and watching. Not when they could easily get more. Lauren considered that, to stay alive in the coming days, she'd be better to do what April did, and make herself indispensable to the men, Neil especially. But she was damned if she was going to do that. She was so angry at them, and at herself for having been dumb enough to get herself caught, that she wanted to make them wish they'd never set eyes on her.

In the center of the floor were stacks of food, tools, camping equipment and a variety of other items acquired from their looting sprees. Lauren thought about those beautiful houses in the woods, isolated from each other and easy prey for this gang, taking them out one by one. It was the equivalent of going out shopping with unlimited credit. All three were dressed in the finest outdoor clothing from the most expensive brands. Neil had even taken the trouble to shave, priding himself in his new identity. Lauren got the sense he'd never had it so good, in spite of his affected philosophical musings.

"These aren't the end times. These are the beginning times. A new beginning. You want to ask yourself a question: do you want to be part of the new, or the old?"

Lauren wanted to tell him he was talking garbage, but the gag prevented that.

"Only you can make that choice," he continued. "The old has been laid to waste, and seriously, who wants to go back to that? Watching the clock, worrying that you'll be late for work. Paying endless bills. Insurance. Tax. It was never ending. And for what? A 401k retirement plan that's never going to be enough to fund what you really want to do in life, and which you've wasted most of your life waiting for."

He put his hand on her thigh.

"It doesn't have to be that way, and there's no need to wait any more. Might as well live for the moment. Enjoy life. And each other. There's no shame in that."

Lauren wriggled his hand off. Neil appeared amused. Reaching into his top pocket, he pulled out a cop badge.

"This is the old order," he said, tapping the badge. "This guy begged for his life when we caught him. He'd shed his uniform and was running away. Forgot all about that Protect and Serve crap. He didn't have any faith that all them folks in DC would be able to bring the old order back. And he was right." Neil toyed with the badge. "All their levers of power have gone. You see, they never had the power they thought they had. It was all an illusion, and people could have overturned it if they'd risen up like they should have. But they were just sheep." Neil tossed the badge and it clattered to the floor. "We're all animals really, but there's different kinds. Better to be at the top of the apex than down at the bottom eating the grass, I say. I like my meat." He thrust his hand between Lauren's legs. "You'll like my meat too, if you just let yourself. Give it up and taste the pleasure. Because why not? Enjoy it. There's no point screaming, because no one's going to hear you."

Lauren didn't waste time screaming. As Neil tried to pull her pants off, she bucked and kicked, arching her body, bringing her knees up against him and headbutting him whenever he got close enough. Pinning her down, he slapped her a few times, but she continued to struggle with all her strength until he sprang back, touching his bleeding lip from where she'd banged her skull against him.

Picking up his rifle, he aimed it at her. "Keep still, or I'm going to put one right through you."

The gag had come loose in the struggle and Lauren shouted back, "Go to hell!"

He looked for a moment as if he would pull the trigger, his face twisting in anger to reveal the kind of person he truly was, the fake persona disappearing. To do so, however, would rob him of the living body he wanted to make his.

He turned to look at little Daniel. "Hey you! Kid! Come here."

Daniel looked up, confusion on his face. "You stay right there, baby," said April, still fidgeting. "Stay close. The man don't want you really. He wants a little pleasure, that's all. And we can give him that. You stay close."

Lauren, her face burning and her head spinning, wondered what the hell she was talking about. April's words didn't really make sense. As her vision cleared, however, she noticed something she hadn't seen before. Thrown about in her struggle and coming to rest in a different location, she had a clearer view of April's hands, and suddenly the constant fidgeting made sense.

April almost had her hands clear of the zip tie.

Neil, too angry to notice anything amiss, strode over, grabbed Daniel by his coat hood, and yanked him over until he had the boy dangling in his hand. Pressing the barrel of the rifle against the child, Neil addressed Lauren. "Last chance. You lie still, or I'm going to fill this little shit full of lead."

"Baby," screamed April, rolling over and fighting to pull her hand all the way out of the tie.

Lauren looked up at Daniel, realizing it wouldn't make any difference. The choice of whether he would live or die was ultimately hers.

That was the moment the Ruger hidden down the front of Daniel's coat slipped out and clattered to the floor.

There was a moment of stunned silence all round. Several things made sense to Lauren, then. Like why April had been declared 'clean' when she was searched by Bud back at the river. Lauren, distracted by her shame, thought she'd simply misheard. But April, hugging her boy, had slid the pistol into his coat. It was why he was hugging his stomach. And why she urged him to stay close.

"You son of a -" began Neil.

He never got to finish. Coiling herself like a spring, Lauren kicked out hard with both tied feet, connecting with his leg and knocking it out from under him. Both he and Daniel came tumbling down, the rifle sliding along the floor.

Daniel scampered away, Neil clambered over Lauren to reach for the Ruger, and Lauren swung her legs, kicking the pistol towards April. Neil smashed his elbow down onto Lauren's face as a punishment, and April yanked her hand free.

Lauren didn't see too clearly what happened next. Her nose had been crushed and her eyes were streaming. She simply heard the pistol shot, and felt Neil jerking back.

Blinking hard, she saw Neil gasping like a landed fish, a spreading pool of blood on his chest. His legs spasmed, and he flopped over onto his face, staring at the floor and trembling.

April had the gun in her hand, but her legs were still tied. Momentarily shocked by what she'd done, she turned when she saw Tyrone running for his shotgun. She fired, but Tyrone was over ten yards away, and that was too much for her rudimentary aim. The bullet went wide and Tyrone, ducking, reached his shotgun and blasted back.

His aim turned out to be as bad as April's, and he took out part of the wall paneling behind her.

She fired again, causing him to run for cover, and he fired back, hitting a pillar this time. Bud, a little further back, pulled out his revolver and fired, but he couldn't hit anything either. As they traded badly aimed shots, Neil gave one last twitch and died.

Lauren knew this one sided battle wouldn't last long. It would only take one lucky hit and April would be down. Jerking her body, she tried to break the ties on her arms and legs. The plastic cut deep into her wrists, and no matter what she did, she couldn't do what April had done. The tie was too strong and too tight. Her legs, however, had more power, and she twisted and stretched the zip tie, even as it sliced into her flesh. Straining hard, she finally snapped the plastic. Rolling over and jumping up, she careered into the wall, held herself up, then began rubbing the tie holding her wrists against an exposed steel beam.

Pounded by near misses, April finally remembered the training Lauren had given her and held the pistol steady in a two handed grip. Aiming carefully, she fired as Tyrone leaned out from cover, catching him in the shoulder. The shotgun flew up into the air and Tyrone staggered back. April fired five rapid shots. Only two connected, but one was to Tyrone's throat. He dropped like a sack, gurgling, his hands vainly trying to stem the blood flow.

Bud, having emptied his chamber and hit nothing, decided it was time to go. April fired a hasty last shot as he headed for the door, but she couldn't track him and the bullet flew wide. With her legs still tied, she couldn't follow him.

Lauren rubbed the tie furiously against the pillar and strained against the plastic until it finally snapped. Without hesitation, she snatched up the hunting rifle and ran to the door.

The stars lit the sky, and a new moon shone up the side of the pickup, which was parked at the edge of the wood. A silhouette moved against the reflection. Lauren lifted the rifle and put her eye to the scope. The wide scope gathered and focused the little extra light, revealing the vague figure of Bud running for his life. Lauren aimed for center mass and squeezed the trigger. There was a loud crack in the night, and the figure fell as the large caliber round knocked him down.

Lauren would once have said she'd never shoot a fleeing man in the back. April was right, though. These weren't normal times, and he was still a threat.

Working the bolt action to load another round, she approached him. He lay perfectly still, and after prodding him a few times, she checked his pulse.

Nothing. He wasn't a threat anymore.

Back inside, April hugged Daniel tight and sobbed. Lauren thought something had happened to the boy – so many bullets had been flying, he might have been caught in the crossfire. He was nuzzling his mother's neck, however, and appeared to be fine. Lauren lowered herself down to sit cross-legged on the floor, light headed and tasting the blood that dripped from her nose.

"Are they all dead?" murmured April.

"Yes," said Lauren, flatly.

April wiped her eyes. "Oh my God, I didn't think we were going to get through this."

"You did good."

"I tried to get them to leave you alone. I tried to distract them."

"I know. I didn't realize what you were doing. I'm sorry, but I underestimated you."

"Ain't no bother. Oh my God, I can't believe what I just did. I was trying, and thinking, and praying that we'd get out of this. Oh my baby, I'm sorry for what I did."

She hugged Daniel tightly again, and Lauren could see she was still in shock, the post-action adrenaline causing her to blurt out random stuff. Lauren sat quietly, surprised at how calm she herself felt. It was like she was too tired to feel excited about anything anymore.

"How'd you get out of those cuffs?"

"Huh?"

"The cuffs. How'd you get out of them so easily? Mine were so tight, they were cutting into me."

"Oh, them. Watched a video on how to get out of them. Lock your fists sideways when they tie them. More space between the wrists. I told you I was prepping."

Lauren lay down, feeling she could sleep for a week. "You saved the day, April. Smart, smart move."

Daniel broke his long silence. "Smart Mommy."

April wept and rocked him in her arms.

40

As dawn's light filtered in, Daisy shuffled to the window, parting the curtains slightly. She dreaded the thought of seeing a body outside, or the blood trail left by a wounded looter, but there was nothing. Whatever she'd shot at the night before had gotten clean away.

She wasn't sure whether that made her feel better or worse.

The broken window was a problem now. She needed to board it up, but the tools and nails were all in the garage, and she wasn't sure there were any panels in there. She left that side of things to Harold, and the garage was his, just as the house was hers. They'd never kept a car in it. It was just a place for Harold to store his junk.

It might well be a safer place to sleep at night, seeing as the only window was a small pane in the side door. The house was a bad place to be besieged in, she could see that now. Unless she boarded up every single window, there was little to prevent someone getting in if they really wanted to, and she didn't relish the thought of patrolling every room at night to guard against that.

There also remained the pressing problem of food and water, with the latter being the most important. It meant she had to venture out, at some point.

She remembered then that some of those fancy new houses had pools in their gardens. She might not have to go as far as the creek. The water might be chlorinated, but it was possible that it could be drunk. She'd swallowed water at the public swimming pool a few times, and it hadn't done her any harm. At least it was clean and pestilence free.

Leaving the house was a risk, but she had the revolver, and she'd fired it once already. If she'd scared the intruder off, he might have left the area, looking for easier pickings.

And they only seemed to come at night.

"I'm sick of being cooped up, here," she told the children. "We'll clear a space out in the garage and drag a mattress there. We'll sleep safer at night. And we need to go out and get some water."

The children looked at her, a little bewildered. It wasn't clear how much of an appetite they had for exploring outside, but it was down to her to offer some leadership. Glimpsing renewed hope in their eyes, she knew she was doing the right thing. Cowering at home like frightened kittens was bad for all of them.

"Okay, let's do this thing."

Grabbing the keys to the garage, she had the children check the view from all the windows to make sure both the street and the garden were clear. Enlisting Josh to help her move the table away from the back door, she unlocked it and peered out, gun at the ready.

A squirrel scampered up the tree in next door's garden, but otherwise, everything was quiet. She figured that, if they kept all noise to a minimum, they should be able to clear out the garage without attracting attention. There was so much junk in there, however, that Daisy wasn't sure how long it would take. Or what she would find.

No matter, they only needed to clear a space large enough to sleep in. After that would come the riskier job of scavenging.

Making sure the children stayed behind her, she made her way across the lawn, feeling exposed. Looking around, she slipped the key in the lock.

The key wouldn't turn, however, and she berated herself as she realized she'd left the door unlocked. Perfectly normal for the way things were before, but she realized that such habits needed to change.

Opening the door, she peered into the gloom, groaning inwardly at the sight of all the junk. Making rough calculations, she guessed it was going to take longer than she thought to get most of it out.

She stepped in and was immediately bounced back by a blow to the chest. Gasping in surprise, she looked down and saw a knife embedded between her breasts. The knife was tied to the end of a long pole. Following the pole back into the garage, Daisy saw the rough hands that grasped it, and the shadow of the man hiding by the door.

She tried to shout, tried to bring the revolver up, but the excruciating pain in her chest drained away her energy, and she couldn't breathe.

Josh heard the faint sucking noise of the knife going in, but wasn't aware of what happened until his grandma came staggering out, pushed by what appeared to be a pole. As soon as he saw the man pushing it, he froze, recognizing the face as the man who'd confronted him after finding Skye's dead body. The same man he'd seen coming down his street.

Grandma fell, and the man pulled out his improvised spear and stabbed her again.

"Get me some food," he bellowed at the children.

In spite of being dehydrated, Josh urinated involuntarily in his pants.

The man reached down to pluck the revolver from Grandma's limp grip. "You know where it is," he snarled. "Show me."

Josh stared at his grandmother, traumatized. Mouth open, she gazed sightless at the sky.

The man pointed the revolver at Josh, the barrel looking large and ominous. "Get some," said the man. The gun trembled in his hand, and he looked crazy. When Josh, rooted to the ground, failed to move, the man turned the wavering gun to Lizzy. "Get me some food or I'll shoot the little girl."

For a moment, Josh didn't know what to do. Then he grabbed Lizzy's hand. "Run," he shouted, pulling her along.

The gun boomed, and a clod of earth jumped up nearby. Josh ran straight to the fence and threw himself over, his hand arrested when Lizzy stopped dead. She couldn't get over the fence by herself.

Josh reached over and grabbed her, dragging her over, and the gun boomed again, taking a chunk out of the fence. Stumbling over on the neighbor's lawn, Josh pulled Lizzy with him behind a bush and towards the path at the side of the building that led to the road. Risking a glance behind, Josh saw the man running, spear in one hand, gun in the other. The man clumsily hurdled the fence, tripped over, landed flat on his face, then got up again to continue the pursuit.

Out on the road, Josh picked up the pace, but his sister dragged behind, barely able to keep up. He wasn't going to be able to outrun the man this way. Deviating right, he dashed past a house and into a garden, jumping over flower beds. At the fence, he lifted his sister over and clambered after her, grabbing her hand and running again. The man ran into the garden after them, panting heavily, and Josh led his sister across more flower beds, past a pool and out onto another street. Turning left, he dragged his sister along then turned left again, back into the houses, running through a gap into another garden. He couldn't see the man behind him, so he scrambled over a fence again, across a yard and back onto his own street. In this way, he zigzagged through the neighborhood until, certain he'd shaken his pursuer, he dodged into another garden and behind a pair of wheeled trash cans.

Trembling and heaving for breath, he listened for any sign that the man might be close, but all he could hear was his own heartbeat pounding in his ears.

Lizzy curled up against him, sobbing uncontrollably.

"Come on, dammit!"

Lauren pushed hard against the pickup, trying to get it to roll.

The yard behind the mill was small, and the pickup had been parked at one end of it. Lauren assumed that, with a good push, there was enough room to push-start the vehicle. That was how the men must have done it. The track that led out to the road was too bumpy.

Loading all the supplies they could find into the back of the pickup, April got into the cab and put it into gear, depressing the clutch. On her own, however, Lauren struggled to move the vehicle. Straining until she thought her veins would pop, she got it rolling, but it was moving too slow. Running out of yard, April released the clutch to see if they had enough momentum to start the engine.

They didn't. The vehicle juddered to an abrupt halt. Lauren slapped her hand on the truck in annoyance.

"There's got to be an easier way to do this," said April, leaning out of the cab.

Lauren, sweating, tightened the hunting rifle strap and walked round to the front, putting her hands on the bull bar. Birds twittered in the woods and the sun beat down. "Backwards now," she said. "Put it in reverse."

April rolled her eyes. She'd lost count of how many attempts they'd made. "Okay, have it your way."

Engaging the right gear, she pushed on the clutch and signaled. Taking a deep breath, Lauren pushed against the truck until her face was puce.

The Cessna's engine ran beautifully as they crossed the Davis Straits. With clear skies and good visibility, Rick took a turn at the controls. Gleaming icebergs sailed serenely below them in the blue waters. In spite of the positive view, Rick was impatient to get home, and he wanted to open the throttle.

Kowalski wouldn't let him touch it, however. He was running the engine lean to max out the range. Flying at ten thousand feet, it felt like they were barely moving at all. When the Canadian coastline crept into view, Rick's angst grew.

He felt so close, and yet so far.

41

As a young boy, Josh liked to imagine himself as a soldier in Vietnam, hiding in the foliage amid the tropical heat. He played with toy soldiers in his bedroom and watched war movies. It wasn't that he ever imagined becoming a soldier himself, and he never played at soldiers with the kids in the neighborhood – though they were never interested anyway, and he often felt excluded from the groups.

He played by himself because it was his one connection with his dad, his only way of mentally being with him. His dad's homecomings were a chance to curl up with him and watch movies, and he'd accompany his dad to the PX in Fort Bragg, surrounded by Humvees and marching recruits. Outside the base, his dad didn't bother with military trappings. Josh never saw him in uniform, and even his friends from the unit, when they came to visit the house, could have been guys from the bowling club. None had regulation hair cuts. Josh got the impression sometimes that his dad hated the army – the rules and the pomp – and acted like his own unit didn't belong to the army at all. He didn't talk about his work and he never flew a flag on his lawn.

As Josh got older, the homecomings would be more muted. His father always seemed tired, and Josh didn't curl up with him anymore. They did less together, and his dad watched movies alone while Mom worked longer hours. The purpose of his father's absences somehow got lost in all that. It was like he was now an oil rig worker or engineer, away on long jobs. When most of the troops came home after 2011, other soldiers in the neighborhood got rotated less, and the subject of war faded from the news. His father, however, continued to go out, disappearing for months. Playing with toy soldiers carried less meaning for Josh. Once he reached secondary school, he observed what was cool and what was not, and hung around the edges of new fashions and the obsession with personal appearance and fitting in with one subculture or other. But it all seemed transient and pointless. None of it moved him in the same way as playing with soldiers had.

Because once upon a time, that actually meant something. And his dad felt like his dad, and not just some visiting stranger.

Sitting now in the foliage of a bush, Josh remembered what it was like to be younger, sitting in the dark in his own garden with Mom calling for him to come in, then searching for him with threats of no supper.

He felt a pang for those lost days. Parched with thirst and weak from hunger, he tried to bring them back, recalling the feelings of certainty and security, when it was safe to imagine being somewhere more dangerous. And just pretend.

No such luck, now. With the crazy guy still on the loose, Josh and Lizzy had relocated, moving away from whatever noise they heard in the distance as objects were thrown and windows broken. The cloudy sky blocked out the stars and brought a darkness so total, Josh thought his eyes were permanently shut. Thunder rolled in the distance, and the air was humid and thick.

Lizzy slept fitfully, waking in starts and putting her arm out to check her brother was still there. He was all she had now. One by one, people had been taken out of their lives, and the loneliness of responsibility weighed heavily on Josh.

It was down to him now, and he didn't really know what to do. The night dragged on, but ideas – productive ideas – failed to come.

Rain drops started to patter on the leaves above his head. Pessimistically, he thought this was the last thing they needed, stuck outdoors as they were. It was only when the rain came down harder that he realized the opportunity. Shaking Lizzy awake, he slid out from the bush and lay down on his back, his mouth open as he tried to collect as much moisture as he could.

The deluge drenched his face and he held his hands out, catching the water and splashing it into his mouth. Soaked through, he pulled Lizzy out from the bush and cupped his hands, refreshing her dry lips.

It was all he could do to keep from laughing.

When the morning came, the sun emerged and steamed the moisture off the grass. Josh woke, damp and cramped. Shaking the bush, he licked at the last drops that came down. He couldn't believe his eyes when he saw what else he was shaking.

Cucumbers. They'd sheltered the night in someone's cucumber patch, and hidden under the large leaves were young, two-inch long cucumbers.

Like most kids, Josh had never been into salad, but he didn't hesitate to pick this new-found bounty before his eyes. Crunching into one, he savored the tart, juicy taste. Within seconds, he and Lizzy devoured the meager pickings. But there was more. Attached to the fence was a tomato vine. Most of the large fruit had been picked, presumably by the owners before they evacuated. Small green tomatoes, however, had budded since and, while not ripe, they tasted like heaven to the two starving children. Josh scoured the garden for more, then realized other gardens might contain the same.

Galvanized, he dragged Lizzy over the fences, searching. Most folks, it seemed, didn't bother growing their own food, but he did find an apple tree. Most of the lower offerings had been taken but, telling Lizzy to keep watch at the foot of the tree, he began to climb. Tucking his hoodie into his pants, he filled it with crisp, red apples and climbed carefully down, cautious not to crush them as he grasped the branches. Sitting in the shade of the tree, they gorged themselves until their stomachs ached and they felt lethargic and sleepy.

The house the garden belonged to was a two story new-build. Josh gazed at it thoughtfully. Urging his sister to follow him, he walked to the back door and peered in.

"What are you doing?" whispered Lizzy.

"There could be more food in there," said Josh. He picked up a stone garden ornament.

"Josh, don't," said Lizzy when she saw what he was about to do.

Josh stood back and heaved the ornament through the pane of the door, smashing it. Leaning forward, he sniffed the warm air that escaped through the hole he'd made. It was musty but it didn't smell bad.

Hopefully it meant there were no dead bodies inside. Reaching inside, he unlocked the catch and opened the door, beckoning to Lizzy.

"I don't want to go in," she said. "We shouldn't be doing this."

"It's empty," said Josh. "They're all empty."

"It's against the law," said Lizzy seriously.

Josh looked sadly at her. "There are no laws any more. We have to survive, Liz. That means doing things like this. Come on, it's safe."

Taking her by the hand, he entered a hallway. Lizzy stopped, refusing to go any further. "I'm scared," she said.

"Wait here, then."

Josh searched the kitchen and pantry. Unsurprisingly, he found nothing, and didn't expect to find anything anyway. He wasn't really looking for food.

He was searching for weapons.

From a wooden block, he drew a chef's knife. It felt sharp, with a reassuring weight in his hand, but he couldn't see himself entering into hand-to-hand combat with it. Not against that creep who'd murdered his grandma and hurt Skye.

He needed something more substantial.

The man had never been far from Josh's thoughts. Last night, desperate and weak, he only wanted to get away from him. Now, on a full stomach, he wanted more. The memory of what the man had done, burned. Running away meant leaving the area, and if his mom was really going to return, he had to be sure she could find them.

He also didn't want her to arrive at the house with that creep inside, waiting like he had for Grandma.

No. One way or another, he had to go.

He searched the rest of the ground floor. By the fake fireplace, he found an ornamental poker, but it didn't impress him. In the back room there was a full sized pool table with a rack of pool cues. He hefted one, liking the weight and the swing. It was okay, but he would have preferred a baseball bat.

Back out in the hall, he took Lizzy's hand and walked to the stairs. Seeing the knife he was carrying, she balked, but he persuaded her to follow him. Upstairs, he searched the dressers and closets. He was looking for a gun cabinet. It was a long shot, considering that the evacuees would have taken any guns with them, but maybe the people hadn't been at home when the storm struck. They were pretty wealthy, so maybe they were away on a business trip like Mom. Or perhaps they had another home somewhere. He tapped the walls for any hidden compartments or safes, but came up empty handed. He'd seen an advertisement once for hiding a rifle in a drop-down panel beneath a shelf, and searched those as well, but didn't find anything so exotic. A whip and handcuffs hanging at the back of a closet showed what was more to the owners' tastes, but it wasn't really to Josh's.

He was considering how to get into the attic space when he heard a creak on the stairs. He looked around and saw Lizzy wasn't with him anymore. He'd left her in one of the other rooms and he guessed she was trying to sneak back downstairs.

"Lizzy," he called, going out onto the landing.

He froze when he saw the man on the stairs, pointing Grandma's pistol at him. The man gave him a nasty grin, holding up a freshly eaten apple core.

"I knew I'd find you in the end," he said.

42

Before dawn, the Cessna was already crossing the US border. Rick had overridden Kowalski's objections to taking off while it was still dark. Passing over the Hudson River, the little plane flew by the blackened skyscrapers of New York, multiple empty window frames staring bleakly at them. Taking his turn at the controls, Rick opened the throttle and Kowalski, apart from looking at him, said nothing.

Below them, the New Jersey turnpike stretched south, and Rick thought about Lauren. Container trucks and trailers lay with debris in a wide circle around, like a giant fist had squashed each one, scattering its goods. Empty packaging blew across the highway, and groups of either looters or refugees moved about, looking like ants.

He hoped she wasn't down there.

Lauren was furious at having lost so much time. Frustrated at being unable to start the truck in the mill yard, they'd been forced to push it along the rutted track to the road, struggling to move it every time the wheel sank into a hole. It took them hours. When they finally got the truck started on the smooth highway, they'd lost most of the day and had to stop at nightfall, having traveled only a few miles. The truck had no working lights and they were too exhausted to go further. As soon as they had enough light to move in the morning, Lauren took the wheel and put her foot down.

Barreling down a road, they approached a town and saw a barricade across the highway, manned by armed men.

Lauren wasn't willing to negotiate passage.

"Get down," she told April.

Seeing what she was about to do, April grabbed Daniel and sank down off the seat, eyes wide.

Lauren lowered herself behind the steering wheel, weaving the vehicle erratically.

The barricade guards lifted their weapons hesitantly, unsure if this was a bluff. When the vehicle's momentum indicated it wasn't, they took aim and fired. The windscreen shattered, showering Lauren in glass, but she kept her foot on the gas, aiming for a weak spot in the barricade. The guards scattered and the pickup smashed its way through, bumping over the debris. Lauren fought with the wheel to keep the vehicle straight and powered through the center of the town, the engine roaring as bullets pocked the bodywork.

43

Holding a terrified Lizzy at gunpoint, the man forced Josh to climb back up the apple tree. "Get me as many as you can," he said.

Swaying on the thin upper branches, Josh reached for an apple, certain he was going to fall. After dropping one apple down, however, the man ordered him to get more. Wobbling precariously, Josh edged out for another. He knew that if he fell, the man would only send him up again, and the look on Lizzy's face compelled him to keep trying. He wanted to throw the apples down at the man's head, but knew it would do nothing. Worse, he feared the retaliation. Or what the man would do to his sister. Angry at himself for having been caught so easily, Josh leaned out further than he would normally have dared.

The man ate the apples voraciously, the barrel of the revolver pressed firmly against Lizzy's skull. When he judged Josh had gotten enough, he ordered him down.

"You're pretty useful," he said. "Let's see if you can do something else. Walk on ahead, and if you run, I'm just going to shoot the girl. Don't think that I won't."

Walking out onto the street, the man pointed to another house. "That one, there," he said.

It was the house that Josh had seen the chairman outside of. The one with the bodies in.

"The stink was too much for me," said the man. "But you can go in. Check out the kitchen, and don't try anything funny."

Reluctantly, Josh went up to the front door. The thought of what lay inside turned his stomach. Slowly, he turned the handle.

The stench hit him immediately and he wretched, throwing up the contents of his stomach.

"Bad, ain't it?" chuckled the man. "Now that you're empty, you should be able to get in there."

Spitting out pieces of apple, Josh covered his nose and ventured in.

The reek of death caused him to vomit again, bringing up acid and bile. Dropping to his hands and knees and coughing, he crawled to the kitchen.

Grabbing a towel to cover his face, he reached up into a cabinet and fumbled around, his eyes streaming. His hand fetched up on a can and he ran out of the house, dropping it on the stoop.

"Sweet Jesus, that ain't enough," said the man in disgust. "Get a bag, boy."

Drawing in the clean outside air, Josh braced himself and went back in. A frantic search through the drawers produced no bags, so he just grabbed more tins and threw them out the door.

All the time he was trying to think of what he could do about the man. A hunt for weapons in the house was out of the question. Josh didn't want to come across the bodies that were most certainly in an advanced state of decay. There was a knife on the counter, but it was too big to hide on his person and Josh had the same doubts as before about using it against the man. He couldn't think of a way he could harm him while he still held onto Lizzy.

Opening the windows to clear some of the odor, Josh threw out bags of pasta, flour and sugar. As they broke open and spilled on the paved path outside, he heard the man protest, but Josh was in a hurry to get out of there. Emptying the cabinets of everything he could see, he finally grabbed a sack of rice and a bottle of oil and staggered outside.

The man, gripping Lizzy's neck tightly, aimed the revolver at him. "That was just plain careless," he said. "Now get back inside and find some containers to put the flour and sugar into. I ain't licking it off the ground. Hurry up, before the ants get to them."

Wearily, Josh did as he was told, scooping up powder and grit. Then he went round the back to fetch a wheelbarrow as ordered, and loaded up the food.

The rest of the morning was spent going into every house and clearing out anything edible he could find and wheeling it back to the house, the man casually following him. There was very little to clear out, and the only houses that yielded substantial finds were those where the occupants had died before they could eat their supplies. As Josh wretched and coughed outside each such house, the man lay on the lawns, waving the revolver at his sister's head and laughing softly.

"That'll teach you," he kept saying. "If you'd have done as I asked when I first asked you, this would all be over. Hell, we'd have had food for all of us. Could be we'd be sitting down at a picnic, like one big happy family."

Josh glowered, but could do nothing.

By midday, the man felt they had enough food and marched the children back to the house. Sitting in Grandma's chair with Lizzy on his lap, he opened a can of peaches. "Get yourself something to eat, boy. You're going to need the energy for this afternoon. You're going to discover what a hard day's work is like."

Josh sullenly stared at him. Hungry as he felt, he wasn't going to give the man the satisfaction of his compliance.

The man sneered. "Have it your way. But you'll learn."

Pulling the knife out of his belt – the same knife he'd used to kill Grandma – he spiked a peach slice with it and ate. He watched Josh as he did so, the revolver still in his hand, and Josh watched him back. Amused by Josh's defiance, he speared another peach slice and held it to Lizzy's mouth.

Lizzy recoiled from the offering on the blood stained blade, and Josh started at the sight of the knife so close to his sister's face. There was a click as the man cocked the revolver.

"You'd better eat, girly," he said. "Your loving brother wants you to grow up healthy and strong."

Lizzy's eyes welled up with tears, staring at her brother. Josh wanted to rush in to save her. He wanted to smash the man's face to pulp.

Swallowing her sobs, Lizzy delicately closed her lips around the peach slice, sliding it off the knife.

"There, that's good," said the man. "See? It's not so hard."

The man finished off the rest of the can, chomping triumphantly.

"There's a bucket in the hall," he told Josh. "Get me some water. And not from some pool. I like it fresh. Get yourself down to the creek."

Josh didn't want to leave Lizzy, and her eyes implored him not to go, but the revolver was still cocked, and still aimed at her head. Silently willing her to understand, he edged out of the room, grabbed the bucket and ran out the front door.

He slowed to a walk when he was out of sight of the house. He had no intention of going to the creek. Instead he looked around at some of the houses he'd entered, his thoughts focused on what could be useful to him.

The clock ticked in the house. The man clicked his teeth. Lizzy turned her neck slightly to loosen his tight grip. She didn't dare move more than that.

The man de-cocked the revolver. He tapped the barrel against the table a few times. He scratched his beard growth. He twitched his leg.

"Jesus Christ," he exclaimed. "That clock is going to drive me crazy."

He tapped the revolver against the table some more. Scratched his beard again. Twitched his leg until his heel was hammering on the floor.

"That's it. I've had enough," he said, springing up. Pushing Lizzy before him, he steered her to Grandma's bedroom. Grabbing the clock, he tossed it through the window, smashing the glass.

"That's better," he said.

Lizzy stood stock still.

"Time flies, huh?" he said, laughing to himself.

Lizzy didn't reply.

"Jesus, you're no fun. I thought kids were supposed to be fun."

He exhaled loudly and clicked his teeth again.

He pulled the drawers out in a dresser, shaking the contents loose, kicked the bed to move it, then rifled through the clothes in the closet. "What's the point of having all this crap?" he said. "Ain't no use to me now, is it?"

Unaware that it was supposed to be, Lizzy averted her gaze to avoid seeing her grandparents' belongings treated like dirt.

Bored of the bedroom, the man steered her towards the kitchen, looking out into the garden. Lizzy shut her eyes, not wanting to see the body of her grandma still lying by the garage. She was finding it difficult to breathe now, and it wasn't because of the man's grip. Terror froze her lungs, and she thought she was going to have an asthma attack like her friend Dorothy used to have.

"Now that there is what happens when people get unreasonable," he said. "That your grandma? Huh? Well, it's a shame, but a man don't take kindly to being shot at."

Quivering with tension, Lizzy snapped. "You broke into our house."

"You can speak, then? I was starting to wonder. Broke into your house? Yeah, same as you and your brother were doing when I caught you. What goes around comes around, kid. Ain't no point complaining now. Live by the sword, die by the sword, that's what I say."

The man laid the revolver down on the kitchen counter and twirled it a few times. Lizzy didn't know much about psychology, or drug addiction, but she knew something wasn't right with him. He couldn't keep still. There was no telling what he was going to do next. Lizzy's gut was heavy with the thought that neither she nor Josh were going to make it to nightfall. Josh especially. The man had a special grudge against him. Lizzy bit her lip.

"You gonna cry now?" he said, snatching up the revolver again. "Jeez, your grandma's been dead since yesterday. Get over it. When my grandma died, it didn't bother me much. I was doing a spell inside, at the time, but the news was no biggie. I didn't like her that much, anyway."

He dragged her along with him until they were in her bedroom.

"Are these all your pictures?" he said, a touch of wonder in his voice.

Lizzy opened her eyes. For the past few days she'd been drawing constantly, and her pictures were lined up the full length of one wall.

"Now, I like these." He peered closer, like an art aficionado. "You sure draw a lot of planes and cars."

Several of the pictures featured different shaped planes, flying alone in the sky. The cars all had two women in them, their hair swept back in the breeze.

"Why's there a bear in every car?" he asked. "And two women? Does that mean something?"

Lizzy refused to answer.

"I used to like drawing when I was inside. Took lessons. You need more perspective on some of these. Get the angles right."

Lizzy had no idea what he was talking about.

The man sorted through the drawers, just like in the other room. "Not even a lighter," he said. "Doesn't anyone smoke around here?" The man snorted in disgust. "Hey, that boy's taking his time. You don't think he's run off, do you? Seemed to be awful keen to get out of the door. You think he's gone and left you? I got a brother who'd do that."

The man stopped, as if troubled by a memory.

"Oh yeah, he'd do that."

He steered her back to the living room. He was checking the soil of the dead potted plants to see if there was anything hidden there when Josh returned, his bucket full of water.

"About time," said the man. "Drop it right there and get me a cup."

Josh backed away slowly to the kitchen, trying to control his breathing. His heart hammered. Fetching a cup he returned, holding it out for the man.

"What's the matter with you boy? You look like you need a crap real bad. Something wrong with the water? You trying to poison me, is that it? You take a drink first, and I ain't taking no for an answer."

Josh made an effort to control his nerves and approached the bucket, dipping the cup. Without hesitation, he drank it.

It tasted of chlorine, but it could have been worse. Leaving the cup by the bucket, he stepped well back.

The man eyed him suspiciously, and Josh focused his gaze on Lizzy, trying to see if she was okay. She looked back at him, and her eyes widened, as if she saw something wasn't quite right about him. Josh put on his best fake smile for her, but that only made her more concerned.

The man put his arm over Lizzy's shoulder, using it to pick up the cup while keeping her pinned to him with his elbow on her chest. The revolver remained in the other hand, pointed to one side. He took a sip of the water, savored it, then spat it out.

"Jesus, this is pool water! What the hell have you been doing all this time? You could have been to the creek and back three times by now."

Josh wasn't listening. He was reaching to the whip tucked into the back of his pants. Taking the handle, he shook it out to uncoil it, and then lashed out with it.

In the house where he'd found it, he'd practiced over and over, trying to get it to wrap around the target right. When he used to watch Indiana Jones movies with his dad, he'd practice the same thing in the garden with a piece of rope, and got pretty good with it. Right now, his heart was in his mouth as he realized he only had the one chance.

He was aiming for the revolver. He thought if he could entangle it and yank it out of the man's grip, he could get it himself. His aim wasn't quite so good, though. The synthetic whip lashed the man's hand instead, without wrapping itself around anything.

The man reacted like he'd been stung by a bee, jerking his hand back and releasing the revolver.

It tumbled to the floor. Like a released spring, Josh dived forward, groping for the weapon. The man danced around, still pissed about his hand, and Josh's fingers grasped the revolver, jerking it back when the man tried to kick him.

Josh had never fired a gun. Didn't realize how heavy the trigger would be on double action. Aiming for the man, he fired the gun, jerking it sideways at the same time. A chunk of plaster blew out by the man's head. By the time Josh realized he'd missed, the man had grabbed Lizzy and run out the front door with her.

Recovering too slowly, Josh scrambled up, dashed out after him, and stopped dead.

The man was crouched behind Lizzy on the lawn, and he had the knife pressed up against her throat.

"Oh, I should have known," said the man, disappointed and angry. "Something wasn't right about you when you came back. I should have seen that. Smart move, but you ain't smarter than me. Put the gun down now, or I swear I'm going to slit your sister's throat from one ear to the other."

Josh was under no illusions that the man would let him live if he put the revolver down. Nor even his sister. Holding the gun in both hands, and determined to hold it steady, he aimed it at what little he could see of the man's head. The gunsight looked huge, covering most of the man's skull and some of Lizzy's too.

The man crouched lower. "Don't do it, boy. You know you ain't got it in you. You'll hit your sister. Or I'll kill her and use her body as a shield. Either way, she's dead."

The gunsight wavered. Holding the gun out straight, he couldn't keep it steady, and the longer he waited, the heavier it felt. He could barely see the man's head now. Lowering the sights, he targeted the arm that held the knife, but the sights wavered between that and Lizzy's chest.

"I'm going to give you three seconds. Then, by God, I'm going to kill you both."

Josh held his breath, trying to keep the sight still.

"One!"

The gun wobbled, the trigger finger slick with sweat.

"Two!"

Josh had to take the shot, but he couldn't decide where to shoot. No matter where he aimed, Lizzy was there.

A drone began in his ear, getting louder. There was a sudden burst of sound, and a shadow passed overhead, an engine roaring. Looking up, Josh saw a plane passing so low over the rooftops, he thought he could reach up and touch it.

The man glanced up and laughed. "Time's up, boy. It's a beautiful sight, but I win."

44

Kowalski flew close to the center of Charlotte, and Rick looked out in dismay at the devastation. It was no different from the other cities, but to Rick it meant more, because this was where his family was. Bringing the plane down low, Kowalski lined it up with the Andrew Jackson Highway, trying to find a large enough gap between the abandoned vehicles. Touching down on the asphalt and leaving a wake of prop-blown litter, he taxied to a halt, leaving the engine running.

Rick and Scott were ready to leap out immediately. Leaning into the cockpit, Rick shook Kowalski's hand. "You have no idea how grateful I am," he said.

"I've got an idea how much," said Kowalski modestly.

Scott bumped fists with the pilot. "You're still an asshole, though," he said.

"Yeah, but it takes one to know one," grinned the pilot.

"Good luck, man," said Rick.

"You too. You'd better get moving."

As Kowalski opened the throttle and turned the plane around, Rick and Scott double timed it up the embankment and vaulted fences as they raced through neighborhood gardens.

Equipment jangling on his vest as he ran, Rick glanced apprehensively at the deserted streets, the downed power lines, the evidence of looting: everything he saw mocked him for arriving too late. Feet pounding as he careered round corners, he spurred himself on, his anxiety heightening by the second.

Reaching the head of the street where his parents-in-law lived, he scanned the houses, finally catching sight of a figure. As the scene swam into focus, he discerned the awful scenario he'd been dreading.

Some guy was on the lawn, holding his beloved daughter at knife point. Josh was aiming a pistol that was too big for him at the man, looking like he was going to shoot his own sister. Rick wanted to shout, but he was too far away. He skidded to a halt, snapping his rifle up to aim, but the range was too great to be sure of a clear shot.

Aiming anyway, the world dragged its feet in slow motion as his heart went into overdrive. He witnessed his son's wavering, unsteady hands. Saw the horror on his daughter's face as the knife was pulled tight to her throat. Rick's finger squeezed on the trigger, taking up the slack, all the while making calculations for the fall of shot.

A shadow fell across the scene as the Cessna roared low over the street, and the man looked up, moving his head clear of Lizzy's. Rick was about to take the shot when Josh's gun cracked, and the man jerked his head further back, a gout of blood arcing from his cheek. Lizzy wrestled herself free and took a step away. The man fell backwards, putting an arm down to catch himself, his body sagging, the knife flashing in his hand.

Rick didn't wait to see if the man was able to get up again. Pinning him in his sights, he pounded the trigger several times. Alongside him, Scott did the same. The man jerked and twisted as the bullets ripped him up, and he kept falling. Rick emptied his magazine until the body bounced and lay still.

Overhead, Kowalski made another low pass, waggled his wings farewell, and turned for home.

45

Lauren didn't arrive until it was nearly dark. Obstructions on the road, a leaking radiator and, at one point, a blowout, slowed her down on the numerous and confusing back roads. Pushing the ailing pickup to its limits, a high pitched knocking coming from its engine, she screeched round the last corner and onto her parents' street, skidding to a halt outside the house. She was astounded to see her husband in a rocking chair on the porch, cradling his children like babies, who were curled asleep on his chest.

It was like a mirage. Dumbstruck, Lauren got out of the cab, moving cautiously lest she disturb this dream. Her husband gazed at her, the saddest of smiles on his face. Lauren gazed back, the years falling away as she beheld the man she fell in love with a lifetime ago.

The children woke and, upon seeing her, uncurled themselves and rushed over to her. They looked exhausted, dirty and haggard. Their haunted eyes, especially, broke Lauren's heart. Clasping them to her, she broke down, sobbing. "I'm sorry. I'm so sorry."

Kissing them profusely and mussing up their greasy hair, she hugged them tight, as if she could squeeze every bad memory out of them. Wiping away the tears that blurred her vision, she focused on her husband, getting up slowly from his chair.

"Rick? What... how?"

"He's magic, Mommy," said Lizzy seriously. "He made an airplane."

Like some gaunt cowboy from an old Western, he ambled towards her, a faraway look in his eyes. Moving towards him, Lauren paused, hesitant. As he came closer, she tenderly touched his bearded face to see if he was real.

"For the record," he said, "I'm sorry too."

They embraced slowly and kissed fiercely, forgetting where they were for that one, precious moment.

"Where have you been?" she whispered.

"Away," he said, brushing a tear from her cheek. "In more ways than one. But I'm back."

Lauren rested her head on his shoulder. She recognized Scott by the front door, and he gave her a curt acknowledgment that, yes he was here, and no he wasn't going to get in the way of their tender moment. The grateful smile on her face melted when she noticed the broken windows, and that no one else emerged from the house.

"Where's Mom and Dad?" she said.

Rick shook his head gravely, and Lauren's eyes welled with fresh tears. "I should have been here," she cried.

"You did what you had to do," said Rick.

"I know, but..."

Rick put a finger to Lauren's lips. "It's done. We've both made mistakes, but we're here now. Got to focus on the future."

Lauren wanted to rage and shout. She wanted to scream at the sky for the damage it had wrought. For what it had done and what it had taken away. Getting a grip of herself, she took a deep breath and wiped her cheeks. "Yeah," she said. "The future."

She looked around. At her children. At April. At the abandoned, leaf blown street.

"The future," she murmured again.

It was going to come, no matter what. It didn't care what she thought about it. Her feelings and fears weren't about to make it change its mind. Nor its course. No other option but to prepare for it.

No other option at all.

"Winter's coming," she said. "Do you think we'll be ready?"

"Oh yeah."

Lauren nodded slowly in approval, her mind made up. "Okay. We'll talk more later. Let's get the gear out of the truck."

End

You have just finished reading *Solar Storm*, Book 1 of the Survival EMP series. Book 2, *Solar Winter*, is out now, following the survivors of the first book as they face the challenge of what comes after.

If you want to receive an exclusive email notification of further releases in the series, subscribe to my VIP List and get early warning of a bargain, pre-release price. Alternatively, give my Facebook page a like for similar news and updates.

Hope you enjoyed the book.

VIP List at: www.roblopez.co.uk
Facebook: www.facebook.com/roblopezbooks

What follows is the sample first chapter for the next book in the series, *Solar Winter*.

Solar Winter – Sample Chapter 1

With its old-fashioned charm and relative isolation, it could have been paradise.

Hugging the banks of the slow-flowing Cape Fear River, the hundred-acre farm was a snapshot of what it must have looked like when Scottish settlers came to this part of North Carolina, clearing the trees and planting their first crops in the loamy soil. Deer would have poked their inquisitive noses out of the surrounding woods, and flintlock muskets would have belched smoke to bag the first wild turkeys. Maybe the settlers would have seen Indians across the wide river, or paddling in their war canoes to trade pelts for trinkets, one warrior tribe to another. Wood would have been chopped and sawed, with chisels cutting notches for interlocking pieces. Barns and outbuildings will have been erected by multiple hands working in community. They would have been smaller, perhaps, than the large cypress barn Sergeant Rick Nolan was currently looking at, but the principle was the same. Running his hand along the rough, knotted fence, he pondered for a moment the grim train of fate that had brought him here.

The farm was paradise lost. The cleared fields, the rough pastures and the surrounding woodlands were filled with tents, tarps and strung washing. Flies hovered over the stinking latrine pits. Garbage littered the ground. Rowboats arriving from upriver unloaded stores on the bank, guarded by disheveled cops and unshaven soldiers. Shotguns and batons were wielded to keep back the crowds of people who gathered in the hope of getting food. A sheet hung on the side of the barn, crudely painted lettering proclaiming the presence of FEMA camp 107.

Many such camps existed now, and the Cape Fear River was the highway that linked them all. Since the solar storm fried the grid and put most vehicles out of action, the rivers returned to their traditional role of carrying freight. The only problem came from finding enough freight, and enough boats, to feed the exploding riverbank populations. The nearby city of Fayetteville, its store shelves bare, emptied its citizens toward the camps, and more came from farther afield. People arrived faster than the food, and even Fort Bragg, just fifteen miles to the north-west, struggled to cope. Not since the Civil War had so many military minds been forced to contemplate the age-old problem of how to supply massed armies using just hoof and oar. Except Civil War logisticians never had to contend with the issue of feeding every civilian as well. Plus, they had the advantage of steam power, trains and the telegraph.

Rick walked through the debris of cardboard packaging and empty MRE pouches. Vacant faces stared as he passed by in his dirty, bloodstained cargo pants and body armor – vaguely military, but not quite so. Questing eyes tried to ascertain whether he was an authority they could trust, or somebody they should be avoiding. Paranoia hung heavily over the clustered family groups in their sagging tents. Lone wolves prowled the camp, either because they were looking for something or because there was nothing better to do. Scavengers picked at the trash, hoping to find a crumb that somebody had missed. Patients lay in rows outside the medical tent, triaged by overworked nurses who had to choose between those they could help and those they couldn't. Anybody with a fever was left to sweat it out. Pamphlets trampled into the dirt warned of the risk of cholera from drinking untreated water. Bodies with sunken eyes and wrinkled hands lay by burial pits, patiently waiting to be interred. Grave diggers leaned on their shovels and hiked their kerchiefs over their noses as they waited for a bedraggled minister to bless the dead.

The inside of the cypress barn was stuffy and rank, with straw laid down on the concrete floor. In the stalls were mothers with young babies, given priority shelter under the high beamed roof. Rick strode past them all until he found Dee.

The last time he'd seen Dee, she was the bubbly blonde with the Meg Ryan hairstyle, joining him and the other guys from his small unit as they fraternally celebrated the end of another tour, taking over the bar of Carlos's joint in the early hours of the morning. Walt had proudly announced the news of her pregnancy, and got down on his knee to propose to her, theatrically pulling a ring from his pocket. After the tears and the hugs, they toasted the engagement and Walt's goofy smile as he contemplated fatherhood.

It seemed so long ago.

Dee's hair was dark at the roots now, and as wild as the hay left in the iron feeding cage at the end of the stall. The baby in her arms was swaddled and sleeping, its little mouth opening and closing as it sucked on an imaginary nipple.

Dee looked up as Rick's shadow fell across her. Wonder glowed on her features as recognition dawned, and she glanced behind him, looking to see who else had arrived. Her face crumpled when she realized Rick was alone, and the glow faded.

"They said you'd never make it back," said Dee, her voice breaking. "Now I wish you hadn't found me, because I know what you're going to say. I wanted to keep hoping."

"I'm sorry," said Rick heavily. He took a pair of metal ID tags from his pocket and held them out to her. "I did everything I could."

Dee took the tags, tears cutting tracks through the dirt on her cheeks as she ran her thumb over the embossed name and number of her fiancé. "Walt always said your team was the safest place to be. Said you would always lead them out. I wanted to believe you'd bring Walt back."

Rick didn't want to correct her on any of those points – didn't want to admit out loud the mistakes he felt he'd made. "I'm sorry," he said again.

"How many of the others made it out?" she asked.

"Just me and Scott."

Each word weighed a hundred pounds, and Rick felt guilty about being able to say them. A bunch of guys now couldn't. He gazed at the baby, remembering when his own children looked like that, and of the vow he made to keep them protected. He was sure Walt would have made the same.

"We need to get you out of here," he said.

Dee wiped her face and stared into the distance. "They said I couldn't get onto the base. Couldn't verify my ID because the systems were down. Said Major Connors was unavailable. Unable to contact him."

"We're not taking you to the base. We've got someplace else."

"I thought they'd take care of me, you know? Serving the flag and all. Thought they'd take care of their own."

"Forget Connors. You're as much a part of my team as Walt was. We take care of each other."

"They wouldn't let any of us in. There's a bunch of us here. It's so messed up."

Rick kicked at the straw with his boot. "None of that stuff matters now. You're coming with us."

The baby stirred, and Dee uncovered her breast to feed it. "Where to?"

Rick glanced around, aware that this conversation wasn't as private as he would have liked. "Somewhere that isn't here."

"Is it far?"

"Kind of."

"Secure?"

"It's a work in progress."

Dee moved the baby into a more comfortable position as it fed. "I can't really travel now. Maybe in a few months."

"Might be too late, then."

"It's too soon to go. It was tough enough getting here. I don't have a whole lot of energy, and I'd only slow you down. You're better off leaving me."

"I wouldn't leave a dog here."

"I'm not your dog, Sergeant Nolan."

Rick looked at her. Saw the defiant gaze, the protective embrace of the child.

"You know that's not what I meant."

In the opposite stall, another mother looked up and threw a glance of admonishment, like she didn't believe him.

"I've got friends here," said Dee. "We look out for each other. You know how that works, right?"

"I do."

Dee stroked the baby's head. "I didn't mean to patronize you. Just wanted to let you know how things are. I'm grateful you found me and all, and … told me about Walt. I …" Her voice broke again, and she squeezed her eyes tight to stop the tears. "I'm sorry. I'm trying to keep it all together. I knew something like this would happen. I just *knew*."

She dissolved into sobs, and the baby, sensing her distress, quit feeding and started crying too. The other mothers gathered around to console her, and Rick stepped back.

"I'll wait outside," he said to nobody in particular.

Down by the river, a fight had broken out, and the cops responded with batons, knocking a couple of guys down and pushing back a crowd that threatened to surge toward the supply boxes being carried to the farmhouse. Insults and hand gestures were thrown at the authorities. Around the camp, heads turned lazily toward the noise, like it was a regular occurrence.

Rick waited until the disturbance died down and a simmering indolence returned to the scene. A woman holding a baby came out of the barn.

"She says she wants you to go," said the woman.

Rick stared at her for a while but kept his thoughts to himself. Nodding once, he walked off.

Scott waited by the camp gate, looking like a hobo who just happened to find some body armor and a rifle. Lack of food left him more rangy and pop-eyed than ever, with a beard so unkempt it would have made a backwoodsman blush. Holding onto two bicycles, he chatted with two soldiers who also looked a little worse for wear. Walking up to him, Rick retrieved his M4 carbine and Glock.

"Is she coming?" asked Scott, turning from the conversation.

Rick shook his head, slinging the carbine and holstering the pistol.

One of the soldiers, a corporal, stepped forward. "Man, I just want to shake your hand. I can't believe you made it back from Syria."

Rick glared at him, as if he'd broken some protocol.

"They were just curious," explained Scott, knowing well the look on Rick's face. "No harm in telling them."

"Yeah, man," said the corporal. "It's a pretty amazing story."

"Then just keep it to yourself," said Rick brusquely. "There's guys out there who still haven't made it back, and folks here still waiting for news. I don't want them hearing rumors and hanging onto false hope."

"No, sure. I understand. But damn, what a journey. You guys are Delta Force, right? Real hardcore."

Rick clamped his jaw and Scott hastily intervened. "The corporal here was just telling me how things have been at the camp."

"Uh, yeah," said the corporal, glancing from one to the other. "It's been pretty bad, man. The other day, they were rushing the fences, demanding to know why we were getting fed more than them. I mean, do I look as if I'm getting my three meals a day? The pounds are falling off me, man, but some jerk spread the rumor around that we were withholding rations from them, so there we were, pointing rifles and yelling at them to stand down. Seconds away from a massacre, I tell you. Can't say I'd be sorry to administer some ballistic therapy to a couple of assholes in particular. They do nothing but bitch and whine, and they're getting the others riled up. Captain says we'll be getting some relief soon, but I ain't seeing none." The corporal leaned in and lowered his voice. "We've had guys skipping out, and I don't blame them. My folks are in Michigan and I ain't had word on how they're doing. If this keeps up … well, you know what I mean."

Rick certainly did. The system was breaking down, even here, and soon there'd be nothing to put back together, no matter how much people tried. He thought about Dee and contemplated going back one more time to try and persuade her. At least for the sake of the child.

On the other hand, he remembered her defiant look, and suspected he wouldn't get far with that. He wasn't good at persuasion. Didn't have the patience for it, which was why he was a soldier, not a diplomat.

By the camp gate was a wooden outbuilding, the side of which was covered in creased photos, hand drawn pictures and written notes – all pleas to locate missing loved ones, or to let others know they were here. A door opened and an officer who looked more disheveled than Scott stepped out, scratching his groin and dragging a pump-action shotgun.

The corporal groaned. "Looks like Captain Asshat's woken again. Stays in that shack whenever there's trouble outside. Says he's doing vital administration, but I think he's just jerking off. Started off highly strung and he's getting flakier every day. If the girl don't want to go with you, you can take him instead. It'd make my life easier."

The captain looked around until he fixed indignantly on the group at the gate. "Corporal," he shouted, "why are those civilians still armed?"

"They're not civilians, sir," called back the corporal.

The captain didn't appear to believe him and strode over, holding the shotgun out in both hands like a baton. "Who are you?" he said, addressing Rick. "Identify yourself."

Rick glanced back at him. "Sergeant Rick Nolan, 409522002."

"Why are you out of uniform?"

"Just back from deployment. Sir."

The captain appeared affronted that Rick didn't turn around to address him properly. "Where were you stationed?"

Rick rolled his eyes at Scott. "That's classified."

"What's your unit?" blustered the captain.

"That's classified too. Sir."

The captain circled around until he was face to face with Rick. "What gives you the right to be out of uniform, soldier?"

Rick didn't bother making eye contact. "You don't have to concern yourself with me, Captain. Simply go back to your shack and carry on with your job. Or exercise your wrist, I don't mind."

Rick took hold of his bike and made to move off, but the captain jumped in his way.

"I know your type," said the captain contemptuously. "You think that just because you're special forces you can disregard the chain of command. Stand to attention when I'm talking to you."

Rick narrowed his eyes at him. "Out of my way, Captain."

The captain failed to heed the warning. "That's an order, soldier. You either show me written confirmation of your assignment or I'll be forced to arrest you for insubordination and being absent without leave."

Rick kneed him savagely in the groin. As the captain doubled up, gasping for breath, Rick plucked the shotgun out of his hands and tossed the weapon to the corporal. "You want to be careful there, Captain. You'll give yourself a hernia."

The captain collapsed to his knees and Rick mounted his bike and cycled past the bemused soldiers. Scott tipped them a salute and followed behind.

"I'm guessing you're pissed that Walt's girlfriend didn't want to join us," he said, drawing up alongside.

"I promised Walt I'd check in on his kid. Doesn't feel right to leave them here."

"Yeah, I know, but what can you do?"

Nothing, and that was what irked Rick. Autumn leaves drifted down off the trees, carpeting the road now that there was no traffic to disperse it. Three miles up the road they passed the tractor and trailer they'd seen earlier on the way to the camp. The tractor was a little old Ferguson, low tech enough to still be running after the EMP, but it had broken down and the farmer, black oil stains on his hands, was still leaning over the engine, a ratchet wrench dismantling another engine component. Attached to the tow hook was a huge trailer loaded with grain, two soldiers riding shotgun on the top. They looked bored.

If this was the best that could be done, the future did indeed look grim for the half million people waiting in this part of North Carolina alone. In the rest of the state, the population ranked at ten million, a twentyfold increase since the pre-industrial era when people lived in small homesteads.

Never an optimist, even Rick was overwhelmed by the thought that most of them weren't going to make it through this first winter. It was entirely possible that his own family would be among them.

End of Sample

By the Same Author

The Alien Infiltrators Series
Amped
Assembled
The Tollon Codex
Bunker 51
Arctic Run
The Alien Infiltrators Collection: Books 1-5

Dystopian Space
Callisto

Undead UK
Remember Me Dead
Hunting The Dead

Survival EMP
Solar Storm
Solar Winter

78696334R00144

Made in the USA
Middletown, DE
05 July 2018